BR
OF THE HEART

A NOVEL IN THE HAVEN HOLD SERIES BY

SHELLEY PENNER

RCN Media Publishing

Brothers of the Heart by Shelley Penner © 2021 by Shelley Penner & RCN Media

Haven Hold Eye Logo © 2020 by RCN Media. All rights reserved.

Haven Hold Series is a ™ of RCN Media.

All rights reserved. No part of this publication may be reproduced, distributed, or transmitted in any form or by any means, including photocopying, recording, or other electronic or mechanical methods, without the prior written permission of the publisher, except in the case of brief quotations embodied in critical reviews and certain other noncommercial uses permitted by copyright law. For permission requests, write to the publisher, addressed "Attention: Permissions Coordinator," at the address below.

At the beginning of some chapters are snippets from songs. Those songs' lyrics were used without the permission of the rights holder. RCN Media acknowledges. The usage is intended to bring more context to the story at hand and RCN Media or associates are not capitalizing on their use. If issues or concerns arise from this, please use the contact below to make it known. Thank you.

First Edition: April 2021

RCN Media was founded in 2015 by Colton Nelson. It is a publishing company for adult, young adult and children's books. The RCN Media logo is © 2015 by Colton Nelson & RCN Media. If you require bulk orders of an issue with an RCN Media contact, feel free to contact them with the info below. Special discounts are available on quantity purchases by corporations, associations, and others. For details, contact the publisher at the email address below.

Cover artwork © 2021 by RCN Media.

Artwork created and adapted by Shelley Penner © 2021 by RCN Media. Some rights reserved.

Colton Nelson was the head of production and is the promoter for this novel. For any comments or to contact the author you can reach them through him (contact below) or you can contact RCN Media.

Contact:
www.rcn.media
(250) 206 0356
nelsoncolton16@gmail.com (subject: "Brothers of the Heart")

1 3 5 7 9 8 6 4 2 0

To Gail, the sister of my heart and my brother, Dave, who told me, "It doesn't matter what other people think of you, it's what you think of yourself that counts." Those words of wisdom from a sixteen year old had a profound impact on my life.
- *Shelley Penner, April 2021*

Bright Blessings!
Shelley Penner

BROTHERS OF THE HEART

SHELLEY PENNER

Chapter One

I hope you never fear those mountains in the distance
Never settle for the path of least resistance
Livin' might mean takin' chances, but they're worth takin'
Lovin' might be a mistake, but it's worth makin'.
   ~Lee Anne Womack

Near the top of the grey stone wall that encircled Haven Hold, Jesse Hayes stood on the guard-walk, scowled at the grey, watery landscape. *Guard duty again*, he thought disgustedly. This year at last, the hold council had decided to allow Jesse serve as a shepherd, and he felt frustrated by the seemingly endless delay in their departure. The spring weather continued too cold and damp to risk taking the new lambs out where they would have little shelter. He glanced over at the relaxed figure of his partner, Hutch Ingram, blurred by the rain as he paced the guard-walk a few yards away. Jesse's frown eased and his face softened into a smile. He was going to miss Hutch. His amiable, easy going partner felt like a big brother to Jesse, even more than his natural brother, Sev. Over twice Jesse's age, Sev spent so much time away, training the shepherds, the brothers barely knew each other. But perhaps over the summer Jesse would have the chance to spend time with Sev and get to know him better. If the plagued rain would ever stop.

Hutch came and stood beside the boy, peering off toward the west. Jesse wondered what his partner stared at so intently. He could see nothing out there himself but sheets of rain. Their mutant friend, Daniel, had visited yesterday and was not due again for two days, so Hutch could not be looking for him, and besides, Daniel always came from the north or the east. Over the winter months the mutant had become a frequent and welcome visitor at Haven Hold, and since the naming ceremony, when the assembly accepted him as guardian for Kelda and Davin's newborn son, Little Daniel, he seemed more at ease within the hold. The mutant took an intense interest in the growth and development of his namesake and often visited the nursery to cuddle and play with the baby. Yesterday though, he had arrived soaked to the skin from checking his snares in the rain and wanted to get home quickly and dry off.

Jesse strained his eyes, trying to spot what had caught Hutch's attention. He started to hear some odd sounds and thought he saw vague shadows moving behind the curtain of rain. As he watched, the forms gradually became visible through the mist. Wagons . . . lots of them. Kithtrekkers!

Isolated in the wilderness, Haven Hold saw few trade caravans. Nearly two years had passed since the last Kithtrekkers had visited. Caravans brought exciting news of the outside world, the doings of city folk in more civilized regions, stories and songs about faraway places and strange customs. They also brought goods the holders would otherwise never see, cottons and exotic foods from the balmy south, metals unavailable locally and badly needed for the smithing of tools and weapons, medicines that grew only in other climes, lead, gunpowder and cartridges for making ammunition, and salt from the western sea, used in the preserving of foodstuffs.

Many of the Kith traders also had entertaining skills as jugglers, acrobats, balladeers, dancers and actors. The holders, eager for diversion not of their own making, packed the performance tent night after night, enjoying the rich variety of entertainment. For the three to six days of the caravan's stay, a holiday atmosphere pervaded the hold, and they temporarily suspended most non-essential work.

As the two guards watched, more and more wagons rolled into sight, drawn by heavy draft horses. When the first wagon had almost reached the walls and the end of the train still had not emerged from the mist, Jesse said in a strained voice, choked with excitement, "It's the biggest caravan I've ever seen!"

Hutch grinned at his enthusiasm and replied, "Aren't you glad now that you're not up at the Meadows? You'd best go find Aaron and the rest of the council. They'll want to come out and greet the traders."

Jesse turned and pounded down the stairs, shouting the news to the men working inside the barn. Hutch shook his head ruefully. Their three years of partnership had done much to curb Jesse's headlong impetuosity, but sometimes in his excitement the boy forgot to act with a modicum of adult dignity.

By the time the first wagons came to a halt outside the gates, a small crowd had gathered to welcome them. Aaron Tayler and Tadi Hayes made their way forward as the driver of the lead vehicle climbed stiffly down and turned to greet them, a muscular man, not especially tall but built like a bull, with a grizzled beard and shrewd blue eyes. He reached out amiably to shake hands with the council members.

"Greetings. I'm Jericho Smith, caravan master. We have thirty-two wagons and about a hundred and fifty head of stock. If we are welcome, we would very much appreciate being shown where we can set up camp. It's been a long, wet, miserable day."

"You are welcome indeed," Aaron replied cordially. "You can set up right here on the flats in front of the gates if you wish. The south pasture remains free for your animals. It would please us greatly if you and your people would join us for supper once you get settled, and if you wish to bed down within the Haven, I'm sure we can accommodate you."

Jericho smiled, grateful for the generous offer. "The meal we gladly accept, but the shelter I regret we must decline. These wagons are our homes as well as our livelihoods. We would not want to leave them undefended in this wild, mutant-infested country."

"As you wish. If you need any help setting up your camp, I'm sure some of our young men would gladly assist." He picked one of the grinning boys out of the crowd and said, "Rennie, perhaps you could stay and guide our guests to the great hall when they're ready."

Hutch and Jesse watched from the guard-walk as several of the women hurried off to help the head cook, Cochita Sorenson, prepare for the last minute, unexpected dinner crowd. A few of the young people stayed to watch and speculate with anticipation on the contents of the wagons as the Kithtrekkers quickly, expertly formed them into a tight circle. With the wagons in place, the young holders moved forward to help unhitch and feed the draft animals, which the traders then corralled near the walls in a quickly built, temporary enclosure made out of ropes and metal rods. It seemed a flimsy structure, but these animals were well trained and tired from a day's work. This was all routine to the Kith and they accomplished each task with swift, economic efficiency. They released the trade stock to graze in the south pasture, watched over by a pair of trader guards. When they had cared for all the animals and set a watch on the wagons and the corral, the Kithtrekker traders gathered in a group and headed for the hold.

Jesse watched enviously as Rennie led the guests across the courtyard and into the great hall. "Wouldn't you know it!" he groused. "Stuck up here on guard duty at a time like this. I bet they'll be telling all kinds of interesting stories in there."

Hutch grinned and put his arm around the boy's shoulders, reminding him, "Oh, well, tomorrow Hedy and Rennie will be stuck up here and you will be free to browse to your heart's content through the fair and listen to all the stories and songs you want."

Jesse brightened at the prospect and Hutch turned to stroll away along the wall until he overlooked the temporary corral. In the failing light he could see the shadowy figures of two trekker lookouts, and he called down to them.

"Hey! You fellas hungry? Once these slow-birds finish stuffing themselves, they'll be relieving us for dinner. You're welcome to join us. My partner is eager to hear some tall tales from the civilized lands."

He caught a flashing gleam of white teeth in the dimness and a quick laugh. "Sounds good to me! I wasn't looking forward to reheated, overcooked stew again."

"Well, I'm afraid that might be all that's left after this crowd gets finished, but at least you won't have to reheat it yourself. We'll meet you at the gates as soon as you get relieved."

"We'll be there."

Quite some time passed before the traders began to straggle out of the hall, a few at a time. The night guards, Rad Tayler and Skeet Sorenson, finally came to take over the watch, so preoccupied discussing the tales they'd heard over supper that they barely acknowledged Hutch's all clear. Hutch and Jesse stood by the half-open gates, waiting for the caravan guards, and eventually they appeared, five of them, two from the pasture, two from the paddock, and one from the wagons. The first pair looked like twins, tall, almost as blond as Hutch and nearly identical. They introduced themselves as Mik and Bel Haerigan. Their companions gave their names as Kaese Messick, a lean whip of a man, Martel Smith, Jericho's son, and Zach McKenna, a slender, silent youth with a brooding, almost sullen look. Hutch introduced himself and his partner, then the two holders led the way into the great hall. Most of the tables lay empty now, but small scattered groups still sat in conversation. The kitchen crew had cleared off the buffet table, so the young guards made their way to the kitchen, where a flock of women chattered busily while washing up. Cochita caught sight of the young men and bustled forward, calling her helpers over to assist.

"We kept it hot for you," the cook said, as the women removed several bowls from the warming oven and placed them on the big kitchen table. Carly plunked down a stack of dishes and utensils.

"Help yourselves," she said bluntly, "we're busy."

Cochita scolded her for being rude and she looked startled. She had not intended rudeness, she had simply said what she meant.

"This looks wonderful," Mik said, scooping potatoes onto his plate. "There's nothing like a friendly welcome and a hot meal after a day of slogging in the rain."

The others chorused a heartfelt affirmation. What with the short notice, Cochita had no time to make anything fancy, but the food was good and plentiful and much appreciated by the hungry guards. For the first few minutes they ate in silence, but once they had taken the sharpest edge off their appetites, Hutch asked casually, "So what's the news from the capitol? Is the governor stomping the masses as usual?"

The traders grinned and shook their heads ruefully. "That he is," Mik said. "He raised taxes again this year. It's getting so a man can hardly make a decent living in the cities. If he earns four credits a day, the government takes two."

"And now," added Kaese, "they've started an annual trade fair in the capitol -- three weeks after harvest when folk can come from all over to buy, sell and trade their goods directly, without dealing through Kithtrekkers like us. What people don't seem to realize is that the government takes a bigger cut of their profits than we ever have. It's really eating into our business in those parts."

"Yeah, the damned government has to stick their noses into everything and make life as difficult as possible for the ordinary man," Bel grumbled. Jesse listened wide-eyed, glad they had no need to worry about such things at Haven Hold.

"Yes, and if it's not the government, it's the damned raiders we have to worry about," Kaese added morosely.

"Do you get attacked often?" Hutch asked with concern.

"A year never goes by when we're not attacked and a few of us killed or injured. And in truth, we're safer than most caravans because we're bigger. Remember Hadly Ranning and his caravan?"

"Sure, they've been coming every year for as long as I can recall. We missed them last year when they never turned up."

"They got attacked coming through West Pass last fall. Wiped out."

"Wiped out!" Hutch cried in horror. He had friends amongst those people.

"Every last one. This stupid policy of slavery is beginning to backfire. In the past year five uprisings have taken place in different parts of the country . . . one in this very territory. Two hundred slaves at the Sardiz iron mines revolted. They massacred fifty guards and escaped into the hills. Most have probably turned to raiding by now."

Even with Haven Hold's isolation, Hutch had heard of the Sardiz iron mines. They had a reputation for brutal treatment of slaves. Getting sold to the mines was as good as a death sentence. The holder felt more empathy for the slaves than he did for the dead guards, despite the shocking news about Ranning's caravan. But he could not express such sympathies to these traders, who obviously had little fondness for mutants of any description.

"I think the government should organize local militia groups to go into the hills and wipe the damned mutants out of existence," Bel growled. Hutch felt chilled by the cold-bloodedness of the suggestion. He sent Jesse a warning look to keep him quiet.

They finished their meal and the ladies cleared away the remains while the young men continued to converse. Mik and

Kaese did most of the talking for the traders, with Martel and Bel saying little and Zach remaining silent throughout. Despite his silence, or perhaps because of it, Hutch felt intrigued by the dark, moody youth. Some elusive quality about him reminded the holder of Daniel, though he could not quite put his finger on it. The resemblance was certainly not physical, beyond the fact they both had dark hair. The similarity lay not in their attitudes either, for Daniel, even at his most distrustful, never seemed sullen. Hutch finally shrugged it off without ever realizing that sense of familiarity came from his instinctive talent for recognizing strays.

Later, after seeing the traders home and barring the gates, Hutch began strolling back across the courtyard, when he heard Aaron's voice calling him from over near the barns. He paused, waiting for the council leader to catch up. Aaron smiled, the excitement of a trade fair infecting even him.

"I've just been looking over the livestock with Hal and Cam, seeing what we have to trade. It's a good thing this weather delayed the shepherds."

Hutch eyed the council leader curiously. Aaron surely had not waylaid him to tell him this.

"These trekkers have had considerable troubles with raiders. They seem to have a rather strong dislike of mutants. Perhaps you should warn Daniel to stay away as long as the caravan remains here."

Hutch smiled, pleased by Aaron's concern for his friend. "Daniel won't likely come with the caravan here anyway. He's too wary of people. I plan to take his bread to him."

Aaron nodded doubtfully but realized Hutch would do whatever he deemed necessary to protect his friend.

*   *   *

The holders wakened early as usual the next morning, but found the traders up and about before them, busily setting up their tents and booths in the pre-dawn chill. The sky had cleared overnight and it looked like an excellent day for trading. The holders felt eager to see what the caravan had to offer, but little individual trading could take place until the council finished dealing with the caravan committee. Few of the Haveners had any personal belongings to trade. Almost everything was communally owned. One or two individuals had marketable skills, such as Denys Sorenson, who carved beautiful figures out of ordinary firewood, or Sev, who made his potent brandy out of little more than a few wild berries and a bit of honey. But the primary craft of the Haven, for which they had some repute, was weaving, and while the skilled work got done by a handful of men and women, the materials and the labor of preparing them belonged to all.

Since most holds operated communally, the traders had worked out a method of barter that seemed to satisfy almost everyone. The ruling body of the community presented the goods they had to trade, and after a bit of haggling they settled on a certain number of credit tokens in return. These small coins minted by the Kithtrekkers from cheap metals had little real value but represented the value of the goods exchanged. The hold council would then bargain for supplies necessary to the running of the hold. After that, they divided remaining tokens according to the individual customs of each community. In the Haven it went three ways, one third going to the household to buy medicines, foodstuffs and crafting materials, one third to the farm to buy livestock and tools, and one third was divided amongst the assembly, so each member might enjoy the entertainment and make some small purchases for themselves.

Through the first part of the morning the different divisions of the community busily prepared their goods. Hal Sorenson, Tadi Hayes and Aaron culled the flocks and herds for trade animals. Neely and a clutch of weavers went through every bolt of cloth they had made since the last trade fair, choosing and discarding. In the kitchen and pantries, Cochita ransacked the dwindling food supplies for items that might be considered exotic treats in other territories, and Margit, the hold's healer, hunted through her supply of herbs and roots for medicines that might be hard to come by elsewhere. Fortunately, the mutant, Daniel, had kept her abundantly supplied with bitterberry leaves throughout the winter, since the plant was an evergreen. Those healing leaves had brought Daniel and the holders together. In the Haven, they had never seen the bitterberry plants that grew at higher elevations atop the wall of the plateau that surrounded Haven Hold Valley, in dangerous territory inhabited by vicious raiders. Over the winter, the healer had filled a multitude of ceramic jars and vials with her healing bitterberry ointment, aware it would become a valuable trade item and much sought after once its marvelous virtues became known.

By midmorning the holders had their goods assembled for the traders and the bargaining began. Jesse felt little interest in watching the negotiations, so he dragged Hutch away to wander through the fair, talking to people and examining their wares. The older boy still had a few trade tokens from the last caravan, and all traders of good repute honored the Kithtrekker coins. Hutch bought a pair of small, savory egg pies for Jesse and himself and they paused to eat them beside a bright, colorful tent, examining its gaudy facade curiously. A woman in her thirties opened the door flap and emerged. She looked a perfect match for her tent. Her bright, multicolored dress looked beautiful but odd, as if sewn together from pieces of other clothing, like a crazy quilt. She had a wealth of thick, curly black hair tied back with a red scarf. She saw the young men watching and gave them a seductive smile.

"What do you sell?" Jesse asked bluntly. Hutch reddened and almost groaned out loud at the boy's naive tactlessness. But the woman answered without shame or offense.

"I tell fortunes. Would you like me to tell yours?"

"Uh . . . no thanks," Hutch answered quickly, urging the fascinated Jesse to move on.

"I will do it for free this time, since we are not really open for business yet," she offered, raising her tent flap invitingly. Hutch eyed the dark opening suspiciously. He shook his head again and said, "No thanks."

"Aw, come on, Hutch! She says it's free," Jesse protested. The woman dropped the flap, smiling as if amused, and waved to a group of small tables and benches set up a few feet away for those customers wanting to sample the cooked foods offered in the next booth.

"Perhaps you would prefer a reading in the open, under the revealing light of the sun?"

One look at Jesse's pleading face and Hutch gave in. The three of them had barely settled themselves at a table when a tiny woman appeared from the food tent with a pot of tea and three small cups. Hutch reached for his scanty tokens, but the tiny woman shook her head, saying, "For Elyan's customers, no charge." She disappeared back into her tent.

Elyan poured and they sipped the hot drink, strangely but pleasantly spicy. The Kithtrekker woman studied them speculatively.

"The young one first, I think. What is your name?"

"Jesse," the boy answered quickly. She smiled at his eager innocence.

"Give me your hands," she said gently. She cradled his hands in her own, palms up, examining them minutely. "You have a courageous heart." She paused, releasing his left hand to trace a line on his right palm. "You have risked death for someone you love." Again she hesitated, then continued softly, "You will risk it again. Before a year has passed you will get a chance for the great adventure of which you dream, the chance to prove your courage." She stared a while longer at his hand before releasing it, saying, "That is all."

Jesse felt a little disappointed by the briefness of the prediction but flattered by the talk of courage and adventure. He moved aside so she could take Hutch's hands, watching for a moment as she studied them. Then Jesse noticed the dark, curly-haired youth from last night crouched against the wheel of Elyan's wagon, making quick, vigorous strokes with charcoal on a piece of parchment. Jesse wandered over to see what he was doing.

The Kithtrekker woman examined Hutch's hands as carefully as she had Jesse's. "You have a very special talent," she murmured. Hutch snorted in amused self-deprecation and she looked up at him sharply. "Do not underestimate the value of your gifts. You have the power within you to bring peace and happiness to several very sad and lonely people. But you also have the power to destroy them." She looked down at his hands again. "Three of those you hold dear will face grave danger, each at different times, and you will fear greatly for them. Only your heart can show you how to help them. Also, there is another . . . you will meet him soon . . . one who needs your tolerance. Remember, situations and people are not always what they seem."

Hutch watched her as she studied his hands seriously. That she believed every word seemed obvious, but he wondered how much credence he should give it . . . all this talk of his special talent, when he reckoned himself about as talented as a mud puddle. At last she released him and sat back with a sigh. She gazed intently into his eyes and said, "The lives and dreams of others rest in your hands. Be gentle. Dreams are easily shattered and difficult to mend. Trust your heart." Without another word, she rose and entered her tent, pulling the flap shut behind her. Hutch stared after her, bemused.

Jesse trotted over and thrust something into his hands. "Hutch, look at this."

The blond holder frowned absently at the piece of parchment, then his gaze sharpened as he realized what it was, a perfect likeness of his own face, rendered in just a few economical strokes. In the picture he wore an expression of gentle amusement, just as he had while listening to Elyan's prediction for Jesse.

"Where did you get this?"

The boy just pointed to where Zach still crouched against the wagon, scribbling away, half a dozen sketches scattered at his feet. Hutch strode over to stand behind him, watching him work. The outlander seemed not to mind. In fact he seemed oblivious. He quickly sketched the fortune teller's tent, the way the light fell across the wind-rippled cloth and spilled out over the ground, creating a shadow like a bird of prey about to take flight. He finished in a few strokes and sprayed it with a clear liquid from a small atomizer. Zach glanced up, noticing the holder for the first time. With a guilty start, he scrambled his sketches together and thrust them into a binder. He snatched the one from Hutch's hand, starting to shove it carelessly in amongst the others.

"Wait, I . . . I'd like to buy that one," Hutch protested weakly, sure it was worth far more than he could afford. Zach looked at him as if he was crazy.

"I don't sell them. Why would you want it anyway? It's just a bunch worthless of scribbling."

"Worthless! How can you say that? You have an incredible talent there!"

The young man looked away, plainly convinced Hutch was only flattering him.

"I have a friend I would really like to give that picture to," Hutch said slowly. "I've only got..." He pulled out his credit disks. "...Three tokens. But I can get more this afternoon."

Zach crouched silently, head down, fingering the edge of the binder as though hoping Hutch might go away if ignored. He slowly drew out the sketch and examined it. He really had created an excellent likeness. He had captured that big brother quality that seemed innately Hutch. He thrust the picture at the holder, saying, "You can have it. No charge." But as Hutch reached out incredulously, the outlander looked up and added, "On one condition." Hutch waited.

"You'll sit for another?" Zach finished wistfully. Hutch grinned, delighted with the bargain.

"Done!"

For the next two hours they strolled about the fair grounds and camp together, Hutch doing most of the talking and Zach doing sketch after sketch. Rarely did the outlander find such a willing model, and never one so natural and unselfconscious. Jesse had long since gotten distracted by more interesting sights and wandered off on his own. Hutch and Zach eventually ended up sitting atop the knoll where the holder first met Daniel. The outlander began drawing the trader camp spread out below, with the walls of the hold behind. He seemed to go into a kind of trance of concentration while he worked, making it harder than ever to get a word out of him.

"Do you mind if I look at your drawings?"

Zach grunted absently, waving a hand at the binder in invitation, and went on with his drawing. Hutch began to leaf through the sketches with great interest, unaware how unusual it was for Zach to allow anyone to see them. The drawings appeared in no particular order, pictures of the caravan and the traders next to ones of beggars on city streets and others of a farm. Hutch recognized a sketch of Elyan and another of Jericho. The next drawing depicted a street urchin about Jesse's age or a bit younger, dressed in rags, with an expression that showed a sad mixture of childish vulnerability and hardened cynicism. The following sketch portrayed a younger child, also a girl, feeding a flock of chickens and laughing as sparrows flew down and boldly stole some of the seed. A series of facial portraits came next, each one making Hutch feel he almost knew these people. Zach finished his latest sketch and turned to study Hutch's face hungrily, watching for his reactions. The holder came across an arresting face that reminded him strongly of Aaron at his most intimidating. But this man showed none of the underlying compassion that softened the council leader's sternness.

"Who is this?" Hutch asked curiously. Zach's face darkened and he turned away, answering grimly, "My father."

Surprised by the reaction, the holder quickly passed on to the next page, asking no further questions. Toward the bottom of the pile he found a group of three sketches that made his jaw drop in horror. Crude and passionately rendered, each showed several dark figures silhouetted against a burning farmhouse, dancing in demonic ecstasy over the tortured and mutilated bodies of a man, a woman and two young girls. The three drawings looked almost identical, each with a splattered stain of red across it.

"Zach! What is this!"

The outlander turned sharply in response to Hutch's dismay. When he saw what the holder was looking at, he quickly snatched up the binder and shoved the three drawings to the back, saying, "Those aren't supposed to be in here." His hands shook as he tied the binder closed. Hutch watched with concern and sympathy. The drawings obviously meant something very personal and painful to the outlander.

"Your family, Zach?"

The young man froze, then slowly nodded. "After the raiders killed them," he said softly, "I joined a group of mutant hunters, hot to get revenge and stop the bastards from doing the same to others. My father probably would have considered it the only right thing I've ever done in my life. It took me about two weeks to realize the mutant hunters didn't give a damn about stopping raiders. They just wanted to capture as many slaves as possible and sell them as high as they could."

"So you quit?"

"No. They told me to burn off. I wanted to kill raiders and they wanted to sell slaves . . . a conflict of interests."

"Do you still hunt mutants?" Hutch asked uneasily. Slavers occasionally followed or travelled with the caravans, knowing the rich cargo drew raiders like flies to honey. But Zach shook his head.

"No, I'm not much of a tracker or a hunter. I was just an extra gun to the slavers. I signed on with the caravan as a guard and roustabout. But if I do happen to see any mutants, I'll sure enough blow them back to hell where they belong."

"Not all mutants are raiders, you know," Hutch reminded him worriedly. Zach gave him a strange look.

"Maybe not, but I've never met one I would turn my back on." He rose. "I'd best get back to work and earn my pay. Thanks for posing." He turned abruptly and headed down the hill.

"You're welcome," Hutch called to his retreating back. "And thanks for the drawing."

The outlander waved briefly without looking back. Hutch wondered how this moody young man could ever have reminded him of Daniel.

Chapter Two

When he was a man, my father would stand,
I never saw him run,
There wasn't anyone could make the man bend;
And the strength of his will was a tool of his trade
And he did his work well.
~Gordon Lightfoot

Hutch returned to the hold and carefully deposited the portrait in a safe place before heading to the kitchen to check if anyone needed help. The kitchen remained the hub of the household and was rarely found empty. Any messages or requests for assistance would be left there. He found Cochita bustling about, just finishing preparations for a cold supper before heading out to enjoy the festival atmosphere of the trade fair.

"Has anyone requested a strong back and a pair of willing hands?"

"Aaron asked a while ago, but he got Rad and Joshua to help him. Most everyone is over at the fair anyway. If you need something to do, I could use an escort."

"It would be a pleasure and an honor, mistress," Hutch drawled, thrusting out his elbow for her in a humorously exaggerated manner. She whipped off her apron and patted her hair.

"Do I look alright?" she asked, her eyes sparkling with excitement.

"A vision of loveliness, my dear. No one would guess you're a grandma!"

She laughed and slapped at him playfully. "You're just full of feathers and nonsense, Hutch Ingram! Oh, I almost forgot!" She went to the bowl of tokens on the table and took out a handful for each of them, then slipped her arm through Hutch's and off they went.

The overdue spring sun had burned away the few remaining clouds, leaving the day deliciously warm and summery. Nearly the entire population of the hold crowded onto the fairgrounds. As Hutch followed Cochita from booth to booth, he spotted Neely enthusiastically haggling over a bolt of lustrous white fabric printed with large red flowers. Printed fabric remained a rarity to the holders since they possessed neither the equipment nor the knowledge to produce it themselves. A little further on he saw Margit deep in conversation with a white haired woman outside the stall that sold herbs and medicines. The next booth attracted Hutch's interest and he drifted from Cochita's side to have a closer look. The stall held a surprising assortment of goods, ranging from scented soaps and candles to perfumes and oil lamps. The latter caught Hutch's eye, and after a bit of dickering, he purchased a small spirit lamp the size of his cupped palm, a crock of scented oil and a plentiful supply of wicks. When he turned, Cochita had disappeared, so he wandered off alone, unconcerned. The range of merchandise seemed awe inspiring. He saw booths selling jewelry and metalwork, and others with embroideries and fine lace. One stall sold every kind of weapon imaginable, from tiny throwing knives no longer than Hutch's middle finger, to rifles with a bore that looked like they could blow a man in half. Another held furs and leathers and offered the services of a bootmaker. In the next stall, a sharp eyed woman with a hawkish demeanor sold fabric goods, everything from raw fibers to already woven materials. The small tent adjoining dealt in dyes, dying materials and mordants. Several stalls offered food, a variety of the familiar and the exotic. Hutch bought a small packet of dried, honeyed fruits and strolled along munching on them, his other purchases tucked under his elbow. He breathed deeply, taking in the mingled scents of spicy cooking, exotic perfumes, herbs, leathers and livestock. The atmosphere of the trade fair seemed so far removed from the day to day life of the hold that it felt almost other-worldly. Hutch found himself wishing he could share it with Daniel.

He spotted Jesse over by the livestock, watching while Zach put a magnificent sorrel stallion through his paces at the end of a lunge line. The boy glanced up at his partner, then back at the horse.

"Isn't he something?"

"That he is!"

"Aaron says we're going to get him to service Sarantha."

A crowd gathered to watch the handsome animal, and Hutch could see the stallion's growing nervousness as the audience increased. Zach didn't seem to notice until the horse suddenly shied and began to dance with fright. Hutch thrust his packages into his partner's arms, saying, "Take these home for me, will you, Jess?"

Without waiting for a reply, he pushed his way through the crowd. Zach had gone hand over hand up the line toward the horse's head, but the animal saw him coming and began to rear in fright, lashing out with his forefeet, narrowly missing the outlander's head. As the horse came down, Zach tried to grab him by the halter, but the animal jerked his head away and reared again, out of control. Hutch moved in on the stallion's other side, and as the animal came down, caught the halter and hauled his head down firmly, speaking in low, soothing tones, stroking the beast's sweaty neck. The stallion quieted instantly. Hutch glanced across the horse's neck at the outlander.

"You alright, Zach?"

The young man appeared shaken and shamed, but he nodded and said, "Fine. Let's get him out of here."

Together they led the jittery horse away to a quiet spot and picketed him. In silence they rubbed him down, one on either side, until he stopped fidgeting and trembling and began to calmly crop the grass.

"Thanks, Hutch. If anything happened to this horse I would be in deep trouble. This animal is Jericho's pride and joy."

"No worries. You could have handled it. You just need to be a little more sure of yourself. Let him know you're not afraid so he knows he can trust you to protect him."

"I guess I'm just not good with animals. Or much of anything else," Zach said ruefully. "I grew up on a farm. My father must have wondered what he ever did to deserve such a misfit for a son."

"Different people have different talents, Zach," Hutch said seriously, disturbed by the self-contempt he heard in the outlander's voice. "What you do with a piece of parchment and a bit of charcoal is nothing short of miraculous. I would consider it a gift just to be able to see that way, let alone put it on paper."

Zach smiled shyly, the first smile Hutch had seen on his face. "You're the only one who's ever seen them."

Hutch felt astounded. "But why? Your sketches are beautiful! You should share them. I bet you could make a living doing people's portraits."

The smile died and Zach's gaze dropped. "It's just a bunch of useless scribbling," he muttered. "I used to hoard every scrap of paper I could get my hands on, and bits of charcoal from the fireplace. I would find a quiet spot and draw for hours, then hide the pictures under my mattress." He leaned against the horse, staring at his hands unhappily as they shredded a piece of straw. "My father caught me at it one time. He thrashed me until I could hardly stand, then he forced me to tell where I'd hidden the others. He made me burn them all. A sinful waste of time he called it. After that I was more careful, but I could never stop. It's like there's something inside me that has to get out."

Hutch shook his head seriously. "He was wrong, your father," he said earnestly. "It would be a sinful waste of your talent if you didn't use it."

Zach searched Hutch's face and saw that he sincerely meant it. The outlander smiled crookedly. "Thanks," he said softly. "I guess you're as good with people as you are with animals."

Hutch grinned in return. "Maybe that's what my special talent is. Elyan said I have one, but I've seen rocks with more talent."

Zach came out from behind the horse and gave Hutch a friendly slap on the shoulder. "If you listen to Elyan, everyone's got a special talent. Come on, I think I owe you a beer."

*   *   *

The next day was bread day. Early last spring, Daniel had saved the lives of Jesse and his sister Neely when they were attacked by a monstrous beastman. About a month later, the mutant had warily approached the hold and made a trade deal with them – medicinal bitterberry leaves in exchange for a loaf of bread every three days. But with the caravan parked outside the hold gates, Hutch knew his mutant friend would remain at a distance. In most of the seven territories, mutants were considered less than human, fit only for slavery. Daniel had worn chains and felt the lash more than once in his life. It made him wary and suspicious of strangers.

As soon as the loaves came out of the ovens, Hutch packed up the small gifts he had bought for Daniel and headed for the hidden valley. He felt certain the mutant remained too gun-shy to come near the traders, but the fear that something might go wrong had lingered in the back of his mind all yesterday. The trekkers' obvious hatred of mutants made him nervous and he wanted to ensure that his friend stayed safe. When he entered the side canyon, he walked right past the entrance to the hidden valley where Daniel made his home and had to backtrack to find the mouth of the tunnel, well hidden by a line of bushes. Hutch had only used it once before, when Daniel led them through from the other side carrying Kelda Sorenson on a stretcher after a terrifying encounter with Rogan's Raiders. As Hutch emerged from the hidden tunnel into Daniel's pocket valley, his eyes went immediately to the lean-to that sheltered the entrance to Daniel's home. A small, shadowy figure darted away from it, headed for the trees. Hutch recognized that figure instantly, recalling in a flash the slavers this creature had killed and horribly mutilated. A jolt of horror shot through him. Daniel! That monster had come from Daniel's home! Hutch bolted across the clearing, cutting the intruder off from the trail to the rim, bringing his rifle to bear. The small man stopped dead, glaring at the holder with evil intensity. Throbbing pulses of malevolence pounded at Hutch like a heartbeat.

Darius faced Hutch's rifle with his shoulders hunched and his hands raised, teeth bared in an attempted smile. He felt too scared to cover his repellent gaze, the only real defense he had, and to Hutch his attempts to make himself look less threatening only served to make him appear more predatory. The holder broke into a cold sweat and his finger tensed on the trigger.

Inside the cave, Daniel was busy cleaning the cold ashes from the fireplace when Darius' telepathic cry for help knifed through his head. He dropped the leather bucket full of ashes, snatched his knife from its sheath and lunged for the entrance, crashing into the lean-to in his haste. He found Hutch with a rifle aimed at Darius, finger tightening on the trigger.

"Hutch, no!"

The holder heard his anguished cry and tore his gaze from his deadly adversary long enough to assure himself that his friend remained unharmed.

"Daniel, thank God you're alright!"

"Don't shoot him, Hutch! Please, don't shoot him."

The holder stared at Daniel in consternation, but his trigger finger relaxed a little. Daniel sheathed his knife and strode toward them, edging slowly between his two friends, his empty hands raised. Hutch lowered the rifle.

"He's not what he appears to be, Hutch. He's my friend."

Daniel felt desperately afraid such an admission might mean the end of his friendship with Hutch, the end of trust between them, but he was not about to watch Darius die to preserve that trust. He felt the telepath come up behind him and lean against him, shaking, and he reached back to touch the little man reassuringly.

"You told Aaron he was not your friend."

"I didn't really know him then. He came to visit me about a week later. Near scared the living flame out of me. Then he came again in midwinter." Daniel hesitated, then asked anxiously, "Do you still trust me?"

Hutch looked startled. "Of course I trust you. It's him I don't trust."

"He's not a monster, Hutch. He's really sort of special. His name is Darius Dreamweaver."

"But what about the way he killed the slavers?"

"The slavers got what they deserved. He's a telepath, Hutch, a psi mutant. He was in mental contact with Alanna while they were . . . abusing her. I suspect he's the only thing that kept her sane. Will you give him a chance?"

The holder studied the appeal in his friend's eyes and slowly nodded. "Alright, Daniel. You trust him. And I trust you. I'll give him a chance."

Daniel relaxed and smiled with relief. "Come on inside then. I'll make some tea and the two of you can get acquainted."

They turned together and headed toward the cave, but after a few paces, Daniel realized the telepath was not with them. He turned back and Hutch stopped and looked back too. The little man stood where they had left him, shoulders hunched and head down.

"Darius?"

"Hush you friend. Holder hate I."

Hutch regarded the telepath in uneasy surprise. "I don't hate you," he said, "I'm just a little scared of you."

"He's willing to give you a chance, Darius, but you have to give him a chance too."

Darius gazed at Daniel stonily, and even the peripheral menace of that gaze shook Hutch. But the little man's eyes dropped again almost immediately. Daniel caught the holder by the arm and drew him toward the cave.

"It's alright," he said, "he'll come when he feels ready."

Hutch made himself at home on a cushion of hides while Daniel cleaned up the spilled ashes and started a small fire in the cold hearth, putting on water for tea.

"It's a defense you know, that look of his," Daniel told Hutch as he worked. "He has almost no control over it. The more scared he feels, the more threatening he appears. It's a kind of camouflage, like protective coloration."

"Are you saying he's harmless?"

"No, he's not exactly harmless. He can fight like a wolverine if he's cornered. But he's not the vicious killer you think he is."

Hutch watched as Darius crept in silently, hands shading his eyes, and went to crouch in the corner by his bed. For the first time Hutch noticed the second bed and his eyes widened in shock. "He lives here with you?"

"Yes. He came during the winter storms, in trouble, with nowhere else to go. He would have died if I refused him shelter. Then after a while I didn't want to."

Hutch felt stunned. Daniel, who trusted almost no one, trusted this evil looking little gargoyle enough to share quarters with him. It seemed almost beyond belief. There had to be more to Darius than met the eye.

"Can he hear my thoughts?" Hutch asked with uneasy curiosity. Daniel shrugged.

"Why don't you ask him?"

The holder regarded Darius uncertainly. "How about it, Darius? Can you hear my thoughts?"

"Color," the little man grated, continuing to shield his eyes. "Some word."

Hutch turned to Daniel in puzzlement. "Color?"

"Near as I can make out," Daniel explained, "we all project some of our surface thoughts. Those he can pick up from anyone close enough. Mostly he just sees emotions. He sees them as colors surrounding us like a kind of halo. To understand deeper thoughts, he has to establish a deeper link. A blast of anger or hatred directed at him through such a link could kill him. As far as I know, the only people he's established that kind of rapport with are myself and Alanna."

Daniel poured the tea, made with sage and chamomile to soothe their nerves after the recent, tense confrontation. He carried the first cup over to Darius. The little man took it with one hand, continuing to hide his eyes with the other. Daniel felt concerned by the mental silence from the telepath since his panicked cry for help.

"Are you alright, Darius?"

The little man answered hesitantly. "Hush you friend. Want to kill I. No hurt you friend." At the same time Daniel received a mental wash of blue-grey shame and despair. He replied with a sense of reassurance and love, but the telepath's fears remained unrelieved. Daniel poured two more cups of tea and took one to Hutch, seating himself near the holder.

"Darius thinks you will try to convince me that he's not worthy of my friendship." Daniel gazed into Hutch's startled grey eyes seriously. "*He* thinks he's unworthy. He is convinced that if you force me to choose between you, I'll choose you."

Hutch felt appalled. "I would never ask such a thing of you!"

He sipped his tea, thinking as he studied the shadowy, hunched figure in the corner. His natural empathy for those outcast and unwanted began to overcome his fear of this repellant little man. If, as Daniel said, the telepath had no control over his strange and terrifying defenses, the small man must have few friends.

"Darius," Hutch said gently, "Daniel would not care for you if you were unworthy. The very fact that you are his friend makes you worthy of his friendship. And if I tried to use *my* friendship with him to destroy yours, *I* would be the one worthy of rejection. I would never do such a thing."

The telepath peeked at Hutch from beneath his hand. Daniel felt a wistful questioning and said with a grin, "You'll have to ask him that yourself."

Hutch looked from Daniel to Darius, confused by the silent part of the exchange. The telepath lowered his hand and turned the full force of his gaze on the holder. Hutch swallowed hard and braced himself to meet that baleful glare.

"You friend Dan-yel. Dan-yel friend I. Be you friend I, Hush? Be friend all?"

Despite the total lack of vocal or facial expression, Hutch sensed the hopeful longing in the question. He turned to Daniel and saw a similar hope reflected in those leaf-green eyes.

"Yes, I think so," he answered slowly. "We can all be friends."

He by no means felt convinced that Darius presented no threat, but he trusted Daniel. For Daniel's sake he would try to accept this strange little man and call him friend. The telepath continued to stare at Hutch until Daniel noticed the holder's growing uneasiness.

"Darius," Daniel said softly, showing the little man the holder's discomfort. Darius dropped his gaze instantly, radiating apology and humble admiration.

(*Nice color. Holder nice man.*) he thought to Daniel. The mutant grinned at Hutch.

"He likes your colors."

"My colors? What are they?" the holder asked curiously.

Daniel went silent for a moment, smiling, then he began to translate what Darius showed him. "You're mostly green and a sort of rosy pink. There's a lot of yellow too, like sunshine. Little touches of purple and a few splotches of orange."

"What do the colors mean?"

"I'm not sure exactly," Daniel hesitated. "Each color seems to mean several things, depending on the shading and circumstances. Green is . . . compassion, sympathy, courage, peacefulness. That rosy color . . . I'm pretty sure that's love, or affection, or friendship. The reds and oranges are pretty confusing. There's so many variations and they're mostly pretty violent. I suspect the orange in your colors is from Darius looking at you." Daniel felt another wave of shamed apology. "It's alright, Darius. We know you can't help it."

Hutch studied the small man. Darius had covered his eyes again and the holder felt a stab of pity for him. What a horrible curse to live under. As he had done so many times for Daniel, Hutch changed the subject to try and ease Darius's discomfort.

"Did you know there's a Kithtrekker caravan at the Haven?"

Daniel smiled. Smiles came more easily to him these days. "We knew. We have heard it, seen it, smelled it, and kept a healthy distance."

"I figured you would," Hutch said, relieved. "It might be a good idea to keep a sharp lookout for slavers and raiders too. These caravans sometimes draw both."

"We'll do that. Thanks for the warning."

"I brought something for you." Hutch began to delve into his pack and handed Daniel his loaf of bread, payment for the medicinal bitterberry leaves the mutant had provided over the past year.

"Thanks, I thought we would have to go without for a while." Daniel wrapped the bread in a piece of thin, oiled leather to keep it from drying out. But Hutch had not finished. He drew something else from his pack and handed it to Daniel, who examined it carefully.

"What is it, Hutch?"

"It's a spirit lamp. Here, I'll show you."

The holder filled the shallow depression with water, then added a thin layer of perfumed oil. He inserted a wick in the float and lit it. As it burned, a light, cheerful scent filled the room like a fresh breeze, lifting their spirits and producing a calming effect, a feeling that all was well.

"If you light it just before you go to sleep, it burns all night and helps to drive away bad dreams."

Daniel had received few gifts in his life. He felt deeply touched by his friend's thoughtfulness and concern. "It's really special, Hutch. Thank you. You needn't worry about my nightmares though. I haven't had one since Darius moved in with me."

Hutch's brows rose in surprise and he turned to regard the telepath, thinking he would be more likely to cause nightmares than prevent them. Daniel understood the holder's incredulous look, and affection for both his friends warmed his eyes.

"He is the Dreamweaver. He guards my sleep."

The telepath sat staring at the small flame of the lamp as if entranced, but he felt their attention on him and he said in his harsh, flat voice, "Pretty. Feel good."

Daniel got a faraway look, thinking about the magical rainbow visions Darius had gifted him with. "We have shared memories," he said with a dreamy smile.

Hutch felt a twinge of jealousy. Daniel had so rarely shared memories with him, he knew little more about his friend's past than when he'd first met the mutant. But the memories Daniel shared with Darius were the ones of Hutch, of Jesse and Neely and a few of his mother, Jaylene, the rare happy memories he treasured. Daniel cleared out a niche and carefully lifted the small lamp to place it there. As he turned back, Hutch handed him a piece of parchment.

"This is for you, too."

Daniel held it up to the light and his eyes widened. "Hutch! It's incredible! It's just like you. Darius, look at this." Daniel crouched and the telepath came and leaned against his shoulder. Darius reached out one finger to almost touch the portrait.

"Blue man," he said. "Hurt inside. Like Dan-yel."

Hutch looked startled. "What do you mean, Darius? I'm not hurt. And I'm certainly not blue. What does blue mean anyway?"

"Blue means unhappy, lonely. I think he's sensing whoever made the drawing. Who did it anyway? One of the traders?"

Hutch told them about the morning he had spent with Zach and the three horrible, tortured sketches amongst his collection. He also told them of the incident with the stallion and Zach's story about his father. Daniel shook his head.

"This father of his sounds a lot like someone I used to know."

Hutch waited hopefully. Daniel so rarely talked about his past and Hutch felt reluctant to try breaching the wall of reserve that rose whenever the subject came up. As usual, Daniel went no further. He sensed his friend's curiosity, but the past still held too much power to hurt him, his memories too painful to share. Not even with Darius had he shared those bitter remembrances. The little telepath had enough problems of his own. Daniel felt no need to burden either of his friends with the painful roots of his nightmares. He rose and put the portrait of Hutch in the niche, carefully placing it away from the flame. In the soft glow the picture seemed almost alive. He turned back abruptly with a grin and asked hopefully, "Can you stay for supper, Hutch? My snares caught a pair of grouse this morning and we have fresh biscuit root and greens."

"Sounds good. I'd love to. If it's alright with your roommate that is." Darius froze beneath his questioning glance, staring at the floor tensely. Hutch turned to Daniel in puzzlement. "Did I say something wrong?"

Daniel didn't speak for a moment, communicating silently with Darius, then he answered slowly, "He thinks you're mocking him."

"Mocking him! Why?" Hutch asked in dismay.

Daniel studied him hesitantly, not sure if he should shock the holder with the story of Darius' past. But he could see Hutch felt genuinely distressed that Darius would think him cruel enough and petty enough to resort to ridicule.

"He was raised by wolves," Daniel said softly, "after his family abandoned him. I guess in the pack he always held lowest rank, the one who had to bow and scrape to all the others. He figures he's still bottom rank and he doesn't understand why you would treat him with the respect due a superior."

"Raised by wolves!" Hutch repeated in awe and wonder. "I swear to you, Darius, I meant no mockery or disrespect. And I certainly don't rank higher than you here. This is your home . . . I'm just a guest."

Darius looked at him with stony black eyes. The telepath's gaze had lost much of its power now that he no longer feared the holder, and Hutch was growing used to the idea that the threat was mostly illusion. He met that baleful glower without flinching.

"Friend, Hush. You stay."

Dinner tasted delicious, the grouse succulent and tender, the biscuit root crisp and the greens a welcome change after winter months of stored roots and dried vegetables. Afterwards, as they relaxed together in satisfied comfort, Hutch brought up a question that had puzzled him and many others for months.

"Darius, how did you get out of that root cellar last summer?"

Hutch waited through a long silence, realizing the telepath was probably sending to Daniel, using him as a translator. Daniel groaned suddenly and Hutch sat up sharply in concern.

"Ah, Darius!"

Then Hutch noticed the telepath shaking, his eyes tightly shut. What the hell was going on here? The moment ended and Daniel turned haunted eyes to meet the holder's worried gaze. He shook his head slowly.

"They had no idea what they were doing when they put him in with those monsters. The slavers were furious and he was the only available target. They hurt him, Hutch. God! And *I* told Aaron to let those bastards keep him! The only thing that saved him was the dark. They couldn't see him, but he . . . well, he can't exactly see in the dark, not with his eyes, but he senses colors, kind of a mental vision. He found a piece of slate splintered away from the floor . . . cut his foot on it while he was trying to keep away from them. That's what he used to kill them. He was fighting for his life, Hutch. If they hadn't beaten him to death, they would have burned out his brain with their anger and hatred."

"What about the, uh . . . mutilation?"

"He did that after they were dead, in revenge for Alanna. Darius has a very straightforward sense of justice."

"And the door?"

"Well . . . it's a bit confused, but near as I can make out, he slid the bolt with his mind."

"He can move things with his mind?" Hutch felt awed and appalled by the possibilities of such a talent.

"I've never seen him do it. Apparently it takes a great deal of energy and concentration. He only uses it in emergencies because it leaves him exhausted. He figured he was going to be killed in the morning, so he had nothing to lose."

Hutch contemplated the telepath, still huddled and shaking from the horrible memory, and his sympathy grew. "I'm glad you escaped, Darius. I don't know what the council might have decided to do with you, but I'm glad they didn't get the chance."

Hutch felt a slight flutter in his head, soft as a butterfly kiss, gone almost before he became aware of it. He felt startled but experienced none of the terror Daniel had first felt when he realized what that touch meant. Hutch had grown up secure and sheltered by a loving family and friends. He had never in his life been deliberately hurt or betrayed, so he had none of the built up layers of emotional defense Daniel had been forced to erect over the years just to survive. It was the casual, irresistible breaching of those defenses that had thrown Daniel into a panic when Darius first contacted him mentally.

The touch the holder felt remained brief and did not return, and Hutch soon forgot it. Darius had not been trying to establish real contact. He didn't quite trust the holder enough for that. The telepath had only been searching for assurance of Hutch's sincerity.

When Hutch finally said good-bye and started for home, twilight had already faded into night. If he stayed any longer, someone would surely notice his absence and begin to worry. As he made his way through the darkened forest, he felt a strange uneasiness, as if something followed him, watching. An owl hooted softly a few yards away and he stopped to listen intently, unused to traveling the woods at night. But he heard no sound that seemed threatening or out of place, so he continued on. Then, as he drew near to the river and the end of the trees, he detected a soft rustling in the brush to his left. He tensed, waiting in the shadows, his rifle steady, aimed at the source of the sound. A small shadow detached from the deeper darkness and padded forward a few steps . . . Darius. Hutch could not see the telepath's fixed glare, but he felt the power of that gaze even in the dark. Facing this menacing little gargoyle in Daniel's home was one thing, knowing Daniel and trusting him to control this strange being. To face the little monster out here in the darkness alone was something else again. All Hutch's fears and doubts suddenly seemed saner and more reasonable than the sympathy he had begun to feel back at the cave.

"Why are you following me, Darius?"

"Friend, Hush. Alone you. Dark. Not safe."

Hutch lowered his rifle, sorry for having displayed his distrust, shamed for having doubted Daniel's judgement.

"You came to escort me home?" he asked, grinning a little in surprised amusement.

"You Dan-yel friend. Dan-yel need. Keep safe. You hurt, Dan-yel hurt. Not want Dan-yel hurt."

The telepath's voice seemed softer, less grating out here in the open. His speech had improved a lot over the past months, with Daniel's help. He no longer scrambled sentences unless he became excited or upset. Hutch had understood perfectly. For the first time he realized the friendship between the telepath and the mutant was not so one-sided as he had thought, not just Daniel kind-heartedly sheltering another misfit, more homeless and outcast than himself. Darius loved Daniel. If the telepath possessed no other redeeming qualities, that one alone would be enough to ensure Hutch's tolerance, perhaps even his friendship.

"Dan-yel not need I."

Hutch sensed sadness in that quiet statement. He sank into a crouch, resting his rifle across his knees.

"Darius, maybe Daniel needs to be needed too."

The small man thought silently about his telepathic connection with Alanna, who had lived through hell after she was captured and raped by the slavers last summer. He thought about how good it felt to be able to help her, to make her happy, if only for a few moments. He realized Hutch was right. The telepath padded hesitantly closer, longing to touch that gentle green and rose aura, but afraid of seeing it flare into orange and red because of his nearness. Hutch didn't move. His colors remained steady as Darius slowly reached out and touched him lightly, his pale hair, his cheek, his shoulder, then started to withdraw. The gentleness of the gesture caught Hutch by surprise and he captured the telepath's small hand in his own. Darius stiffened, but the holder's grip remained light and unrestraining.

"Darius, I'm sorry for any unkind thoughts I may have had about you. I'm sorry if I hurt you or scared you." The holder paused and grinned a little. "I think I'm beginning to see why Daniel figures you're special. You really are not what you appear to be, are you?" Darius didn't answer, so Hutch went on. "I suspect your injury or death would hurt Daniel as badly as mine would. I love him too, and I don't want to see him hurt either. If you are ever in trouble and I can help, I will." He squeezed the telepath's hand gently, then released it and rose. Darius looked up at him and Hutch ignored the feeling of discomfort that gaze caused. As he started off again, the telepath padded silently alongside, and the holder realized the small man was determined to see him home safely. He turned south, following the edge of the forest, knowing Darius would feel more comfortable in the protection of the trees. They travelled together in companionable silence until they reached the spot where Hutch had to turn west and move out across open ground to reach the hold. He sank to a crouch again with his rifle across his knees, regarding the small shadow that was Darius. For a moment neither of them spoke as they listened to the sounds of music and laughter coming from the fair grounds.

"You'd best not come any further, Darius. It's not safe for you. I'll be fine."

The telepath reached out again to touch Hutch's hair, like spun silver in the moonlight. "Nice colors," he said.

Hutch smiled. "What are your colors, Darius?"

After a moment of startled silence, Darius answered, "Can't see. Dan-yel say rainbow."

"A rainbow! Did you know that rainbows are a symbol of hope? You take care of yourself, friend. And take care of Daniel for me."

Hutch touched Darius lightly on the shoulder and said good night, then strode away across the open, rolling hills toward the lights of the fair and the hold. Darius watched him go, spinning out a fine mental thread, a lifeline connecting him to Hutch. If the holder was ever hurt or in trouble, Darius would know, just as he did with Daniel and Alanna.

Chapter Three

Every time I change direction,
Every footstep asks the question,
Does this take me closer or further away?
On this long and twisted journey
Every passing moment finds me
Wondering will I find my home someday.
~Unknown author

The weather continued warm and sunny, and the shepherds left at last for the Meadows with the flock. Hutch stood at the stock gate, watching them disappear down the river trail, feeling a part of himself being torn away. He had said a quiet good-bye to Jesse and wished him luck, smiling at the suppressed excitement in the boy's eyes. Jesse would soon learn there was nothing exciting or adventurous about babysitting a bunch of sheep. Hutch already missed him. He enjoyed Jesse's company, and after almost three years together, he would find it hard to be without his partner. The last of the flock disappeared down the river trail and Hutch started to turn away when he heard a voice call out to him. He turned and found Zach watching.

"Can I talk to you?"

"Sure, Zach. Is anything wrong?"

"No, I . . . just need to talk to you."

"Alright, let's go get some breakfast and take it up on the hill."

They bought a pair of meat pies, a handful of dried fruits and a mug of cider each and carried it up to the knoll overlooking the hold and fairgrounds. They sat side by side, eating in silence. Hutch studied Zach's moody expression curiously. The outlander felt his scrutiny and met it with an uncertain smile.

"What did you want to talk about, Zach?"

He looked away, seeming unsure of himself, as if he didn't know quite how to begin. At last he said, "You know the caravan is leaving tomorrow?"

Hutch nodded. "I heard."

Zach began pulling up blades of grass and shredding them nervously. The silence continued for several long moments, then finally he said, in a barely audible voice, "I've heard your people sometimes take in outsiders."

Hutch nodded. "We have eight adopted members right now. It helps to keep us from getting inbred. The hold was originally established by only five families, and we're all pretty inter-related by now."

Zach pulled up another blade of grass and carefully ripped it to pieces. "Would you accept me?"

Hutch could feel the tension in him, the expectation of rejection. "I would accept you, but it's not up to me. I could present you to the council, but you would have to have a sponsor . . . either a senior member of the assembly or a council member. Once the council had interviewed you and approved the sponsorship, you would make a verbal agreement with the council and your sponsor for a trial period. At the end of that trial period, your sponsor would bring your petition before the assembly, and one of the five families would offer to adopt you."

"And if no one wanted me?"

"Someone would want you, Zach. You would have to completely disgrace yourself to be that undesirable."

"Believe me, it's not outside the realms of possibility."

"Zach, don't!"

The unusual sharpness of Hutch's tone startled Zach.

"Don't what?"

"Don't talk about yourself that way. You're a good man with a lot to offer."

"You don't even know me."

"Maybe not, but I like you, and I'm not often wrong about people. If you're really serious about this, I'll talk to the council members and see if anyone would be willing to sponsor you."

"Thanks, Hutch. I really appreciate it."

"There is just one thing, Zach. We're not mutant haters. We don't shoot anyone unless they attack us. Raiders live up on the rim, but peaceful mutants live there as well. We don't like mutant hunters or slavers and we don't pay to have our neighbors murdered or enslaved."

Zach went white and his eyes dropped.

"No offense intended. If you prefer, no one else needs to know about your mutant hunting days. I just want you to realize that once you are accepted, you can't go around shooting mutants just because they are mutants."

The outlander sat with his head turned away in silence. Finally he answered, "What do you want me to say? That I won't hate mutants anymore? I can't help it. Every time I think about what they did to my family, I just want to blow the whole plague-ridden lot of them off the face of the earth!" His voice broke and his hands clenched into fists.

"I'm not asking you to stop hating raiders. Or to forget what happened to your family. I'm just telling you, if you want to find acceptance in the Haven, you have to be a little more receptive to the idea that mutants are just people, some bad, but some good as well. They don't all deserve to die."

Zach offered no reply, so Hutch continued. "One of my dearest friends is a mutant. His name is Daniel." He told the outlander how the mutant had saved Jesse and Neely from the beastman, about the trade agreement and how Daniel had been captured by slavers and dragged to the hold in chains. He continued with the story of how Daniel had tricked a band of Rogan's Raiders and rescued five captive holders, including himself. He even told Zach about the naming ceremony, where the entire assembly accepted the mutant as guardian for Little Daniel, his namesake. Hutch wanted to ensure that Zach understood Daniel had the support and loyalty of the entire hold, not just himself.

"He is a good man, Zach . . . the very best. We owe him more than we could ever possibly repay."

The outlander thought for a moment in silence. "I suppose it's possible a few of them aren't killers," he admitted grudgingly. "I've never met any I would care to trust."

Hutch shook his head helplessly, discouraged by the solid wall of prejudice. But he felt sure that once Zach actually met Daniel, the outlander would recognize the mutant's integrity.

"What about the Kithtrekkers? Don't you have a contract with them?"

"I expect they'll be glad to see the last of me. Things always seem to go wrong when I'm around. Bel says I'm a jinx. Maybe your council would be wiser to turn me down."

"Horse shit! Zach, don't do this to yourself. If you go before the council talking like this, they *will* turn you down. Anyone who trusts himself so little can be dangerous."

Their eyes met for a moment, then Zach looked away and muttered, "Sorry."

Hutch shook his head in exasperation. "I'll go ask around about a sponsor. I'll find you later and let you know what I've turned up."

*   *   *

Zach was mucking out the stock enclosure when Hutch returned a few hours later, accompanied by a middle-aged man with dark hair, greying at the temples, and sharp, intelligent blue eyes. The man's right leg had been taken off at the knee and he stumped along on a wooden peg.

"Zach McKenna, this is Tadi Hayes," Hutch introduced. "Tadi is a member of the council."

They shook hands and Tadi said, "I understand you're looking for sponsorship."

"Yes, sir."

"Do you mind telling me why? Most of our young men would jump at the chance to travel with a caravan, seeing new places, experiencing different cultures."

"I guess I just don't have a traveler spirit."

"But why us? You must have stopped at a dozen holds on the way here."

Zach shifted uneasily, not sure what to say. "I've watched you all these last few days. There's a feeling here . . . like home, like family. My people are dead." He flicked a glance at Hutch, then with his eyes on the ground he said, "I miss them. I would like to be part of a family again."

Tadi smiled with friendly sympathy. "A good reason, lad. I'm sorry about your people. Come to the hold after supper and we'll introduce you to the rest of the council."

Zach regarded him wide-eyed. "You mean that's it? You'll sponsor me?"

Tadi looked amused. "What did you expect?"

"I don't know. I guess I just thought it would be harder."

Tadi gave him a friendly pat on the shoulder, a paternal gesture of reassurance and approval that Zach could not remember ever receiving from his father. Then the councilman turned and limped back toward the gates. Hutch grinned at Zach. "I have duties for now, but I'll meet you at the gates later and escort you to the council meeting. Good luck!" He turned and loped away, headed for the kitchen. It was bread day again and he was due to make another visit to Daniel and Darius.

Zach quickly completed his chores, then went in search of Jericho. He found the caravan leader in his wagon, just finishing lunch with his taciturn wife, Meshandra. When Zach told them about the sponsorship, Jericho seemed less pleased than expected.

"We'll be sorry to lose you, son. But if this is what you want, we'll not stand in your way. I realize you've not been exactly happy with us."

Several unfortunate incidents had occurred for which Zach had taken the blame, though they had come about through no fault of his. Part of the problem had been the bad weather, putting everyone in a foul mood, but part also had been Zach's own attitude. He had accepted the blame without protest, as if he actually believed himself at fault.

Jericho rose and went to the token chest. He counted out a generous handful of coins and put them into a drawstring pouch, then handed it to Zach.

"Your wages until now. You are a good lad, Zach. Don't ever let anyone tell you different."

Zach took the pouch hesitantly. "They haven't accepted me yet."

"I can think of no reason why they would refuse you. If you need a recommendation, I will gladly give it. And son, if this doesn't work out for you, we will be back next spring. You would be welcome to join us again."

*   *   *

When Zach arrived at the hold gate just after supper, Hutch awaited him as promised. Zach felt so nervous he almost decided to call the whole thing off. But Hutch smiled reassuringly, so Zach swallowed a few butterflies and followed him into the hold. The great hall stood empty except for the members of the council, seated at the large table at the head of the room. Hutch stopped before them and Zach stood at his shoulder, trying not to show how uncertain he felt. Tadi smiled at him and he felt a little better. Then Aaron stood up to face them and Zach's mouth went dry. The council leader looked enough like Zach's father to be his twin, and the youth suddenly wished himself anywhere but here.

"So, Hutch. I understand you are presenting a petition for sponsorship. Would you introduce us to your friend?"

"Yes, sir. Members of the council, this is Zach McKenna. Zach, you have already met Tadi. This is Margit Ingram, our healer . . . " The grey haired woman smiled pleasantly and shook hands with Zach. "Cochita Sorenson, whose wonderful cooking you have already sampled . . . Alison Kendle, our head of agriculture . . . and Aaron Tayler, the council leader." Zach shook hands with each in turn, carefully avoiding Aaron's stern gaze, in case he saw there the same contempt he had so often found in his father's eyes.

"So tell us, Zach," Aaron began, "where are you from?"

"A small town called Aspengrove, about five days south of the capitol. My folks had a small farm a few miles out of town."

"How old are you, Zach?" Cochita asked.

"Sixteen."

"Young to fend for yourself. Why are you not with your family?"

"They're dead." Zach's eyes fell, not wanting them to see the still fresh pain in him. "Killed by raiders last spring."

"How is it that you survived this attack?" the dour, hatchet-faced Alison asked.

Zach flushed red with guilt and shame, feeling himself accused somehow. "One of the horses had gotten loose, my father's favorite colt. He sent me on foot to catch it. It took a long while and by the time I started back, it was dark. When I got out of the trees, I could see the house burning," his voice broke. "The colt was too young to ride, so I ran all the way back, but . . . it was too late. They were already dead." Zach stood with his head bowed, hands clenched at his sides. The council members exchanged silent glances of sympathy.

"We're sorry about your family, Zach," Margit said gently. "Do you have no other kin?"

"None I know. My mother mentioned an uncle I think, somewhere in South Desert Territory. I've never met him though. I don't think he even knows I exist."

"How are you connected with the Kithtrekkers? Do you have a work contract?" Aaron demanded.

"Yes, sir..."

"We have no wish to antagonize the traders, you know. If they are unwilling to release you, you will have to finish out your contract before we will consider a sponsorship. And we are not fond of contract deserters or runaways either."

Zach focused on Aaron's forbidding visage for a moment, unnerved by the uncanny resemblance to his father. Desertion would never have occurred to him, but once more he felt himself being accused. "I've already talked to Jericho. He's willing to terminate the agreement. He said he would give me a recommendation if I needed it."

"Are there any warrants out against you in the territories?"

"No!" The question bewildered him. Why were they treating him like this? Jericho was wrong. They were going to refuse him, he knew it. Suddenly he felt Hutch's hand on his shoulder, warm and reassuring. It steadied him.

"Do you have any skills?" Alison demanded.

Zach's heart sank to his boots. He couldn't do anything well enough to call it a skill.

"No, sir."

Before anyone could bring up another question, Hutch quickly interceded. "Uh . . . sorry to interrupt, but that's not strictly true. Zach is an artist, and in my humble opinion, a very good one."

Zach stared at him, taken aback. He would never have considered himself an artist, and his drawing was hardly a useful skill. It was more like a vice, a bad habit.

"You say you grew up on a farm," Cochita said. "You must know farm work."

"Sure," Zach shrugged.

"Do you have survival skills?" Aaron demanded.

"Sir?"

"Can you hunt, fish, build your own shelter, find your own food in the wilderness? Do you know how to stay alive with raiders on your trail?"

"I've done some hunting," Zach answered uncertainly. "I'm a pretty fair shot."

"Do you hate mutants?"

The sudden shift of topic threw him for a moment, but he recovered quickly, remembering what Hutch had told him this morning. He answered carefully, "I hate raiders."

The council members exchanged another look. "If you came face to face with a mutant, would you know whether or not he was a raider?"

"I don't know. I've never seen any other kind of free mutant."

"Has Hutch told you about Daniel?"

"Yes, sir."

"You understand then that this man, this mutant, is very special to us? That he is a trusted friend?"

"Yes, sir."

Aaron faced the other council members. "Do you have any other questions for Zach?"

They shook their heads and Margit said, "I'm satisfied." Aaron turned back to the youth.

"You realize of course that you have to be sponsored by a senior member of the community? I'm afraid Hutch doesn't yet qualify. Do you have a sponsor?"

Zach hesitated and glanced at Tadi uncertainly. Tadi had remained silent throughout the interview, but now he spoke up. "I will sponsor him, Aaron."

"Very good." Aaron nodded, then said slowly and formally, "Zach McKenna, do you swear to abide by the laws and customs of this community, deferring to the advice of your sponsor?"

"Yes, sir."

Hutch nudged Zach from behind and whispered, "I so swear."

"I so swear," Zach repeated, his heart doing acrobatics. He couldn't believe they were actually going to accept him.

"Do you swear to protect and defend the lives and property of Haven Hold to the best of your ability?"

"Yes, I so swear."

"Do you understand the conditions and limitations of the sponsorship contract?"

Zach hesitated. "No, sir."

"Tadi, would you like to explain it to him?"

Tadi nodded and took it up. "Sponsorship is a kind of trial period, to let us get to know you, and to give you a chance to be sure our way of life is really what you want before you commit yourself. The time period varies, sometimes lasting until the next trade caravan comes by, which could be anywhere from six months to two years. During this trial period you will be appointed a guide to help you get acquainted with our laws and customs and to teach you any necessary skills you may be lacking. If we find for any reason that we wish to terminate the agreement, it must be brought before a general council and voted upon. You, as the petitioner, have the right to break the agreement at any time simply by leaving. When the trial period ends, if there are no immediate offers of adoption, I, as your sponsor, will bring your petition before the assembly. Any member of the assembly over the age of twenty-five can adopt a new member. Do you agree to these terms?"

"Yes, sir."

"Do you have any questions you would like to ask?"

"No, sir."

"Very well," Aaron said. "Since you already know Hutch and he has indicated his willingness, we are assigning him as your guide. Congratulations, Zach, and welcome to Haven Hold."

"Thank you, sir. Uh . . . when should I . . . move in?"

Aaron smiled at his diffidence. "You can go and get your things now if you wish. Hutch will show you where to stow your gear and where you will sleep. On the other hand, if you wish to spend one last night with your trader friends before they leave in the morning, you are welcome to move in tomorrow. I would like you here for breakfast though, so we can introduce you to the assembly."

A slow smile spread across Zach's face as he realized it was actually happening, they had accepted him. "Yes, sir. Thank you."

Hutch put a hand on his arm and drew him away as the council members began to rise and disperse to their regular evening activities.

"Well, what do you want to do, Zach? I'll give you a hand if you want to move your gear tonight."

"Thanks, Hutch. I would like to say goodbye to a few people, but they will all be packing up to leave, so I might as well move in tonight."

"Would you rather I didn't come with you? Maybe you prefer to say your good-byes in private."

"No, I . . . I would like you to come." Zach smiled shyly. "Good-byes can be hard. It would be nice to know I have a welcome at my back."

Hutch laughed at his odd way of putting it, but felt quite willing to give moral support, so they headed off to the fairgrounds together. They found Jericho at one of the food stalls, sitting at a table, drinking tea with the caravan's committee members and making plans for tomorrow's pull out. The caravan master saw the young men coming and rose to greet them.

"How did it go, Zach?"

"They accepted me."

Jericho noted the surprise and wonder in the young man's dark eyes. "Of course they did. Why would they not? Congratulations, lad."

The others seated at the table murmured good luck and farewell too, but Zach suspected they felt relieved to see him go. They still blamed him for an incident over a month ago when the stock had stampeded during a thunderstorm. A wagon was badly damaged and Davi Lassiter's leg broken. Zach had been on watch when the herd, spooked by the storm, erupted into motion. He had done his best to stop them and had succeeded in turning them away from the main camp, but Lassiter had parked his wagon outside the circle, on the bank of the river. The surge of the thundering herd had pushed it over the edge, sending it crashing into the water. Furious at the loss, Lassiter had blamed Zach. The young outlander made no attempt to defend himself from the unjust accusations, having learned from his father that protest only brought more grief. After that it seemed like Zach got blamed every little thing that went wrong, until he acquired a reputation for being bad luck.

Jericho shook hands with the youth, then pulled him into a quick, rough embrace. He had never believed Zach responsible for any of the misfortunes but felt a man had to learn to stand up for himself.

"These holders better treat you right, or by God, they'll see some hard trading come next spring!"

Zach grinned, moved by the gesture and the words, but self-conscious before the watching audience.

"Thanks, Jericho. I'm going to miss you."

"And I you, boy. Good luck."

Zach backed away a few steps, almost running into Hutch, then turned on his heel and headed for the tent he shared with Bel and Mik.

"He seems very fond of you," Hutch observed as he lengthened his stride to keep up with the outlander.

"He's in the minority," Zach answered dryly.

When they arrived at the tent, they found Mik and Bel both present, packing in preparation for tomorrow's early start.

"Hey, Zach! We've been wondering where you disappeared to," Mik greeted him amiably. Bel glanced over with a sour expression as Mik continued, "I wonder if you would consider riding herd for me tomorrow. I'd like to drive for Maeve and snuggle up to Sylvy for a while." He flirted his eyebrows and grinned rakishly.

"Sorry, Mik. I'll be staying here."

"Staying here!" Mik gaped as if Zach had said he was going to fly to the moon.

"I've got a sponsorship contract with the hold."

"Well . . . I suppose if that's what you want . . . " Mik said uncertainly. A Kithtrekker to his bones, to Mik a settled life seemed incomparably drab. "Are you sure?"

"Shit! Don't argue with him!" Bel snarled. "He might change his mind!"

Hutch frowned at the blatant hostility. Mik whirled on his brother in fury.

"Shut up, you braindead plague rat!"

Bel glared back at him for a second, then stalked out of the tent, shoving Zach out of the way as he passed. Seething with anger, Mik watched him go and then turned to Zach and Hutch.

"Sorry about that. Don't mind him, kid. He's just burnt because Davi Lassiter kept him supplied with junk weed. He's been getting a bit ragged since we left Lassiter ground-tied." Mik had always stood by Zach, even when Bel began spreading rumors he was a jinx.

"I'll be sorry to see you go . . . or stay. Whatever! I hope things work out for you, Zach. Good luck, and we'll see you next spring." Mik offered a friendly handshake, then headed off to find his brother and try to talk some manners into him.

Zach began shoving his few belongings into a knapsack, avoiding Hutch's curious gaze. The holder waited in patient silence, wondering over the cause of the hostility, but sure Zach would rather not talk about it yet. Zach hooked his pack over one shoulder and gathered up the binder that held his sketches, glad not to have to answer any curious questions.

"I have one more stop to make."

He led the way to the edge of the fairground, to a booth already half dismantled by a small, brown-skinned woman with frizzy hair and snapping black eyes.

"Hey, Cinda," Zach greeted her softly.

"Hey, Zach. I hear you're leaving us," she answered in a velvety southern accent.

"That's right. I wondered if I could still buy some paper from you. And char sticks."

"And fixer?"

"Yes."

"Well, everything's all packed up, but for you, Zach, I'll dig it out. How much would you like?"

Zach handed her the pouch of tokens Jericho had given him. "As much as this will buy." Her eyes widened and she hurried off to fill his order.

"We do have paper in the hold, you know," Hutch said.

Zach shifted uneasily. "I wouldn't want to waste it."

Hutch shook his head in amused disbelief. "What you do is not a waste of paper, Zach."

The youth shrugged and turned away. The thought of having to face Aaron and justify the use of hold resources for his scribbling seemed more than he could handle. Cinda returned a few moments later with several bulky packages wrapped in thin paper. Hutch took them, since Zach already had his hands full.

"I've included a paper mold, chemicals and instructions to make your own, just in case you run out."

"But, Cinda! Won't you need them?"

Making and selling paper was her livelihood. She never sold her molds and chemicals. "I have plenty," she answered. "And I can get more at the annual Gathering this winter." Then she quickly reached out and hugged Zach. "Consider it a farewell gift. I wish you every happiness, honey. Maybe when we come back next spring you can do my portrait again and you'll let me see those drawings of yours at last."

"Thanks, Cinda. I'm going to miss you more than anyone."

"Way they treated you, not many deserve to be missed. You take care of yourself, and don't let anyone push you around this time."

"Goodbye, Cinda."

"Bye, Zach."

Chapter Four

Dreamweaver, I believe you can get me through the night;
Dreamweaver, I believe we can reach the morning light;
Fly me high through the starry sky, Maybe to an astral plane,
'Cross the highways of fantasy; Help me to forget today's pain.
Ooh, Dreamweaver, I believe you can get me through the night.
~Gary Wright

In the mutant village high on the plateau above Haven Hold Valley, Alanna felt the sudden involuntary tightening of her abdominal muscles. With her birthing time drawing near, such contractions had come off and on now for over a month, but this time seemed somehow different. She went on with her work, waiting. The sensation came again, rippling across her belly. Menda, her mother, noticed the far away, listening expression on her face and her slight quiver of discomfort.

"Alanna?"

The girl turned and smiled. "It's starting," she said. Menda hugged her excitedly.

"I'll go get Narsii and Daana."

"There's lots of time, Mama."

Alanna had feared Narsii, the village healer, since early childhood, when she accidentally stumbled in on an operation in progress. Only five years old at the time, Alanna had innocently wandered into the hut of her favorite uncle and found Narsii bending over him with a blood-stained knife in her spidery hand. He died that night. Alanna had known he lay ill from a festering wound, but for years afterwards she remained convinced that Narsii murdered him. Even after she grew old enough to understand what she had seen, a deep rooted fear of the woman persisted. Alanna had no wish to spend any more time in the healer's presence than absolutely necessary. Menda however remained adamant. She had felt relieved and delighted when her daughter finally, inexplicably accepted her pregnancy, the result of getting raped by slavers. Menda longed for a grandchild to cuddle. If her body had still been capable, she would have had another herself.

The healer and Daana, the midwife, came and bundled Alanna and her mother off to the previously readied birthing hut. They refused to allow the girl any activity, not even her basket weaving. She spent the afternoon and evening in utter boredom while they constantly checked and fussed over her, timing the contractions that gradually grew closer and closer together, coaching her and trying to prepare her for what was to come. With nothing to distract her from the increasing discomfort, the hours dragged at a torturous pace. Just before suppertime, her water broke and they gently cleaned her up and insisted she eat something to strengthen her for the coming ordeal. She felt little appetite, but she accepted a cup of hot soup, then spilled most of it when an unusually strong contraction caught her by surprise, causing her to double over in pain.

As the evening lengthened into night, the contractions grew increasingly painful and closer together, assaulting her in waves that rose, peaked and broke, sliding back into oblivion. The three women coached her constantly now, bathing her sweaty face and neck, telling her how and when to breathe, praising and encouraging her. Time lost all meaning. The hours ran together into eternity and the night and the pain seemed endless. She felt like her back was breaking, like she was being torn apart from inside. The pain became constant and went on and on with no relief and no apparent result. The agony built until she felt sure she would die. She was only vaguely aware of the worried glances exchanged by the women, but then Narsii said something that cut through the fog of pain and exhaustion like an alarm whistle.

"Something is wrong. The baby's not coming. It must be tangled in the cord or positioned incorrectly. We may have to use the knife."

Alanna's heart leaped with panic and she grabbed her mother's hand, squeezing with the strength of terror until Menda winced. "No! Mama, no! Don't let her cut me! Please don't let her cut me!"

Menda stroked her sweat-dampened hair and spoke soothingly. Alanna suddenly convulsed as the pain mounted excruciatingly, and for the first time a scream ripped from her throat and shattered the pre-dawn stillness. Alanna felt herself sinking into a deep well of darkness and panicked, sure she was dying. She was just about to surrender to the pain-free promise of that darkness when she felt a flutter, like the soft beating of wings against her mind.

"Dreamweaver," she muttered. "My Dreamweaver."

The women thought her delirious and Narsii hurried out, heading for her dwelling to get her knives. Alanna sank through a cloud of rosy pink to settle into the warm, comforting embrace of her dream friend, pain and fear far away in the real world. He soothed and reassured her and she felt a trusting confidence that everything would be fine now. He gently drew her forward to that place where he had once before shown her the innocence and beauty of her child. She felt that precious spirit once again, sensing the wrongness of its positioning. There was a feeling of urgency and tremendous pressure. The Dreamweaver guided her and together they gently pushed and turned the tiny being into the proper position. Something eased as the baby at last began her journey down the birth canal. The contractions began to come in waves again, seeming natural and almost gentle after the torturous pressure. Alanna felt the rise and fall of them and rode the crest like a cork in the tide, but she felt no pain. Her Dreamweaver protected her.

Narsii returned to the birthing hut to find Daana and Menda excitedly coaching and encouraging the girl as the contractions returned to normal. Alanna lay with eyes open, but she seemed totally oblivious to her surroundings, her features fixed in an expression of serene wonder.

"I don't know what happened, Narsii," the midwife exclaimed in amazement. "I've never seen anything like it. Something just seemed to change suddenly, almost as if the baby shifted by itself. Then the contractions returned to normal. The baby is on its way!"

Alanna and the Dreamweaver stayed with the little one, monitoring her progress down the birth canal. Alanna could sense him gently reassuring the baby, comforting her shock as she entered the chill of the outside world and was received into the loving hands of her grandmother. For a few moments the Dreamweaver strained to hold that three-way connection now the baby was no longer a part of Alanna's body. The girl felt his awe, his excitement and wonder, sensing it in rainbow washes of color. He wrapped her in a bright blanket of rosy pink, like an embrace of love and admiration, and she hugged him back. (*I love you, Dreamweaver,*) she thought to him. He seemed shy and apologized wordlessly for having taken so long to reach her. She got the impression he had been far away and had not realized she was in trouble until things started to go wrong.

"Alanna! Alanna!"

A voice called sharply to her. The Dreamweaver reluctantly began to withdraw and she sent a wistful thought chasing after him, (*I will always love you*.) Then he was gone and the real world came crashing in. She felt like an army of norps in heavy boots had used her for a floor mat. Daana gently placed the baby in her arms and she held it close, lovingly.

"It's a girl," the midwife announced. The new mother smiled, wondering what Daana would think if she said she had known since midwinter that the baby would be female. She cuddled her daughter and thought about a tiny rose bud opening and blossoming in the sunlight.

*   *   *

Zach lay rolled in his blankets between Hutch and Tadi, thinking about the events of the past day, his first day as a sponsor. He listened to the soft sounds of the sleeping shepherds all around him and remembered waking that morning in the hold with Hutch's friendly smile to greet him. They had risen at dawn to go out and wave goodbye to the Kithtrekkers, calling a final farewell to Jericho, Mik and Cinda. When Aaron introduced Zach at breakfast, the assembly received the news of his sponsorship with amiable acceptance. Everyone welcomed him and tried to make him feel at home. Over breakfast, Tadi suggested to Hutch that they take Zach up to the Meadows that afternoon, to show him something of the valley and introduce him to Sev and the shepherds. They decided to spend the night and the next day at the cottage, returning the following morning in time to introduce Daniel when the mutant came on his regular visit.

Later that morning, as Hutch gave him a tour of the hold, Zach heard mention of Daniel countless times from various people, all anxious to make sure he understood the fondness they felt for the mutant. The constant repetition began to wear on his nerves. At last, after lunch, they left the hold and headed north, into the deep, cool shadows of the forest. In the bush country where Zach grew up the woods had seemed a fearful place, full of escaped slaves and raiders. But these cool, fragrant evergreen woods seemed serene and peaceful. Zach enjoyed the trip immensely, soaking up the beauty and tranquility of the forest, savoring it, wanting to hold it forever.

When they reached the cottage, Sev and the shepherds greeted them with friendly hospitality, and Zach was once again cordially welcomed into the community. After a simple meal they enjoyed an evening of music, laughter, elderberry brandy and storytelling, during which Zach heard once again the story of Daniel beginning to end. At last they all retired for the night, except Jesse Hayes and Cal Sorenson, who stood on night watch. Zach felt too keyed up to sleep. His mind overflowed with images and impressions of the day: the feeling of friendly acceptance from the assembly; the orchard at the hold in full bloom, all frothy pink and white; the noisy tumbling of a group of children playing in a grassy garden behind the main building of the hold; the cool, green serenity of the forest path and that sense of being a part of nature; Hutch laughing at a joke made by one of the shepherds. Tadi seemed everything Zach had always wished his father would be . . . kind, considerate and accepting. And Hutch felt like the brother, the companion he'd never had, growing up with only younger sisters and far from the nearest neighbour.

Zach finally drifted into a light doze, anticipating the days and months to come when he would get to know these people better.

An unfamiliar sound jolted him awake and he lay listening intently. But most sounds in this environment seemed unfamiliar to him, so he relaxed again, preparing to go back to sleep. Then one of the dogs started barking, followed by a chorus of others. Sev jumped up and headed for the door before the shepherds even woke, with Hutch not far behind him. Zach scrambled up to follow with Tadi at his shoulder and the rest of the shepherds tumbling out of their beds in confusion. Sev had stopped on the porch to listen and take his bearings, then he plunged away into the darkness. One of the dogs let out a sudden scream of pain and the racket from the others scaled up into pure hysteria. A shot came, then another.

Zach followed Hutch, crashing and stumbling through the brush, tripping over roots and getting slapped in the face by unseen branches. He devoutly hoped that whatever lurked out there could see no better in the dark than they could. He stopped for a moment, discovering he had lost Hutch in the dark. He listened but heard nothing except a faint rustling in the bushes to his right. Zach suddenly realized most of the noise of passage had been his own. He squinted, straining to make out details of the landscape. An almost full moon stood overhead, covered by a blanket of high fog which filtered and diffused the thin light. Zach took two uncertain steps in the direction he thought Hutch had gone. His footsteps sounded incredibly loud in the tense silence. He stopped, heart pounding in near panic. His hands, clutching the rifle the holders had given him, felt clammy with nervous sweat. He had followed Hutch blindly, and now had only the vaguest notion where he stood in relation to the cottage. If he moved, he would only get himself more lost and possibly attract whatever danger the night held. He did the only thing that made sense . . . he kept still and waited for Hutch to come back for him. Time seemed to telescope, seconds into hours, as he waited, every sense alert, every nerve taut. This place that only a few hours earlier had seemed so calm and peaceful now seemed filled with menace. Gradually the frogs and crickets returned to their late night serenading and the feeling of imminent danger eased. Zach caught a faint sound of movement and a flicker of motion. His heart leaped like a landed fish and he clutched the rifle tighter, afraid to use it in case he shot Hutch or one of the young shepherds.

"Zach?"

He recognized Hutch's low voice and sighed with relief. "Here," he called in answer. The holder made his way forward in near silence.

"Sorry I left you behind. I feared for Jesse."

"Is he alright?"

"He's fine. Raiders took a sheep. Killed our best dog too. Poor old Shep. He was almost as old as Jesse, but he would not stay behind. Most of these younger dogs are descended from him, but none are as smart or as brave as he was."

They headed back to the cottage, and by the time they arrived, the others had returned as well. Jesse and Cal, though shaken, had insisted they could complete their shift. Sev stayed out to patrol the area. Hutch, Tadi, Zach and the other four shepherds sat up for a while discussing the attack, too excited to sleep. A raid on the flock was not a common occurrence. The last had come three years earlier and resulted in the death of Martin Tayler. Wild game remained too plentiful to make the dangers of poaching attractive, especially when the holders went much better armed than most mutants. Tadi made some herb tea to calm their nerves and eventually they went back to bed, but they got little sleep that night.

*   *   *

Birdsong echoed cheerfully through the woods and the sun was doing its best to burn off a thin layer of high fog when Daniel set off for the end of the main valley. He breathed deeply as he glided between the trees, enjoying the tangy, earthy scents of the vernal woods. Spring was his favorite time of year, a time of hope and renewal, when the earth once more released her bounty.

Today Daniel planned to climb to the rim and pick a fresh supply of bitterberry leaves for Margit. He knew her supplies must be low after the trade fair. He looked forward to visiting the hold again, to seeing his friends and playing with Little Daniel. It never failed to amaze him how quickly the baby grew and changed.

He had decided to take the cliff trail this time because it lay closer to where the bitterberries grew, and because he planned to stop along the way to tag the camas plants again. They had provided a welcome addition to his winter diet with their sweet caramel flavor, and Darius loved them. As Daniel emerged from the north end of the narrow, rocky pass, he thought about Sev and the shepherds. Hutch had told him Jesse worked as a shepherd this year. Perhaps on the way home he would stop in for a visit, but for the time being, he ghosted past unnoticed.

He continued northward, staying within the shelter of the trees, skirting the Meadows until he came to a spot where the woods bordered a small clearing. Just to his right through the trees he could see a patch of red and white that seemed out of place. He froze, all senses alert, then slowly moved closer to investigate. The carcass of a sheep lay just at the edge of a grove of alders. Daniel stepped cautiously forward and crouched to examine the remains of the animal and the signs surrounding it. He saw tracks of numerous small scavengers, and some of the bones had been gnawed, but the animal had obviously died by a human hand. It had been gutted and skinned and most of the meat removed. The butcher had worn moccasins, a different style from Daniel's. The holders for the most part wore boots. The sheep killer had to have been an outsider . . . possibly a raider. With a sudden stab of concern for Sev and the boys, Daniel quickly rose, prepared to run to the cottage and make sure all was well. He never got the chance.

*   *   *

After breakfast, Zach and Hutch set out to look around for any signs of last night's marauders. The woods seemed once more peaceful and unthreatening. Under the brightness of the morning sun, the fear and violence of last night had a far off, dreamlike quality. Zach suggested they separate to cover more ground. In a way, he was testing Hutch's confidence in him, seeing if the holder would trust his ability to take care of himself in this unfamiliar environment. Hutch agreed without hesitation, not about to do anything to lessen Zach's deplorably low self-esteem. He let the youth go off on his own, but stayed fairly close, just in case the inexperienced outlander ran into trouble.

Zach headed in a westerly direction, carefully scanning the ground for any signs of human passage. He had no training as a tracker, but he had a sharp eye and would not miss any obvious clues. He liked wandering alone in the forest. It gave him a fleeting, illusory sense of competence and self-confidence, with no one to notice if he made a mistake, or to blame him if things went wrong. It was just himself and Mother Nature, and he felt her welcoming him home like a prodigal son.

Zach reached the grove of alders just a few moments ahead of Daniel and spotted the carcass. He hesitated, wondering what he should do. How could he signal Hutch without alerting any raiders that might still lurk in the area? He studied his surroundings uneasily, wondering if the innocent beauty hid a deadly danger. As he stood undecided, he saw a flicker of movement in the trees near the carcass. A figure emerged from the woods and knelt beside the dead sheep. Zach recognized Daniel instantly. In the past two days the holders had inundated him with stories and descriptions of the mutant, until he felt sick of hearing about it. Zach's eyes narrowed suspiciously as he watched this man the holders spoke of so fondly. The evidence seemed to point to the conclusion that Daniel was taking advantage of the holders' trust to raid the flock unsuspected. Perhaps he was even in league with raiders. Zach raised his rifle and took careful aim. He had no intention of shooting Daniel. He intended only to send a bullet buzzing past his ear to scare him off. Then the evidence would remain, plain for anyone to see, and Zach would make sure Hutch and Tadi realized how dangerous it was to trust a mutant. His finger tightened on the trigger. Daniel rose abruptly just as the shot shattered the stillness, echoing through the forest. The mutant vanished and Zach froze, uncertain. Had he actually hit the man? Hutch appeared suddenly at his elbow.

"What is it? What were you shooting at?"

Zach stared at him with a sinking feeling. "It was your mutant friend. He was one of the poachers," he said, indicating the remains of the sheep.

Hutch paled. "You shot at Daniel?"

"He killed one of your sheep," Zach said defensively.

Hutch grabbed a handful of the outlander's shirt front and yanked him closer, snarling into his face, "You stupid brain dead outlander! Don't you listen? Daniel would never kill one of our sheep, and even if he did, we owe him! If he wants a goddamn sheep he can flaming well have one!" Hutch dragged Zach over to the carcass. "Damn you, Zach! He's going to think we've betrayed him, that we've turned against him!" He released the youth and bent to examine the evidence.

"This animal's been dead for hours. See? Daniel didn't kill it any more than you did."

Daniel's bow lay beside the carcass and Hutch picked it up with a sudden chill of fear. He scanned the ground quickly and stiffened, eyes widening in horror when he saw smears of blood leading into the trees.

"You hit him! You actually hit him!"

Hutch turned to face Zach, staring at him as if seeing something foul that had just crawled out from under a rock. "You mutant-hating son of a dag bitch!" The holder's voice sounded flat, almost emotionless in its anger. "You get back to the cottage and tell Sev what happened and be quick about it. And you'd better pray that Daniel doesn't die, because if he does, I'm going to kill you."

The holder whirled and ran into the trees, following the blood trail. Zach watched him go, stunned by the depth of Hutch's anger, filled with a sense of dread and despair. He had done it again. It seemed he could do nothing right. He had not meant to shoot the mutant, but it had happened. All he could do now was try to help any way he could. He turned and started loping back toward the cottage.

*   *   *

Daniel staggered and his shoulder struck a tree, spinning him around. He fell, landed on his back and lay there, stunned, staring up at the lacy patterns of foliage. But the instinct of the hunted drove him with an urgency that brought him unsteadily to his feet to stumble on. He made no attempt to hide his trail. He was deep in shock, both physical and emotional, and his only thought was to run. He knew the shooter would follow.

When he heard the rifle crack and felt the powerful blow strike him in the side, knocking him off his feet, one crystal clear thought imprinted itself on his mind. He had been shot by a holder. No raider would so advertise his presence within hold territory. Few local raiders had rifles or ammunition to begin with. It had to have been a holder. Moving purely on instinct, he had rolled into the trees and lurched to his feet, one hand pressed against his side where the bullet had entered just below the curve of his ribs. His thoughts reeled. Why? What had he done? He had trusted them! Again. Betrayed again. He ran, more from the unbearable pain of shattered trust than from the hunter on his trail.

Daniel's side grew soaked and sticky with blood and he left a trail a child could follow, but it didn't matter. This wound he could not fix himself, and he was alone. His life felt like an empty, desolate wasteland of aloneness. Every friend he had ever known had either died or betrayed him. Every event in his life had led inevitably to this moment. The holders had struck the mortal blow. This wound would kill him whether the hunter found him or not.

He moved at random, barely conscious. Each time he fell it took longer to get to his feet again. He could feel himself growing weaker as the life drained out of him. A root caught his dragging foot and he stumbled and fell again, landing face down. Daniel groaned as the spreading numbness in his right side awakened in a blaze of fiery agony. He lay in a gathering pool of blood, feeling sick and dizzy, waiting for the pain to subside enough so he could get up and go on. His shoulder rested against the tree that had tripped him, and he used its rough trunk to haul himself to his feet again, then stood clinging to it, waiting for the world to stop spinning. Suddenly he knew he could go no further. The time had come to make a stand.

The old pine he clung to had partially rotted out to form a shallow cavity. He wedged himself into the hollow and crouched there with his hunting knife in his hand, a pitiful weapon against a rifle, but at least he would die facing his enemy with a weapon in hand. He waited, his left hand clamped against the burning pain in his side, waiting to see whose familiar face would come bearing his death. He heard quick footfalls coming along his back trail and blinked hard, trying to clear the darkness from his vision. A figure came into view, rifle in hand, blond head bent, following the blood trail. Daniel groaned softly.

"No! Ah, Hutch! No!" he whispered in anguish. It felt as if every blow ever struck against him in his life, every rejection, every bitter betrayal had all combined to deal one tremendous blow to his scarred and battered spirit. For an instant everything went dark and he sank, drowning in a black sea of despair. His one true friend had betrayed him. He wanted to die. But something drew him back, some stubbornness in him that would not accept an easy surrender.

*   *   *

Miles away, up on the plateau, Darius trotted homeward, happy and weary from the birthing. He felt the sudden shock of the bullet as it struck Daniel and the tremors of emotional pain transmitted along the lifeline. The little telepath began running along the rim, heading for the refuge and the nearest, safest route to the valley. His friend was in trouble. Weariness forgotten, he hurried along at a distance-eating trot. Daniel was hurt. Daniel needed him. A few miles further on, Darius got brought up short, as if he had slammed into a stone wall. All his muscles went rigid with pain as Daniel's mental cry of agony and despair fed back along the lifeline in a tidal wave of black and grey. Darius stood frozen as the echoes of anguish faded away, sure he had heard his friend die. But the lifeline remained intact. He started to run again, throwing himself into high speed, burning his already depleted energy reserves at a tremendous rate, straining to reach his friend before it was too late.

*   *   *

Hutch loped along, heart clenched with fear as the trail continued and he failed to catch up with the mutant. There was so much blood. He heard a low groan and looked up . . . saw his friend.

"Daniel!" He ran forward and Daniel raised his knife defensively. Hutch stopped dead, disconcerted.

"Why, Hutch?" the mutant groaned softly, his face a mask of pain that came from something deeper than the wound in his side. With a shock like a punch in the gut, Hutch realized Daniel thought the shot had come from *his* rifle. He flung the weapon aside as if it had suddenly turned into a poisonous snake.

"Daniel! You can't believe that *I* would shoot you!" Hutch cried, moving closer, empty hands out beseechingly. Daniel's left hand came up as if to ward him off, shiny and slick with blood.

"Oh, Lord!" Hutch groaned at the sight. He moved in beside his friend, ignoring the threat of the knife. He couldn't believe Daniel would harm him. He touched the back of that bloody hand.

"Please, Danni. Let me help you!"

The holder's trust was well founded. Betrayed or not, Daniel would rather cut off his own hand than hurt Hutch. The mutant submitted with numb despair as his friend drew him from the hollow of the tree and laid him out on the ground. With shaking hands Hutch peeled back Daniel's bloody shirt to examine the wound. He had seen bullet wounds before, usually in the bodies of dead raiders, but never before in the living flesh of someone for whom he cared. It seemed such a huge, gaping wound, a raw, red mouth opened up in Daniel's side to spew out his life's blood. It looked deadly. Hutch's heart cramped in grief and fear as he realized his friend might not survive.

"Leaves! Daniel, do you have any of those leaves?" he demanded, gently trying to rouse the dazed mutant.

"Medicine pouch," Daniel mumbled.

With feverish urgency, Hutch fumbled through Daniel's sundry pouches until he found the right one. He sprinkled the greyish leaves thickly over the wound, gently pressing them against the gaping hole, wincing when Daniel shuddered. The blood at last stopped flowing. Hutch sliced a strip from the hem of his cloak to bind the leaves in place, then wrapped the rest of his cloak around the mutant's shivering body, praying that Sev would hurry.

Daniel opened his eyes and looked up at Hutch, pupils dilated with shock and pain. "Hutch, I'm so cold."

The holder sat down with his back against the tree and carefully drew Daniel up so the mutant lay against the warmth of his chest, dark head resting in the hollow of his shoulder. He wrapped his arms around his friend to warm him and pressed his cheek against the springiness of Daniel's hair.

"I love you, Danni. Don't die," he pleaded softly.

His quiet words penetrated the fog of desolation in which Daniel's broken spirit wandered. Like a colored thread in a world of black and grey, they wrapped around Daniel's heart, binding the shattered pieces once more into a whole. He was not alone . . . Hutch loved him . . . friendship remained intact.

Daniel relaxed in Hutch's arms, supported, warmed and comforted by his friend's love and strength. He surrendered to the physical pain, accepting it with a calm, peaceful confidence, trusting Hutch completely, knowing his friend would defend him from further harm. He no longer wished for death, though he had no fear of it. For his friend's sake he would fight for life with all the stubborn courage he possessed.

It seemed like hours passed before Hutch heard Sev calling him distantly. He shouted in answer to guide the hunter to them. Seconds later, Sev appeared, running with a folded blanket stretcher in one hand, closely followed by Jesse and Tadi, stumping along on his wooden leg as fast as he could manage. They gathered around anxiously, Tadi kneeling on Hutch's right and Jesse on his left.

"How bad is it?" Sev asked.

"Really bad," Hutch answered brokenly. "I don't know if he can make it."

Tadi caught Daniel's chin gently and turned his head until their eyes met. Daniel struggled to focus. Hair had fallen across his face and the older man gently brushed it aside.

"You hang on, son," Tadi said softly. "If you take the high road now, you're going to leave behind a lot of sorrowful people."

Daniel blinked up at him dazedly. He felt their love and concern wrap around him like a blanket, warm and protective. It no longer mattered who had shot him or why. The holders were still his friends. He was not betrayed.

They eased him onto the stretcher and picked it up, Sev in front and Hutch behind, where he could watch his friend's shallow breathing and know he yet lived. Tadi retrieved Hutch's rifle and carried it slung across his back.

"Jesse," he said, "you'd best get back to the flock. Your duty is there."

The boy met his father's eyes with an expression of stubborn defiance. "No, sir. I'm staying with Daniel until I know he's going to be alright. Zach can take my place."

Tadi gave Jesse a stern look. The boy didn't back down, but his eyes took on a pleading expression. Tadi sighed and nodded. "Alright then."

The trip back to the hold became a torturous nightmare. Hutch feared and expected at any moment to see the rise and fall of his friend's breathing cease. Daniel remained conscious most of the way, and each step became exquisite agony. The bullet burned like a coal of icy fire in his gut and every step seemed to drive it deeper. He tried to keep silent, knowing any sign of his pain was like a knife twisting in Hutch's heart, but an occasional stumble or misstep on the rough trail would wring a tortured moan from him. He prayed for the peace of unconsciousness to find him, but the agony just went on and on. At last, as they neared the place where the trail leveled out along the bank of the river, he felt a familiar mental flutter.

"Darius," he muttered. No one heard him or understood except Hutch. The blond holder watched his friend's face relax at last as he slipped into merciful unconsciousness, and Hutch silently blessed the little telepath.

Hedy and Rennie stood lookout that day and they saw the stretcher party coming long before it reached the gates. Rennie ran to get Margit and found her in the laundry room helping with the washing. The women all dropped their work and rushed out to see whose husband or brother or son had been injured. Margit met the stretcher party at the gate and bent over her patient for a brief examination.

"What happened?" she demanded, lifting Hutch's cloak to see the mutant's blood-soaked side.

"Zach shot him!" Hutch answered, his voice rough with anger and fear for his friend. Margit glanced sharply at him, disturbed by what she heard in his tone. But she had no time to worry about that now.

"Take him straight to the surgery," she said briskly. "Jesse, go see if you can find Kelda. She should be either in the classroom or the nursery."

The boy complied instantly, sprinting across the courtyard as if raiders chased him. They carried the stretcher through the infirmary and into the tiny operating room, setting it down on top of the surgery table. Sev and Tadi backed against the wall and watched as Margit quickly cut away Daniel's buckskin shirt and gently peeled off the crude bandage and leaves to expose the ugly wound. Jesse and Kelda appeared in the doorway and Margit glanced up. The small surgery was getting crowded.

"Out! All of you except Kelda. Wait in the hall or something. This is going to take time."

They filed out obediently, all except Hutch, who stood at the head of the table, his hands resting on Daniel's shoulders.

"You too, Hutch. Out."

The young man stared at her impassively. "I'm not leaving him."

Margit studied Hutch for a moment, seeing the immovable determination in him, a kind of blank calm that would accept no argument. The only way to remove him would be to drag him bodily from the room. Such an act would cause more harm than allowing him to stay.

"Alright but be quiet and keep out of the way."

The two healers quickly scrubbed up. Margit took a bottle of clear, colorless liquid from a shelf and poured a few drops onto a small square of cloth, then laid it over Daniel's nose and mouth to ensure he remained unconscious throughout the operation. Kelda unwrapped the pre-sterilized instruments and laid them out, ready for use. Hutch kept his eyes fastened on his friend's quiet face as the operation began.

Outside in the corridor a small crowd gathered, anxiously awaiting news. Tye had returned from a hunting trip and now paced restlessly up and down the hallway. Jesse sat with his back to the wall, hugging his knees, with Neely next to him, fidgeting with anxiety. They had waited for hours already. Sev had reluctantly left to go back to the Meadows. To leave the inexperienced boys unattended for any lengty time seemed unwise, especially with raiders in the vicinity. Tadi promised to bring news to the cottage as soon as they knew something definite. They had decided to leave Zach at the Meadows for a few days until the anger that rocked the hold quieted a little. If Daniel died, Zach would not be forgiven. Even if Daniel survived, it seemed doubtful whether the mutant-hating outlander would ever find acceptance now.

Davin Mattias came striding down the corridor for the third time to ask, "Any news yet?" This time he stayed to wait with the others. He leaned against the wall, thinking about the mutant. He loved Daniel's gentle playfulness with the baby, his shy wonder at being allowed a place in their small family. Davin closed his eyes and uttered a silent prayer. Not a deeply religious man, prayer came to him seldom and not easily. The last time had been when his pregnant wife fell into raider hands, and Daniel had become the miraculous answer to that prayer.

At last the infirmary door opened and Margit slipped out to lean wearily against the wall, gazing into the anxious faces gathered around her. "Well," she said in a tired, discouraged voice, "I have removed the bullet and repaired the damage to his organs, but he has lost too much blood. It's between Daniel and the Creative Flame now. If he survives until morning, we can begin to hope."

They all looked at each other in worried disappointment. They had hoped for better, more definite news. Neely started to cry and Tadi put one arm around her and the other around Jesse.

"Don't worry," he said, "that young man is a survivor. He'll not give in without a fight."

The crowd gradually dispersed to spread the news and return to neglected duties, thoughts heavy with concern for the young mutant. While stories of his daring rescues had been talked about for over a year now, most of the holders had actually only known him for a few months, since the naming ceremony. In that short time he had unknowingly, in his shy, quiet way, found a permanent place in their hearts. They valued his steady courage, his willingness to risk everything to help someone in trouble. They each felt that if he died it would somehow diminish their own lives.

* * *

Sometime past midnight, Jesse rose and moved silently through the darkened corridor, unable to sleep for worrying about Daniel. He reached the infirmary door and slipped inside. A lamp burned on the night table beside Daniel's bed. The mutant's face looked paper white against the stark contrast of his jet black hair. He looked dead. With a stab of fear, Jesse hurried forward to check him, to make sure he was still breathing. The rise and fall of his chest seemed shallow but steady. Hutch lay slumped, half on a chair and half lying on the edge of the bed, sound asleep, emotionally exhausted. Several people had offered to sit up in his place, but the young man refused to leave his friend's side. Jesse pulled a blanket from one of the beds and laid it over his partner, then crawled into the cot next to Daniel's. He wanted to stay nearby in case any change occurred.

Sometime close to morning, Daniel finally woke, rising to consciousness slowly like a deep sea diver rising from the depths.

He opened his eyes and stared up at the wooden ceiling, thinking vaguely that it should be stone. Where was he? Gradually the memory came back to him. Someone had shot him. The holders had been taking him to the Haven. This must be the infirmary. The burning pain in his side had eased, replaced by a dull, throbbing ache. He felt unutterably weak and tired. He rolled his head a little to the right and saw Hutch, asleep with his head pillowed in his arms just a few inches from Daniel's hand. The rest of the memory returned in a rush . . . Hutch's warmth comforting him, the holder's soft voice saying, '*I love you, Danni. Don't die*'.

With a great effort of will, Daniel raised his hand a few inches to touch the pale gold of his friend's hair. Hutch woke with a start, feeling that light touch. He sat up abruptly, blinking sleep from his eyes. He had not meant to fall asleep. Daniel's eyes were open and the smile on his face brought a leap of hope to Hutch's anxious heart.

"Danni!" Hutch gripped his hand and Daniel squeezed back weakly.

"I'm sorry, Hutch," he whispered.

"Sorry?" the holder repeated in puzzled alarm. Was Daniel giving up, saying good-bye?

"I'm sorry I doubted you."

Hutch smiled with relief and reassurance. "I understand, Danni. You were in shock. I know you've been hurt and betrayed before."

Daniel smiled weakly. "I've never had a true friend before, Hutch. You will have to forgive the mistakes of inexperience."

Hutch swallowed hard and his fingers tightened on Daniel's hand. "I'll forgive you anything, Danni. Just don't die."

The mutant's smile turned to a crooked grin. "I'll try not to."

Jesse sat up, awakened by their low voices, and they noticed his presence for the first time. The boy scrambled out of bed, almost tripping over the trailing blankets in his haste. He went to his knees at Daniel's bedside, reaching out to touch the mutant's shoulder.

"Daniel! You're awake! Are you alright? You're not going to die?"

"I'll be fine, Jesse," Daniel replied, then focusing on Hutch he added in a wry voice, "I promise on my life's blood, what I have left of it, and on my honor, if I ever had any, that I will do my best to stay alive."

"I've never met any man more honorable than you, Daniel."

"Yeah," Jesse added, "but you are coming up a little short on the life's blood."

"Which reminds me," said Hutch, "Margit left this awful potion I'm supposed to pour into you now you're awake. She says it will increase production of new blood." He gently lifted Daniel's head and shoulders and held the cup to his lips. The mutant made a face but drank the bitter brew without argument.

"Argh! That's awful. Next time just tell her I died in my sleep."

"It would break her heart. She loves you as much as we do."

Daniel blinked up at Hutch in mild surprise, his eyelids beginning to droop as drowsiness overtook him.

"She does?"

"She's not the only one either," said Jesse. "You should have seen the crowd waiting in the corridor while Margit patched you up."

"You have more friends here than you realize," Hutch said softly. Daniel's eyes closed and he fell asleep with a peaceful smile on his face.

*   *   *

At the edge of the forest, hidden in shadow beneath the trailing branches of a big evergreen, a small figure huddled, watching the distant hold. Darius had followed the holders this far as they carried Daniel to the Haven. The telepath had seen the love and concern the holders felt for his friend and knew Daniel lay in good hands. But Darius also knew Daniel was very badly injured. The small man longed to be near his friend, to guard him against pain and help him in his struggle for survival. But Darius feared the holders and this seemed as close as he could safely go. It was not close enough. He could not make any real contact from this distance. All he could do was focus on Daniel's lifeline and listen for any change.

Toward morning rain began to fall softly, drops pattering and dancing amongst the leaves and grass blades. Darius huddled deeper into his cloak and shivered in the dampness. He sensed a stirring as Daniel began to surface and the telepath rose stiffly, prepared to risk approaching the hold if his friend needed him. He listened tensely with his inner hearing, but detected no sense of fear or unbearable pain, no echoes of that terrible, despairing cry. Darius felt answering tremors down Hutch's lifeline and realized the blond holder must be with Daniel. The tenuous contact flooded with a sense of peace and security as Daniel sank once more into sleep. Everything was fine. Hutch was there. Hutch would take care of Daniel. Darius turned for home, reassured at last. He stumbled with exhaustion and hunger after his high-speed run and the second long, sleepless night, but hunger and weariness remained old, familiar enemies, and he would never have another friend like Daniel.

*　　　　*　　　　*

Hutch dampened a cloth in a basin of water and bathed Daniel's burning face. For two days now the mutant had balanced on the thin edge between life and death as fever raged through his already weakened system. Hutch trembled with exhaustion. He had not left his friend's side since they returned to the hold. Meals were delivered to the infirmary for him, but they mostly went back untouched. He had little appetite with Daniel lying so close to death. Margit, Neely and Kelda helped to nurse Daniel, bathing and caring for him, urging Hutch to get some rest while they relieved him. But the young man stubbornly refused as long as his friend lay in danger, though he felt helpless to aid in the mutant's desperate struggle to survive.

In actual fact, his presence did more good than he knew. When Daniel tossed in delirium, muttering and crying out to people from his past, reliving old hurts and betrayals, Hutch would answer him gently, soothing and comforting him, each time drawing him back from the brink of despair that would have spelled his death. The holder learned more of his friend's background from those fever dreams than Daniel would ever realize. The more Hutch learned, the more he wondered that Daniel had ever been able to trust him.

Late on the afternoon of the third day, Margit came in to check on her patient and found Hutch reeling with exhaustion, barely able to sit upright in his chair at the mutant's bedside.

"Hutch, you're killing yourself. Go and get some sleep," she ordered him, "And eat something. You'll not do Daniel any good by making yourself sick."

The young man glanced up at her with burning, feverish eyes. His face twisted. "I can't. Aunt Margit, what if he dies? What if I go to sleep and he's gone when I wake? What if he has another nightmare and he needs me? I have to stay with him."

Hutch drew a deep, shaky breath that sounded close to a sob. Margit put her arms around him and held him, heart filled with sympathy for his fear and grief. He had not called her Aunt for years, and his use of that title now spoke to her of his need for comfort and reassurance.

"Alright, Hutch. I know you love him, but you have to get some rest. At least lie down for a while. Here, you can use the next bed. Then you'll be close if there's any change. I'll stay right here with him, I promise."

She drew the young man to his feet and over to the cot, and in his exhaustion he had no strength or will to resist. He collapsed onto the bed, determined not to fall asleep, to just rest awhile.

"Promise me, Margit . . . promise if I fall asleep you'll wake me."

"I swear that if he needs you or if there's any change for the worse, I'll wake you immediately."

Hutch fell asleep before she finished speaking. She laid a blanket over him and stood watching him for a moment. Margit had married once, years ago in her younger years, to a man she had loved deeply. But he died before they could produce any children and she never remarried. Years later, Margit's brother and his wife had died along with seven others when a fever epidemic swept the hold, leaving Tye, Hutch and Carly orphaned. Tye had been fourteen, nearly a man, but Hutch was only ten and Carly eight. Margit had taken them under her wing and mothered them as her own, so that now Hutch felt more like a son to her than a nephew. She brushed a stray lock of pale hair from his brow lovingly, then turned and began the sad task of changing Daniel's bandages.

Margit spent the rest of the afternoon and evening bathing Daniel and laying cool cloths against his pulse points, trying to bring down his temperature. She felt desperately worried about him. Blood loss weakened his resistance and the fever undermined the healing process, dehydrating him and slowing the renewal of vital fluids. If the fever didn't break soon, she feared they would lose him.

Neely came to take over at bedtime and noted with relief that Hutch lay asleep. "Oh, thank goodness!" she cried. "How did you manage to get him to rest at last?"

Margit smiled wryly. "After a time the body asserts its own will." She gave Neely a few brief instructions, though the girl had been helping all along and knew the routine.

"If he begins to dream or hallucinate, or if he starts to get any worse, wake Hutch immediately. I gave him my word on it. Then come and get me."

Margit headed off for bed, feeling older than her years. A crushing sense of helplessness overwhelmed her. She felt very fond of Daniel and she doubted he could survive until morning. She feared what his death might do to Hutch. If Daniel died, Zach's life would be in danger, and not just from her nephew. The Haveners were a friendly, hospitable group, but when one of their own was threatened or injured, they tended to close ranks, and Zach remained an outsider, a stranger, while Daniel had unknowingly become as much a part of the community as anyone outside the assembly could.

Chapter Five

Where your love is, put your heart,
Guard these moments well;
Where your dreams are, put your hopes;
You know they will not fail you;
Where your love is put your heart;
Oh, what would you do
If your dreams came true?
~Chris DeBurgh

Sometime well on toward morning, Neely woke with a start from an unintentional doze. She rose immediately to check Daniel. She felt his forehead and found it much cooler, almost normal. With a sigh that rose from the depths of her soul, she lifted his hand and pressed it against her cheek, closing her eyes as tears of relief welled up. When she opened them again, Daniel gazed up at her with sharp awareness and a touch of gentle amusement.

"Angel of mercy," he whispered, his voice thready with weakness. She smiled and stroked his cheek.

"You were for me once, remember?"

"How could I forget? You were the most beautiful thing I had ever seen, and Jesse threatened to kill me if I touched you."

"I love you, Daniel," she said, rubbing her cheek softly against the back of his hand. His smile faded and he gazed up at her with mingled apprehension and despair, aching to believe, but fearing it too. He felt sure he must have misunderstood her, afraid to allow his hopes to rise only to have them crushed. He knew love between a mutant man and a normal woman was strictly forbidden.

"You . . . love me?"

"Yes. I love you."

"But I'm a mutant . . . spawn of the devil. You barely even know me."

"I know you, Daniel. I don't care if you are a mutant. I don't care if you are the devil himself. I know your kindness, your loyalty and your courage. I know you have been desperately hurt more than once by those you trusted, but in spite of them, in spite of their cruelty and injustice, you still have a gentle, caring heart."

Daniel felt astounded and flattered by her assessment of him, so contrary to his own self-image of an unattractive, unwanted outcast, isolated and reserved, terrified to trust enough to love anyone. Anyone except Hutch. Somehow the holder had managed, in less than a year, to overcome the barriers and defenses Daniel had spent a lifetime building.

"Hutch?"

"He's in the next bed."

Daniel turned his head and saw a thatch of pale hair above the edge of a blanket. "Is he alright? He isn't sick, is he?"

"No," Neely smiled, loving him all the more for his concern. Hutch remained very dear to her as well. "He's just exhausted. He hasn't slept in four days. We've all felt sick with worry for you, so don't you dare die!"

Daniel stared at her, astonished by her vehemence. "I won't die," he assured her, "I promised Hutch and Jesse." He smiled, completely unaware of how close he had come to breaking that promise. She still held his hand, and she began once more to rub her cheek against it. He found the caress subtly erotic, awakening feelings he felt too weak to act upon even if it had seemed safe to respond. She saw the wistfulness in his eyes, the awakening of safely buried dreams. She bent over and kissed him lightly, stroked his hair back from his forehead and gently brushed his eyelids closed.

"Sleep," she whispered, and he obediently lay with his eyes closed, breathing in the subtle perfume of her until he fell into a gentle, natural slumber.

*   *   *

Margit woke early the next morning and went straight to the infirmary to check on Daniel. She felt surprised and grateful not to have been awakened in the night to attend a dying patient. She found him sleeping peacefully, his temperature normal and his pulse weak but regular. Margit breathed a sigh of relieved tension, thankful that her fears had not come true.

Neely slept in her chair, one of Daniel's hands clasped in hers. Margit smiled and didn't wake her. She turned to check on Hutch. He too still slept soundly, thank goodness. After the past four days, he needed all the rest he could get. Margit left them to their slumber and went for breakfast with a lighter heart. Once everyone had gathered for the meal, she stood and announced before the assembly that Daniel's fever had broken and he seemed out of immediate danger. Barring unforeseen complications, he would recover. A rousing cheer rocked the room and echoed down the corridors. It penetrated the depths of Hutch's exhausted sleep and triggered a dream.

He crouched deep in the bowels of the earth, following a dark, constricted tunnel. He knew the way out and longed to turn around and seek the sunlight, but Daniel lay up ahead somewhere in the darkness and needed help, so Hutch crawled on through blackness as thick and suffocating as syrup. He could hear voices somewhere ahead, shouting and chanting, and he knew they spelled danger for his friend. They intended to do something to Daniel, something terrible.

Hutch crawled until he came to a place where the path dropped away before him. From far below came a dull reddish glow, reflecting off the rocks around him. The chanting rose from those abysmal depths, ominous and chilling. He crept to the edge and looked over. Just a short way below him ran a narrow ledge, and on it, Daniel balanced precariously. The sheer, slick cliff offered no way up. From below, swarms of faceless people began climbing towards him, intent on reaching the mutant and dragging him down . . . down into hell. Daniel looked up, fear and desperation on his face, and saw Hutch. His expression changed to one of hope, of trusting confidence that somehow the holder would save him. Hutch reached down to him and Daniel stretched to his full height, straining to reach his friend's fingers. Mere inches separated them, and the savage hordes from below climbed closer.

Hutch swung out further over the edge, clinging to safety with one hand and his toes. He caught Daniel's wrist and their hands clasped. Hutch started inching his way backwards, pulling Daniel up with him. But suddenly the chanting stopped. The hordes from below swarmed up the cliff. Hutch knew their identities, even though they wore no faces . . . all the unknown people from Daniel's past, the betrayers, the slavers and mutant haters, all the cruel, unjust people who had hurt his friend. And they wanted him again, wanted to drag him down into hell where they could torture him forever. Hutch tried to hurry, but Daniel was heavy and his own hold on safety remained tenuous at best. Suddenly the crowd reached the ledge and they started to pull at Daniel. Hutch saw *their claws sink into Daniel's back, his legs, his sides. Blood welled and ran down his body. They pulled harder, dragging Hutch perilously close to the edge. Daniel gazed up at him, pain and despair in his eyes . . . and love.*

"I'm sorry," he whispered, and let go. His hand, slick with blood, slid out of Hutch's fingers. The mutant disappeared beneath the tide of savage humanity and Hutch screamed, "No, Danni!"

His cry brought Neely to her feet before she even fully woke. Hutch sat bolt upright on the bed gasping and shaking, his eyes wild and crazy with grief. His cry had wakened Daniel too.

"Hutch?" the mutant asked softly, his voice weak, but filled with concern. The holder turned stiffly and regarded him with a strangely blank expression. Neely put her arms around Hutch and hugged him.

"Was it a bad dream, Hutch?"

Slowly, the young man came fully awake and realized that it *had* been only a nightmare. "Mother of Mercy, what a dream!" he cried, slowly running his hands over his face. Rising shakily, he went to crouch by Daniel's bedside. He clasped the mutant's hand in a firm grip and strengthened his friend's weak hold with his other hand.

"Don't ever let go, my friend," he said with earnest intensity. "I would rather go down with you than watch you go down alone."

Daniel grinned crookedly. "I hadn't planned on going down. You want to come up with me?"

*   *   *

Zach threw another scoop of old straw and manure onto the heap and dropped the shovel. Picking up the handles of the barrow, he wheeled it out to the growing pile beside the barn and dumped his load. Two weeks had passed since the shooting and eight days since Tadi and Tye had returned Jesse to the Meadows and escorted Zach back to the hold. The outlander had fared well enough with the shepherds. They only knew an accident had happened and Daniel had been badly injured. When Sev returned he said little, treating Zach with polite reserve and telling the boys nothing. While the young shepherds had their suspicions, especially since the outlander no longer carried a rifle, they took their cue from Sev and left Zach alone.

Zach pushed the empty wheelbarrow back down the dimly lit aisle and started mucking out another stall. Though alone in the gloomy barn, he felt less lonely than he did in the dining hall filled with people. No one had spoken a word to him since his return, except for Tadi telling him what to do. He had weeded and hoed acres of garden, mucked out barns, cleaned and repaired harness, doing whatever task they assigned without protest or complaint. He spoke even less than he was spoken to, feeling like an unwanted ghost, invisible and totally ignored. He found it hard to remember that feeling of belonging he'd experienced on his first day as a sponsor. It seemed years ago. The anger of the holders felt like a thunderstorm hovering over his head, waiting to strike like a bolt of lightning.

He had seen Hutch only from a distance. The blond holder avoided him like the plague. Then yesterday Zach had come face to face with him in the corridor. They both stopped and stared at each other, and Zach opened his mouth to say something, to apologize, or to tell Hutch he hadn't meant to do it. But Hutch just glared at him with grim self-control, then turned on his heel and stalked away. Any shreds of self-esteem remaining to Zach crumbled. He had failed again before he even began. He had been wrong and he knew it. He had jumped to a false conclusion, and acting in his usual blundering manner, he had shot an innocent man, if any mutant was ever really innocent. Zach deeply regretted the incident. If he could have changed it he would have.

He turned and dropped another shovel load into the wheelbarrow, stiffening as he noticed the three grim figures standing at the entrance to the box stall. He recognized Rad Tayler but didn't know the others. His heartbeat quickened. Lightning was about to strike.

Rad swaggered forward threateningly with the other two flanking him. "So, mutant hater, I see they've got you right where you belong . . . in a dung pile!"

Zach brought the shovel up instinctively in defense.

"What you gonna do, outlander? Bash some heads?"

Rad wrenched the shovel from his hands and Zach offered no resistance. He had no wish to aggravate his situation by injuring anyone else. The holder threw the implement into the corner and moved forward menacingly.

"Don't worry, mutant hater, we'll give you more chance than you gave Daniel."

He started to throw punches at Zach. The outlander countered them easily, backing away, but Rad had not yet begun to get serious. He toyed with the youth, taking his measure. Zach had little experience with fighting. He'd had no brothers to wrestle with, no companions except his younger sisters. Rad eyed the openings in his opponent's defenses and suddenly drove his fist into Zach's stomach. The youth doubled over and Rad hit him hard between the shoulder blades, driving him to his knees, then kicked him in the side and sent him skidding across the floor. The other boys moved in then and the three of them started kicking Zach . . . not hard enough to do serious injury, just hard enough to hurt, to bruise him. Zach grabbed a foot aimed for his chest and twisted, and one of the boys lost his balance, crashing against the wall. Rad kicked the outlander in the face, splitting the skin over his left eyebrow and sending his head smashing into the side of the stall. Zach saw dancing lights and curled into a defensive knot, trying to protect his most vulnerable parts. They continued to punish him for a few moments, but with the end of his resistance the fun went out of it. At last they left, Rad giving him one last hard thump in the ribs and saying, "Enjoy your bruises, mutant hater. Try to imagine what it feels like to be gut shot."

Zach just lay there in the filthy straw, dazed and hurting all over, stunned by the violence of their hatred. He felt a sudden aching desire to see Cinda's smiling face again, or Mik's friendly grin, and wished he had never left the caravan. He heard footsteps approaching, the arhythmic step, thump of Tadi's wooden leg. Zach managed to push himself up so he leaned against the wall. He felt sick and suddenly the small amount of lunch he had managed to choke down came spewing back up. Tadi glanced into the stall and found him lying on the floor retching helplessly.

"Lord of mercy, Zach! What happened?"

Zach didn't answer . . . he couldn't. Tadi hurried to his side and held him, supporting him until the convulsions stopped coming. Then the councilman caught him by the chin and gently wiped the blood and filth from his face with a clean handkerchief. Zach refused to meet his eyes.

"Rad did this, didn't he? That boy is like a lightning rod. He seems to absorb other people's anger and focus it into violence. Damn him! He's not going to get away with this!"

Zach turned his face away. This had nothing to do with Rad, he thought, it was himself . . . he was the one drawing misfortune and disaster like a lightning rod. Rad was just one bolt of lightning. Maybe he had deserved this beating, as he had always seemed to deserve his father's punishment. Everything that happened to him, everything that went wrong around him, was his fault. He stared at the wall with blank, expressionless despair. Tadi was reminded of what he had seen in Zach at that first meeting, what had prompted him to take on the responsibilities of sponsorship. Zach had a lost look, a starved look that had nothing to do with a need for food.

"Come on, lad. We'd best clean you up and get Margit to examine you."

Tadi aided the boy to his feet and supported him as they made their way out of the barn and across the courtyard. The bath house remained deserted at this time of day and no one disturbed them as Tadi helped Zach wash off the worst of the grime. The youth still seemed shaky and unsteady on his feet when they had finished, so the councilman once more supported him as they headed down the corridor toward the infirmary. The door stood open with Margit nowhere in sight. Zach caught a brief glimpse of the mutant, asleep in one of the beds, then Tadi hustled him into the surgery and pushed him down onto a wooden chair in the corner.

"Stay there," he told Zach with a stern, warning look. "I'll go find Margit."

After he left, Zach slumped in the chair, deliberately concentrating on the pain of his abused body to take his mind off the ache of having won a dream and then lost it. He thought about the mutant lying in the next room and wondered what made this man so special. So maybe he had helped the holders a few times, that didn't mean his plans included no treachery. It could all have been part of a calculated plan to win the holders' trust and make them vulnerable to attack. Mutants just could not be trusted.

Simple curiosity drew Zach to his feet and sent him limping into the next room. He stood at the end of the bed gazing down at the sleeping patient. Daniel did not look like a raider. He didn't even look like a mutant. In repose his face had a strong, sensitive beauty that made Zach's fingers ache for a char stick and a piece of paper. The mutant's eyes flickered open and looked straight at him and Zach froze, transfixed by those alien green orbs, pupils huge with sleep like black bottomless wells. Puzzlement swam in them, and growing wariness. Zach felt that gaze penetrating to his very soul, seeing all his guilt, his failures, his shameful inadequacy, stripping away his thin human disguise and seeing him for what he really was, a nothing, a small, insignificant zero. He started to back away, heart pounding in his ears. He felt faint.

"Zach!"

Tadi's voice rang out sharp as a whip crack and Zach jumped and staggered as if he'd been shot.

"I told you to stay put!" The councilman strode forward like an avenging warrior. Zach backed away, shaking.

"I just wanted to see him," he muttered.

For an instant Tadi saw the fear, the hurt in his eyes, then that mask of sullenness slipped back into place. But that one glimpse acted like a bucket of ice water, cooling Tadi's anger. He stopped and searched the youth's face. Zach averted his eyes.

"Alright, you've seen him. Let's go."

Margit had entered the room right behind Tadi and she bent over the mutant, checking his condition. "Are you alright, Daniel?"

He gazed up at her in bewilderment. "Of course. I'm fine. He didn't do anything. Why is Tadi so angry? Who is he anyway?"

"Shhh. It's alright. His name is Zach McKenna. Tadi sponsored him for membership, though I doubt he'll find acceptance now. He is the one who shot you."

"Zach? He's the artist?"

Margit's brows rose in surprise. "I believe there was some mention of his being an artist."

"Hutch told me about him," Daniel said, frowning thoughtfully. "Raiders killed his family."

"Yes. We should have known better than to sponsor him with such a background. We might have guessed he would be a mutant hater. We told him about you, Daniel. We described you to him and told him you were a friend, but he shot you anyway."

"You would have turned him down because of me?"

"Because of you and Alanna and all the other mutants in these parts who are not raiders." She smiled. "We value you, Daniel." She brushed his cheek gently and he stared up at her, wide-eyed.

"I'd best go see to Zach. Some of the boys got a bit rough with him. He roused a lot of anger against himself when he hurt you."

Daniel had noticed the cuts on the outlander's face and the darkening bruises. Zach did not look like a mutant hater. Daniel had seen plenty of that kind, but he had detected none of that iron hostility in the youth's expression. Zach had looked like a scared kid, lost and alone. Daniel couldn't find it in his heart to feel any anger toward him.

* * *

Zach sat on the end of the surgery table and Tadi leaned against the wall in silence.

"Take your clothes off," Margit said brusquely, and turned away, busying herself searching the cupboard for the last jar of bitterberry ointment. Supplies were sadly depleted since the trade fair, and now her supplier lay injured. She found the jar and stood gazing at it for a moment doubtfully, then put it back, deciding that Zach would just have to suffer his lumps. She turned back to him and found him sitting on the table again, stripped to his underwear. His back, ribs, arms and legs looked mottled with angry red patches of beginning bruises. She gently probed his contusions, making sure no serious injury had occurred. He kept his eyes on the floor and she could feel him trembling faintly with pain and tension.

"No broken bones," she announced, forcing his head up so she could examine the cut on his forehead. She painted it with antiseptic and felt the lump on the back of his head, deeming it not serious.

"You'll live. But you're going to feel very sore and stiff for a week or so."

Rad and his cronies had been more brutally thorough than she expected. She seriously doubted the beating had stemmed from any real regard for Daniel. Rad never appeared to care too deeply about anyone but himself.

"You can put your clothes back on."

She turned back to the cupboard and took down a number of ceramic jars. In a small square of cloth she placed a pinch of herbs from each jar, then twisted it into a pouch and tied it closed. She held it toward Zach, saying, "Here, ask Cochita to make a tea for you with this. It will settle your nerves."

He backed away, fists clenched at his sides, shaking his head in refusal. The thought of asking the cook or anyone else in the hold for even so small a favor seemed more than he could bear. Margit frowned and Tadi reached out to take the medicine.

"I'll see that he gets it," he said grimly and started to shepherd his young charge out of the room.

"One more thing, Zach," Margit said, eyeing the youth narrowly. "Daniel is off limits. Leave him alone. I don't want him upset.

*   *   *

After that, Tadi kept a closer eye on his young sponsor, making certain no further harm came to him. Rad and his two friends got severely reprimanded and put on night guard duty for three months. In their off hours they had to clean the privies and do other assorted, unpleasant tasks. It didn't improve their tempers any, but it left them little time to harass the outlander.

Zach noticed he was seldom left completely alone. Tadi always seemed to hover somewhere nearby, conspicuously busy, but always present. The youth wondered bitterly if Tadi thought he might try to sneak back to the infirmary and finish the mutant off, or if his sponsor just didn't trust him to do his work properly unless someone watched. It never occurred to him that Tadi might be protecting him.

In the meantime, Daniel's strength improved daily and Margit began allowing him other visitors besides Hutch and Neely. One of the first was Tye. The hunter cocked his chair back casually, put his feet up on the night table and began regaling Daniel with a story about the magnificent stag he had stalked a few days earlier. He had spent hours working his way close enough for a clean shot, and when he finally had the beast in his sights, the animal turned and looked straight at him as if aware of his presence all along. And Tye could not fire. The stag seemed just too magnificent to kill. It would feel like killing the spirit of the forest. Daniel's eyes warmed with understanding and approval. Tye would never have told this story to Sev, or any of the other hunters. They would have thought him amusingly insane. He suspected that to most of them the animals were just food on the hoof. But somehow he had known Daniel would understand. He glanced around to make sure Margit was out of sight, then pulled Sev's flask from his pocket, saying with a twinkle in his eye, "Sev left this for you. First time I've ever known him to part with it. Said he figured it would do you more good than all Margit's smelly concoctions."

Daniel grinned and took a sip, enjoying the fruity fire of it. He was really beginning to appreciate this potent stuff. "Tye," he said, suddenly turning serious, "is Hutch alright?"

The hunter's eyebrows rose in surprise. "You probably see more of him these days than I do. Why do you ask?"

"I don't know. It's just . . . he seems different. Sort of sad I guess . . . like something's been taken out of him. I'm worried about him, Tye."

"Alright, I'll have a talk with him, see if I can find out what's wrong."

Tye visited a while longer, until Margit came and shooed him out so Daniel could rest. The hunter headed straight for the guard-walk, where he knew Hutch stood on duty. Daniel's concern had started an answering ripple of worry in his own mind. Now he thought about it, Hutch had seemed unusually subdued and serious lately, as if he'd had all the humor knocked out of him. Tye nodded to Ray Sorenson, Hutch's partner for the day, and strode past him.

"Hutch, can I talk to you?"

The young man leaned against the wall, staring out toward the desert, but he turned at the sound of his brother's voice. "Sure, Tye. What about?"

"Well, it's about you really. Daniel's worried about you."

Hutch grinned and shook his head. "He's lying in the infirmary half dead and he's worried about *me*?"

"Yes, well, he got me thinking, and you know, you have been unusually quiet lately. You want to tell me what's wrong?"

Hutch hesitated, not sure he could put into words this thing eating at his heart. "You know I have never hated anyone in my life." He met Tye's eyes and the hunter nodded. Hutch went on unhappily, "When we were carrying Daniel back from the Meadows and he was in so much pain . . . all I could think about was how much I wanted to kill Zach for making him suffer like that.

I still feel like smashing Zach's face every time I see him. It scares me, Tye."

"Ah, well . . . I don't think he's very popular with anyone these days. Did you know Rad and a couple of his friends kicked the sparks out of Zach the other day?"

The news startled Hutch. He had not gotten close enough to the outlander to notice the bruises. He slapped the top of the wall in pain and confusion.

"Damn it, Tye! I'm so mixed up about this whole damned mess! I hate that son of a bitch for what he did to Daniel. But Zach was my friend, or at least he was starting to be. I liked him. Hell, he wouldn't even be here if it weren't for me. And now, if the council and the assembly decide against him and cancel the sponsorship contract, which they probably will . . . he'll be out the gates and on his own. And he can't survive out there, Tye. He hasn't got the training. He doesn't even own any weapons."

"Maybe they won't cancel the contract."

"How much chance do you think there is of that? I don't know. A part of me feels sorry for him, 'cause right now everyone hates his guts, including me. A part of me is saying, no, it isn't right, he's only two years older than Jesse. He doesn't deserve to be exiled to his death. But another part of me wants to hurt him, to see him suffer the way he made Daniel suffer. It's making me sick inside. I don't know what to do. I feel like I'm the one who's had the sparks kicked out of him."

Tye laid a comforting hand on his brother's shoulder. "I wish I knew what to tell you. I guess it's not really up to us anyway. All we can do is cast our votes and see what happens."

"But how can I vote against him, knowing he'll probably die out there? And if they let him stay, how do I know he won't try to hurt Daniel again? If I vote for Zach I'll feel like I'm betraying Daniel."

"If the vote goes against Zach, I can't believe the council would send him off without weapons or supplies. He'd make it alright. And if they let him stay, I doubt he'd be stupid enough to try anything against Daniel again. Not after the reaction he got this time. He can't be a total fool."

"Maybe you're right," Hutch said, some of the tension going out of him. "Maybe you're right. But I won't rest easy until this damned trial is over. I dread it. I feel like, either way it's decided, I'm going to lose something important."

*   *   *

Zach knew about the coming trial and awaited it with equal dread. When Tadi returned to the Meadows to pick him up, his sponsor took him to a private spot and had a long talk with him . . . or to him. He gave Zach little opportunity to speak, and when Tadi questioned him, the undercurrent of angry accusation was enough to freeze any words of defense in his throat. His sponsor warned him about the sort of reception he could expect when they got back to the hold . . . told him that, as soon as Daniel recovered enough to attend, a hearing would take place to decide whether the sponsorship contract should be cancelled. Tadi had not speculated on the outcome, but Zach held no illusions. He had felt surprised when they accepted him in the first place. Now they had good reason to throw him out, and he felt little doubt they would do just that. But no caravan waited to welcome him back. The Kithtrekkers lay weeks away now and he would be alone and unarmed in country swarming with dangerous mutants and wild animals. As cold and desolate as his life appeared right now, he felt no desire to die.

*   *   *

As time passed and Daniel's body slowly healed, almost every member of the assembly stopped in to wish Daniel well, some merely popping in and out to say hello, and others staying to talk for hours, until Margit sent them away. Rad swaggered in one day about a week after Zach's beating, and casually informed Daniel that he needn't worry about that damned outlander, they had taught him a good lesson. The mutant frowned with chilly disapproval and said, "Don't do me any favors, Rad. Not unless I ask for them."

One day, Davin and Kelda brought Little Daniel to visit. Six months old now, the baby looked plump and rosy and seemed vitally interested in everything. His big blue eyes fastened on the mutant's familiar face and he smiled a heart-melting baby smile, reaching for his namesake. He had missed his play sessions with Daniel. Kelda sat him on the edge of the bed and Daniel held him and played with the little fellow until he hiccupped and giggled with delight. He gave a little cry of protest when the time came to leave and Kelda picked him up. She stood for a moment, hugging her baby and gazing down at the mutant, who smiled shyly back at her. She bent impulsively and kissed him lightly on the forehead. Daniel gave her a startled look and cast a nervous glance at her husband, who stood at the foot of the bed. But Davin just smiled and nodded his agreement when Kelda said, "We love you, Daniel. We're so glad you're on the mend."

Neely and Hutch visited every day, the girl usually in the afternoons, and the young man later in the day to keep Daniel company through dinner and the evening. Unused to remaining idle, as Daniel's strength gradually returned he felt increasingly bored and restless. Neely showed him how to card wool, and he sat propped on pillows, combing out mounds of raw wool, while she sat and knitted and chattered about the excitement and wonders of the trade fair or the goings on of the hold. Sometimes she sang to him. Daniel loved the sound of her voice, and once when the song was one dimly remembered from childhood, he even joined in tentatively, his voice soft and unsure, but true.

He loved to watch her knit, fingers flying, needles clicking a staccato rhythm while a garment seemed to grow like magic. One day she brought an extra pair of knitting needles and taught him the basic mechanics. When Hutch came in that evening, carrying their supper tray, he laughed to see Daniel sitting propped on pillows, knitting like a little old granny. The mutant grinned and held up the completed strip, full of dropped and uneven stitches.

"Don't laugh," he said, "the first sweater I make is for you. And you'd better wear it!"

*   *   *

Nearly three weeks passed after the shooting before Margit deemed Daniel strong enough to sit through a general assembly. She walked into the infirmary one day during a rare moment when no visitors were present, and found him out of bed, leaning on the night table, trying to stand on his shaky legs. After that she allowed Hutch and Tye, and sometimes Davin, to take him for short walks, just around the room at first, then later, up and down the corridor, so his legs could regain their strength. At last she told Aaron he was ready and the council leader called the general assembly.

Hutch and Tye found Daniel sitting up in bed that evening, braiding strips of rawhide into a rope for Tadi. The mutant glanced up and grinned as they entered.

"Did Margit send you to make sure I stay in bed?"

Tye smiled, but Hutch continued to look serious, even worried.

"Not this time," the older brother answered. "Aaron has called a general assembly meeting in the great hall. The council wants you there."

Daniel frowned, a feeling of unease growing in him. The flood of friendly concern over the past weeks had done much to relax his wariness but could not completely undo the damage of the past. One glimpse of the expression on Hutch's face warned him this would not to be a pleasant experience. He tried to remember if he had done or said anything to offend them and wondered if he would have the strength to make it back to his refuge if they turned him out.

"Why do they want me? What's this about, Hutch?"

The holder hesitated, avoiding Daniel's eyes, and the mutant's alarm grew.

"It's about Zach," Hutch said finally. "A hearing to decide whether he'll be allowed to complete his sponsorship. We've been waiting for you to grow strong enough to attend . . . as his accuser."

"His accuser! I'm not accusing him of anything!"

"Well . . . as his victim then."

Daniel thought about that scared, battered kid who had stood at the end of the bed watching him. It had felt like seeing an image of himself not too many years ago. A feeling of dread came over him. He did not want to do this.

"We brought some clothes for you," Tye said. "We'll give you a hand getting them on if you need it."

"I've been dressing myself since I was two years old," Daniel replied wryly, "I think I can manage." But in the end they had to help him with his pants. He could not bend far enough to get his legs into them. He raked fingers through his ragged hair and Hutch handed him a comb.

"We'll have to get Cochita to give you a proper haircut one of these days," Tye observed critically. "Let's go. They're waiting for us."

The two holders walked on either side of Daniel, ready to support him if he needed it. When they entered the great hall, the assembly already filled the room, seated and murmuring in quiet conversation. Still weak and unsteady, one glimpse was enough to start Daniel's heart pounding. Before the naming ceremony they could not have gotten him into that room without dragging him. As it was, he barely managed to enter with a kind of shaky dignity. He felt like he was walking into one of his nightmares.

The council sat behind the large table at the head of the room. Just to the right of the doorway a pair of chairs waited, and Hutch guided Daniel to one of these and sat down beside him. They had the council on their right and the assembly on their left. Opposite them, across the width of the room, Zach sat in another chair, hunched in sullen misery.

Once Tye had seated himself amongst the assembly, Aaron rose and the room went still. The council leader turned his gaze on the mutant and smiled. "It is good to see you on your feet again, Daniel."

Daniel smiled back uncertainly as a murmur of agreement arose from the assembly. Aaron held up his hand for silence and they quieted.

"We gather here tonight to look into the shooting of our friend and neighbor, Daniel, and to decide the fate of his attacker, Zach McKenna. The details of the incident and possible extenuating circumstances remain unfamiliar to most of the assembly. The members of the council will question the defendant and the accuser. Then members of the assembly will have an opportunity to forward questions to clarify any points that remain uncertain."

He strode out from behind the table and stood facing Zach, tall and intimidating. The youth kept his eyes on the floor, afraid to look at Aaron and see his father's face staring back at him accusingly.

"Zach McKenna, three weeks ago you terminated your work contract with the Smith caravan to take up sponsorship with this hold. Is this correct?

"Yes, sir."

"When you brought your petition before the council, we asked if you understood the value we place on our friendship with Daniel. You told us you did. Is this not so?"

"Yes, sir."

"When you accepted sponsorship, you took an oath, swearing to abide by our laws and customs and to listen to the advice of your guide and sponsor. Do you recall taking that oath?"

"Yes, sir."

"Did your sponsor and guide, as well as dozens of other members of this assembly, not advise you that Daniel is a trusted friend?"

"Yes, sir."

"And yet, the first time you laid eyes on Daniel, you shot him."

Zach glanced up at Aaron briefly, opening his mouth as if in protest or denial, but then his eyes dropped again and he whispered, "Yes."

"Speak up. The assembly wishes to hear what you have to say."

"Yes, I shot him!" Zach cried.

Daniel cringed inwardly at the trapped expression on the youth's face. This scene looked all too familiar. It haunted his sleep, except in his nightmares it took place in a dimly lit barn and he himself stood accused, alone and undefended.

"You knew it was Daniel when you shot him?"

"Yes," Zach answered dully.

"Then why?"

Zach met Aaron's eyes for an instant and again he started to speak in protest, "I didn't . . ." But meeting the council leader's stern, forbidding gaze, he faltered, recalling his father's voice growling, *'No excuses, boy! Learn to accept the consequences of your actions'*. His gaze fell to the floor again and he answered, "I thought he killed one of your sheep."

"Zach, we don't kill people for poaching," Aaron said firmly, "not even mutants. Especially not friends." After a moment's pause, the council leader continued, "Could you not have questioned him? Or just held him there until Hutch or Tadi came to straighten it out? You gut shot him, Zach! Do you have any idea what a terrible way to die that is?"

A low angry murmur swept the assembly. Zach's hands tightened in white-knuckled tension on the arms of the chair. For a brief instant his eyes locked with Daniel's and the mutant's stomach knotted at the anguish he saw there. But the outlander said nothing, just stared at the floor again, his face a stiff mask. Aaron sighed at his unresponsiveness and turned to face the mutant.

"Daniel, can you tell us your side of the story? Just tell us in your own words what happened."

Daniel told them briefly, "I started out for the rim to pick bitterberry leaves for Margit. When I saw the dead sheep I stopped to investigate. It appeared to have been killed by raiders. I got worried about Sev and the boys, and I was just going to run to the cottage and check on them when I heard the shot. The bullet knocked me down, so I rolled into the trees and ran."

"Did you see who fired?"

"No."

"Did you think it was the raiders?"

"No. Raiders don't often use rifles. Too hard to get ammunition."

"So you thought *we* had fired on you . . . that we had turned against you."

Daniel's eyes focused on him briefly. "Yes."

Aaron nodded and turned to Hutch. "You arrived shortly after the shot was fired?"

"Within seconds."

"Can you tell us what Zach said when you arrived?"

"He said he had shot at Daniel, that Daniel was one of the poachers. I thought Zach meant he had fired a warning shot. Then I found the blood and I knew he actually hit Daniel."

"And what did you do then?"

"I sent Zach back to the cottage for help, then I went after Daniel. At first I didn't realize how badly he was hurt. I just feared he might think we had turned against him, and that he would disappear and we would never see him again."

Aaron nodded once more, then turned and tipped his head to the healer. "Margit?" He returned to his seat and Margit rose to take up the questioning.

"Zach," she spoke gently, "I understand you lost your family in a raider attack?"

He eyed her warily, not sure why she would bring up the death of his family, whether it might help or hinder his case. But he felt somewhat disarmed by her gentle manner after Aaron's sternness. He swallowed hard and answered, "Yes."

"Your parents? Brothers and sisters?"

"Two sisters, my mother and father." His voice shook a little.

"Zach, do you hate mutants?"

He blinked, startled by the question when it seemed everyone had taken for granted that he hated mutants. He answered carefully, "I hate raiders."

"Have you ever met a free mutant who was not a raider?"

"No."

"Would you have fired at Daniel if you had not known he was a mutant?"

"I . . . I don't know. I thought he was abusing your friendship, taking advantage of your trust to raid the flock unsuspected."

"I understand the flock was raided just the night before the shooting?"

"Yes."

"And when you saw Daniel examining the dead sheep you thought him in league with the raiders?"

"Yes."

"So you believed you were defending hold property, as you swore to do?"

Zach nodded. "Yes."

Margit looked thoughtful and returned to her place. Cochita rose and the questioning went on. And on. The cook brought up the fact that Zach had gone to the cottage and sent help for Daniel, even though he must have realized the anger the holders would feel over the shooting. At that time the caravan lay only a day away and Zach could have just deserted the sponsorship and avoided facing the consequences of his act. Then Alison took over, and his first question was, "Do you think a sheep is worth a man's life?" He went on from there, battering Zach with blunt, tersely worded questions until the youth felt so shaken he simply shut his mouth and refused to speak. Then finally the last council member rose and came forward -- Tadi. Zach hunched deeper in his chair, wishing he could just die and get it over with. Tadi was the only person since the shooting who had treated him with any real kindness. If his sponsor started to grill him the way the others had, he feared he might shame himself before the assembly by breaking into tears. He could not take much more.

"I have only one question for you, Zach," Tadi said quietly. "In light of the treatment you have received in recent weeks, do you still wish to continue with the sponsorship contract if the assembly will allow it?"

Zach gazed up at him in silent misery, wondering why he bothered to ask. The assembly would not vote for the sponsorship anyway.

"Well, Zach?"

"Yes." He had nowhere else to go. He would die alone in the wilds without weapons. Tadi nodded and squeezed his shoulder encouragingly. The touch startled Zach, and he realized he was not entirely alone in that hostile room. He had at least one ally. Tadi returned to his place and Aaron stood.

"Are there any further questions from the council?" They exchanged glances and shook their heads. "Any questions from the assembly?" No one moved or spoke.

"Very well then," Aaron went on. "The council has decided to put this matter before the assembly. Tadi has agreed to honor the contract if the matter is so decided. However, if the assembly chooses to cancel the contract, we will provide Zach with survival gear and an escort out of hold territory." He paused a moment and total silence filled the room. "We have however decided not to put this to a vote. Such an exercise seems pointless. We all know what the outcome would be. None of us really got to know Zach before this happened, and feelings are still running high. We wish to be totally fair to Zach. Therefore, we are going to give you a period of time in which to stand and speak for him. If only three voices are raised on his behalf, the contract will be honored." Aaron seated himself and reversed a sand clock on the table. "When the sand runs out the time is finished."

At first Zach gazed out over the assembly in vague hope, but as the sand dribbled away and no one rose to speak, his tenuous belief in miracles faded. He looked at Hutch, but the blond holder sat like a statue, staring at his tightly clasped hands, and Zach knew he would find no help there. The mutant's eyes had gone glassy and he looked deathly pale. Zach looked to the sand clock. The last of the sand dimpled as it funneled swiftly into the base.

The trial had proven almost as much of an ordeal for Daniel as it had for Zach. He felt the youth's hopeless despair as if it were his own. He knew how it felt to face a hostile crowd, defenseless. After a time, he fell into a trance of misery, hardly aware of the questions and Zach's responses. He felt lost in a nightmare that would not end, unable to wake up. His wound began to ache with a fierce throbbing. When Aaron upended the sand clock and time began spinning away in silence, Daniel knew with certainty that the past remained inescapable. He felt like he was drowning.

Hutch sat immersed in his own torment, torn between the responsibility he felt for Zach and his protective concern for Daniel. At first he remained so wrapped in indecision he didn't notice Daniel's increasing distress. When the mutant groaned softly, Hutch sat straight up in alarm. Daniel trembled, his face set in a grimace of pain.

"Daniel, what's wrong?"

In the quiet room his alarm drew every eye. They all heard the mutant's anguished whisper, but only Hutch sat close enough to hear his words.

"Don't do this to him! Don't do this to me! Please, don't do this to me!"

"Daniel, what's wrong?" Hutch asked again, but Daniel couldn't hear him. He was lost in his own private hell, staring at Zach's despairing face and seeing his own childish ghost, helplessly, hopelessly searching a sea of hostile faces for some shred of sympathy.

Tye and Neely came to their feet and Margit advanced half way around the council table when Daniel suddenly rose unsteadily and stood swaying. Hutch leapt to his side in an instant, supporting him.

"I know I am not a member of the assembly, and I have no right to speak . . ."

"Nonsense," Aaron interrupted, "you are the victim in this matter. Your words carry more weight than anyone's."

Daniel stared at him for a moment, appearing dazed and slightly lost.

"Go ahead," Aaron encouraged him gently. Daniel turned and scanned the crowd self-consciously.

"I wish to speak for Zach."

His words initiated a murmur of surprise throughout the room, and from the corner of his eye, Daniel saw the outlander straighten and give him a hard, suspicious look.

"He is young and inexperienced. He comes from a society much less tolerant than yours, more violent. In the settled lands the only free mutants a normal would see have turned to raiding to survive. You don't make friends with them, you kill them before they kill you. He doesn't understand that not all mutants are like that. When he shot me, he probably thought he was doing you a favor, protecting you from treachery." Daniel searched Zach's face for some response, some confirmation, but all he saw was confusion and distrust. "He's just a boy. He made a mistake. Please, give him another chance."

Daniel gazed at the five council members beseechingly and they studied him for a long moment, then exchanged glances amongst themselves. Aaron rose and scanned the assembly searchingly, judging their reactions. Then he turned his eyes to the mutant and said, "Your compassion and forgiveness are a credit to you, Daniel, and an example to us all. The council will have to deliberate on this. We will retire to the kitchen for a time to discuss it. Please bear with us."

The council filed silently out of the room. Daniel sank shakily to his seat again, feeling suddenly weak and exhausted. Hutch squeezed his arm in a warm grip, limp with relief.

"Why didn't you speak for him, Hutch?" Daniel asked. "I thought he was your friend."

"He tried to kill you, Danni. How could I consider him a friend after that?"

Their eyes met and Daniel saw a depth of pain in Hutch that filled him with dismay and remorse.

"You thought I would consider it a betrayal," he guessed, realizing for the first time how deeply his distrust had wounded Hutch. His friend looked away and said softly, "I don't ever want to hurt you, Danni. I don't ever want to see you hurt again."

"I believe you, Hutch. I swear I will never doubt you again. If you held a gun to my head and pulled the trigger, I would die believing you did it out of friendship."

Hutch smiled and answered, "I'd as soon shoot myself."

Their eyes connected in a glance that confirmed the bond between them, then they both relaxed and waited in silent companionship and understanding, each of them drawing strength and comfort from the other.

The crowd muttered in quiet discussion as the time dragged slowly. Zach saw the earnest exchange between Hutch and the mutant, though he couldn't hear their words. He studied Daniel with a suspicious scowl. What was the mutant up to? Why had he spoken? If he had left things alone, Zach would be on his way to the hold boundary by now with an armed escort. Why did the mutant want Zach to stay? Was he making plans to exact his own revenge at some future time of his own choosing? The outlander shivered, remembering what remained of his family after the raiders finished with them. He could not honestly believe any mutant would help a normal out of compassion, especially when that normal had nearly killed him.

At last the council filed back in and took their seats. Aaron remained standing. "We have decided to allow Zach to complete his sponsorship," he announced. The audience gave a collective sigh, but it seemed hard to judge what emotion prompted it. Zach's eyes widened in surprise. He had not really expected the mutant's plea to do any good.

"However," Aaron continued, "we have two conditions. If either of these conditions is not met or is unacceptable, the contract will be cancelled." The assembly waited in silence to hear the details. Aaron turned to address Daniel. "We had not intended to approach you about this until you were fully recovered, but your plea on Zach's behalf, and our decision concerning him, have caused us to revise our timing."

The mutant frowned in puzzlement. What was Aaron getting at?

"Time and again you have proven yourself to be a man of courage and integrity. We have come to hold you in very high regard. When you lay close to death, we prayed for your recovery, and when Margit announced that you were out of danger, an impromptu assembly took place and a certain idea was put forth and voted upon with unanimous approval."

"Aaron, quit feathering and get to the point," Margit scolded. "Daniel should be in bed."

The council leader turned and gave her a quelling glare that didn't faze her in the least. He faced Daniel again, scowling with irritation. The mutant waited, puzzled, totally unsuspecting of what came next.

"We wish to invite you to become a member of our assembly. Because you have already proven yourself a man of honor and loyalty, we are willing to waive the usual trial period of sponsorship. All five families have tendered offers of adoption. Will you accept our invitation?"

Daniel regarded him blankly, unable to comprehend what he had just heard. "You . . . you want me to . . .?" His throat closed on the words, leaving him speechless. His heart raced and he trembled with hope and fear that he had misunderstood. Since early childhood he had dreamed of belonging to a community that would love and accept him. He had never dared to hope that dream might come true.

"But . . . I'm a mutant," he reminded them.

"It doesn't matter," Aaron replied gently.

The words echoed and re-echoed in Daniel's mind. He could not believe he had heard them. His whole life, everything that had ever happened to him had hinged on the fact he had been born with mutant eyes. The past winter had been the happiest in his life, being accepted by them, included in their celebrations and evening gatherings. But he had always felt like an outsider. Now a door opened and a hand beckoned him into the warmth and shelter, inviting him to become a member of the family, not just an occasional guest. And he felt afraid . . . afraid to believe, because if that belief was shattered, it would kill him as surely as any bullet. He cast a glance at Hutch in mute appeal. His friend smiled encouragement and reassurance but said nothing. This decision had to be Daniel's alone. The room waited in tense silence to hear his response.

"I . . . I accept," he said in a low, shaky voice.

The assembly erupted in joyous cheers that rocked the room. Hutch hugged him with fierce gentleness, careful not to hurt his half-healed wound. Over his friend's shoulder, Daniel caught a glimpse of Zach's face, twisted with pain and envy. Daniel could almost read his mind. This mutant got it all handed to him with ribbons, while Zach, a normal, teetered on the verge of being cast out as undesirable. Daniel understood the youth's pain and jealousy better than he understood the holders' love.

Aaron held up his hands commandingly and the tumult gradually ebbed. The gruff, forbidding council leader smiled at Daniel with warmth and gentleness. "Welcome home, Daniel."

More cheers and shouts of affirmation and welcome ensued, but this time they subsided quickly and Aaron continued.

"Back to the issue of Zach's sponsorship," he said. "The first of our two conditions has been met by Daniel's acceptance of our invitation, which we had planned to make in any case. The second condition must be agreed upon by both Zach and Daniel. If either of you find this stipulation unacceptable, the contract will be cancelled." He studied each of them briefly and said, "The second condition is that the two of you agree to work together as partners."

Hutch gave a small cry of alarmed protest, which Aaron ignored. Stunned silence filled the room. The council leader turned to Zach.

"An indiscriminate hatred of mutants presents a danger to us all. Those mutants who have peacefully co-existed with us for generations would not take kindly to being shot at. Daniel has taught us that mutants can be not only harmless and peaceful neighbours, but loyal, courageous friends. We can think of no one more capable of teaching this to you. Also, he is a master of the techniques of survival, skills you would do well to learn."

Aaron turned then to the mutant. "Daniel, this is not a condition of your acceptance. You have that in any case. We understand the dangers to you in what we are asking and I assure you, if you wish to refuse this condition, we will not think less of you."

"If I refuse, what will happen to Zach?"

"We will give him survival gear and escort him out of Haven Hold territory."

Daniel and Zach eyed each other warily. The outlander felt repelled by the proposal, not because Daniel was a mutant, but because they all seemed to think he was so damned perfect. Zach had had a lifetime of trying to measure up to impossible standards. But the alternative seemed even less appealing . . . probable death out in the desert at the hands of raiders. Daniel thought about the dangers of an unwilling, hostile partner at his back. The holders were willing to give the outlander another chance, but only if Daniel would. Zach might betray him, but somehow the thought of betrayal concerned him far less than it used to. He no longer stood alone. He had loyal friends to support and defend him.

"I accept," he said, gazing at Zach with steady courage and newfound confidence. The outlander saw that unwavering gaze as a kind of threat, a challenge that, under the circumstances, he could not possibly hope to win. But he had little choice in the matter.

"Zach?" Aaron questioned.

The outlander bowed his head in surrender. "I accept."

"Very well. Since you are both fairly new to our ways, we are assigning Hutch as a guide for the two of you. He will explain our rules and laws and the responsibilities of partners, to each other and to the hold. If you have any questions and Hutch is unavailable, feel free to ask any adult member of the assembly."

He paused for a moment, then queried, "Does the assembly or the council have any other questions or suggestions to offer?"

After a moment's silence, a male voice spoke up from the anonymity of the crowd, saying, "I suggest you take that mutant-hating son of a plague mother and hand him over to the Rogan's Raiders. You're setting Daniel up for the kill."

The stillness of shock lay over the assembly and Zach looked as if he had been punched in the stomach. Aaron glared out over the assembly like a thunderstorm. He recognized that voice.

"On your feet, Rad! Have the guts to show your face when you speak!" the council leader roared. The young man stood up, red faced and insolent. This middle son of Aaron's had proven a trial from the day he was born.

"You are out of line, Rad. It seems three months of night duties and cleaning privies are not enough to shift your attitude. We'll make it four months. And if I hear of any more harassment of Zach by you or your friends, you will be doing it for the rest of the year. Do I make myself clear?"

"Yes, sir."

"I think you owe Zach an apology."

Rad glared at the outlander as if it was all his fault and said a very grudging and insincere, "Sorry."

"Now sit down and keep your mouth shut unless you have something constructive to say."

Rad sat, seething with resentment and humiliation.

"My apologies to the assembly and the council, and to you, Zach, for my son's rude and unseemly behavior. Now, if no one has any further comments, we will adjourn this meeting."

No one offered anything further. Everyone seemed uneasily satisfied with the council's decision. Hutch kept silent about his misgivings only because of Daniel's apparent wish to help Zach.

"I declare this meeting adjourned."

The crowd rose and surged forward to welcome Daniel and congratulate him, but Margit stood up and banged angrily on the table and everyone came to a halt.

"I do *not* want to see a mob scene!" she snapped. "Daniel is still not well and this has been a very difficult and exhausting evening. If you wish to give him your congratulations, I suggest you visit him tomorrow, a few at a time."

Daniel, nearing collapse, felt profoundly grateful for her intervention. Tye appeared beside him, and with Hutch supporting him on the other side, he headed gratefully for the peace and solitude of his bed. Zach watched them leave with Neely following, dancing with delight and excitement over Daniel's acceptance. The outlander felt adrift and no less unwelcome than he had this morning with the ordeal of the trial still ahead of him. A hand came down on his shoulder and he jumped, almost flinching away. Tadi drew him to his feet.

"Come on, lad. You look like you've had about all you can take."

The councilman guided Zach toward the kitchen with a comforting, fatherly arm around his shoulders. They found the kitchen blessedly empty and peaceful. Tadi brewed a pot of tea. Handing a steaming cup to Zach, he said, "Here, drink this. It will settle your nerves. They were pretty rough on you."

Zach's hands clenched nervously around the mug. "Thanks," he said, low voiced. "Thanks for . . . not abandoning me."

Tadi acknowledged him with a serious nod. The youth seemed lost, bewildered.

"Why did he do that? Why did he speak for me?"

"Daniel?" Tadi frowned. "I don't know. Maybe you should ask him."

Zach swallowed hard. "Is he . . . am I allowed to see him now?

"He's your partner, Zach. You're allowed to see him. But I suggest you be very careful what you say and do. Your position here is by no means secure."

Chapter Six

And if you call me brother now,
Forgive me if I ask,
Just according to whose plan?
And when all has come to dust
I will kill you if I must,
I will love you if I can.
~Leonard Cohen

The morning after the trial, Daniel woke feeling distressingly confused and uncertain. He had spent a restless night reliving in nightmares a tangled mixture of memories from his own traumatic childhood ordeal, intermingled with those of Zach's trial. Toward the end of last evening, he had experienced everything through such a haze of emotional and physical exhaustion that now he felt unsure exactly which memories were real and which were merely products of his subconscious scars, or dreams of wish fulfillment. Soon after breakfast, Aaron came to see him and found the young man lying on his back staring up at the ceiling fixedly, a strange, remote expression on his face.

"Good morning, Daniel."

Green eyes glanced at Aaron vaguely and the young mutant pulled himself into a sitting position. "Good morning," he said in a subdued voice. After that first quick glance he avoided Aaron's eyes.

"You seem upset this morning. What's wrong?"

Daniel regarded him uncertainly. "Dreams," he answered, "I had the strangest dreams. I don't know what's real and what's not."

"Dreams about the trial?"

Daniel nodded.

"Dreams about being invited to join the assembly? About accepting Zach as your partner?"

Daniel's eyes widened. "It...it wasn't just a dream then? It actually happened?"

Aaron smiled and patted his knee reassuringly. "It really happened. That's why I'm here now. I wanted to arrive ahead of the usual crowd of visitors so I could see you privately, to tell you about the adoption ceremony and the options you have in the way of bonding ties."

"Bonding ties?" Daniel repeated blankly, still struggling to believe the reality of their acceptance.

"Bonds that tie you to the hold, that make you family . . . kinship ties." Aaron hesitated a moment, then went on apologetically, "I am sorry we had to bring this up at the trial. We meant to make the invitation on a happy occasion, not during such an ordeal as last night. We had planned to wait until you gained enough strength to leave the infirmary. The cherry picking festival is only a few weeks away. It would have been a more fitting occasion. I believe we'll plan the ceremony for then anyway. A bonding is similar to a joining ceremony. Have you ever seen a holder joining?"

"No." Such ceremonies had taken place when Daniel was a child, but his presence had never been welcome.

"Well, in a joining a man and woman make vows of love and support to one another. In a bonding ceremony you make similar vows to your adopted family, and they to you."

Daniel thought about it in silence for a while -- thought about all his closest friends amongst the holders, Hutch, Neely, Tye, Cochita, Kelda and Davin and Little Daniel, Jesse, Margit and Tadi. "Who?" he asked. "Who would be my family?"

"That's one of the things I wanted to talk to you about. With so many offers, we thought it only fair to leave the choice up to you. The council has received five offers, one from each founding family. Denys and Cochita have offered for the Sorenson family. I know you are fond of Cochita, and Denys is a good man. Margit has offered for the Ingram family. Her husband died years ago and left her childless. She would dearly love to be able to call you son. Alison Kendle also lost his spouse some years back when the hold suffered a fever epidemic. He has two daughters, Serene and Hedy, but he would like very much to have a son."

Daniel considered the sour-faced councilman with dislike. Something about the man set his teeth on edge. Daniel felt Alison's questioning of Zach last night had been unnecessarily brutal. Aaron continued, "Then there's Ross and Zanna Hayes. You may not know them as well as you know some of us. Ross is Tadi's brother. Tadi wanted to offer for the Hayes family himself, but being Zach's sponsor, he felt it might create a certain conflict of interest and responsibility. And your final choice would be my wife, Gemina, and myself. We would be proud to have you."

Daniel struggled to take it all in. The invitation still had a surreal, dreamlike quality to him. More than anything, he felt the need to get out alone in the woods to think, to gain some perspective on this strange trick life played on him. But he knew that was impossible. He just didn't have the strength yet.

"I don't understand," he said, his face reflecting his bewilderment. "Why do you all want me? No one has ever wanted me before, not even my own father."

"You are a good man, Daniel. If no one in your past could see that, well it's their loss and our gain. The shape and color of your eyes are no more important than Little Daniel's extra toes. It doesn't change what you are."

"What I am and always will be is a damned mutant!"

"No. What you are, and no doubt always have been, is a good, compassionate human being. Not many people these days would risk their lives for two total strangers, especially if they thought such action would bring them nothing but grief. Not many would fight alone against a number of raiders, even to save a friend. And what you did last night for Zach proves it again. I can think of few people who would willingly forgive a man who had tried to kill them."

"He's just a boy. When I look at him, I see myself the way I was three or four years ago. I suspect we're a lot alike, Zach and I."

Aaron shook his head. "I can't see it myself. I notice more similarities between you and Hutch."

Daniel's eyes widened. "Do you think so?"

An amused smile softened Aaron's craggy features as he recognized the pleased note in Daniel's voice. The mutant obviously admired Hutch a great deal.

"Tell me, Daniel . . . if Zach had shot Hutch instead of you, would you have been so quick to forgive?"

Daniel's face went blank for an instant, then he answered flatly, "I would have killed him."

Aaron nodded. "I think that's pretty much how Hutch felt too, and more than a few others as well. If you had died, we might have had a hard time keeping Zach alive long enough for a hearing."

*   *   *

The first days following the trial saw little change in the holders' attitude toward Zach. Evenings felt especially uncomfortable, when people gathered in small, friendly groups to play games or work on some joint project, or just to talk. And later in the dorm he would have to listen to the cheerful bantering of the young men as they prepared for bed, friendly teasing from which he was excluded. Mealtimes seemed the worst though, having to enter a room full of people who hated him and try to choke down a meal in crowded isolation, surrounded but ignored as if he didn't exist. His muscles became constantly knotted with tension, and more often than not food would just lay in his stomach like lead until it came back up an hour or so later. He had buried more than one meal in a back corner of the tranquility garden behind the main building. He took to avoiding meals whenever he could, lingering to finish his work, or sitting alone in the tranquility garden until mealtime ended.

Zach tried to see Daniel a few times, but the infirmary seemed always full of visitors, and he could not bear the thought of facing the man in front of witnesses, all watching with hawkish intensity for any sign of hostility toward their pet mutant. At last, five days after the trial, Margit began allowing Daniel to sleep in the dorm and wander about the hold unattended, with strict instructions not to overdo it. With the mutant's presence in the dorm, the young men's attitude toward the outlander shifted subtly. The change seemed hard to pin down, but Zach noticed the difference. They seemed to stop treating him like the mutant-hating outsider who had shot their friend and begin to see him instead as Daniel's partner, Daniel's problem to deal with in his own way. They still excluded Zach from their joking and friendly roughhousing, but it was like they saw Daniel and Zach as a unit now, and they backed off, allowing the mutant room to handle his partner without the subtle pressures of their personal feelings about the youth.

One morning, soon after Daniel had graduated from the infirmary, Zach lingered too long in the dorm, trying to avoid having to go to the great hall for breakfast. Rad came wandering in off night guard duty and found him still there. The holder glanced around the room and an unpleasant smile spread slowly across his face.

"So . . . all alone, are we?"

He advanced swaggeringly, eyeing Zach with arrogant self-assurance. Zach backed away warily. The only exit lay behind Rad. In a quick, sudden movement, Zach tried to dodge past the bully, but the older boy caught his arm, twisted it behind his back and slammed him against the wall with bruising force.

"Going somewhere, mutant hater?"

Rad increased the pressure on the captive arm until Zach felt sure it was going to separate at the shoulder, but he refused to give the bully the satisfaction of hearing him cry out.

"You told Tadi it was us beat you up, didn't you, you little shit. Having to clean privies for four months doesn't do much to improve my temper." He gave Zach's arm a savage wrench that drew a grunt of pain from the outlander, then released him and yanked the youth around, slamming him back against the wall again. Zach took a swing at Rad, but his right arm hung temporarily useless and his left-handed blow had little power behind it. Rad countered it easily and laughed in his face.

"You'll have to do better than that, runtling. You fight like a damned girl! Go ahead, fight me. Yell and shout and make a big scene. We don't like troublemakers here, and when I tell them you started it by bad-mouthing Daniel, who do you think they'll believe? I might end up cleaning privies for the rest of the year, but you'll be out the gate . . . `cause I belong here and you don't." Rad enjoyed the trapped despair on Zach's face. "And if you tell Tadi about this, you'll get worse next time!"

At that moment, Daniel walked through the door. He had visited the bath house to wash up before breakfast and now returned to find one of the clean shirts the holders had given him. As he entered the room, he saw Rad pinning Zach to the wall, leaning against him threateningly.

"Rad!" Daniel called sharply.

Both boys glanced around and the holder eased up on Zach, backing away a little. He grinned at the mutant as if they were good friends.

"Just keeping him in line for you, Daniel. Warning him not to try anything against you when you're out there alone in the woods with him."

Daniel eyed Rad coldly. "I told you before, don't do me any favors."

"Hey, just trying to help. This mutant-hating son of a plague mother already shot you once."

"I seem to remember you almost did the same not much more than a year ago, and for much the same reasons."

Rad looked disconcerted. "I didn't know you then," he protested.

"Neither did Zach. It doesn't matter anyway, Rad. You don't fool me in the least. I've seen your kind too often before. You're not doing this for me, you just like to push people around and you figure Zach doesn't have the option of fighting back. Well, I'm warning you, norp! You lay a hand on my partner again and I'll break it!"

Rad regarded Daniel uncertainly, not sure whether to laugh or feel nervous. The mutant could barely stand up straight yet and his shirtless torso was still wrapped in bandages. But the steely expression in his green eyes warned the holder not to try calling his bluff. Rad started to back down, seething with anger and resentment.

"Ungrateful mutant slime! If my father hears about this, you'll both regret it!" He stalked past Daniel with a furious scowl. Daniel turned to his partner.

"You alright, Zach?"

"Fine. I don't need a goddamn mutant babysitter! I can take care of myself!"

Daniel felt taken aback by Zach's resentment. "I'm sorry. I didn't mean to interfere. I just thought you looked like you could use a little help. That's what partners are for."

Zach looked away. Daniel shrugged and went to hunt down the shirt he had come for. The youth eyed the whip scars on his back with horrified fascination for a second, then quietly left the room. He did not want Daniel suggesting that they eat breakfast together. He passed Rad in the corridor and the holder didn't speak, but he gave Zach an icy stare that said they had unfinished business.

Zach headed for the tool shed. He knew the routine now and Tadi no longer needed to tell him what to do each day unless it was something different. Zach put the shovel into the wheelbarrow and pushed it toward the barns. First cleaning out stalls in the morning, then he would hoe and weed the gardens in the afternoon. He had always been a good, steady worker. Not as fast or efficient as his father would have liked, but then, nothing he did had been good enough for his father. Sometimes the unspoken disapproval would get him so tied up in knots that he fumbled even the simplest, most routine chores. The cows would sense his tension and refuse to let down their milk, the horses would get skittish with his hands on the reins. His father would glare at him in contempt and his self-esteem would fall another notch. Tadi had surprised him profoundly one day by patting him on the shoulder approvingly and telling him he was doing a good job. After that, Zach even began to enjoy the work.

*   *   *

Daniel's morning became the essence of boredom. Margit had warned him not to do anything too strenuous, so he spent the morning sitting in the weaving room, carding wool for Neely while she worked the spinning wheel. After a while the inane chatter between Carly and her cousin Meta began to get on his nerves, and by midmorning it finally drove him from the room. He wandered into the kitchen, where he found Cochita making pies.

"Please," he cried, "give me something to do before I go crazy!"

Cochita laughed and gave him a bowl of apples to peel. She ruffled his hair, burying her fingers in his thick mane.

"Will you let me cut your hair, Daniel?"

"Sure," he answered with a pleased, self-conscious grin, "Tye says I look like a sheepdog."

"Not a sheepdog," she smiled, going back to making pastry. "More like a . . . " She hesitated musingly.

"A curlmup? A hairybear?" he offered in humorous self-deprecation. A hairybear was a bristly, furry caterpillar, and a curlmup was a small rodent that looked like a walking mop, named for its defensive habit of curling up and playing dead when threatened. Cochita chuckled.

"No. Have you ever seen a lion?

"I'm afraid I'm not that well-travelled. I hear they live in the deep south. Saw a picture once though, in a book. Mean looking critter! Big teeth. Still, I suppose there is some resemblance around the eyes." They both laughed.

Once they got the pies in the oven, Cochita sat him down on a chair in the middle of the kitchen and began to trim his ragged locks. "This looks like you cut it with your hunting knife."

"I did. Scissors are hard to come by out there. Barbers are even harder."

He liked the feel of her hands. Her touch had a loving quality that brought out a fierce ache of nostalgia. In appearance she looked nothing like his pretty, petite mother, but something about her reminded him so much of Jaylene. He felt more comfortable with Cochita than he did with anyone in the hold except Hutch. Suddenly he knew with firm conviction that this was the woman he wanted for his bond mother.

"Cochita . . . " He hesitated, and she heard the serious, troubled note in his voice.

She left off fussing with his hair and moved around in front of him so she could meet his eyes. "What is it, Daniel?"

"Aaron told me about my . . . bonding choices. I don't want to . . . offend anyone. Or hurt anyone's feelings . . . "

"You won't, Daniel. We would all love you to be a part of our families, and those who are not chosen will be disappointed, but no one will be offended."

Daniel gazed up at her with a worried expression, not yet convinced. "I like Denys a lot but . . . Aaron has helped me a great deal. I guess I felt a little afraid of him at first, but he makes me feel . . . almost normal."

"Daniel, you are normal," Cochita smiled, stroking his hair. "If you wish to choose Aaron, I'm sure he'll feel very pleased, and Gemina too."

"Gemina?" Daniel barely knew Aaron's wife. "No, I want you for my bond mother."

Cochita looked startled as she at last comprehended his problem. "Bonding parents are usually couples," she said thoughtfully. "Or widowed singles. Still, I don't see any reason why it couldn't work just as well. After all, you are an adult. It's not like you're a child who needs a united family circle. And it would give you kinship ties with two families instead of one. Three actually, if Hutch and Tye stand up for you, as I'm sure they will."

"Stand up for me?"

"Volunteer to be your bond brothers."

Daniel's eyes widened in wonder. "Aaron never mentioned that part." He started to grin. "There is nothing I would like better than to have Hutch for a brother. And Tye."

*   *   *

At the noon meal, Serene Kendle sat down across from Daniel. He didn't know her well, but he had seen her a few times with a crowd of children around her. She and Salla, Tadi's wife, shared the task of teaching and caring for the smaller children, the ones too young to spend a whole day at lessons. A plain, rawboned young woman, Serene had a long, horsey face and lank hair pulled back into a loose braid. She had unfortunately inherited Alison's looks, but she had a shy, gentle manner and the children adored her. She smiled uncertainly at Daniel.

"Neely tells me you're at loose ends this afternoon and in need of something to do."

"That's right. I think I'll expire from boredom if I have to listen to one more minute of Carly and Meta talking about city fashions, jewelry and hairstyles. Margit won't let me do anything," he complained. "And carding wool lost its appeal long ago, even for Neely."

Serene laughed. She had a beautiful, low, throaty chuckle that bubbled up from somewhere deep inside her. It felt infectious and brought an answering smile to Daniel's face.

"I'm taking the little ones across to the big orchard this afternoon. Would you like to come along? The children would love it. You're their hero."

Daniel shifted uneasily. "Don't know that I've ever been considered a hero before."

Serene smiled. "It doesn't matter," she said, "these little ones are not demanding of their heroes. I expect to many of them, I'm a hero too. And I'm about as heroic as a mouse! Will you come?"

"I would like to. But I have to warn you, I don't have much experience with children."

"You'll do fine. I promise I won't leave you alone with the little beasts." She chuckled again and he decided he could easily grow very fond of this young woman.

After dinner they went to the nursery to collect the children. Little Daniel recognized his guardian immediately and gave a small crow of delight. He scooted across the floor with astonishing speed and pulled himself part way up, clutching at Daniel's breeches. The young man picked him up and he settled contentedly into Daniel's arms, babbling baby talk while Daniel listened with serious attention. When Serene had the children organized, Salla came to take the little one. He screamed in protest, reaching for Daniel, and Salla smiled at the expression on the mutant's face as she held the squirming child.

"Don't worry," she said, "he'll settle as soon as you're gone. You can play with him after you get back."

They made a hasty retreat from the nursery and started off along the river path, leading the old bay mare, Daisy, swaybacked and gentle. If the youngsters got tired, they could ride. The sun felt warm and it was a glorious day. The children darted about, exploring and playing tag, their sweet, shrill voices cutting the still heavy air like birdsong. The seven children ranged in age from three to five years. The youngest, Peri Kendle, seemed a placid, serious little boy who walked along stolidly without entering into the games of the others. After they had gone a little way, he quietly slipped his hand into Daniel's, gazing up at the mutant with an expression that seemed childishly trusting, yet oddly mature in its gravity. Daniel smiled down at him and he faced forward again, trotting along on his short little legs, taking three steps for every one of the mutant's. Before long Daniel could see him beginning to tire.

"Would you like to ride?" he asked the child. Peri looked up at Daisy and shook his head. He had never sat on the horse alone before. She looked so tall and her back was so broad. Daniel crouched beside the little boy.

"On my shoulders?" he asked softly. Peri's eyes widened and he nodded wonderingly. Daniel lifted the child onto his shoulders, feeling the movement pull at his half-healed wound. He rose to his feet and Peri grabbed a double handful of his dark hair for balance, squealing with delight and apprehension.

"Serene, look! Look at me! I'm bigger than you! I'm bigger than everybody!"

The other children began to dance around Daniel.

"Me too! Me too!"

"It's my turn, Peri. Get down."

"Can I have a ride too?"

Daniel stared helplessly at Serene and she laughed at the expression on his face. Then she took pity on him and clapped her hands for attention.

"Come, children! Poor Daniel's just gotten out of the infirmary. You can't expect him to carry all of you. That's why we brought Daisy."

So the older children went up on Daisy's back, five in a row, and Serene carried little Fawn Ingram on her own shoulders. Before long the children got bored with just sitting and came tumbling down off the mare's back again to bounce along the trail, picking up treasures and bringing them back for examination and explanation. They seemed so delightfully exuberant that Daniel couldn't help grinning over their antics and the funny things they said. Peri patted him on the head and said, "Nice horse. Much better than Daisy." Daniel laughed.

They reached the bridge that crossed the river into the big orchard, and Hymi Sorenson, the oldest, decided he had to show the others his bravery by climbing up and walking along the rail. The drop to the water seemed not a long one, but the current here ran swift and deep.

"Hymi, get down," Serene called sharply. Daniel caught the boy around the waist and lifted him down.

"Keep your feet on the ground, little man," he said. "If you fall in, you'll be fish food."

"Fish food!" the boy repeated and giggled. The others found it riotously funny as well and they all went into gales of laughter as they galloped across the bridge and into the dappled shade of the fruit trees. Daniel and Serene set the two youngest children on their feet and let them run off after the others. Daniel sank down and leaned against the trunk of an apple tree with a sigh. He felt a lot more tired than he should after the easy walk. Margit was right, he was far from his full strength yet.

A few minutes later the children came dashing back, shrieking with joyous abandon. Serene clapped her hands for attention and said, "Lesson time." She sat down, her skirts pooling around her, and the children quieted instantly, seating themselves in a semicircle. Peri flung himself into Daniel's lap and Serene saw the mutant wince.

"Peri," she scolded, "you hurt Daniel. You all have to remember, Daniel has been injured. He's not all well yet, so be careful."

The little boy turned and looked up at his hero, lower lip beginning to tremble. "I'm sorry," he whispered.

"It's alright," Daniel smiled and hugged him. "I forgive you."

Layla dropped an armload of flowers into Serene's lap and sat down beside her.

"Thank you, Layla! These are lovely!" the teacher exclaimed. "Now, does anyone remember what the lesson is for today?"

Little brows puckered in concentration as they tried to remember.

"Same," Peri said.

"That's right," Serene smiled at him, "different and the same." She laid out a row of flowers from her lap. "Zindle, can you tell me which one is different from the others?"

The little girl moved forward and studied the array seriously, then chose the one yellow flower out of a row of pink.

"Very good, Zindle. And tell me, are the others all the same?"

The child shook her head solemnly.

"Which one is different?"

The flowers were all pink, all the same species, but the little girl pointed to one that looked crushed and mangled. "Squished," she said.

Serene laughed and praised Zindle and the lesson went on, with each child given a question or problem to solve, according to their level of knowledge and ability. Daniel listened in fascination.

He had learned all his early lessons from his mother. He had never been welcome to join the other children in a group like this. He found the interaction between the youngsters intriguing, and he gained the impression they learned almost as much from each other as they did from Serene. After a while she released them to run and play, warning them to stay in sight.

Daniel dozed in the shade for a while, never so deeply asleep that he was unaware of the high, piping little voices. He heard a delighted giggle and opened his eyes to watch Layla chasing a bright, black and yellow butterfly about the grove. She had her hands out as if to grasp it, but several times when she could have caught it, she just shooed it until it fluttered away again. Hymi came galloping up and saw what she was doing.

"I'll catch it for you, Lally!" he shouted, and took a wild swing at the bright insect, snatching it from the air. Grinning with pride at his accomplishment, he held it out to her. She stared for an instant in shocked dismay at the crushed and broken thing he held in his grubby paw, then she let out a high pitched shriek of grief and fury. She smacked poor Hymi across the face so hard he sat down abruptly, too stunned even to cry. Serene caught the last bit of action.

"Layla Ingram! *That* is no way to act! Now you apologize to Hymi."

Layla's round little face took on a set expression of stubborn defiance and she shook her head.

"Fine," said Serene, "then you can just sit over here by this tree and think about what you did until you figure out why it was wrong, and when you're ready, you can come and say you're sorry."

The boy sobbed now, holding his reddened cheek. Serene picked him up and comforted him for a moment and soon he ran off to play again, the incident forgotten. But Layla sat under her tree looking stubborn and defiant. Daniel saw a silent tear slip down her cheek. He rose, carefully picked up the tattered remains of the butterfly and carried it over to her. Wordlessly, he dug a small hole with his knife and helped her bury the insect. She placed a flower in the tiny grave and pushed the earth back into the hole. Layla started to sob and Daniel cuddled her and told her gently, "You know, Hymi didn't mean to hurt it, or you. He thought he was helping you."

"It looked so pretty," she mourned, "and he broke it!"

"I know," he comforted her, "but he didn't mean to. He didn't understand. He thought you were trying to catch it, and he didn't know it would break so easily. You hurt him. You really hit him hard and he didn't know why."

She rested against Daniel for a while, thinking about it as her sobs tapered off into hiccoughs.

"Do you think you could forgive him?" he asked gently. "He was only trying to be your friend."

She nodded. Daniel helped her up and she asked pleadingly, "Will you come with me?"

"Sure." He rose stiffly to his feet and she took his hand. Hymi saw them coming and ran to meet them.

"Can you play now, Lally? It's no fun without you."

"I forgive you, Hymi," she said with a hint of queenly condescension. "I'm sorry I hit you but you shouldn't have killed my flutter-by."

Hymi looked crestfallen. "I'm sorry, Lally. I didn't mean to hurt it."

Layla glanced up at Daniel with a grateful smile and a look that said her faith in him had been justified, then she ran off to play. Serene strolled over, smiling.

"For someone with so little experience, you do very well with children."

He grinned at her. "They're easier to deal with than most adults. More direct and honest. They say what they mean and act accordingly."

She smiled her agreement, watching her charges with great affection. After a while she clapped her hands again and they all came running. "Snack time," she said. Everyone sat down in the shade and Serene passed out the cookies and strawberries Cochita had packed for them. They chattered like little magpies while they ate. Layla came and leaned against Daniel's shoulder, studying his face with an expression of fierce concentration as she fed him a fat strawberry. She leaned closer until their noses almost touched, staring into his strange green orbs.

"You have pretty eyes," she said.

He nearly choked on the berry. No one had ever told him his hated mutant eyes looked pretty. Serene laughed at his startled expression. "Like you said, direct and honest."

"Will you tell us a story, Daniel?" Peri asked hopefully.

"A story," Daniel repeated, disconcerted. "They certainly know how to keep you off balance too." He gazed around at the eager little faces, turned up to him like flowers to the sun, and tried to remember some of the stories his mother had told him as a child. But it seemed so long ago. "I'm sorry, I'm afraid I don't know any stories," he told them regretfully.

"You could make one up," Layla suggested. Daniel gazed at Serene helplessly and shrugged. "I'll try."

He thought about their lesson earlier, different and the same. A bird fluttered down into one of the trees nearby and took an experimental peck at a half-ripe cherry. The motion caught Daniel's eye and he said, "Do you see that bird?" They all turned to look. "One day, a bird just like that picked a cherry and flew away with it in his beak. He carried it away up onto the rim, searching for a safe place to eat it. But after a while he got very tired -- so tired that the cherry dropped out of his beak and landed in the forest. The bird flew away and left the cherry lying in a little patch of sun, surrounded by dark evergreens. Sometimes it rained and sometimes the sun warmed the cherry, and it put out little roots and started to grow. It sent up a little branch and one little leaf, and then another. Soon a tiny tree grew from the cherry. The evergreens watched curiously as the cherry tree got bigger. She looked so different from them, with her flat, broad leaves and thin branches reaching up to the sun instead of trailing toward the ground like theirs. Fall came and they watched in wonder as the cherry tree's leaves turned red and dropped off. They laughed and mocked the little cherry tree, saying she would freeze standing naked like that in the winter cold. The little cherry tree felt sad and ashamed. But a small fir tree felt sorry for her and said, 'Don't worry, I'll protect you. I'll cover you with my green branches and shield you from the winter winds.' And so, when the cold weather came, the little cherry tree slept in the shelter of his strong branches, safe from the heavy snows that piled up and weighed down the proud evergreens. When spring came at last, the evergreens felt worn and tired from fighting the cold and the winter winds. The little cherry tree woke up and put out bright green leaves and little white buds. The evergreens felt too tired to notice the song the soft spring breezes sang. They just stood sadly with drooping branches. But the cherry tree lifted her branches to the warm sun and played with the wind and sang back to it, singing a song for her friend the fir tree, telling him of hope and renewal and the warm, lazy days of summer soon to come. Her little white buds burst into blossom and she sang of the joy and wonder of life. She looked like a little girl in a white, lacy festival dress. Her beauty and her happy singing lifted the spirits of the evergreens, and they realized . . . it's alright to be different. Sometimes it's even nice. And after that they always protected her from the winter winds so she grew big and strong, and she always sang to them in the spring. But the fir tree always remained her best friend."

Eight pairs of solemn eyes gazed back at Daniel in silence and he reddened a bit, wondering if his story was acceptable. "Oh, Daniel," Serene breathed softly, "that was beautiful. You are an excellent storyteller. Right, children?"

They chorused their agreement. Hymi piped up, "That was a girl's story. I liked the one about the duck better." But then he turned and put his arms around Layla. "I'll be your best friend, Lally. I won't let you get cold."

She pushed him away, frowning. "It's summertime, silly! I'm not cold."

The rest of the afternoon passed in idyllic peace, with the children playing quietly together, building a hold with rocks and using smaller pebbles and sticks for people and animals. When at last the time came to pack up and leave, the children seemed tired and considerably quieter than on the walk there. The older ones went up on Daisy's broad back and the two littlest once more rode Daniel's and Serene's shoulders. As they crossed the bridge, Daniel felt Peri begin to wilt. The little boy sagged until his cheek rested against the top of Daniel's head, sound asleep. Serene smiled and said, "We have really enjoyed having you with us."

"I have enjoyed being with you," he answered. "This has been one of the best days of my life. I will always remember it." Serene reached out shyly to rub his shoulder. "You will have lots of days like this. And even better ones." He smiled, believing her.

Chapter Seven

When you're weary, feeling small,
When tears are in your eyes,
I will dry them all;
I'm on your side
Oh, when times get tough
And friends just can't be found.
~Paul Simon

All through the long, hot afternoon, Zach labored in the outer gardens. Sometime after noon, Tadi came stumping out to where Zach worked, and without a word, settled a straw hat onto the boy's head. He smiled and said, "Can't have you getting sunstroke." Then he turned and stumped away again.

By the time the supper bell rang, Zach worked in the side court garden within the hold walls. He just kept hoeing as others headed in for the meal. A moment later, Daniel and Serene entered through the gates with the children and Zach paused for a moment to watch them. Serene lifted Fawn down from her shoulders and set the little girl on her feet, then took Peri from Daniel. She began herding her weary flock into the hold while Daniel led Daisy toward the horse barn. Zach turned away and went on with his hoeing, feeling depressed and confused. Ever since the trial he had taken every opportunity to study the mutant, trying to figure out why he had spoken up. It made no sense. The only possible reason Zach could think of was revenge. Once Margit deemed the mutant well enough, Daniel would take Zach out into the woods to teach him survival skills . . . alone with a man he had nearly killed. It would be so easy for the mutant to murder him and make it look like an accident or the work of raiders. The holders loved Daniel. They probably wouldn't even question it. But the more Zach saw of Daniel, the more difficult he found it to picture him in the guise of a vengeful killer mutant. He just looked and acted so normal. Even his eyes seemed not that hard to get used to. And he was always so unfailingly kind. If he harbored any resentment over the shooting, he hid it very well. It put Zach's nerves on edge.

Over the past few days since Daniel's release from the infirmary, every time Zach saw him he was helping someone, though in his convalescent state he had little strength or endurance. He seemed always in the right place at the right time and he seemed to do everything well. Zach began to feel a certain envious admiration for the man. Daniel seemed everything Zach had always wished he could be -- tall, confident, competent and respected. The mutant even carried himself with an unconscious air of nobility. He moved with the grace of a panther and the confident dignity of a young king. He made Zach feel like a scrub pony partnered with a thoroughbred.

Daniel came out of the barn and started toward the dining hall, then noticed his partner still working in the garden. Everyone else had long since gone in for supper. He walked across the courtyard and came up behind Zach with his usual silent tread, then hesitated. The youth seemed so prickly, Daniel felt unsure how to approach him.

"Zach?" he questioned quietly. The youth's shoulders tensed and he stopped hoeing but he didn't turn.

"Aren't you coming in to eat?"

"I'm not hungry," Zach muttered.

"You never showed up for breakfast, and I didn't see you at dinner either. You have to eat sometime."

Zach didn't answer, he just started hoeing again, slashing at the weeds as if they were deadly enemies. Daniel winced as the tops came off three carrots. He asked softly, "Is it because of me, Zach? Because you don't want to sit at the same table with a mutant?"

The youth stopped and turned slowly to face him.

"We don't have to sit at the same table you know, just because we're partners. You have to eat, Zach."

"It's not you," the youth said, casting a glance in the direction of the great hall. He turned away again. "I'm just not hungry." He felt ashamed, as he always did with Daniel. He went back to hoeing, carefully avoiding the carrots. Daniel hesitated, then turned and walked slowly toward the hall. He had recognized that expression on Zach's face. Sometimes when he looked at Zach it felt like looking into a mirror that reflected his past.

As soon as Daniel left, Zach headed for the tool shed and put the hoe away. A need deeper than hunger drove him. He quickly went to the dorm and gathered drawing materials, then almost ran to the gates and out of the hold.

A little while later, when supper ended, Daniel emerged from the hall carrying a cup of apple juice and a plate he had filled for Zach, but the outlander no longer worked in the garden. The guards had just been relieved and Daniel called to them as they sauntered across the courtyard.

"Did you see where Zach went?"

Hedi answered, "He's outside, up on the hill."

Daniel nodded his thanks and headed for the gate. He climbed the knoll and came up behind Zach quietly. The outlander remained deep in creative concentration and neither heard him nor noticed his presence. Daniel put the plate and cup down and glanced over Zach's shoulder. He worked on a sketch of Tadi wearing a warm smile of approval. Half a dozen other sketches lay scattered around. Daniel noticed one of Rad, looking arrogant and contemptuous, then spotted one of his own face. He picked it up curiously. Zach had drawn his head and shoulders, with one hand upraised as if in benediction. The portrait gave an impression of wide-eyed innocence and benevolence. Daniel snorted in amusement and said, "You make me look like a plagued saint!"

Zach, startled out of his trance, spoke and reacted without thinking. He snatched the picture from Daniel's hands and snapped, "Sometimes you act like one. You make me want to puke!"

Daniel recoiled from the hostility, dismayed by the depth of the resentment he saw in Zach's eyes. The youth went back to his drawing, and when next he glanced up, Daniel had left. Only then did Zach notice the plate and cup the mutant had left beside him. He lifted the napkin and looked at the food, still warm. It smelled delicious and his empty stomach cramped with hunger. Zach felt a wave of shame wash over him and any lingering doubts he might have held about Daniel faded. This simple gesture of kindness was not the act of a vengeful man.

Zach sat alone on the hill until twilight began to fade into darkness. He tried to draw, but nothing turned out right and he ended up wasting paper, so he just sat and brooded over the way his life was going, thinking about Daniel and dreading the day the lessons would begin. He almost wished the mutant *would* just shoot him and get it over with. It tied him in knots, the thought of having to try once again to measure up to someone else's impossible standards of perfection. At last he headed for the gate, realizing if he didn't go inside soon he would locked out, and with Rad on night duty, he probably would not get back in before morning.

He went to the dorm and put his sketches away, sliding the binder beneath his mattress. Then he headed for the kitchen with the empty dishes. People had gathered in groups in the sitting and weaving rooms, but as usual, they ignored Zach as he passed by in silence. When he reached the great hall, he felt surprised to find it also occupied. By this time it usually lay deserted. A few small groups sat at tables, talking and playing dice or card games. Zach hesitated when he saw Hutch and Daniel standing in conversation, half way between himself and the kitchen door. The mutant saw him and gazed at him with a troubled, wary expression. Hutch noticed and glanced over his shoulder, spotting the youth hovering uncertainly in the doorway. The blond holder nodded to Daniel and said something and the mutant turned away, moving toward the kitchen. Hutch strode toward Zach purposefully and the outlander tensed, wondering what Daniel had told him.

"Alright, Zach. You want to tell me what happened?"

"What do you mean?"

"Daniel's upset about something. I can tell. He said he was going to take you some supper and he came back looking like he'd been slapped in the face. What did you say to him?"

Zach stared at Hutch, paralyzed by the accusing tone of his voice. Neither of them noticed that Daniel had returned. The mutant walked up behind his friend and said in a quiet, reproving tone, "Hutch! Zach is my partner. If we have a problem between us, we'll work it out ourselves."

Daniel put a hand on Hutch's shoulder and smiled to take the sting out of his words.

"I don't need a mother hen."

Hutch looked disconcerted. This was the first time he'd ever heard anything approaching criticism or disapproval from Daniel. Then he realized his friend was correct. As their guide, Hutch could advise them if asked, and make sure they understood their responsibilities to one another, but he had no right to interfere in their personal relationship.

"You're right, Daniel. My apologies to both of you."

"Accepted," Daniel said warmly, then he turned to Zach. "We were just about to make a pot of tea. Would you like to join us?"

Zach felt trapped. He wanted to say no, but knew he had little choice. Hutch would not accept another rebuff to Daniel, and Zach needed to go to the kitchen anyway, so he nodded reluctantly and trailed after them. While Hutch made the tea and Daniel found the mugs, Zach washed his own dishes and left them drying on the counter. Daniel saw him hesitating uncertainly and beckoned him over.

"Come and sit with us, Zach."

He slid in beside Daniel because, mutant or not, Daniel felt more like a friend right now than Hutch did. Daniel handed him a cup of steaming tea and Zach wrapped his hands around the mug nervously.

"So what did Margit say about this trip to the refuge?" Hutch asked Daniel, continuing a conversation started at supper. Daniel made a face.

"She says I can go as long as I take my time and don't carry anything. She's upset about me carrying Peri back from the orchard this afternoon." Daniel grinned. "By the time she thinks I'm ready, Peri will be old enough to carry me!"

"Maybe we should wait a bit if she thinks it's too soon."

Daniel shook his head, turning serious. "No, I'm worried about . . ." He hesitated and glanced at Zach's downcast face. "I'm worried about Darius," he finished quietly. "He must think I'm dead, or I've deserted him."

"He knows you're fine. I've been visiting every six days or so, taking him bread. I just told Cochita you had a friend you shared with and she never questioned it. I've been letting him know how you're doing."

Zach's eyes went from Hutch to Daniel, puzzled by the sense of secrecy surrounding this third person they discussed. Hutch eyed the outlander uneasily, his distrust plain to see. Daniel noticed and told him, "Zach is my partner, Hutch. He has to know about Darius sooner or later. Why didn't you tell me you were visiting him?"

Hutch looked a little uncomfortable. "I wasn't sure how you would feel about me going there when you weren't around."

"I trust you, Hutch. I trust you with my life and I trust you not to hurt anyone I care about. I would have asked you to visit Darius, but I wasn't sure how much *you* trusted *him*."

Hutch smiled. "Darius and I have a mutual understanding. I haven't told him about your adoption though. I figured you would want to break that news to him yourself. He's missed you a lot. He'll be awful lonesome there all by himself."

Hutch immediately regretted his words, seeing the upset, concerned expression on Daniel's face.

"Maybe moving to the hold isn't such a good idea."

Hutch frowned in alarm. "You do want this adoption, don't you, Daniel?"

"More than I've ever wanted anything in my life. It's just . . . Darius has been so alone all his life. And I'm the only real friend he's got. He needs me, Hutch."

"You can still be his friend, Daniel. We can visit him often and make sure he doesn't feel lonely, that he's got everything he needs. And I had this idea . . . I'm not sure what you'll think of it, but since Darius was . . ." He hesitated, glancing at Zach uncertainly. The outlander started to rise, feeling distrusted and unwelcome, but Daniel caught him by the arm.

"Stay, partner. Please. You're in this too, or you soon will be." Daniel could feel the tension singing through Zach like electricity and he mistakenly assumed it was from distaste at his nearness, his touch. He carefully removed his hand and said to Hutch, "Go ahead. Tell us your idea."

"Well," the holder continued, "since Darius was raised by wolves . . ."

Zach suddenly wondered who or what Darius might be.

". . . what do you think about giving him a puppy? Luma had a litter two months ago. They're just about the right age. It's not quite the same as a human friend, but at least it would be company for him."

Daniel felt stunned by the simplicity of the solution. He started to grin. "Hutch, you're a genius! That's a brilliant idea."

"Glad you like it," the holder replied with relief. "Now I hope we'll hear no more talk about moving to the Haven being a mistake. What do you think? Should we do it tomorrow? Do you feel up to it?"

"I feel fine."

"How much gear do you have to bring back? Will we need help?"

"No, I'll be leaving most of it for Darius. You and Zach should be able to carry it. I'd like to keep the refuge a secret for Darius's sake. You will come with us, won't you, Zach?"

The youth felt surprised to be given a choice. "Sure. If you want me to. If it's alright with Tadi."

*   *   *

The next morning, Daniel kept an eye on Zach, and when the youth started to head out to work again without eating, Daniel followed him.

"Zach!"

The outlander turned, scowling. Daniel caught up with him and said sternly, "Remember when Hutch said I was the senior partner and you had to do what I told you, within reasonable limits?"

Zach nodded unhappily.

"Well, I'm pulling rank, junior. I'm telling you to come and eat breakfast. I think that's well within reason. You can't keep starving yourself like this."

An expression of dread came over Zach's face and Daniel said softly, "I know it's hard, Zach. I know what it's like to be ignored, treated like an outcast. But the more you avoid them, the longer they're going to treat you that way. You have to give them a chance to get to know you. Things won't stay this way forever."

Zach studied the mutant impassively, hiding the surprise he felt at the understanding and sympathy in those strange green eyes. They were beautiful eyes, Zach suddenly realized, the bright yellow green of sunlight on new leaves, clear and honest and filled with friendly concern. They held a taut wariness as well, and the youth recalled his rudeness of yesterday with a flush of shame.

"Are you coming?" Daniel asked, and Zach nodded. He followed his partner back inside and down the corridor to the great hall, taking a deep breath to brace himself before entering. The room seemed crowded and noisy. They helped themselves at the buffet table and Zach just took a little fruit and a small bowl of oatmeal. He knew his stomach could not handle much. It was already beginning to cramp. He kept his eyes lowered as he followed Daniel to a seat and slid in beside him. Glancing up, Zach met Tadi's eyes, smiling approval at seeing the partners together. The youth relaxed a little, some of the tension going out of him. Neely sat on her father's left and Tye on his right, and to Zach's surprise, the hunter acknowledged him with a nod of welcome. Hutch sat on Daniel's other side, and he greeted them cheerfully.

"Mornin', Daniel, Zach. I've just been telling Tadi about our little trip this afternoon."

"It sounds like a fine idea," Tadi said. "I'm sure Zach could use a break from the routine. You just take it easy though, Daniel. There's no point in pushing yourself before you're ready."

"I'm fine," Daniel insisted. "I'm really not as fragile as Margit seems to think."

"That may be, but Margit is a fine healer, and she usually knows what she's talking about." Tadi paused and gazed thoughtfully at his sponsor. "I hear you've had more trouble with Rad."

Zach's eyes widened and he glanced quickly at Daniel.

"He didn't hear it from me, partner, I swear."

"It doesn't matter where I heard it. Zach, why didn't you tell me?"

The youth swallowed hard and muttered, "He already hates me. The more you punish him, the worse it's going to get."

Tadi exchanged a worried glance with Daniel and the mutant nodded in silent agreement.

"Alright, I'll let it pass this time. But you can't just go on letting him use you for a punching bag. If it happens again, tell me!"

"It won't happen again," Daniel said with quiet determination.

They all looked at him as he continued to calmly eat his breakfast. Zach felt a confused stirring of resentment and relief. The corner of Tadi's mouth quirked up in a smile and he said, "Try not to do any serious damage."

Daniel just nodded.

After breakfast, Zach had more gardens to hoe and weed. The hold planted extensive gardens in order to feed a large number of people through an entire year. As he started walking across the courtyard to the tool shed, Daniel called to him.

"Zach, wait. Before you start work, come and see the puppies with us."

The youth hesitated, then went to join Hutch and Daniel as they headed for the kennel. At this time of year the kennel usually lay deserted, since the dogs went to the Meadows with the flock. But this year Luma had stayed behind to care for her new family. The three young men crouched in the clean straw carpeting the kennel floor and watched the seven puppies wrestling and tumbling about.

"The last of old Shep's sons and daughters, I guess," Hutch said sadly. "He was a good dog. The best I've ever known. What do you think? Which one should we take?"

The puppies all looked like black and white balls of fuzz on short, stubby legs. The differences between them seemed minimal except for one standout, a tiny male, half the size of the others. He caught Zach's eye immediately and the youth watched as the runt tentatively tried to join in the rough play and got bowled over and trampled by his bigger brothers and sisters. Daniel shook his head.

"I don't know, Hutch. They all look pretty much alike. What do you think, Zach?"

"What will happen to the rest of them?" Zach asked hesitantly.

"Tadi will start training them as soon as he thinks they're old enough. When the flock comes back they'll get some real practice, and then next year they'll go to the Meadows for more training and experience. The year after that most of them will be traded to the first caravan that comes along. Tadi and Sev have quite a reputation as trainers. We'll get a good price for them."

Zach watched the puppies seriously for a moment, brows drawn together in thought. "That little one," he said, "the runt . . . won't they be less likely to notice or get upset if he disappears?"

Hutch and Daniel exchanged a glance and the blond man nodded. "Good point. We'll take him. Poor little fella looks like he's having a pretty rough time of it anyway. Pretty tough competition, eh, little scrap?" He picked the puppy up and it chewed on his thumb, growling ferociously. Hutch frowned and said, "Shep was a runt too. I remember when my father and Tadi picked him out. I remember how pleased they seemed over the deal, and Tadi said courage and intelligence have nothing to do with size. Shep sure proved him right. I've got a feeling this little fella's going to be just like his father."

Chapter Eight

I've heard it said that people
come into our lives for a reason
Bringing something we must learn and we are led
To those who help us most to grow if we let them
And we help them in return.
Well, I don't know if I believe that's true
But I know I'm who I am today
Because I knew you.
~Julie Osborn

Throughout the morning, as Zach worked in the gardens, he found himself looking forward to the afternoon's trip. When the bell sounded the dinner call, he stopped for a moment and considered going in for the meal, but then he just turned away and continued working. A little while later he nearly jumped out of his skin when a voice suddenly spoke up behind him.

"Dinner time, Zach."

The youth whirled. "Stop sneaking up on me!" he cried accusingly.

Daniel backed off a pace and the wariness in his eyes intensified. "Sorry," he said wryly, "I'll try to stamp my feet next time."

Zach's anger deflated and left him once again feeling shamed.

"Are you going to come and eat?" Daniel asked. Zach gazed at him in misery, searching for some way to refuse. Finally he nodded in resignation and followed his partner back toward the hold.

Again, the meal was not as uncomfortable as Zach had feared. They once more sat with Hutch and Tadi. Neely was busy helping in the kitchen and Tye had gone off somewhere on a hunt, but Serene and Hedy shared the table with them and the talk remained light and amiable. Tadi and Daniel made an effort to involve Zach in the conversation, and while he didn't say much, at least he didn't feel excluded.

As soon as dinner ended, the three young men went to the kitchen. Cochita had gotten the bread into the ovens early, knowing the boys needed an early start if they were going to keep an easy pace for Daniel and still get back by suppertime. She packed the loaf into a linen sack, along with some pastries for Daniel's mysterious friend, and a few extras for the young men . . . to keep up their strength on the hike, she said.

"Now don't you let Daniel overdo it," she admonished Hutch and Zach. "I'm counting on you to bring him back in one piece and on his feet."

"I promise if he gets too rambunctious, we'll sit on him," Hutch assured her with a grin.

Zach and Daniel went to the kennel and smuggled the pup into the outlander's knapsack, while Hutch went to the armory. The holder returned with only two rifles. He handed one to Daniel, but the mutant refused it.

"I've never used one before. Do you know what happened to my bow?"

Hutch shrugged and shook his head. "Tye went back for it, but found it gone. Sev says it's not at the cottage. We don't know what happened to it."

"Damn! That was a good bow. I guess I'll have to make another." He still refused the rifle though, so Hutch reluctantly handed it to Zach.

"Take care what you use it on this time. If you hurt Darius I will personally tie you in knots and throw you in the river."

"Hutch!" Daniel reproved him gently. "Ease off."

"Sorry," the holder said, but he made the apology to Daniel, not Zach.

They started off with the youth trailing, all his pleasurable anticipation crushed by Hutch's undisguised distrust. They let Daniel set the pace, and for the first part of the trip he moved with a brisk stride, eager to reach the welcoming embrace of the forest. When they left the river path and moved into the trees, Daniel slowed and then stopped and just stood there, eyes closed, breathing deeply the familiar, comforting scents of home. Hutch studied him worriedly.

"Are you alright, Daniel?"

"Fine," the mutant sighed, "I just can't imagine how anyone could spend their whole life in a city or town and never go into the forest, never know this feeling. It's like . . . " He hesitated, groping for words to describe it.

"Like being wrapped in your mother's arms," Zach supplied, then turned bright red, embarrassed to have expressed such feelings. His father would have jeered. But while Hutch looked surprised, Zach saw neither ridicule nor contempt in his eyes, and Daniel smiled warmly in agreement.

"Exactly."

They continued on, the shared emotion making Zach feel a little less like a tag-along. When they neared the mouth of the box canyon, Hutch drew Daniel to a stop.

"We should warn Zach," he said.

The youth stiffened. "You don't have to warn me," he cried, "I'm not going to shoot anyone!"

Hutch recognized the hurt in his voice and regretted his earlier sharpness.

"Easy, Zach," Daniel said, "that's not what Hutch meant. Come and sit down and we'll tell you about Darius."

Daniel sank down to sit cross-legged on the mossy ground and Hutch crouched beside him. Zach sat stiffly on a log, avoiding their eyes.

"Darius is . . . a little different," Daniel began. "He's a psi mutant."

Zach regarded him blankly.

"A mind mutant. Physically he's pretty normal looking. At least he has all the right parts in the right places and proportions. But he thinks a little differently, more in pictures and emotions rather than words. He has trouble with words. He's a telepath, or an empath . . . I'm not sure just what you would call it."

"You mean . . . he can hear thoughts? See inside people's heads?" Zach asked with growing dismay. He did not want anyone prying into his head, picking out all his shameful secrets.

"He can hear some surface thoughts, but he can't invade your privacy without endangering himself," Daniel assured Zach. "What we wanted to warn you about though is this involuntary defense he has. He radiates a sense of evil, of deadly danger. He can't control it except by covering his eyes. If he's scared or upset, it gets stronger, but don't let it convince you, because it's just a disguise. He is not evil. He's one of the gentlest, most beautiful people I've ever known. He has the intelligence of a grown man, but the heart and soul of a child." Daniel searched the youth's face for a moment, then added, "He is my friend, Zach. You have to promise me that, no matter what happens, you won't harm him."

The youth met Daniel's eyes and said, "I promise," determined to die himself before he harmed anyone again. Hutch's mouth tightened and Zach could tell what he thought by his sour expression.

"Alright," Daniel replied, "just remember, we wouldn't let him hurt you anymore than we would want you to hurt him." He rose in one graceful movement and Zach stood up, feeling awkward in contrast.

*   *   *

Darius lingered in the cave, waiting for Hutch, expecting him to come today. He felt the holder's presence as Hutch emerged into the little valley, and the telepath started to go to meet him. But then he sensed another aura, one vaguely familiar that he associated with the portrait of Hutch and with the scene of Daniel's shooting. Darius had gone the next day to examine the place, picking up lingering vibrations, trying to understand what had happened. He realized this person with Hutch was the one responsible for hurting Daniel. Darius retreated fearfully to the back of the cave. Then suddenly he recognized Daniel's aura, just emerging from the tunnel, and his heart leaped with joy. But he remained in hiding, confused by the presence of his friend's attacker.

As the trio moved toward the lean-to, Hutch said, "He usually comes to meet me. Maybe he's not home."

Zach didn't even have time to feel relief before Daniel replied with glad conviction, "He's here." A bright rainbow of joy and welcome had bubbled into his head the moment he entered the valley. "He's in the cave but he's a bit wary because of Zach."

Daniel entered the cave first, followed by Zach and then Hutch. No fire glowed in the hearth and the cave seemed very dark. Zach felt an oppressive sense of danger the moment he entered. He could dimly make out a small, dark figure in the shadowy depths of the room. Waves of malevolence pounded at him and sweat beaded on his forehead, but he kept his rifle pointed resolutely at the floor.

"It's alright, Darius," Daniel said soothingly, "these are friends."

"Hush you friend," a harsh voice grated out of the dimness. "Evil norp hurt Dan-yel." Darius made a threatening motion toward Zach and the rifle came up instinctively, without conscious thought. Daniel caught it by the barrel and aimed it away from Darius, keeping a tight grip on it. But Zach kept his finger away from **the?** trigger and offered no resistance.

"He made a mistake, Darius. He's my partner now. Look at him. Do you see any evil in him?"

Zach felt the weight of the telepath's gaze intensify and he froze in panic. After a moment the feeling of malevolent threat began to subside a little and the paralysis locking him in place eased. He wrenched the rifle from Daniel's grip and fled the cave. Daniel yelped as the gun sights ripped into his hand, and he gazed after the youth in dismay. Hutch swore and started to go after Zach, but Daniel caught his arm and held him back.

"Hutch, don't be angry with him. Remember the first time you faced Darius? Just let me handle this. You talk to our friend here. See if you can calm him down a little."

Zach had not gone far. Daniel found him outside the cave entrance, leaning against the cliff, white faced and shaking.

"Zach?" Daniel put a hand on his shoulder, but the youth shrugged it off.

"D-don't touch me!"

Zach suddenly noticed the blood dripping from the mutant's right hand and his eyes widened in horror . . . dropped quickly to note the smear of blood on the gun sights. He winced. Daniel noted his dismay and said, "It's fine, Zach, it's just a scratch. Please, come back inside. Hutch is calming Darius. I swear he won't attack you."

The outlander seemed calmer now, almost subdued. He took a shaky breath and nodded, and when his partner gestured toward the doorway, he preceded the mutant into the cave, leaving his rifle outside. He felt like he was entering a lion's den with the animal in residence. He found Hutch seated on a pile of hides with his back against the wall. Darius crouched at his side, listening seriously as the holder tried to explain the concept of partnership. Daniel waved Zach to another seat and settled himself near his partner. As the outlander sat down, something moved against his back and he heard a soft whimper. The pup had slept so quietly during the trip, they had all but forgotten him. Zach swung his pack off and gently drew the little animal out. Darius became instantly fascinated and moved closer to see better. Zach put the little dog down and shrank away from the telepath.

"Cub," Darius rasped. "You cub, norp?"

"Darius, my partner's name is Zach."

The telepath blinked at Daniel. "Sack. You cub, Sack? Mama dead?"

"No . . . the mother's not dead."

"You steal cub?"

Zach glanced at Daniel nervously, not sure how to respond. In a way, they had stolen the pup. Daniel smiled reassuringly and answered for him.

"We brought him for you, Darius. A friend for you, to keep you company."

The telepath picked up on the impression Daniel was only visiting. "Dan-yel not stay?"

"I'm sorry, Darius, I can't. Come here, my friend. I have memories to share."

The small man sat next to him and Daniel closed his eyes, falling easily into rapport with Darius, showing him all that had happened in the past weeks -- the shooting, his illness and slow recovery, the flood of concern and love from the holders, the ordeal of the trial and its resulting in an offer of adoption and partnership with Zach. He let the telepath see Zach as he did, as a lonely, scared kid with nowhere else to go, in danger of being cast out if Daniel refused partnership with him. Daniel showed Darius how happy he felt with the holders, how their acceptance fulfilled a lifelong dream. And he shared his treasured memory of his day with the children.

(*Understand.*) Darius expressed a surge of great happiness for Daniel, but a strong sense of loss, of loneliness, seeped in around the edges, trying hard to stay hidden.

(*I wish you could come with me, Darius. I will always be your friend. We'll visit often, Hutch and I, and Zach. I promise. We won't let you get lonely, and the puppy will keep you company.*) He showed Darius an image of the kennel with the little runt getting trampled and shoved aside. (*He needs you.*) Daniel's thoughts colored with distress and concern for his friend's happiness. Darius sent a warm wave of reassurance washing over him, relieved that he would not lose Daniel completely.

Zach watched the silent exchange while Hutch got up and quietly laid a small fire and heated water for tea. The puppy began to whimper, apprehensive in this strange environment and lonely without his brothers and sisters. Zach picked him up and cuddled him, gently ruffling his fur. It felt somehow reassuring to comfort someone else's fears. Hutch brought Zach a cup of tea and the youth glanced up nervously, expecting to see anger. But Hutch's expression remained carefully neutral. The tea tasted of chamomile and helped to soothe Zach's jittery nerves. The puppy began attacking his hand, chewing valiantly at the base of his thumb. The pup's funny, baby awkwardness and obvious determination to subdue this tricky five-legged beast managed to draw a rare smile from the youth. Zach became so engrossed with the little animal's antics, he didn't notice at first when Daniel and the telepath emerged from their shared trance. He heard his partner's soft voice thanking Hutch as the holder offered a cup of tea, and glancing up, he met Darius' glare. The feeling of threat had greatly lessened, but enough remained to draw Zach's nerves up taut. The telepath made no hostile move, just crouched in front of Zach, watching him and the puppy.

"Cub like Sack. Sack not evil. Dan-yel pot-ner. Not hurt Sack."

Hutch handed Darius a steaming cup and the small man gazed up at the holder. "Hush friend Sack?" he asked, sensing the uneasiness between them. Hutch studied Zach with a veiled expression and the outlander met his eyes, needing to hear him say yes, but knowing he wouldn't.

"I suppose," Hutch answered neutrally. His ambivalence looked like a strange, muddy puddle of mixed color to Darius.

Daniel began quietly gathering his belongings. Most of his gear he would leave for Darius, the cooking utensils, the bedding, the dishes. He took only his weapons and those things that held personal meaning for him . . . the portrait of Hutch, Neely's shirt, the spirit lamp, a pair of half-finished deerhide boots.

Darius continued to watch Zach and the puppy, making the youth increasingly uncomfortable. Zach started to hand the little animal over to him and then hesitated.

"You won't eat him, will you?" the youth asked suspiciously. He felt a single strong pulse from the telepath's defense system and flinched. Daniel turned to watch them with mild amusement.

"You've shocked him deeply," he said. "Darius was raised by wolves, remember. Wolves love their young. They'll adopt orphans quicker than any other species, including people. Sometimes they'll even foster the abandoned young of other species, as they did with Darius.

"Cub be friend I," the telepath rasped, "be pot-ner. Not hurt Cub."

Zach reluctantly surrendered the pup to him and Darius held the pup gently, communicating silently with him. The puppy started licking his face, tiny tail wagging joyfully, and the little telepath began laughing his strange, wheezy laugh. Coming from that expressionless face, with its fixed glare, the sound unnerved Zach almost as much as that threatening defense, but Daniel grinned, pleased to hear the happy sound.

Hutch got up and studied the piles Daniel had made of his belongings. Daniel had decided to take much of his stockpile of hides and furs. Darius would never need them, and the holders could make use of them.

"You're making three piles?" Hutch demanded. "You're not supposed to carry anything."

"Don't you start treating me like an old woman too. The day I can't carry my share is the day the flame will go out."

Hutch shook his head. "Zach, get over here and tell your partner he's being a damned fool!"

The outlander glanced from one of them to the other uncertainly. He eyed the three piles. "There's not that much. Hutch and I can carry it."

"I know you can carry it. I could carry it all myself if I had to. I'm not going to stand around like a dorf while you two do all the work." Daniel began tying up the three packs, not willing to argue the point further.

"I suppose when you collapse you'll expect us to carry you as well," Hutch said sourly. "You're going to put yourself back in the infirmary, my friend."

Daniel ignored him. He shouldered one of the packs and handed one to each of his companions.

"I'm fine, Hutch. What do you think I did before I had you and Margit to fuss over me? This is not the first time I've had to recover from an injury, and I did it without any friends to fetch and carry for me."

"Stubborn, pigheaded fool!"

Daniel grinned. "Mother hen!"

Hutch shook his head in defeat and gave in. Daniel went to one knee in front of Darius and put his hands on the telepath's shoulders.

"I have missed you, my friend. I promise I won't stay away long. I'll come every few days to visit. If you need me, can you get close enough to the hold to contact me?"

"Night time. Dark. Holder not see."

(*I love you, little brother. If you need me, you know I'll come.*)

A warm cloud of rosy pink pressed against Daniel's mind, like a mental hug, and he sensed a wordless promise in return. (*Danyel be careful. No more hurt. Be happy.*)

"I will," Daniel said aloud, briefly embracing the little man, feeling once again that zinging sensation of exchanged energy as their auras mingled. Darius stood near the entrance to the cave with Cub at his feet, watching as the trio disappeared into the exit tunnel. Daniel went last, and he turned and waved once before he left.

The three young men took their time on the trip back, with Hutch setting the pace to ensure Daniel didn't push himself too hard. Before long, Daniel's pack began to feel heavier and heavier.

In actual fact, it weighed little more than Peri, but they were travelling over five times the distance and he was still only half recovered from a near mortal injury. As his weariness increased, he just kept on in stubborn silence, refusing to admit defeat. Hutch, in the lead, didn't notice, and Zach, trailing behind, mostly kept his eyes on the ground, watching his footing over the uneven trail. Daniel began to get lightheaded and his legs started to feel weak and unsteady. "Hutch!"

The holder was back at his side instantly and Zach's head jerked up, startled. Hutch took one look at Daniel's white face and said, "You'd better sit down, my friend, before you fall down." He helped Daniel to a seat and removed his pack.

"Why didn't you say something? We could have stopped for a rest. Dammit, Zach, why didn't *you* say something? You were supposed to keep an eye on him. He's your partner. You're supposed to care about him."

"Hutch," Daniel said sharply, "stop ragging on Zach! This is my own damned fault! You and Margit were right, I admit it. I promise I'll settle down and take up knitting for the rest of my life. Or until Margit says I'm alright, whichever is shortest."

Hutch's frown relaxed into an amused smile. "Everyone in the hold will be wearing the strangest sweaters." He searched out the pastries Cochita had sent for them and handed one to Daniel. "Zach," he asked, "do you want anything to eat?"

The youth sat with his back to them, arms wrapped around his knees, shoulders stiff and hunched. He shook his head. Hutch sighed and said, "I'm sorry I yelled at you. You were no more at fault than I was."

Zach didn't answer and Hutch exchanged a glance with Daniel then shrugged. The sweet pastry brought a quick surge of renewed energy to Daniel, and after a short rest he began to feel considerably better.

"I suppose we should get moving," he said. "If we don't get back by supper time, they'll start to worry."

Zach rose immediately and shrugged into his pack while Hutch gave Daniel a hand up. The outlander snatched up his partner's pack as well and started down the trail without a word to either of them.

Chapter Nine

...I know for certain, every time you fall,
You will rise again above it all.
You'll wake to a different drum
In a place to call your own.
Your world is shaking, but a day will come
For a dream to take you home.
~John Saich

Two more weeks of warm, sunny weather passed, and Daniel continued to heal and recover his strength. The cherries ripened and soon the time came to harvest them. The day before the cherry festival and Daniel's bonding ceremony, Tye headed out alone, early in the morning. The only one of the holder men with no regular partner, Tye preferred to go out alone because he liked to wander farther afield than most of the holders. He was also the only one besides Daniel who made regular trips to the rim. He liked to explore, to see new places, but today he had a mission that involved neither hunting nor exploring.

Hutch, Daniel and Zach spent the day helping with the cherry harvest. Margit forbade Daniel to climb the ladders or lift the full, heavy baskets. As usual, he chafed at her restraints, but Hutch made sure he kept his feet on the ground and didn't overdo it again. Evening found the three young men sitting together on the hilltop opposite the gates, relaxing quietly, watching the sunset and eating cherries. Daniel had begun to include Zach in whatever evening activity or socializing he was involved in. The youth remained silent, often ill at ease, but he rarely refused Daniel's invitations.

Hutch suddenly sat up straighter. "Here comes Tye," he said, "I wonder where he's been all day." Then he noticed the second, smaller figure. "Hey, he's got Jesse with him!"

Hutch scrambled to his feet with a wide grin and trotted down the hill to greet his partner. Daniel followed right behind him for a moment, but he paused and turned back to ask, "Are you coming, Zach?"

The youth trailed along reluctantly, sure Jesse would be far from pleased to see him again. When Tye and Tadi returned Jesse to the shepherds' cottage after the shooting, the boy made it quite clear, without actually saying anything, that he considered Zach the lowest form of life to crawl the earth.

Hutch and Jesse met with an exuberant whoop from the boy and a huge bear hug that turned into a brief wrestling match. When Daniel reached them, they broke apart, and Jesse shyly embraced the mutant.

"You didn't think I'd miss the chance to have you for a brother, did you?"

Daniel just laughed and hugged him back. "It's good to see you, Jesse."

"It's good to see you too, alive and on your feet again. You really had us worried there for a while."

"Well, I'm fine now. You remember Zach, don't you?"

Jesse eyed the outlander and his expression shifted to something coolly neutral. "I'm not likely to forget him."

"He's my partner now."

Daniel's tone held a note of mild warning, and Jesse smiled crookedly.

"Understood."

Tye interrupted impatiently. "Can we take this inside? I'm parched as an old bone. I could use a cup of tea and a few of those cherries."

*   *   *

The next morning the hold buzzed with excited preparations for the bonding ceremony and the festival. Cochita and a small army of helpers prepared last-minute delicacies for the feast. Everyone got out their best festival clothing and the ladies ransacked the tranquility gardens and the nearby fields collecting flowers for their hair. Hutch and Tye were Daniel's attendants for the preparations, and the blond holder insisted that Zach, as Daniel's partner, should help too. The outlander would just as soon have avoided the whole affair, preparations and all.

They stayed with Daniel throughout the long morning, trying to ease his nervousness. About midmorning they took him to the bath house and helped him with the purification rites, which consisted of little more than a very hot bath with special soap and fragrant oils. Daniel complained jokingly that Margit was going too far . . . now she wouldn't even let him take a bath by himself. When they finally allowed him to emerge from the pool, they wrapped him in a big, white towel and briskly rubbed him dry. Hutch handed him the ceremonial clothing, a pair of loose, drawstring pants and a tunic shirt, both of white linen. Daniel put them on, feeling strange and awkward in the unfamiliar clothing. Tye rubbed a little scented oil into his damp hair and combed his thick mane into a semblance of order. The three attendants stood back and surveyed him critically.

"You'll do," said Tye.

Hutch sounded a little more flattering. "You look great!"

Zach said nothing. He got an odd expression on his face . . . not resentment or envy, but a kind of concentration and a strange sort of hunger. Daniel smiled at him, puzzled, and Zach looked away. The three attendants quickly finished their own wash up, then they all headed for the dorm. Daniel paced nervously while they donned their festival finery. The hold fell silent, empty except for the guards outside. Everyone gathered in the orchard, eagerly awaiting Daniel's arrival. As the young men exited the hold, the guards called good wishes to Daniel and he waved, then suddenly noticed they had lost his partner.

"Where's Zach?"

Hutch scowled and glanced back toward the gate. "Do you want me to go roust him?"

Daniel remained silent for a moment, then shook his head slowly. "No. This must be hard enough for him as it is, watching me get everything he hoped for. Let him skip the ceremony if he wants."

Zach had in fact planned to skip the ceremony if he could, but when he saw Daniel all scrubbed and dressed, the white ritual garments accentuating the sun-darkened tan of his skin and the raven-wing blackness of his hair, the young outlander felt an overpowering urge. He waited until the others left, and in their excitement his absence went unnoticed. Once alone, he quickly removed a thick sheaf of paper from his stash and a wrapped package of char sticks, then hurried out of the hold.

By the time Zach reached the bridge, the crowd was so busy giving Daniel a noisy welcome that no one noticed the youth's arrival, which suited him just fine. He found a sturdy old apple tree that gave him cover and a good vantage point and he climbed into its branches, settling himself comfortably with his back against the trunk. He unwrapped his char sticks and began to draw. He remained marginally aware of the words of the ceremony as Daniel and Cochita made vows of support and comfort to one another, then Daniel and Aaron. That gave Zach pause for a moment. Why would Daniel choose Aaron for his bond father? Zach shuddered, shook his head and went on with his sketching, tucking each drawing to the back of the sheaf as he finished them.

The ritual continued, and Tadi, acting as master of ceremonies, announced, "A man needs brothers to stand by his side, to defend him and to teach him the joys of sharing. Bereft is the man with no brother to guard his back. Who will stand beside Daniel as his bond brother?"

Zach paused briefly to watch as Hutch, Tye and Jesse stepped forward and stood at Daniel's right side. Again vows were exchanged. Then Tadi said, "A man also needs sisters, to teach him gentleness and to help him understand the ways of women. Lonely is the man with no sister to comfort him. Who will stand beside Daniel as his bond sister?"

Kelda, Serene and Hedy moved forward to stand on Daniel's left. Zach closed his eyes and leaned back against the trunk of the tree, a pain in him too deep for tears beginning to rise to the surface. His sisters . . . his little sisters . . . hardly more than babies. He saw again the scene he had come home to, the blood and the tortured, mutilated bodies. His sisters would never teach him the ways of women; they had never had the chance to learn themselves. Suddenly he wished he had not come. He wanted to be somewhere else, anywhere else. He slid down out of the tree and stumbled away from the ceremony, feeling sick with the memories it had evoked.

The movement in the apple tree caught Tadi's eye and he turned just in time to see Zach slide down and disappear, deeper into the orchard. The ceremony soon concluded and people moved forward to welcome Daniel and congratulate the newly formed family. The mutant was now an accepted member of the assembly. Through his bond parents and siblings he had kinship ties to all five families, and thus to everyone in the hold. He was well and truly a Haven Holder.

Tadi skirted the crowd and went to the tree from which Zach had emerged, puzzled about why the youth had been hiding. When Zach had not arrived with the other attendants, Tadi had assumed the same as Daniel, that the outlander wished to avoid the ceremony. Beneath the tree, Tadi found a single sheet of paper, dropped accidentally during a hasty retreat. He picked it up and turned it over and drew his breath in sharply. It was a portrait of Daniel, done full figure. The mutant stood dressed in the white ritual garments with his hair blowing back and an indefinable sense of wildness about him, the look of an eagle on the wing, or a stallion guarding his mares, proud and untamable. It was marvelous. Tadi stared off in the direction Zach had taken, wondering why the youth had left so suddenly. He carefully rolled the picture into a cylinder and carried it with him as he rejoined the crowd beginning to break up and wander back to the hold for the feast. Tadi felt strongly tempted to show the drawing to Aaron and Cochita, but Zach had been hiding. That fact bothered Tadi. Why did the boy feel he needed to hide what he had been doing?

Daniel noticed Zach's continued absence in the great hall, and he began to feel a twinge of concern. The youth had not skipped a meal in over a week, nor did Daniel have to search him out any longer to make sure he ate. Zach had begun coming in at mealtimes without prompting, and Daniel always saved the place beside him at the table for his partner. But today the feast was in honor of Daniel's adoption and bonding. A special table had been set up at the front of the room for the new bond family, Daniel's family. He could hardly believe it -- he had a family, and not just one he was stuck with by birth, but one he had chosen, who had chosen him, one that accepted him as he was, flaws, mutations and all. His sweetest dreams and fantasies had never felt this wonderful. He had never dared to allow himself such dreams. They would have made his life of lonely solitude unbearable.

At last, just as the kitchen crew finished arranging the buffet, Daniel saw Zach slip into the room and hover uncertainly, searching the crowd, many still standing and talking in small groups. Daniel caught his eye and beckoned him forward. Zach threaded his way between the knots of people until he reached his partner. Daniel smiled at him.

"I was afraid you weren't going to come."

Zach avoided his eyes. "Have you seen Tadi?"

"A few moments ago. He's around here somewhere. Why? Is something wrong?"

"No. I just . . . don't want to sit alone."

Daniel studied Zach's stiff face. The youth almost twitched with tension as he searched the room for his sponsor. In this mob no one would have room to sit alone, but Daniel knew what he meant. All those they normally sat with, all the reasonably friendly faces, would sit at the family table.

"You won't have to sit alone. I want you to sit with me."

Zach glanced at him in surprise. "That table is just for your family."

"You're my partner, Zach. That makes you family."

The youth didn't reply, but Daniel saw him relax a little. Zach wondered what he had ever done to deserve a man like this for a partner. He no longer saw Daniel as a mutant or recognized any similarity between him and the raiders who had murdered Zach's family. He actually liked Daniel, admired him a great deal, but at the same time almost hated him with a kind of desperate jealousy. Daniel was just so damned good. It seemed no matter what a situation presented, the mutant could deal with it, and he always dealt gracefully and fairly. More than fairly.

No one questioned Zach's right to sit at the family table. Hedy sat on his other side, and she chatted amiably with him. As far as she was concerned, the shooting incident had been forgiven, if not forgotten. If Daniel wanted Zach to have another chance, she felt it had to start with forgiveness. Her friendliness surprised Zach and he responded to her shyly. He ate little, picking at his food nervously. Glancing up once, he found Aaron watching him with a speculative look. Zach froze like a rabbit under the eye of an eagle, waiting for the council leader to make some scathing remark or question his right to sit there. But Aaron just turned and made an innocuous comment to Serene about the children. Zach suddenly felt exposed and on display here at the table of honor. His eyes sought out Tadi and found him sitting at the third table on the left with his wife, Salla, his brother and sister-in-law, Ross and Zanna, and Cam Sorenson's family. As if feeling the weight of Zach's attention, Tadi looked up and met his eyes and smiled. That smile always had the ability to ease Zach's tension, but he felt glad when the meal finally ended.

The holders spent the afternoon in games and races and friendly contests of skill. Everyone got involved, from tots to grandmothers. Zach wandered about, just watching and absorbing the excited, holiday atmosphere, soaking up visual images and impressions to digest later and perhaps turn into drawings. For a while he watched the races between the smallest children, almost charmed into a smile by their youthful lack of coordination. When a hand suddenly came down on his shoulder, he jumped like a nervous horse.

"Easy, son, it's just me," Tadi said. "You're wound tight as a fiddle string." He began to gently massage the knotted muscles of Zach's back and shoulders. "I have something of yours," he told the youth quietly. "When you left the ceremony, you dropped something."

Zach stiffened, knowing it must have been one of his drawings. He had noticed one missing when he put them away.

"It's alright," his sponsor said softly, "I didn't show it to anyone or tell anyone you were there. You want to explain why you were hiding? No one would have objected to what you were doing."

Zach had no way of telling him why, no words to explain the feeling of shame attached to his scribbling, the sense of doing something forbidden, so he said nothing. Tadi let it go.

"Come on, Zach, loosen up," he said, continuing to work at the youth's tense muscles. "Come back to the tranquility garden with me. I'll give you a proper massage. This kind of tension is no good. You're going to make yourself sick."

Zach obediently followed his sponsor back inside the walls. They paused for a moment in the courtyard to watch the shooting competition. The holders had set targets up against the wall and a group of men and a few women took turns testing their skill. While Hutch planted three bullets within the center circle of the target, Tye instructed Daniel in the proper way to handle a rifle. As Zach and Tadi watched, Daniel stepped up to take his turn, feeling awkward with the unfamiliar weapon. He aimed carefully, tucking the butt of the rifle close against his shoulder as Tye had demonstrated, and squeezed the trigger. The shot clipped the edge of the target board, sending splinters flying, but came nowhere near the painted rings of the bull's eye.

"I think dinner just got away," Daniel commented wryly, eliciting a spate of chuckles from the group. He ejected the spent shell and raised the rifle to try again. Tadi drew Zach away. Zach would have liked to watch longer. He had never seen Daniel do anything poorly, and it surprised him to see his partner miss, even on a first attempt. He reluctantly followed his sponsor around to the back of the main building. The tranquility garden lay deserted, as Tadi had expected. He led Zach to a sunny patch of short grass and said, "Take your shirt off and lie down on your stomach."

Zach complied slowly, trying not to show his apprehension. It sounded too much like an order from his father when he was in especially deep trouble. He shivered a little, even in the afternoon heat, feeling exposed and vulnerable as he lay face down and defenseless. Tadi knelt and began stroking his back soothingly until he started to relax a little. Then with firm, gentle fingers, the man kneaded taut muscles, working his way slowly from the nape of the boy's neck, across his shoulders and down his spine, then back up again, humming softly in time with his rhythmic motions. As the tension gradually eased out of knotted muscles, Zach's nerves began to relax as well and he grew slightly drowsy, almost dozing off under Tadi's gentle ministrations. After a while, Tadi finished and shifted to sit at Zach's side.

"Roll over," he said, and Zach turned onto his back, squinting up at Tadi, the sun bright in his eyes. The man smiled and asked, "Feeling better?" He began to work on the muscles of the boy's chest and upper arms.

Zach smiled in return and answered, "A lot better. Thanks."

"You shouldn't let yourself get so tied up in knots. Let me know next time it gets bad. I'll do this for you again, any time you need it." He brushed his hand over the youth's prominent ribs. "You should try to eat more. You'll waste away to a shadow."

Zach sat up slowly, feeling more comfortable than he had in years. He had grown used to the pain of constantly tensed muscles until he'd hardly been aware of the discomfort.

"Can I ask you something, Tadi?"

"Anything, Zach. That's what sponsors are for."

"This is personal."

"Go ahead. I'll let you know if it's too personal," Tadi grinned.

"What happened to your leg?"

Tadi glanced down at the wooden peg strapped to his right knee. "Raider got me with a spear. I used to train the boys and dogs at the Meadows, like Sev does. Sev was young then, only a few years older than you. One night raiders attacked and took two of my boys. Sev and I went after them and managed to save Tye. He was only thirteen then and it was his first year as a shepherd. The raiders killed the other boy. I've always wondered if it was my fault, if I could have done something differently to prevent that tragedy. Anyway, the leg never healed and Margit had to take it off, so I retired. Sev took over the next year."

"Were you scared that night at the Meadows when the raiders attacked?"

"Sure I was scared. Only a fool would be unafraid in the face of danger. But I felt afraid mostly for Jesse. He's my youngest child. I don't think I could bear to lose him that same way."

Zach had not realized Jesse was Tadi's son. The tangled relationships of the holders seemed too intertwined for him to even attempt to understand. Everyone was related in some way to everyone else. All births and deaths were meticulously recorded, and when a couple wished to get joined, the council carefully researched their genetic background to make certain they were not too closely related. For this reason, the holders welcomed and adopted outsiders, to enlarge the gene pool and keep it healthy.

But most adoptees were men, since women rarely traveled in these wild parts, except for Kithtrekkers. Thus, the balance of males to females in the hold was a bit heavy on the male side, and every few years a bachelor or two would wander off into the world to find what the Haven could not provide. Often they never came back. When one of these lost sons did return, it became an occasion for great celebration.

"Anything else you would like to ask me?" Tadi questioned.

Zach shook his head, feeling a bit shy and self-conscious.

"Well, I have one for you," Tadi said with a smile. "That drawing you did of Daniel is wonderful. Will you show me some more?"

Zach reddened and seemed almost to shrink.

"It's alright," Tadi said quickly, "don't tighten up on me again. You don't have to show them if you'd rather not."

"It's just a bunch of worthless scribbling," Zach muttered.

"Why do you say that? The portrait of Daniel is superb. When Hutch called you an artist, I certainly didn't expect anything so masterful from someone so young."

Zach hugged his knees and looked away. "My father called them a sinful waste of time. He made me burn them. It felt like burning a part of myself."

"Art is never a waste of time, Zach. Art and music and poetry are all that separates us from the animals. Your father sounds like a hard man."

"He was. Hard as granite, with about as much feeling as a stone."

"Your mother must have been a remarkable woman then, to raise a son like you in the same house with a man like that."

Zach wondered uneasily what Tadi meant by 'a son like you'. He felt sure it was no fault of his mother's that he was such a screw-up, good for nothing but wasting time, a son who couldn't even milk a cow or make a stook that stood up to the first breeze that came along, who couldn't even lock a gate properly to keep the animals in. While his mother had never defended him, neither had she ever scorned him as his father had. Mostly she had just seemed tired, sad, almost indifferent.

"My father was an artist," Tadi said thoughtfully. "Just a dabbler really, but he enjoyed it. He used to design patterns for the weavers to work on their looms. He died about eight or nine years ago of the same fever that took Hutch and Tye's parents. I've still got his paint box. You're welcome to it if you like. I'm sure it would please him to know someone was getting as much pleasure out of it as he always did."

Zach straightened, eyes widening in a kind of breathless hunger. "I've always wanted some colors. I could never afford them until I joined the caravan, and they didn't have any."

Tadi smiled. "I'll go get them for you."

He rose and headed for his quarters. Zach jumped to his feet and hurried to the dorm, quickly pulling his binder from its hiding place under his mattress. By the time Tadi returned with the paint box the young outlander once more sat in the garden waiting for him. The box looked large, about eighteen inches by twenty-four and five inches deep, of polished, hand-carved wood. Zach stroked the lid reverently, fingering the initials carved into its center, 'J.H.' He glanced at Tadi uncertainly.

"Are you sure . . .?"

"I'm sure. It was made to be used and I know he would want this, to pass it on to a worthy successor."

Zach opened the box. Eight fist-sized cakes of color lay arranged in two rows, red, orange, yellow, green, blue, purple, brown and black. They looked almost new. He ran his finger over the yellow, feeling its grainy texture. The inside of the lid had leather straps across it that held a few sheets of paper and a thin metal tray with shallow depressions for mixing paint. A trough between the paint cakes held four brushes in varying sizes, their bristles soft and well kept. Zach swallowed hard, unable to speak. He would not have known what to say if he could. He just picked up his binder, clutching it nervously, then handed it to Tadi as if handing over his soul, which in a way he was. It seemed a paltry gift in comparison.

"Your drawings?" Tadi asked. Zach just nodded.

Tadi carefully undid the ties, handling the binder with the same respect the youth had given the paint box. The first drawings showed the bonding ceremony: Daniel again in the ritual whites, just head and shoulders this time, with a nervous, crooked grin that showed his wry sense of humor; Daniel and Cochita embracing after saying their vows; three little girls like small, dignified princesses in their festival dresses with flowers in their hair, and in the background a small boy reaching out mischievously to tug on a braid; Daniel with his three new brothers; Daniel and Hutch exchanging a smile. You could almost feel the bond between them as a physical force, beyond any need for vows. The last drawing of the festival showed Tadi standing before the assembly, looking fatherly and benevolent as he led them through the ritual.

"These are beautiful, Zach. You have an exceptional talent. May I look at the rest?"

The boy nodded silently.

The next series was a group of portraits of various members of the hold, the ones Zach had done atop the hill the night Daniel brought him supper. Being done from memory, the likenesses were not as good, but they were definitely recognizable. Tadi paused over the sketch of Daniel, intrigued by the otherworldly purity with which Zach had portrayed him, realizing it was more an expression of the youth's feelings than a portrait. It gave Tadi a sense of reassurance. If Zach could see the basic goodness in Daniel, surely the partnership would work out. Tadi's favorite in that series was one of Hedy on guard duty, her bright hair blowing out behind her. She looked like a warrior maiden, resolute and strong willed, but womanly soft. After that the drawings appeared in no particular order. Tadi went through them slowly, enjoying each one. Whenever he came across one that especially interested him, he would ask Zach about it.

"Tell me about this one." This time it was the street urchin with her young, old eyes.

"Her name was Sadi. She was about thirteen I guess. I met her one night when some men chased her down the alley where I was living. I hid her in my room and let her stay the night because she was half frozen and starving. I was spending the winter in the city, trying to pick up odd jobs here and there. The living was pretty thin but I guess I had it better than she did."

Tadi had never heard Zach speak so freely. The youth seldom said more than a dozen words at one time. "What happened to her?"

"She left the next morning. She would come back every once in a while, when she had no place else to go, but she never trusted me. Or anyone else, I guess. I found her one night in the back alley with some brute abusing her. I tried to help and she swore at me. She had taken money to let him do that to her. I never saw her again. She never came back."

Tadi shook his head. "Poor little waif." The next sketch he stopped at showed two little girls leading a milk cow through a grassy field. "Your sisters?"

Zach nodded. "This is Mahree and this is Linnet." His voice sounded husky, pain still close to the surface after this morning's reminder. Tadi examined his unhappy profile sympathetically, then continued on, leafing through the drawings until he came to the last one. He held it up, studying it.

"My father," Zach said softly. Tadi's brows rose in surprise.

"I thought it was Aaron."

Zach nodded. "It scares the spit out of me sometimes. It's like seeing a ghost. I keep expecting him to speak to me in my father's voice, my father's words."

"Has he ever?" Tadi asked gently, knowing that for all his intimidating bluster, Aaron was not an unkind man -- stern sometimes but never cruel.

"Not yet. If he ever does, I'm gone. I'd rather go out and die in the desert. Let the damned raiders have me."

Tadi's brows drew together into a frown of concern. "Just try to remember that he's not your father, no matter how much they look alike. Aaron is a good man, and if you give him the chance, he'll prove it to you."

Zach nodded but said nothing. It seemed he had used up all his words for the moment. Tadi carefully rearranged the drawings in the binder the way he had found them, and tied it closed again.

"They're wonderful, Zach. Thank you for sharing them with me."

"You . . . can keep the one of Daniel," the boy said softly, "if you want it."

Tadi smiled, delighted. "I would love to keep it. Thank you. It's still the one I like best. It's the way I see him too."

They both got to their feet and Tadi added, "I'd best get back to the festivities. Salla's going to wonder where I've disappeared to. You should go and enjoy yourself too. Join in some of the games and races."

Zach shook his head, uncomfortable. "I'm not much good at games."

"You don't have to be good, Zach, it's just for fun. It doesn't matter who wins. Give it a try." He turned and started to stroll away.

Zach called after him, "Tadi?"

The man paused, glancing back over his shoulder, smiling.

"Thanks. For everything."

"Anytime, son. Just remember, I'm here if you need me.

*   *   *

Hutch had been searching since Daniel disappeared a short time earlier. The holder had entered a race and left his friend standing on the sidelines, ordered by Margit to take it easy. When the race ended, Daniel had vanished. Hutch looked for him in each little knot of people surrounding the various games and competitions but could find no sign of him. Worry began to nibble at Hutch's heart, when at last he found Daniel behind the barns, leaning on the stockyard fence, stroking Sarantha's satiny neck. He wore a pensive expression of serious contemplation.

"Daniel?"

The mutant turned with a quick smile. "Thought I heard you sneaking up on me."

"Why are you back here all alone?"

Daniel shrugged. "It just got a little overpowering. Too many people. Too much noise. It's going to take a while to get used to it."

"As long as that's all it is. I thought you looked a little sad just now. What were you thinking about?"

Daniel looked away, frowning slightly. "I was thinking about Neely . . . wondering why she didn't stand up for me today. I really thought she . . . " His voice trailed off. He had tried hard to sound casual, but he couldn't hide his hurt and confusion from Hutch.

"Danni," Hutch said quietly, putting an arm around his friend's shoulders, "don't ever think Neely doesn't love you. She's known you longer than any of us, and I suspect she's loved you that much longer. When she didn't stand up for you today, it wasn't because she doesn't care, it was because she doesn't want to be your sister. Think about it, my friend."

Daniel considered the implications. She was the first woman since his mother to ever befriend him, and while he had many female friends now amongst the holders, Neely would always remain special. He could not deny the aching depth of his attraction to her. Since the first time he had seen her, hurt and bloody but concerned only for Jesse's safety, he had tried in vain to stifle hopeless dreams and fantasies about her. During his time in the infirmary, when she had visited him every day, he had come to believe she really did love him as she claimed. But he had never dared to hope there could ever be more than friendship between them. The holders might like and accept him as a man, but he could not believe they would ever accept a joining between a mutant and a normal girl.

"You should go find her... talk to her, Danni."

He smiled ruefully. "I wouldn't know what to say."

"You'll find something, and Neely's pretty good at filling in the gaps. If all else fails, you could always talk about knitting," Hutch teased. Daniel laughed, his cheerful mood fully restored.

*   *   *

Supper was a casual affair, with banquet leftovers, bowls of salads and plates of cold sliced meats lining the buffet table. The other end of the table held sweets and pastries and plenty of fresh cherries and strawberries. The kitchen crew laid the food out in late afternoon and everyone just helped themselves whenever they got hungry.

Zach spent most of the afternoon alone in the tranquility garden, experimenting with the new colors. After Tadi left him, he had opened the paint box again to marvel over the treasures it held and had been unable to resist the temptation to try them out. For a time he just dabbled and played with the paint on blank paper, getting to know the medium, trying out the different brushes and testing the colors. After a while he took out some of his old sketches and tried applying thin washes of paint to them. The clear fixer with which he had sprayed them kept the charcoal lines from smudging as he brushed over them. As his confidence grew, he used stronger color and the sketches seemed almost to come alive. Time slipped away in undisturbed concentration, and not until hunger brought him out of his concentration did he realize how late it had grown. He reluctantly packed everything up, carefully cleaning the brushes before putting them away.

He went to the dorm and slid his binder back under his mattress and the paint box beneath his clothing on the closet shelf assigned to him. Then he strolled down the corridor to the great hall, wondering if he had been so engrossed he didn't hear the supper bell. But the buffet table still held an abundance of food, and a few scattered groups of people still sat at the dining tables. Zach filled a plate and followed some others headed outside with their dinners. Wondering where Tadi and Daniel were, he drifted into the small orchard, searching for a place to settle. Someone called his name and he spotted his partner sitting further back under the trees with Hutch, Tye, Jesse and Rennie. Zach walked over to join them and Daniel smiled up at him.

"Where have you been all day? Are you alright?"

"I'm fine," he answered, almost smiling. He looked happier, more relaxed than any of them had ever seen him.

"I need a partner for this game. Would you like to play?"

Zach hesitated. He hated games. Mik had sometimes dragged him into card games, and it seemed he always ended up partnered with Bel, who hated to lose and usually did, often blaming his poor luck on Zach. But seeing the hopeful expression in Daniel's eyes, he reluctantly agreed. Hutch partnered with Jesse, while Tye and Rennie paired off. They played with dice, using black and white river stones as markers, but since they were not actually gambling, they just used markers for keeping score. Before long Zach found himself beginning to enjoy the game. Daniel played with reckless abandon, seeming not to care whether they lost or won. In fact, no one seemed very serious about the game. A good deal of teasing and laughter went on, and good-natured moaning over losses, but no one got upset or argued. They just enjoyed the pleasure of playing together. After a while Neely and Hedy joined them and a new game ensued. For the first time since the shooting, Zach began to feel a sense of belonging, of acceptance, at least within this small group.

As the light began to fade, the game broke up and they went to join the larger group gathering around the big bonfire in the center courtyard. They shared stories and songs, and to Daniel's self-conscious discomfort, Serene requested a repeat of the cherry tree story, saying it seemed the perfect tale for the cherry festival. A while later, Alison got out his fiddle and the music became livelier. People began to pair off and dance. Zach found it hard to associate the peppy, cheerful music with the long-faced, morose councilman. Ross Hayes accompanied Alison on a mouth harp and Davin on guitar. For a while Neely played with them on a lap harp, but she wanted to dance, so she soon left the band and drew Daniel into a group forming up for a round dance. He protested that he didn't know how, but Neely accepted no excuses. Soon she had him whirling around the circle with her, laughing and trying to follow what the others were doing without stepping on her toes or getting in anyone's way. Zach watched from the sidelines as more and more people formed circles and joined in the dancing. Suddenly Hedy appeared at his side and caught him by the hand.

"Come and dance with us, Zach." In the dim firelight, she couldn't see how he flushed, but she could see his discomfort in the way he looked down and muttered, "I don't know how."

"Neither does Daniel," she replied. "It's easy, and it's fun. Please, come and try it." She paused, cocking her head. "Listen . . . the music is slowing down. This one is special. Everyone has to take part. Come on, Zach."

He let her draw him into one of the circles, which parted to admit them. He saw others joining in, swelling the other circles, until everyone danced except the musicians. The music slowed a little more and one of the circles broke apart into a string of people holding hands. They wove gracefully through the next circle and it broke apart and attached itself to the end of the line, then went on, weaving through each circle until they all had linked together in a long line. As the line formed a ring around the bonfire, the music went softer and slower and finally ended. The musicians put down their instruments and joined the circle. For a moment the only sound came from the crackling of the fire, then Aaron's voice began speaking quietly, as if to someone standing at his side.

"Lord of Light, we thank you for bringing us safely through another season, and for the bountiful blessings you have showered upon us. We thank you for the life of our very dear friend and brother, Daniel Tayler Sorenson. We thank you for sending us Zach McKenna, a promising sponsor. May your love open his heart and teach him that all men are brothers, no matter what their appearance. We thank you for the safety of our hunters, gatherers and shepherds as they carry out their duties. We thank you for the land which nurtures us and for the sun and the rain and the growth of the crops."

Aaron fell silent, and after a moment his wife, Gemina, on his right, spoke up and offered thanks for the continuing health and safety of her children. And from there it went on around the circle, each person giving thanks for some great personal blessing. Some seemed petty, like Carly's blessing for the jewelry bought at the trade fair. Others seemed sad or poignant, like old Daffer Hayes, whose blessing was that the Lord had led him to this place where he had lived such a long and happy life amongst people he loved, who loved him, and he asked the same blessings on the new son of Haven Hold who had come to fill the place he would soon leave empty. Sometimes long silent pauses occurred as someone searched for their one special blessing. When Zach's turn came, he gazed across the circle at Daniel and the mutant met his eyes and smiled.

"Thank you for my partner's life . . . for not leaving me a murderer. And thank you for a second chance."

Hedy squeezed his hand. Her blessing was simple. "Thank you for my new brother."

Many gave thanks for Daniel's recovery and adoption. When it came his turn to speak, he remained silent for a long moment, trying to find the right words to speak from his heart.

"Thank you for the love of all these friends, for giving me a place to belong. Forgive me for the times I doubted your love. And thank you for the children."

The blessings went on around the circle until they came back to Aaron again. "We thank you, Lord, for your guardianship," he said, "and for the abiding peace of our lives. We ask that you continue to give us the strength to endure whatever hardships and sorrows the future might hold, the wisdom to know what is right in your eyes, and the humility to recognize that all things belong to you. Praise be to the Lord of Light, may the Flame never go out."

In one voice the assembly murmured, "May the Flame never go out." A quiet voice began to sing an ancient spiritual that had its roots far back in time.

"May the circle be unbroken,
By and by, Lord, by and by;
May your love forever bind us,
Though our bodies fade and die;
In the light of your Eternal Flame
Our joyous spirits greet
Those wandering sparks returning
To the circle they complete."

More and more voices joined in and the sound swelled until everyone sang softly. The night and the singing had a hushed, reverent quality, but at the same time a feeling of joy, of oneness. Gradually it subsided into humming and then died away. People began turning to those around them and embracing. Hedy hugged Zach warmly and then turned to the woman on her other side. Zach lost track of the number of embraces he received, many from people whose names he didn't even know. At last the gathering began to break up as the weary holders headed for their beds, feeling tired but somehow renewed. The fire had burnt down to embers and the smell of woodsmoke permeated the mild summer night. Zach stood for a moment, head back, staring up at the clear, starry sky, listening to the sounds of people moving off toward the main building. A quiet voice spoke up behind him.

"Pretty, isn't it?"

He turned, startled. Daniel stood with his head tipped back as well to look at the glittering night sky.

"Sometimes when I can't sleep," he said, "I like to just lie out in the open and watch them move."

"Like watching eternity unfold."

Daniel turned to Zach and the youth saw the starlit gleam of a smile. "Exactly." They walked slowly across the courtyard together.

Daniel spoke again, quietly, "Margit says I can take you out tomorrow and start your training." He added wryly, "If I take it easy."

Zach said nothing, glad the darkness of night hid his dread. He forgot Daniel could see in the dark.

Chapter Ten

It was softer than a whisper, quiet as the moon,
But I could hear it loud as laughter
across a crowded room;
It was gentle as a baby's hand,
But it held me like a chain,
It was softer than a whisper,
When love called out my name.
~Hal Ketchum

Early morning sunlight sparkled off a stream cascading over a rock ledge and into a shallow pool, a favorite watering place for many animals. The woods lay still and peaceful. In a nearby alder, a thrush warbled quietly. A young buck stepped cautiously into the clearing and followed the path down to the water's edge. With a slight hand signal, Daniel indicated Zach should take the shot. The youth took careful aim, then hesitated. He hated hunting, hated the blood and the dying light in the victim's eyes. His father had always scorned and ridiculed him for his 'squeamishness'. Some sixth sense warned the deer and its head came up, ears cocked. Zach squeezed the trigger and the buck leaped into the air and then collapsed, forelegs thrashing. Emerging quickly from hiding, the partners moved forward. The buck saw them coming and panicked, struggling to get to its feet. But the bullet had shattered its spine and paralyzed its hindquarters.

"Finish him off, Zach."

The youth just stared at the thrashing animal without moving. Daniel repeated the instruction. "He's hurting, Zach, finish him off."

But Zach stood rooted in horror, watching the beautiful animal struggling to escape its inevitable doom. When the youth didn't respond, Daniel strode forward and caught the deer by the rack, forced its head back and cut its throat. It sank down and life quickly faded from its eyes, its pain and terror ended. Daniel turned to chastise his young partner, but Zach had disappeared. The mutant shook his head in bewildered despair. Two weeks ago he believed Zach was beginning to accept him a little, even to think of him as a friend. But since the training began the outlander had grown increasingly sullen and hostile, to the point where he barely even acknowledged a simple good morning. Daniel began to wonder if maybe Zach *was* a mutant hater. Or perhaps for some unknown reason he simply hated Daniel.

The mutant cast a regretful glance at the deer, then started out after Zach, hoping the scavengers would not do too much damage before he could return. He could not leave the inexperienced young man wandering alone. Chances of him running into trouble seemed just too great.

*   *   *

Crossing the courtyard on his way to the horse barn, Hutch noticed Zach standing on the guard-walk. The holder paused, frowning. Daniel had planned to take Zach hunting today. Hutch had seen them leave together early this morning. Such an early return seemed unlikely . . . unless something had gone wrong. He started toward the stairs and met Rennie coming down with a worried expression.

"I was just coming to find you," the young guard said. "Zach came in a while ago without Daniel. You don't suppose he . . ." Rennie's voice trailed off uncertainly, reluctant to express his fears. Hutch shook his head.

"If Zach did any harm to Daniel, he wouldn't be stupid enough to come back here. I'll go talk to him."

Hutch ascended the stairs two at a time and went to stand behind Zach. The youth leaned on the top of the wall, staring off gloomily at the distant trees. Zach had been thinking about his time with the mutant hunters, remembering the one raider he had killed. The shot had been clean and the raider died quickly, but not before Zach saw the shock and hurt bewilderment in his eyes. The raider had looked not much older than Zach, and even then, filled with anger and hatred over the recent, brutal murder of his family, the youth had wondered if he had made a mistake. He had gotten violently, horribly sick afterwards, torn with doubt and guilt. The mutant hunters were furious over the killing of a potential slave. They ridiculed Zach contemptuously, telling him to go home to his mama until he grew up. Zach hated hunting. He heard Hutch come up behind him, but he didn't turn.

"Where is your partner, Zach?" Hutch demanded sternly.

The youth jerked his head toward the distant forest. "Out there. I didn't kill him if that's what you're thinking."

Hutch frowned, disturbed by the bitterness he heard in Zach's voice. "That's not what I'm thinking," he answered in a milder tone. "You're not supposed to leave your partner alone out there. You go out with him and you come back with him. What if something happens out there and he needs help? Not very long ago he was lying in the infirmary more than half dead. Whether or not you like Daniel is irrelevant. You have a responsibility to defend him, to guard his back."

Zach turned on Hutch with a tormented expression. "He doesn't need me! He's looked after himself for a long time. If anything happened out there, if we got attacked, he would be better off on his own than with me. He would just end up having to defend us both and I'd probably get him killed."

"You can't be sure of that Zach. Daniel may have managed alone for a lot of years, but it's not been by choice. And anyway, other things could happen besides a raider attack. What if he fell and broke his leg? What if he met up with slavers? Just the fact he was with a normal might be the only thing that would save him. He could pretend to be your slave or something."

Zach snorted and shook his head. "Nobody would mistake Daniel for a slave."

"It would not be the first time, Zach. Daniel has been a slave more than once."

The youth's expression shifted subtly as he remembered the scars on Daniel's back and the story Hutch had told of how the mutant had been captured and abused by slavers. He tried to imagine Daniel in chains, beaten, but it seemed easier to put chains on the wind. There was something wild and untamable about him. Zach suspected Daniel would rather be dead than a slave. He glanced out at the distant line of trees again, suddenly wishing he had not left his partner alone out there. Not that he really cared about the mutant, he tried to tell himself, but if anything happened to Daniel, it would be his fault and he would get blamed.

In actual fact, he *did* care about Daniel, more than he was willing to admit, even to himself. But once the lessons began his own inadequacy had become painfully apparent. It seemed he could do nothing right. Every time he tried to follow Daniel's instructions, he managed to screw it up somehow. It had gotten to the point where he feared looking his partner in the eye, sure he would see there the same contempt he had always found in his father's eyes when he failed. Daniel never failed at anything. He was even becoming reasonably accurate with a rifle. Zach felt he could never compete with or measure up to his partner. But for all his sullen silence and his resentment of Daniel's unrelenting competence and kindness, he would not want to see his partner hurt or enslaved. Hutch saw the sudden, growing concern in Zach's eyes, and the lump of icy anger that had lived in him since the shooting began to thaw.

"Come with me now," he said quietly. "Show me where you left him."

Zach complied without argument, leading Hutch back across the low hills and through the forest to the sheltered hollow where they had killed the deer. He found the spot without any difficulty . . . he had a good memory if nothing else. Daniel was still there. He had butchered the animal and begun packing the meat into the hide for transportation when Hutch and Zach appeared. He glanced up, surprised to see them.

"Hey, just in time," he grinned. "I could use some help with this."

"Daniel," Hutch said sternly, "Zach came home without you."

The mutant glanced at Zach with a puzzled, wary look. "I know."

"You're the senior partner, Daniel. You're responsible for Zach's safety. You should never have let him go off by himself, especially inexperienced as he is."

"Hey, whoa!" Daniel protested. "He was not alone for more than a few moments. I followed right behind him the whole way. I just figured he wanted to be by himself. Or at least that he didn't want *me* with him. So I stayed out of sight. But I watched him all the way to the gates."

Zach stared hard at Daniel and flushed to the roots of his dark hair.

"Of course," Hutch said, relieved. "I should have known you would keep an eye on him. Sorry I jumped on you."

"Apology accepted. Now, are you two going to help me with this or not?"

They divided the burden into three equal portions and headed for home. When they got back to the hold, they went straight to the kitchen, where Cochita bustled about, preparing the noon meal. She released one of her helpers, Deodar Kendle, to give them a hand, and sent them to the pantry to salt down the meat. Deo seemed a friendly, talkative girl, and she kept up a cheerful chatter as they worked, asking the young men interested questions about the hunt and the animals. She seldom volunteered for foraging duties herself. Plenty of others loved it, but she found the woods an oppressive and frightening place.

They cut meat into slabs and packed it into a barrel between layers of salt, working with an easy, natural teamwork that got the chore finished quickly and efficiently. At one point, Deo took Zach to the cellar to get another keg of salt, leaving Hutch and Daniel alone together. After a moment of silence, Daniel turned to his friend with a troubled expression.

"Hutch, I just don't know what to do about Zach. It seems the harder I try, the more he resents me. I thought things were getting better, but since I've started training him, it's gotten worse. Hell, I'm no expert at making friends. You're the first real friend I've ever had, and I've never quite understood how that happened."

"Do you want me to talk to him for you?" Hutch asked, concerned by the discouragement in his friend's voice.

"No," Daniel said quickly. "No, that would only make matters worse. I didn't even mean to mention it, but it's got me so upset, I . . . guess I just needed to express my frustration."

"I had a serious talk with Zach when he came back alone. I don't think he'll desert you again like he did today. I don't suppose you want to tell me what happened?"

Daniel shook his head thoughtfully. "Sorry, you'll have to ask Zach about that. I don't know, maybe I'm just not a good teacher. Lord knows I haven't had much experience at it. It just seems like, no matter what I do, it's the wrong thing. If I tell him he's done well, he looks at me like he doesn't believe me, like he thinks I'm trying to trick him. And if I point out his mistakes, half the time he just walks away and refuses to try again. It's as though he doesn't allow himself any room for mistakes, but he always expects to make them."

"Well, it sounds to me like the problem is with him, not you. The only thing I can suggest is that you sit down and have a good talk with him and thrash it all out."

"Yeah, maybe you're right."

They heard Deo's voice chattering away as the pair returned and they went silently back to work. With the four of them laboring together they soon completed the task. The young men cleaned up the mess while Deo went back to her kitchen duties. As they left the pantry, Daniel spoke softly to Zach.

"Will you come and help me with the hide?"

The youth nodded sullenly. They borrowed a pot from the kitchen and Daniel led the way to the pump in the yard. The hold's water came from an ancient artesian well, cold, pure and sweet. Daniel carefully washed a section of the intestine, making sure to get it scrupulously clean, then poured a little fresh water into the pot. Outside but close against the curve of the wall, he built a small fire and heated the water, explaining to Zach that the brains of the animal had to be lightly cooked and sealed in the intestines to keep them fresh until he could finish preparing the hide for tanning. Then the brains had to be mashed and rubbed into the skin to saturate it. Nothing worked better than brains for tanning a hide. Zach helped him to stretch the skin and hammer in the stakes, then Daniel showed the youth how to scrape away any excess fat and tissue. They worked together in uneasy silence for a time, one at each end of the hide. After a while Daniel asked quietly, "Do you want to tell me what happened out there? Why you ran off?"

Zach faltered for a moment, then continued working without a word. Glancing at his face, Daniel noted an expression of shame. When he felt convinced Zach would not respond, he began to speak softly.

"You know, there is no dishonor in hunting for food. Nor is there any shame in not liking to kill. I don't like killing myself, but I don't like starving either." He glanced at his young partner. Zach had his head down, but Daniel felt sure he was listening. At least it seemed a step in the right direction. "To kill purely for the pleasure of killing is a dishonor, both to the hunter and to the prey. It is a dishonor to be wasteful when the animal has given up its life for you. And it is a shameful thing to allow any creature to suffer needlessly."

Zach closed his eyes, seeing again the pain and terror in the brown, innocent eyes of the deer, seeing its graceful beauty brutally shattered by his bullet. "I don't want to be a hunter," he whispered, feeling sick.

"That's fine," Daniel answered gently, "there is no need for you to become one. But you do need to have some kind of hunting skills if you ever have to survive out there, especially in winter. Maybe we should concentrate on snares. It's not so personal. The prey is usually dead when you get to it."

Once they finished scraping the hide, Daniel sat back on his heels and looked at Zach. "The hide will dry in a couple of days," he said. "Then we have to scrape off the hair and I'll show you how to tan it. You can make all the clothing you need from the skins of the animals you eat . . . everything from hats to boots. You can make tools from the bones, use the sinews for thread, the rawhide for rope, and the bladders and stomachs of the larger animals make excellent pouches and storage containers."

Daniel pulled a pair of sinew thongs from one of his own pouches. He still dressed in his buckskins and deerhide boots, though the holders had given him woven clothing like their own. He just felt more comfortable in the leathers he had worn most of his life. He showed Zach some special knots he used in setting his snares and left the youth practicing them while he went for more water to wash the hide. When he returned he set about scrubbing the skin, cleaning it and checking to ensure they had removed all the fat. Zach sat with his brow furrowed in concentration, working out the difficult knots. When Daniel finished with the hide, he crouched beside the youth to check on his progress. He could feel Zach tensing up as he watched and the youth's fingers turned suddenly awkward and clumsy.

"Relax, Zach. You're doing fine."

The youth finished the complicated sequence and sat stiffly for a moment, expecting Daniel to point out some flaw. But the mutant surprised him by saying, "You have a good memory, Zach. That's great! It took me most of a day to catch on to that one. The Old Man nearly belted me across the room in frustration over it." He grinned, his eyes getting a distant look as he remembered. Those early years with the old trapper had been good times.

Zach glanced up at him curiously. "Your father?"

Daniel's smile died and he said, "No. At times I wished he was, but in the end they seemed like two of a kind anyway." He looked away with a closed, guarded expression and said no more.

*   *   *

Later that evening, Daniel sat alone in the tranquility garden working on a pair of moccasins for Zach, carefully punching holes in pieces of hide and sewing them together with sinew. The soles consisted of three layers of tough rawhide, cut to the shape of his partner's foot and stitched together. Then he made the fringed uppers out of tanned buckskin, cured over a smoky fire so it would dry soft again if it got wet. Daniel frowned, deep in serious thought, trying to understand the problem between himself and Zach. For a while before the training began, Zach seemed almost to depend on him, at least socially, for moral support. Zach still sat with him at meal times, but any pretense of friendliness had vanished. A tension grew between them that Daniel realized came partly from his own wariness. But how could he trust someone whose increasing silent hostility seemed to have no foundation? He needed to do something soon, he realized, but how do you talk to someone who would barely speak to you in more than monosyllables? The situation began to depress him.

Neely came wandering into the garden with a basket of wool and her knitting. She spied Daniel sitting cross-legged in a patch of sunlight, working on something with intense concentration. She sat down near him and he glanced up, smiling absently.

"Where are Zach and Hutch?" she asked. "I hardly ever see you anymore. You're always off somewhere with one or the other of them."

"Tadi asked Zach to help him with something, and Hutch and Tye went to fix that spot in the fence where the cows got out this afternoon."

"Good! I never have you to myself anymore now that you're well. I miss having a captive audience for my chatter."

Daniel chuckled. "Well, I don't miss in the least being stuck in that bed for days and weeks. But you are welcome to chatter to me anytime."

She began knitting and he went on with his own project while they engaged in a friendly, casual conversation. As long as he thought of Neely as just a friend he could relax and feel comfortable with her, but the moment he sensed a hint of anything more between them, Daniel froze up. He loved her, wanted her so badly his body and soul ached with hunger for her. But he could not believe the holders would allow it, even if by some miracle she did want him.

The sun sank below the horizon and they continued to sit and talk about music and spirituality and beauty. Neely told Daniel about a baby thrush Hutch found when they were children. It had fallen out of the nest and been abandoned by its parents. Together she and Hutch raised the little thing, feeding it worms and bugs from the garden, and eventually it learned to fly. In the fall it disappeared and Neely worried about it all winter. Then one spring day she heard the beautiful, liquid song of a thrush in the small orchard, and as she walked amongst the trees, it flew down and landed on her shoulder. After that it came back every spring, building its nest and raising its babies, until one year it simply never showed up and they never saw it again.

Daniel told Neely about the forest and mountains he loved, describing for her some of their beauties and wonders: an alpine meadow carpeted in a multi-colored patchwork of wild flowers; the sun on a misty morning splintering into arrows of light through the branches of a tree; a snow cat mother bravely standing off a pair of dags to defend her kittens. He wished he could tell her about Darius and his magical rainbow visions.

The evening grew dark and chill as a breeze stirred up, blowing in a rainstorm. Neely moved closer, shivering.

"Keep me warm?" she pleaded, snuggling against him. He rubbed the chilled flesh of her arm, feeling awkward and uncomfortable.

"Maybe we should go inside."

"No," she answered quickly, "I like having you to myself for once." She rested her head against his shoulder, gazing up at the stars beginning to wink out as the storm clouds covered them. Her hair tickled his chin and he smoothed it down, loving the feel of her soft curls. He heard a door open somewhere and should have taken it for a danger signal, but her nearness, the sweet woman scent of her, had him mesmerized. She turned her face up to his, just inches away. He responded reflexively, kissing her gently on the forehead. Neely wrapped her arms around him and pressed her mouth softly against his and a fire exploded inside Daniel. He folded her into his arms, breathless and aching with desire. Then some sixth sense made him glance up, and his eyes met Tadi's. Daniel froze, stricken. Neely's father made a gesture the mutant feared to interpret, then turned and went back inside.

Neely felt Daniel stiffen and she hugged him. "What's wrong, Daniel?"

He didn't answer. He thought with anguish about how dearly he loved her, and how loving her could cost him everything, and perhaps already had . . . his friendship with the holders, the love and respect of his bond family, his acceptance here in the valley, even his life. He was a mutant. He would always be a mutant. And she was a normal.

Fat raindrops began pattering down around them. In a strained voice he said, "We'd best get inside before we get soaked."

They quickly gathered up their tools and materials and ran for the shelter of the main building, reaching the doorway just as the rain increased to a downpour. Neely giggled madly over their race and their narrow escape, but Daniel remained sober and silent. She glanced at him, a little hurt by his sudden withdrawal. He seemed distracted and worried, but she felt afraid to ask why, afraid she had been too pushy, afraid he perhaps did not feel the same way about her that she felt about him. They walked side by side down the corridor and into the sitting room without saying a word. Tadi stood in the corner talking with Aaron and he glanced up as they entered. He noted the upset, bewildered expression on his daughter's face and the tense uncertainty in Daniel's green eyes as they met his own and then slid away. Tadi sensed something wrong and had a strong suspicion of the cause. He excused himself to Aaron and crossed the room to meet the young people. He gave Neely a quick, reassuring hug, then turned to Daniel, who met his gaze warily.

"I would like to speak with you, Daniel. Will you join me in the kitchen for a cup of tea?"

The mutant nodded once in agreement. He seemed remote, aloof. Tadi had never seen him like this. Hutch would have recognized that defensive reserve instantly and known that Daniel was afraid.

In the kitchen, they found Cochita helping Serene and a crowd of children make a batch of taffy. The little ones seemed noisy and excited, but tonight not even they could draw a smile from Daniel. His bond mother studied him worriedly. Tadi gave her a reassuring nod and headed for the deserted quiet of the great hall with the young man following. They sat together with the table between them. Tadi silently poured the tea and handed a cup to Daniel.

"Do you love Neely?" Tadi asked bluntly.

Daniel felt a stab of dismay, shocked by the suddenness of it. He was being asked to admit his guilt. His eyes fell and his hands tightened on the mug. "Yes," he replied, his voice strained and barely above a whisper. He didn't see Tadi smile.

"I love her too."

Tadi sipped his tea in silence for a few moments. "At one time," he mused reflectively, "I had hopes she might make a match with Hutch. They have remained friends since childhood and they're still very close. I wanted her to have a man like Hutch . . ."

Any faint hope Daniel might have retained began to fade. He knew he was nothing like Hutch. He was too wild, too stubborn and distrustful. But Tadi continued, " . . . a kind and gentle man, who would put her happiness and welfare before his own. Then when you came along, I knew she and Hutch would never be more than friends. I have known for quite some time that she loves you . . . since well before the shooting. That's one reason why I recommended we adopt you."

Daniel's eyes widened. "You . . .?"

Tadi smiled and nodded. "The assembly agreed unanimously and enthusiastically." Then he sobered. "I just want you to remember though . . . I am entrusting you with the happiness of my only daughter. She is very dear to me. Don't ever hurt her, Daniel. Please."

"I would die first," Daniel vowed, hope blossoming like flowers in the desert. "Does that mean you . . . wouldn't disapprove? It doesn't bother you that I'm . . . a mutant?"

"You are a good man, Daniel, and Neely loves you. That's all that matters to me."

"And Salla?"

"She's known longer than I have. Neely often confides in her. *I* have to guess," Tadi said wryly. "As far as I know, Salla has made no attempts to dissuade Neely." He paused, then asked curiously, "What did you think might happen if we did object?"

Daniel regarded the tea going cold in his cup and tried to speak lightly, jokingly. "Oh, I'd pictured exile, a lynch mob, a firing squad. Judging from past experience, nothing seemed out of the question." It sounded very little like a joke and his expression turned serious. "In the civilized lands I could get shot just for looking at a normal girl in any romantic way."

Tadi leaned forward and clasped Daniel's wrist warmly. "You're not in the civilized lands, son. Why they call it that I will never know. They don't sound very damned civilized to me." His hand tightened on the young man's arm and he said earnestly, holding Daniel's gaze so the young man would see the truth in his eyes, "You are one of us now, Daniel. If you had been Haven born you could not be any more one of us than you are now. I won't say we have not had rare occasions when members have been exiled for one crime or another, but it would certainly have to be a lot more serious than innocently falling in love."

Daniel felt relieved, but he asked uneasily, "How serious?"

"Murder; treason against the hold or the territorial government; rape; unreasonable violence or deliberate cruelty . . . nothing you are ever likely to have to worry about."

"So then . . . when Zach shot me, he would have faced the sentence of exile even if you had already adopted him?"

"In such a case, he would definitely have faced exile, because to get adopted he would have to prove he understood our laws and beliefs and could live by them. We gave him a second chance because, as you pointed out, he is young and inexperienced and he probably didn't understand. He didn't have much chance to learn our ways before it happened."

"Is that why you stood by him?"

"Partly," Tadi mused softly. "I suspect my reasons for supporting him were much the same as yours. He's just a boy. He was going through hell and he didn't have a friend in the world."

Daniel nodded, thinking about his problem with Zach. As if reading his mind, Tadi said, "He's seemed pretty sullen lately. I thought he was getting over that. Has he been giving you trouble?"

"Everything seemed fine until I started training him. Now he barely even speaks to me. I never believed he was a mutant hater . . . he just didn't fit the part. But now I'm beginning to wonder."

"He's a sensitive lad . . . a hard one to figure," Tadi admitted, shaking his head. "Things would be a lot easier if he would just communicate."

"Hutch says I should sit down and have a talk with him. I guess I'll have to try. I'm not looking forward to it though. Getting a response from him is like trying to pet a porcupine. He's so damned prickly I'm likely to get a hand full of quills."

"Well, let me know if things don't improve soon. I'll have a talk with him myself."

"Alright."

"We'd best get back to Neely. She's probably worried sick wondering why you were upset and what I might be saying to you. We'd best go and reassure her."

Chapter Eleven

In my distress...well I wanted someone to blame me;
In my devastation...I wanted so to change;
In my way...disaster was the only thing
I could depend on.
~Stevie Nicks

Daniel examined the snare his partner had just set. They had practiced with the snares for several days now and Zach was getting pretty good at it. He learned quickly, seldom needing correction more than once. But once usually seemed too much for him.

"That's not bad, Zach, just a little low. A rabbit running into this wouldn't get his neck snapped. It would probably catch him around the forelegs, or maybe the head and one shoulder. It would injure him and leave him hanging there in pain and terror for hours, maybe days before you came back to check the snare."

Zach stared at his partner, appalled, then reached out abruptly and wrenched the bit of rawhide from its place. Crushing it into a tangled ball, he flung it in Daniel's startled face.

"Forget your damned snares! Why do I even bother to try? I never do anything right!"

He turned abruptly and stalked away. Daniel gazed after him in dismay and increasing despair. He had tried asking Zach what the problem was, but his partner just retreated into sullen silence and refused to answer. Daniel tucked the snare into his pouch and followed after the angry youth.

"Zach . . . "

The outlander whirled and Daniel dropped instinctively into a defensive stance, half expecting him to lash out. Zach gaped at him in shock, then asked sullenly, "Why did you accept me for a partner anyway? Why did you speak for me at all? I thought at first you just wanted to take your own revenge, but you're always so damned nice you make me sick! Why didn't you just leave it alone and let them do whatever they wanted with me and get it over with?"

"Because you would probably be dead by now."

"So why should you care? Maybe I would be better off."

"Dead is forever, Zach. Things can't get any worse that way, but they sure as hell can't get any better either."

Daniel studied the young outlander's moody features. He sensed there was more to this than just Zach's distaste at being forced to work with a mutant.

"Come on," he said, catching his partner by the shoulder, "it's time we talked this out."

Zach shrugged off the hand but followed without protest. Daniel led the way to a quiet, sunny little glade with a stream bubbling through it, one of his favorite spots. He had often come here in the past to sit and think. He sank into a crouch, back against a big spruce that bordered the creek. Zach sat down in the grass along the bank with his knees drawn up and his arm folded across them, staring at the chuckling stream with a dark, brooding expression, uncommunicative. Daniel sighed, letting the peace of the little glade soak into him while he tried to think of what to say. He was used to dealing with hostility, but always before he'd had the option of walking away, of burying the hurt and pretending it didn't matter. This time he had to meet it head on, and he was not sure he felt up to it.

"Zach, partners are supposed to be friends. They're supposed to care about each other and back each other up if there's trouble." Daniel's only experience with partnership came from watching Hutch and Jesse together. He had envied the brotherly warmth between them. With Hutch, or almost any of the young holders, he might have had that. Instead he had Zach, sullen, hostile and apparently unwilling to even give him a chance.

"People have hated me most of my life," Daniel mused softly. "I guess I should be used to it by now."

Zach hunched his shoulders and turned his head away, saying nothing, not about to make this any easier.

"You asked why I spoke for you at the trial," Daniel said in a low voice. "I did it because I've been there myself."

Zach turned to stare at him in wordless disbelief, wondering what crime his oh, so perfect partner could have committed.

"I was born in a community very much like Haven Hold in a lot of ways, but very different in their beliefs . . . a community of Armageddonists . . . religious fanatics and passionate mutant haters. They truly believed mutants were the spawn of the devil, God's punishment on those who sinned. The only thing that kept me alive was my mother. She was an outsider, a trader's daughter, and she loved me despite my eyes, despite the fact the community shunned her when she wouldn't let my father get rid of me." Daniel shook his head sadly. "Just like drowning unwanted kittens, right?" He found it painful to think about this time in his life, and for years he had suppressed those memories, only to have them resurface in nightmares. "My mother died giving birth to another child . . . a sister I think. They never really told me." He considered it for a minute, trying hard to avoid remembering his grief and panic at losing the only person in his young life who had ever loved him, and the terrifying night that had followed.

"They put me on trial. My father chained me to a post in the barn like some sort of dangerous animal, and they all filed in with their decisions already written on their faces. The bishop asked if anyone would speak in my defense. I sat there for what seemed like eternity, praying that just one of them would have the compassion to see me as a human being and not just some mutant freak. But no one spoke. When the time was up they just filed back out and left me there without a word. I spent the entire night wondering what they were going to do to me in the morning . . . wondering what I had done to make them hate me so much." Daniel's face twisted with remembered pain and he turned it away until he could regain control. "I still have nightmares about that night."

"What did they do to you?"

"The next morning my father came and tied me across the back of a mule. He took me half a day into the desert and then dumped me off like a sack of garbage. He never even untied me. He never even gave me that much of a chance."

"Well, you must have done something to make them treat you like that . . . to make your own father hate you."

Daniel gave Zach a tormented look. "I was eight years old. What could an eight year old do to deserve that kind of treatment?" Daniel's mouth tightened with bitterness. "Only years later I finally realized it didn't matter what I did or said or thought. They just hated me because I existed. Because I didn't fit their perfect image of humanity."

Zach shook his head in dismay, imagining a small boy, alone and defenseless, facing a hate-filled mob. Daniel took his gesture for an expression of doubt. The mutant looked away, saying softly, "I haven't done anything to you, Zach. Why do *you* hate me?"

He didn't see the youth's startled expression or the slow flush of shame that stained his cheeks. Zach knew he had treated Daniel unfairly. He had nearly killed this man, yet the mutant had defended him when no one else would. It was not Daniel's fault that he was such a worthless screw-up, but in a way, Zach had been blaming Daniel, trying to punish the mutant for being all the things he wanted to be himself and never would, never could be.

"Your trial seemed like a nightmare come true, like I was reliving that night all over again. I couldn't just sit there and watch you dying inside while time ran out and no one spoke."

Zach gazed at him in misery. "You should hate me. Why don't you hate me? I nearly killed you and you act like it never happened."

Daniel shook his head sadly. "I learned a long time ago that when you start hating people you end up hurting yourself more than anyone. Besides, Hutch told me what happened to your family, and I've seen what raiders do to their victims." He turned to hold Zach's eyes with a steady gaze. "But I'm not a raider. A mutant, yes, but not a murderer. Please, try to just see me as a man and stop hating me for something I can't change."

"I don't hate you, Daniel. It's just . . . you're always so damned perfect! I can't compete with you. You never make mistakes, you never say or do the wrong thing, you never get angry or scared . . . "

"So damned perfect?" Daniel repeated in wry disbelief. He shook his head. "This is not a competition, Zach. There's room in their hearts for both of us. And you're wrong about me. I have made mistakes. Some have nearly gotten me killed. There's not a lot of room for mistakes when everyone you meet wants to kill you or put you in chains. And I have been angry. And bitter and scared. Hell, I'm *always* scared! Scared I'll wake up some morning and find this has all been just a dream and I'm alone again. Scared *they'll* wake up some morning and wonder why the hell they wanted me in the first place, 'cause I'm just another goddamn mutant! And I'm scared right now, because I have a partner I can't trust, who might or might not help me if I ever get into trouble. Who might someday decide he dislikes me enough to put another bullet into me!"

Zach flinched and went white. They stared at each other for a second, then both looked away. The words lay between them like an open wound. For a long time neither broke the tense silence, then Zach mumbled something so low that even Daniel's exceptional hearing could not make it out over the babbling of the stream.

"I can't hear you, Zach."

The youth turned to him hesitantly, not sure whether he meant he didn't want to listen, or whether he actually had not heard. "I wasn't trying to kill you." He turned away again, unable to watch Daniel's reaction. "I never even meant to hit you. The bullet was just supposed to buzz past your ear and scare you off. But you stood up just as I fired."

Daniel thought about it for a while in surprised silence and remembered rising to his feet just as the shot came. "Why didn't you tell them that at the trial?"

Zach's shoulders hunched. "No one even asked me. They all just assumed I meant to do it . . . even Tadi. I didn't think they would believe me. They would just think I was making excuses."

Daniel nodded slowly, studying Zach with thoughtful eyes. "I believe you."

Zach blinked at him in surprise and relief. He hadn't really expected to be believed. "I would never deliberately let you down if you were in trouble. I'm just such a screw-up. I never seem to be able to do anything right."

"Alright," Daniel said quietly, "so maybe I can trust you. But I can't depend on you until you learn to trust yourself. You can't expect to get everything right the first time, Zach. Some things take practice. It took me nine years to learn what I'm trying to teach you in a few months. You just have to keep trying until you get it right." He pulled the tangled snare from his pouch and tossed it to Zach. "You want to try again?"

The youth caught it and slowly straightened it out, untangling the snarls. He tied the knots the way Daniel had taught him and carefully set the snare, making sure this time not to set it too low. He examined it critically, sure he'd forgotten something or done something wrong. Daniel came up behind him and thrust a stick through the loop, springing the trap. It snatched the stick from his hand and whipped it into the air. He reached out and retrieved the snare, then turned to Zach with a nod of approval.

"That was perfect. Now let's go find a place to set it where it will catch something."

He started to walk away with Zach on his heels, then suddenly changed his mind. Zach almost ran into him as he stopped and turned to face the youth again.

"There's one more thing, Zach."

Dark eyes met green ones with an expression that said, what else have I done wrong?

"A partnership is supposed to be an exchange, sharing, not just me teaching you."

Zach eyed him with dismay, wondering what he could possibly have to offer the mutant. "Do you want me to teach you how to draw?" he offered hesitantly. As a skill it might not have much value, but it was the only thing he could do that Daniel could not do better. His partner's eyes widened in startlement and a single surprised laugh burst out of him.

"I'd as likely be able to learn to fly. No, Zach, I would settle for your friendship." Then he quickly looked away, as if afraid of what he might see in the outlander's eyes. "Or at least your tolerance."

Zach studied his partner's averted face for a moment, finally realizing that, for all his air of confident indestructibility, Daniel was a lot less sure of himself than he tried to appear. The wrong answer now would cut him to the heart. Any desire Zach ever had to hurt Daniel died in that instant. "I'm willing to try for friendship."

Chapter Twelve

Sometimes when I'm all alone
I sing my saddest song,
Lonely, no one to see,
This time, the song is for me.
I can touch your secret place inside,
And still you don't know me.

With the songs that I sing
And the magic they bring,
You've learned to be strong now.
The song sets you free,
But who sings for me?
I'm all alone now.
Where is my songbird?
Who sings her song for me?
~Dave Wolfert and Steve Nelson

A soft breeze rustling through the trees gave musical accompaniment to Alanna's humming. She sat at the edge of the river, dabbling her feet in the water. In the harsh glare of the summer sun she sought the shaded places that offered protection for her pale skin and eyes. The village lay not far off. She could hear other women washing laundry a little upstream from her. The baby beside her gurgled happily. A fuzz of pale reddish hair crowned her finely shaped head. Alanna had named her Freenan, but Nyle called her Bright Eyes and Alanna loved that pet name.

Just last night Nyle had asked her again to join with him. He was a good man and she felt almost ready to give in and say yes, but she knew it would be unfair. She did not love Nyle . . . at least not in that way. If she agreed, it would only be to give Freenan a father protector. Alanna loved another, her Dreamweaver. She'd had little contact with him in the past few months since Freenan's birth. Perhaps it had something to do with the fact she felt happy now. Freenan was a beautiful child, placid and cheerful, a constant source of joy to her mother and grandparents. She made Alanna feel complete. Who needed a man anyway?

But the girl still looked forward to the shy, loving touch of her mind friend. Her daydreams turned to visions of what he might look like. In the slaver's camp there had only been four other men besides the mutant hunters themselves. Alanna knew neither Nyle nor Dickon was her Dreamweaver. That left Daniel, or that repulsive little rat-faced man. In her heart she felt sure Daniel was the one. She dreamed of him, his beautiful green cat's eyes, his gentle, compassionate smile, his kindness. Somehow his image just seemed to fit what she knew of the Dreamweaver, except for one thing . . . that sense of shame her mind friend seemed to feel. Daniel certainly had no reason to feel shame. He was strong and handsome and honorable. He had no reason to hide who he was. But the only other possibility was Ratface, and she could not bring herself to believe that *he* was her gentle Dreamweaver. Ratface had been horrible . . . evil. Though he had never actually threatened her, the menace of his gaze had struck terror in her heart.

Sometimes when she spent time alone like this, she would sense the Dreamweaver's presence. Not actual contact, but an awareness of his presence somewhere nearby, the feeling he watched over her. She wondered if he could see her and wished he would show himself. Closing her eyes, she tried to transmit a feeling of love for him, but felt no response. She didn't know if he was really even there.

Freenan started to fuss, so she picked the baby up and bared one snowy breast. Rocking the baby and humming, thinking about the Dreamweaver, she felt totally at peace. When Freenan was full and content, Alanna laid the baby down a safe distance from the riverbank, then tucked up her skirts and waded in. When the languid current rose past her knees, she bent forward at the waist and began to wash her hair, rinsing the long, silvery strands in the clear water. Suddenly she felt an inexplicable chill down her spine. She straightened, looking around uneasily. The clearing appeared serene and peaceful as ever. When the warning came, it hit her like a blow, staggering her so she floundered in the water.

(*Danger! Save baby!*)

She whirled to look at Freenan and a loose stone moved under her foot so she staggered again, fighting for balance. Panic flared in her, despite the absence of any visible threat. She trusted the Dreamweaver. If he warned of danger, she believed. She began moving quickly toward the shore, eyes scanning the surrounding brush for any sign of threat. And then she saw it. A dark, menacing figure detached from the shadows beneath the trees and darted towards her baby. Alanna let out a shriek of pure terror and outrage, floundering forward as fast as she could, knowing she would never get there in time against the drag of the water. She saw the intruder stagger, snatch at the baby, and strangely, come up short, then turn without touching Freenan and dash back to the safety of the trees, dragging what looked like a heavy rope.

Alanna scrambled up the bank and scooped up her baby, quickly checking to see she was unharmed. Freenan gazed up at her mother, round eyed and startled by the scream and the sudden action. People came crashing through the brush from upstream and from the village, running in answer to Alanna's alarm. She hugged her baby, sobbing with relief. Remembering the Dreamweaver's warning, she sent out a grateful thank you, but received no response. The sense of his presence had gone.

* * *

Hutch jerked out of sleep when Daniel, in the next bed, suddenly shot bolt upright with a low cry. In the dim moonlight Hutch could see the stiffness of the mutant's posture.

"Daniel?" Hutch questioned softly, wondering if his friend suffered from another nightmare. The mutant didn't reply, but he suddenly leaped out of bed and began scrambling into his clothing with an urgency that sent a thrill of alarm through Hutch. He got up, noticing Zach's shadowy form sitting up now too.

"Daniel, what's wrong?" Hutch asked again.

"It's Darius," the mutant answered in a tense whisper. "He's hurt. I have to go to him."

"Wait! I'm coming with you." Hutch hurriedly pulled on his breeches. Zach started to get up, but Daniel went to him and crouched by his bed, saying, "You'd best stay here this time, Zach. Darius is hurt. You two don't really trust each other yet. Hutch will go with me this time. If we're not back by morning, tell them . . . tell them any excuse you can think of. Just don't tell them about Darius, alright?"

The youth nodded wordlessly. In the dim light, Daniel's cat's eyes could see the concern on his partner's face, but he didn't have time now to reassure Zach. Hutch was ready. As the two friends strode silently out of the dorm, they heard a sleepy voice ask, "What's going on?" And Zach's reply, "Nothing. Just a little night hunting. Go back to sleep."

Hutch and Daniel had some difficulty convincing Rad to open the gate for them. In the end, Daniel just left Hutch arguing and unbarred the gate himself. Hutch abandoned the discussion and hurried after his friend, leaving Rad no choice but to lock up behind them. Hutch trotted after Daniel as the mutant disappeared around the curve of the wall. Daniel knew exactly where Darius lay. He sensed a sort of line in his head connecting him to the telepath. He had never before been aware of it, but it had the comfortable feeling of something long established.

He saw a small, dark figure huddled against the base of the wall and went to one knee, gathering his small friend into his comforting embrace. *(Darius! What's wrong little brother?)*

To Darius, his love felt like a cool bath, washing over and quenching the burning pain in his head. He leaned against Daniel, sobbing with relief. Hutch crouched beside them and rubbed the telepath's shoulder soothingly. He leaned forward to whisper in Daniel's ear, "Let's get out of here. We're being watched."

Daniel lifted the small man and cradled him like a child. He was no bigger than a child anyway. They strode swiftly away from the hold, headed for the forest and the sanctuary of the hidden valley. When they reached the safety of the trees, Darius indicated he could walk and Daniel put him down. He seemed a bit shaky and Daniel kept one hand on his shoulder to steady him.

Cub greeted them with obvious relief when they reached the cave, pressing against the telepath's legs anxiously. He knew something was wrong. Daniel quickly built a fire in the cold hearth to give them some light. Darius huddled against the wall and Hutch sat down beside him and put an arm around him comfortingly. The holder didn't have the faintest idea what was wrong, but something plainly was. Even the puppy knew it. He crawled into Darius' lap and gently licked the small man's chin, offering what comfort he could. Daniel sat down on Darius' other side and the telepath leaned against him but made no attempt at mental contact.

(*I'm here, my friend. Tell me what's wrong.*)

Daniel opened himself to that familiar touch, waiting for the old rapport to establish itself. He felt a hesitant contact from Darius, sensed the barriers dropping slowly and gasped as pain hit him between the eyes like a spike driving through his head. Communication with the telepath had never been painful before. It almost startled him into breaking contact before he realized the pain belonged to Darius.

(*Show me what happened, little brother.*)

The story unfolded in Daniel's head as Darius shared the hurtful memory. In the cool depths of the forest he had crouched, hidden in the deepest shadows, just close enough to sense her aura. He often came here now, carrying Cub when the pup's short legs tired. He felt lonely. He missed Daniel's presence in the refuge and knew that, although his friend still loved him, Daniel had a new life now, one in which Darius could take little part. The cave seemed empty. Though Cub made good company and helped a great deal to hold off loneliness, he was not human. So, Darius came here, to be near the only other friend he knew, Alanna. He had to remain careful. With the change of seasons, the villagers became much more active in the woods and he could not afford to be seen. The raiders also became more active, and after last year's disastrous kidnap attempt on the holders, their attentions turned more and more upon Alanna's people. So, Darius would find a safe, secluded spot close to the girl, and while Cub played nearby or slept at his feet, he would stand guard over her. He seldom actually saw her except with his unique inner vision, and he almost never made contact. She felt strong now and happy. She no longer needed him. It would be better for her to forget him and turn to her own kind for love and comfort. But he could not stay away. He loved her too much.

Sometimes he contacted Freenan, sharing her baby discoveries, her pure, innocent contentment when she felt warm, dry and well fed. Darius loved Freenan. He felt in a way that she was his baby too, since he had helped in her birthing and shared her first moments in the world.

On this day, Alanna sensed his light, observational touch, as she often did. The warm wave of love she projected to him almost tempted him into contact, but he resisted sadly, hugging Cub for comfort. The pup licked his chin and wiggled free to fiercely attack a chunk of wood, quickly wrestling it into submission. Darius warned him to stay there and slowly crept toward the river, longing for a glimpse of Alanna and Freenan. At last he could see them through the foliage. He peeked through the leaves, watching as the girl waded out into the river and began washing her hair. As if feeling his cursed gaze upon her, she straightened and looked around uneasily. He started to withdraw, then suddenly noticed a strange aura, cool, passionless and hungry, moving slowly toward the baby. His eyes told him nothing, so he scanned the grasses with his inner sight and encountered the dull, sluggish mind of a green backed snake, a constrictor, almost upon the sleeping child.

He thrust an alarmed lance of warning at Alanna and watched as she floundered in surprise. She glanced at Freenan but didn't see the snake, its head just inches away from the baby's shoulder, black tongue flicking out to almost touch that delicate skin. Alanna started moving shoreward, but too slowly he realized. Once the snake attacked it could have Freenan wrapped in its deadly coils in an instant, and it would not take much pressure to squeeze the breath from that tiny body.

Darius rushed into the open, intent on saving *his* baby. In his concern for Freenan, he forgot to shut down his light contact with Alanna. Her scream as she saw him, and the accompanying tide of red-orange terror and protective fury, swept into his mind like a flash flood of corrosive acid, coupled with a stark image of him as a repulsive, sub-human monster attacking her baby. He staggered and slammed down his defenses, cutting all contacts. It left him head blind, but he could still see with his eyes. He snatched at the snake, catching it just behind the head, then turned and ran, his heart, his head and his spirit seared and burning. Almost blind with pain, he made his way back to where he had left Cub. He had to hurry. Alanna's people would come soon, hunting him. The pup sensed something wrong and came at once, but Darius pushed him away. The snake had wrapped itself around his arm and shoulder, squeezing so tightly his fingers were turning blue. He drew his belt knife and hacked the creature's head off. The body writhed and convulsed, releasing his arm. He dropped it, sheathed his knife and snatched up the fascinated Cub, then turned and, weaving slightly, headed for the only comfort, the only real refuge he had ever known . . . Daniel.

(*Lanna hate I. Think evil I.*) Daniel felt overwhelmed by a sense of unendurable loss, like a deep aching void. She had been Darius's first real human contact, his first friend. She had promised to love him always.

(*Darius, it's not you she hates, it's what she thinks you are. She still loves the Dreamweaver. I think it was a mistake not to tell her who you were long ago. I'm sure she would love you anyway, just as I do. When she saw you, she probably thought you were the danger the Dreamweaver warned her of.)*

Daniel felt Darius' mind uncurl a little from that tightly clenched ball of pain as the telepath considered his friend's words and recognized the truth in them. He relaxed a little more and the pain subsided to a dull ache. Daniel received a warm wash of gratitude from him and the sense he had been comforted as much by Daniel's nearness, his love, as by his words. In Daniel, at least, Darius had one friend who would never forsake him.

While the silent exchange went on, Hutch had rooted around and scrounged up some venison jerky and a few stored roots and set about making a stew, on the hopeful assumption that, if you cared for the body, the mind would heal itself. Cub trotted over, sniffing and whining, and Hutch gave the hungry pup a strip of jerky to chew on, then set some water on for tea.

When at last Daniel and Darius came out of their shared trance, the stew bubbled fragrantly and the tea was ready. Hutch handed them each a steaming cup and asked no questions. They would tell him when they were ready. For now he just laid a gentle hand on the telepath's shoulder and asked, "Are you alright now, friend?"

Darius looked up at him, seeing the real concern in his eyes and coloring his aura. The little man raised his shoulder and pressed his cheek against Hutch's hand for a moment.

"Head hurt. Better now, Hush. You good friend."

When the stew was ready, they all had a little to eat. Cub ate more than any of them, his tail wagging with enjoyment as he wolfed it down. When they'd all had their fill, they lay down to try and get a few hours' sleep before morning. Daniel gave Hutch his old bed and made up a pallet for himself next to Darius. With the warm, reassuring bulk of Daniel at his back and Cub curled against his stomach, the little telepath quickly fell into a deep, healing sleep.

A few hours later, Hutch awakened to a cold nose touching his face. He opened his eyes and Cub licked his face, tail wagging enthusiastically. Hutch smiled and ruffled the pup's fur, rolling out of bed quietly. Sunlight spilled in through the cave entrance. He glanced over at Daniel and Darius and saw that his bond brother was awake. Daniel rose silently, taking care not to wake the telepath.

The two young men went outside and sat in the sunshine with their backs against the sun-warmed wall. Cub strolled out after them and began attacking Daniel's foot. The mutant smiled as the pup chewed on the toe of his moccasin. He told Hutch the story Darius had shared with him last night and the holder shook his head sympathetically.

"Poor little man," he said softly. "What a horrible curse to live under. Will he recover?"

"I think so. He's a pretty tough little fellow. He was almost frozen when he came to me last winter. Half-starved too, but he bounced back pretty quickly. Didn't even get sick. He'll be fine. I just wish . . . "

"I know. You wish we could take him home with us. I wish we could too."

Darius came padding out of the cave to stand blinking at them sleepily. Hutch smiled and Daniel said, "Good morning, little brother. Come and sit with us. The sun is nice and warm."

Darius padded forward and sat between them, taking comfort from the closeness of his two friends, enjoying the humming sensation caused by their overlapping auras. Hutch's seemed to vibrate on a different frequency, adding a harmonic richness to the effect.

"How is your head this morning?" Daniel asked gently.

"Hurt most gone. Be a'right. You have to go, Dan-yel?"

"I'm afraid so. I'm sorry, Darius. We would like to stay, but they will be wondering about us back at the hold. They'll think it pretty strange the way we rushed off in the middle of the night. And poor Zach! We left him to cover for us. I wonder what sort of story or excuse he's come up with."

"I thought the night hunting sounded pretty credible. After all, you can see in the dark." Hutch grinned and turned to Darius. "We'll come back tomorrow to check on you. You rest today. Get lots of sleep and let that poor head of yours heal."

Suddenly Hutch's thoughts flooded with a rosy tide of pink and a feeling of humble gratitude for his friendship. He drew in a breath of wonder and the contact abruptly, fearfully, cut off. This was the first time Darius had ever tried to communicate mentally with the holder. Hutch felt the shy, hesitant touch brush his thoughts again. It reminded him of Layla, hiding and peeking around the corner when she thought she had done something wrong. He tried to project a sense of welcome and reassurance. Hutch could feel Darius' wonder at his trust, his easy acceptance after the painful struggle to establish rapport with Daniel. But Daniel had not really known Darius then, and in those days was only just beginning to learn to trust, whereas Hutch was a naturally trusting person and already a friend, already knew there was no malice in the little telepath.

(*We are both Daniel's brothers, Darius. In a way, that makes us brothers too. I would never knowingly do anything to hurt you, and I know you wouldn't hurt me. I trust you.*)

A joyous rainbow of colors danced through Hutch's head followed by a feeling of confirmation, of promise. Faintly, like a background haze, Hutch could feel Darius' pain, a dull throbbing from damaged sensors and an aching sorrow that would take a long time to heal.

"Ah, Darius! You have beautiful colors too. Daniel is right, you are a rainbow. I can't believe anyone who has ever felt this, who knows you are the Dreamweaver, would ever hate you or fear you. You should tell Alanna who you are."

He received an impression of denial, of fear. If the contact with Alanna yesterday had been deeper, Darius would have died. He still loved her and he would still watch over her, but unless she was in desperate need, she would never again know the touch of the Dreamweaver. And perhaps it would be for the best. She would join with that young mutant who loved her and she would learn to love him in time. She would be happy and Freenan would have a father. For an instant, sorrow welled up and almost overwhelmed Darius again, but the love and nearness of his two friends sustained him.

"You take good care of yourself, little Dreamweaver," Hutch said. "We'll be back tomorrow."

Chapter Thirteen

Lean on me when you're not strong,
And I'll be your friend,
I'll help you carry on,
For it won't be long
'Till I'm gonna need
Somebody to lean on.
~Bill Withers

Daniel hunkered down in the shadows, studying the small patch of forest ahead, and Zach crouched at his shoulder wondering silently why they had stopped.

"Tell me what you see, Zach."

The boy studied the scene, puzzled, looking for something unusual that might have caught Daniel's eye. He shook his head in bewilderment, not knowing what to look for.

"Do you see any signs of life? Of passage?"

Zach looked again, knowing something must be there or Daniel would not have asked. After a moment's study, he offered hesitantly, "There's a broken twig hanging on that bush over there."

"Very good, Zach. Most people wouldn't even think twice about it. Do you see anything else?"

Zach scanned the scene once more, concentrating on the area of the broken branch, knowing whatever had passed must have taken that path.

"Some of the weeds over there look crushed."

"Good. You're very observant. Come and look closer. See if you can tell me what animal passed here."

The youth looked first for tracks, but the tough weeds grew too thick, the ground remained too hard and dry at this time of year to take an impression. He found a few hairs clinging to the hanging twig, short, sandy grey and fine. Zach glanced uncertainly at his partner and Daniel nodded, confident the youth would work out the puzzle. The young outlander backtracked a few yards and found a blurred partial print on a patch of bare, dusty ground.

"Dag?" he questioned.

"That's right. You're going to make a fine tracker with a little more training. Sharp observation is the key . . . picking up on small clues and putting them together to create a clear understanding. You have a good eye."

Zach reddened and turned away. His attitude had improved considerably since Daniel confronted him. He had become much more civil and seemed to make a genuine effort to be friendlier. He still got upset and moody when he made a mistake or failed some imagined test, but he at least seemed willing to try again. He paid sharp attention to everything Daniel demonstrated or told him, appearing genuinely interested in learning. But he still froze up silently whenever his partner praised him. The only way to get around it was to immediately give him something else to think about.

Daniel picked a handful of leaves off a low plant and handed a few to Zach, popping some into his own mouth and chewing with relish. The outlander regarded him in disbelief.

"You want me to eat leaves?"

Daniel chuckled. "Try them. They're good."

Zach cautiously chewed on one of the leaves and found it had a tangy, refreshing flavor. He ate the rest and said, "Not bad, but I wouldn't want to have to live on them."

They walked on, Zach's tread much lighter and quieter with the new moccasins Daniel had made to replace his hard-soled outlander boots. Every once in a while, Daniel would stop and show his partner some useful plant, often digging it up to show him the roots and explain how it should be prepared, either for eating or for medicine. He pointed out any signs of animals, teaching Zach to recognize the tracks of each and telling him of their habits, what type of snares worked best to catch them and whether or not they made good eating. They reached the wall of the rim and followed it for a distance southward until it started to curve away to the east, where they found their path unexpectedly blocked by a fresh rockslide.

"This looks just a few days old," Daniel said, gazing up along the steep, jumbled face of the slide. Suddenly he froze and caught Zach by the arm. "Look up there, Zach. Do you see that?"

The youth looked where Daniel indicated and at first saw nothing. Then his sharp eyes picked out an odd shape that didn't belong there. He drew his breath in sharply. A human hand, coated with dust, thrust up out of the jumble of rocks.

"You stay here. I'm going up to have a look," Daniel said.

"Shouldn't I come with you?" Zach protested, glancing around uneasily. If that was a raider up there, his friends might still lurk nearby.

"No, a fresh slide can be dangerously unstable. You'd best stay here. Get ready to run for cover if you see anything moving besides me."

"If it's that dangerous, why do you have to go up there? He can't possibly be alive still."

"I want to see who he is . . . if he's a raider or one of Oringa's. This seems a bit far south for either. This slide could prove dangerous for the Haven. Once it stabilizes, it'll create another access from the rim, another point of attack for Rogan's Raiders, or any other nasties that want to come crawling down off the plateau."

Zach eyed the disordered rubble of rocks and boulders and splintered trees with a sense of foreboding. "Be careful," he admonished Daniel worriedly. His partner smiled, warmed by the unexpected concern.

"I will. You find the biggest tree you can and get ready to duck behind it if this mess starts to shift again."

Daniel turned and began picking his way carefully up the slope, testing each foothold over the rugged terrain before trusting his weight to it. Zach looked around quickly and found a large spruce just at the edge of the slide area. He stood beside it, watching his partner move slowly upward, head bent, watching his footing. A subtle movement higher up caught Zach's eye, and before his horrified gaze, the mass of rocks began to shift.

"Daniel, run!" he screamed.

His partner didn't look or hesitate, he just whirled and began racing back down the steep slope at a reckless pace, heedless of the risk of a broken leg. Daniel could hear the deep, terrifying rumble and feel the shifting of rocks beneath his feet. This was no time to take care; to dawdle was to die. On his way up he had noted a low, solid outcropping that had survived the last slide. If he could reach it in time it might shelter him.

Zach stood rooted in horror as boulders the size of small ponies bore down on his partner. Daniel fairly flew down the slope, his step miraculously sure over the unstable, shifting landscape. As he neared the safety of the outcropping, he caught a glimpse of Zach's white face staring up at him.

"Zach, you idiot, get under cover!" Daniel dove into the shelter of the solid knob of granite, shrinking back against it as boulders flew around him and over his head.

Zach ducked behind the huge trunk of the spruce and pressed against it, praying it could withstand the assault and praying that Daniel had reached safety. The tree shuddered with shock after shock as boulders struck it and rolled aside or piled up around it, but the forest giant held. Though the bone-deep rumbling seemed to go on forever, it actually lasted less than a minute before it began to die away.

At last it ended and Zach emerged to gaze up the changed slope of the incline. He could see no sign of Daniel. His heart clenched with fear as he scanned the slide for some evidence of his partner. He cast about him for something to test his footing and found a broken branch wedged between two boulders. He wrenched it free and started up the slope, using it like a walking stick. "Daniel!" he called, hoping for some response. To his surprise and great relief, he got one, a muffled shout. He saw Daniel's head and shoulders emerge from behind a pile of rocks, grey with dust.

"You alright, Zach?"

"I'm fine. Are you?"

"Not hurt, but my leg is pinned."

Zach started climbing toward him.

"No, Zach, wait!"

The alarm in his partner's voice stopped the youth in his tracks.

"If this mess starts to go again, you won't stand a chance."

Zach stared up at him. "What do you want me to do?"

Daniel looked away, scared and uncertain. "You could go to the hold for help, but there's no guarantee they could do any better over this mess than you could. It's your call, partner. I just want you to know, if you come up here, you're risking your life."

Zach considered for a moment, picturing a group of holders coming out here to rescue Daniel. What could they do except go up that unstable slope, risking their lives in place of his? Daniel was his partner, his responsibility. Besides, if he went back to the hold, he would have to leave Daniel pinned and defenseless against raiders or any predators foolish enough to try traversing the slide. And there were the airborne scavs, the vicious carrion birds who didn't always wait until the prey was decently dead before picking out its eyes. Zach shuddered at the thought and began to move slowly upward again, concentrating on each step, testing the stability of the boulders with his staff before trusting them. A rock shifted under his right foot and he almost lost his balance. He froze, waiting for the terrifying rumble to start again. He glanced up and saw Daniel watching, the expression on his face hard to read with its greyish mask of dust. Zach continued to pick his way higher, taking his time, afraid each step might prove his last, until finally he reached the granite outcropping that sheltered Daniel. Part of the outcropping had crumbled under the assault and the rubble had encased the mutant's left leg to the knee. Zach gave a sigh of relief as he stepped onto the solid ground on which his partner rested. Daniel leaned back on his elbows and grinned up at Zach.

"Welcome to my aerie."

Zach glared at him, fear and tension from the harrowing climb suddenly translating into furious anger in the face of Daniel's apparent good humor.

"You damned plague-crazy idiot! Do you think it's funny, risking your fool neck just to satisfy your idle curiosity?"

Daniel's eyes widened and he sobered. "I told you I make mistakes."

"Well you don't have to risk your damned life to prove it! I believe you! I don't need this kind of craziness in my life! It would serve you right if I just left you up here."

To Zach's surprise, Daniel looked crestfallen and the mutant said, "I'm sorry, Zach. Thanks for coming after me."

The youth's anger died. He sat down abruptly, shaking with reaction. Daniel watched in silent concern as Zach tried to get a grip on himself, closing his eyes and doing the breathing exercises Tadi had taught him, forcing himself to relax.

"I'm n-not a coward!" he stuttered defensively.

"I know that, Zach! You sure as hell wouldn't be up here if you were."

The youth glanced quickly at Daniel, then away, ashamed. "I'm sorry I yelled at you."

"You had every right to yell at me. I deserve it. It was a crazy, foolish thing to do. I guess I'm just not used to anyone caring if I get myself killed. I promise, it won't happen again." After a moment's silence he added, "Will you get this mountain off my leg so we can get out of here?"

Zach stood up and examined the pile of rubble. He saw a crack between two of the rocks and inserted his walking stick into it. The staff went in a lot deeper than expected. He levered cautiously and detected slight movement, so he threw a little more weight into it. Daniel suddenly fell back with a cry of a pain. Zach froze, white faced. Daniel saw his stricken look and gasped, "It's alright, Zach. It's alright. Just . . . try not to break the damned leg. I think I might need it to get off this rock pile. Somehow I don't think it would be a good idea to try hopping down." He grinned weakly and the youth suddenly realized that Daniel's humor was just a way to disguise his tension and the fear his recklessness might end up costing both their lives.

Zach crouched silently and studied the rubble again. From this angle he could see that the rocks surrounding the leg on either side had protected it from getting crushed when a boulder the size of an anvil came down on top like a capstone. A narrow space separated the boulder from Daniel's leg. Zach laid on his side next to his partner and ran his hand down the captive limb, beneath the rocks, closing his eyes to better picture what his fingers told him. He encountered the obstruction pinning Daniel's ankle against the hard ground and feeling around he found the rough wood texture of the branch. It was situated wrong. Every time he levered on it, it put pressure on the leg. He shifted it to a new position so it was braced against the rocks on either side, then he scrambled to his feet and tried it again, slowly increasing the force, praying the branch would hold. The boulder lifted, began to shift. Daniel felt the release of pressure and quickly slid out of the trap. The branch snapped and the boulder crashed back down, crushing and scattering the lesser rocks that had protected the leg. Zach ducked as rock chips flew at him, then the partners stared at each other, shaken.

"Danielberry jam and a wooden leg," quipped Zach. "That would teach you."

Daniel laughed, as much from relief as anything, and from surprise at hearing something akin to humor from Zach. The young outlander seemed always so deadly serious. Zach helped Daniel to his feet and the mutant carefully tested his weight on the injured leg.

"Just bruised, I think. We'd better get down from here before she begins to shift again."

They made their way carefully down over the rocks, Daniel limping painfully and Zach helping him as much as he could. The slide remained stable and they reached the safety of the trees with heartfelt sighs of relief. Moving quickly aside, well out of range of the danger area, they paused for a moment to catch their breath and relax. Daniel squeezed Zach's shoulder gratefully.

"Thanks, partner."

Zach smiled. Now they were down and safe, he felt good. Just once he had done something right. Just once he had not messed things up and caused a disaster. Maybe there was hope for him yet. For the first time he felt like a valuable part of this two-man team instead of just some ignorant kid who needed a nursemaid.

By the time they neared the hold, Daniel's ankle was beginning to swell and he limped heavily, leaning on Zach. "I don't think we'll be going out again for a while. You'd best resign yourself to cleaning stables again for a few days."

"Better than getting tossed out for losing my partner."

Daniel stopped and frowned at Zach sharply. "Why would they throw you out for something that was my own damned fault?"

Zach avoided his eyes and answered unhappily, "Condition of the agreement. They would only let me stay with you as my partner. Anything happens to you and it's good-bye Zach, and don't come back."

"Not true! They only said we had to agree to the partnership, not that we had to survive it." Daniel shook his head. "I can't believe they would turn you out just because I got myself killed. Not unless you tried to do it for me. These are good people. The least of them has more justice in them than all those pious, self-righteous saints back in that hole where I was born! They promised you a second chance, and I believe they'll give it to you, no matter what happens to me."

He started moving again and Zach moved with him, supporting him. After a moment, the youth said quietly, "Maybe you're right. But I'd rather you tried to stay alive anyway, just in case."

*   *   *

Margit checked the injured ankle and pronounced it slightly sprained and badly bruised, ordering Daniel to stay off it as much as possible for a few days. So Zach went back to hoeing gardens while Daniel lounged about, finishing the boots he was making for Hutch and doing whatever sedentary chores he could find. Zach didn't have to muck out barns though. Rad had inherited that chore. Tadi had begun early training with the pups and he asked Zach to help him. The boy seemed to have an affinity for the little dogs that he lacked with the horses and cattle. The pups trusted him with the naive innocence of the young and he treated them with firm patience that gave Tadi reason to think he might have real promise as a trainer.

After three days of idling, Daniel began growing increasingly restless with boredom. He woke on the fourth day with a sense of impatient determination to get out and do something, head to the refuge and visit Darius or something. His ankle felt much better. The swelling had subsided and his limp was almost gone. Only the colorful bruising remained. After breakfast he wandered out into the courtyard and stood listening to the rhythmic, metallic hammering from Cam in the forge. He sauntered over to watch, hanging back a little uncertainly. Cam glanced up with a cheerful grin. "Mornin', Daniel."

"Mornin', Cam. Mind if I watch?"

"Not at all. In fact, I could use a hand on the blower if you're not busy."

Daniel looked as pleased as any of the children who were usually awarded that chore. He moved into the smithing shed with a kind of uneasy caution, as if afraid he might be doing something forbidden, despite the invitation.

"What do I do?"

The question surprised Cam. The hold children watched his work with fascination from the time they could toddle. Every child in the hold over five years old knew what the blower was and how to use it. "Just pump this up and down when I tell you. It keeps the coals burning hot. Have you never been in a blacksmith's shop before?"

Daniel shifted uneasily and replied, "My father was a blacksmith, but he never allowed me to watch. He said I would curdle the metal with my 'devil's eyes'." Daniel grinned crookedly, trying to make light of something that still hurt in remembrance.

Cam scowled. "Metal doesn't curdle," he snapped bluntly.

Daniel tensed, taken aback by his gruffness. But Cam's anger was not for Daniel, it was for a hard, unfeeling father who would so crush the innocent curiosity of a child.

"You're welcome to watch or help anytime you want. In fact, if you'd like, I'll teach you. I could use an apprentice."

Daniel grinned, delighted. "I would like to learn."

About midmorning, Zach came wandering over to observe their labours. Daniel had his shirt off, his muscular torso streaked with sweat and soot as he hammered away at a misshapen piece of metal while Cam watched and coached him. The mutant glanced up from his concentration and noticed his partner's curious, interested gaze. He grinned and held up a crooked, roughly curved piece of metal with the tongs.

"My first horseshoe, Zach. What do you think?"

Zach eyed it critically and said, "I think I wouldn't want to be the horse who has to wear it."

Daniel laughed and Cam's chest rumbled in a deep chuckle. The mutant thrust the unfinished shoe back into the coals and drew out another, one closer to being finished and much nearer the proper shape. Cam recruited Zach to keep the fire hot, and for the rest of the morning the three of them worked together. Zach felt as fascinated as Daniel and they ended up taking turns at the anvil under Cam's careful guidance. Zach didn't have Daniel's mature strength, but he had a quicker mind and the intuitive instincts of an artist. In the end his work looked finer and shapelier than Daniel's. When the dinner bell rang, Cam said, "Lesson time's over for today, boys. You've both done very well, but I'm afraid I have to get those horses shod this afternoon so Hal can use them tomorrow. Just let me know when you're ready for another lesson."

"We'll do that. Thanks, Cam," Daniel said quietly, while Zach retrieved his partner's shirt from the back of the shop. The youth gave the blacksmith a shy smile of thanks and the two young men headed off to the bath house to wash off the sweat and grime before going to eat. Most everyone had gone to dinner already, so they found the bath house deserted. Zach pulled off his sweaty shirt and tossed it on top of his partner's.

Daniel splashed water over his head and raked his wet hair back from his face. Turning with a smile to speak to Zach, he suddenly noticed a pattern of fading bruises on the youth's ribs and his words died unspoken. Zach looked up, startled, when his partner's hand came down on his shoulder. The youth straightened, face dripping, scared by the unexpectedly hard, angry expression on his partner's face.

"How did you get these bruises, Zach?" Daniel demanded grimly. After a long moment of uncomfortable silence, he said,

"Rad has been harassing you again, hasn't he? Why didn't you tell me?"

Zach just shook his head. Daniel swore and snatched up his shirt, heading for the door.

"Daniel, wait!"

The mutant stopped and looked back, arrested by the desperation in Zach's voice.

"Please, let me handle this myself. If I can't learn to deal with Rad without help, it will never stop."

Daniel gazed at him impassively for a moment, then ordered, "Bring your shirt and come with me."

"What are you going to do?"

"I'm going to teach you a thing or two about dealing with bullies."

Zach slipped his shirt back on and followed his partner out of the building, wondering apprehensively what he had in mind. Daniel led Zach out the gate and then fell into a quick, relaxed trot along the river path, ignoring the faint twinges of protest from his ankle. Zach had no trouble keeping up, but by the time they turned onto the bridge and crossed into the orchard, he felt winded. Daniel was not even breathing hard. Zach flopped down under a tree, trying to catch his breath, but Daniel said, "Don't sit down. Come on, up on your feet, Zach. Walk around 'till you catch your wind."

The youth rose obediently and Daniel paced about the open space under the trees like a caged cat. After a time, he began to speak.

"The problem with bullies is that they're usually bigger or more powerful than you are. They like the odds in their favor, so they tend to victimize those who are smaller or for some reason unable to defend themselves. You're probably right about having to deal with Rad yourself. You have to teach him to respect you, let him know you're not afraid of him. He abuses you because it makes him feel superior, in control. If you can prove to him that he's not, maybe he'll leave you alone." Daniel paused silently for a moment, considering the enemy. "He has the advantage of about four inches, at least thirty pounds and years of experience wrestling with his friends and brothers."

"Thanks for pointing that out," Zach said dryly. "That's exactly what I need . . . self-confidence."

Daniel grinned. "You have a few advantages yourself."

Zach's brows rose doubtfully. "I do?"

"He's overconfident. He figures there's no way you could ever best him."

"He's probably right."

"Also, I suspect you're a lot smarter than he is. He has a temper. You could use that to your advantage. You have to stay cool to think clearly. In a serious fight, losing your temper can get you killed."

"God forbid it should ever get *that* serious!"

"It shouldn't with Rad, but life is long and you never know what twists it might throw at you. It's best to learn early how to dodge." Daniel smiled and said, "Come here."

Zach went and stood in front of his partner. The top of his head came not much higher than Daniel's chin.

"I'll show you a few defensive moves."

For half the afternoon he coached Zach, teaching him how to absorb the shock of a fall by tucking in his head and rolling, how to block blows to the face and body, and to always keep his guard up. They both discarded their shirts and became slippery with sweat in the afternoon heat. Daniel grinned, enjoying the workout, but Zach's face remained intently serious as he focused on absorbing this new skill, imprinting it on his memory so his reflexes would respond automatically, without conscious thought.

"Another advantage you have is your concentration," Daniel said. "You don't let yourself get distracted. That's good, especially if you're up against one man. When you face more than one enemy though, you have to expand your scope of concentration. The next blow could come from any direction. You have to be always aware of your whole environment, the location of each enemy, and anything around you that could serve as a weapon, a distraction or a trap."

He threw a flurry of blows at Zach and the youth countered each one perfectly. "Good," said Daniel, "now hit me." Zach hesitated. "Don't worry, I'll block it. Come on, throw one at me."

Zach took a swing and Daniel twitched aside slightly, catching Zach's wrist in his left hand and giving his partner a gentle poke in the ribs with the other.

"Rule number one," Daniel said with a smile, "never neglect your defenses to go on the offense." He released Zach. "Try it again."

The youth remained warier this time and kept his guard up, studying his partner's stance, looking for an opening. He swung and Daniel twisted his body, catching Zach by the arm and using the momentum of the blow to flip him off his feet. Zach took the fall on his shoulder, tucking in and rolling. He didn't have the momentum to come all the way to his feet again, but he rose quickly, guard raised, ready for the next move.

"Good landing," Daniel praised him. "You learn fast . . . another advantage. When you don't know your opponent's methods, it's important to learn quickly, to stay flexible and adapt to whatever he does."

For once Zach accepted the praise without freezing up. Daniel straightened and relaxed.

"That's enough for today, I think. We'll do this every day from now on. You'll probably end up with more bruises than Rad would ever give you, but the next time he tries to play rough, he's going to get a big surprise."

Zach's face warmed into one of his rare smiles. No trace of the old sullenness or resentment showed in him now. He looked relaxed, almost happy. "The bruises you give me aren't as painful. They hurt the body, but the spirit grows."

Daniel laughed in pleased surprise. "You have a way with words, my friend. You should be a song writer or a poet."

"You never know, I might just try it. I'll write an epic poem: Daniel the conquering hero, wrestles monsters with his bare hands, single-handedly defeats an army of raiders, wins the hearts of ladies, young, old, beautiful and otherwise. Sound vaguely familiar?"

Daniel made a face. "That's all I need. It's embarrassing enough having to listen to the stories all the time. At least they're mostly the truth." He gave Zach a friendly slap on the shoulder and said, "Let's go for a swim and cool off."

They stripped and ran to the river, diving in together. Side by side they raced downstream, driving through the water with long, powerful strokes. At last they turned and started back, fighting the current. Zach, already tired from the unfamiliar exercise of combat practice, began to fall behind. Daniel eased up and paced his partner, making no attempt to best Zach. When they reached the bridge, Daniel climbed out first and gave the tired youth a hand up the steep bank. Zach collapsed, leaning against the trunk of a tree, panting.

"Don't you ever get tired?"

"Sometimes," Daniel admitted. "I seem to remember you having to carry my pack for me not so long ago."

He stretched with the supple grace of a cat. For the first time Zach noticed the fresh, dimpled scar under his partner's right ribcage. He winced and looked quickly away. Daniel didn't notice and strolled over to lie down on his back beside Zach, enjoying the warmth of the day and the lazy, relaxed feeling after the swim. After a while he rolled over, pillowing his head in his arms, and began to fall into a light doze. Zach gazed down at him, studying the white latticework of welts that laced his back. The youth reached out hesitantly and lightly brushed one scarred shoulder. Daniel snapped awake with a startled grunt.

"Sorry," Zach said softly, feeling sick thinking about how much those scars must have hurt. Zach's father had beaten him at times, but never badly enough to permanently scar him, at least not physically.

The intimacy of Zach's touch startled Daniel at first, making him tense and nervous, but he forced himself to relax and trust his partner.

"They really put you through hell, didn't they?"

"Who?" Daniel asked drowsily.

"Whoever did this to your back."

The mutant thought about it for a moment, then answered, "I suppose they thought I deserved it. I never was a very cooperative slave."

"I can't imagine you doing anything to deserve this sort of punishment. You're just too . . ." Zach hesitated, searching for the proper words.

"Too damned perfect?" Daniel quoted him with bitter irony.

"Too damned nice for your own good. It's gonna get you in trouble someday."

Daniel laughed. "It already has. More than once. Isn't that how I got you for a partner?" he asked teasingly. He sensed Zach's immediate withdrawal and it worried him. He flipped over and said, "Zach? I was only teasing."

"I know," the outlander answered unhappily. "You're right though. What good is a partner you can't depend on not to screw things up? You deserve better."

"What are you talking about?" Daniel asked, sitting up abruptly. "You risked your life for me on that slide. And you're learning faster than I would have thought possible. Do you really think the boys from the hold could do any better?"

Zach shrugged, unconvinced, all his earlier feelings of elation and accomplishment crushed by his overwhelming sense of worthlessness. The image of himself as a failure, one who could do nothing right, had been too deeply instilled in him to be so easily undone.

"Have you ever noticed Hutch and Jesse together?"

Zach nodded, so Daniel continued.

"I used to watch them together. I used to dream about having a partnership like that." He turned to Zach earnestly. "Well now I have, and I've got no complaints. None. I couldn't ask for a better partner."

"Not even Hutch?" Zach asked doubtfully, a little jealous of the close bond between Daniel and the holder.

"Not even Hutch. He was the first real friend I ever had, and in my heart he was my brother long before the bonding ceremony. But partnership is a learning experience, a kind of training, and Hutch has already taught me the most important lessons . . . that not all holders are rabid mutant haters, that maybe some of them can be trusted. He gave me the confidence of knowing that I wasn't completely alone, that no matter what happens, I'll always have at least one true friend, one trust that will never be broken. Now it's my turn to teach you . . . that not all mutants are killers . . . that everyone has certain strengths and weaknesses, and we each have to find our own path and learn to trust ourselves and each other . . . that you don't have to measure up to anyone else's ideas of what you should be, you just have to like yourself."

Zach regarded him in silence for a moment, then replied, "I don't believe all mutants are killers anymore. At least . . . I know you're not."

Daniel's gaze turned thoughtful as he stared off into the distant past. "A long time ago, my mother told me I was an empath," he mused. "She said her Kithtrekker family are 'sensitives' and have many varied mental abilities . . . clairvoyance, telepathy, farseeing. She felt disappointed that she hadn't inherited any of that 'talent'. Strange. I haven't thought about that in years."

"So what does it mean to be an empath?" Zach asked.

Daniel glanced at him and shrugged. "It means you feel other peoples' emotions, especially their pain, anger or fear. It makes it hard to walk away from someone in trouble. It . . . also makes it more painful when they hate you for no reason. When your own family hates you enough to abandon you in the desert to die. When the man who raised you to adulthood and taught you how to survive suddenly sells you into slavery. Or when the man you thought was your friend tries to shoot you for the bounty on raiders."

Zach studied his uncharacteristic bitterness and reminded him gently, "What about when everyone loves you? How does that feel?"

Daniel's expression lightened into a slow smile. "That one is new to me," he confessed, "and I have to admit, it feels damned good." Then he leaned back against the tree, his eyes taking on a thoughtful frown. "You know, when Darius first came to the Refuge, he said my nightmare drew him to me. And he said I was the same as him. At the time, I didn't know or trust him, so I didn't understand. But I think he meant we are *both* empaths."

"But . . . you can't hear thoughts like him, can you?" Zach asked uneasily.

"No. Comparing me to Darius is like comparing a raindrop to a river."

Zach thought about the telepath and slowly shook his head. "He scares me. It's not the way he looks. I know you wouldn't be friends with him if he was as bad as he appears. It's the idea he can see inside my head. Every time we go to visit him, I tell myself I won't let it get to me this time, but it always does."

"I told you he won't invade your privacy. I felt much the same way the first time he tried to touch my mind, but in all the time I've known him, he has never tried to pry deeper than I was willing to share. Believe it or not, he has a strong, rather unique sense of ethics. Darius may look like the most evil, dangerous human being you've ever met, but inside he's got the innocence and vulnerability of a child. And his dreamweaving . . . it's like magic. He does with his mind the same sort of things you do on paper. If you could only trust him enough to let him touch your mind, you would see there's not a grain of evil in him."

Zach shuddered at the idea of letting the telepath inside his head. Daniel saw his reaction and smiled sadly. "It's getting late. Are you hungry?"

"Starved!"

"Let's go see if we can scrounge something from Cochita. My stomach is beginning to complain about missing dinner."

Chapter Fourteen

While travelling down life's lonesome highway,
Seems the hardest thing to do
Is to find a friend or two,
That helping hand, someone who understands,
When you feel you've lost your way,
You've got someone there to say,
I'll show you.
~Lionel Richie

"Hey, Daniel!"

The partners paused and turned together, having just returned from a trip to the refuge to visit Darius. Joshua Tayler came trotting across the courtyard toward them.

"A group of us are taking the girls out berry picking after supper," Josh said. "Do you want to come along?"

Joshua looked straight at Daniel while he tendered the invitation, ignoring Zach as if he didn't exist. The young outlander looked away. Over the past weeks, with encouragement from Daniel and Tadi, Zach's self-esteem had begun a gradual climb out of the pit his past had pushed it into, but it remained fragile and easily crushed. Since the incident at the rockslide, he had lost any resentment he had felt towards Daniel. His envious admiration for the mutant had been tempered by the discovery that his partner was only human, capable of making mistakes and needing help and support from a partner occasionally. And Zach had slowly come to the realization that Daniel respected and admired him in return, though he wasn't sure why. A few amongst the holders, however, still treated Zach as if they thought the council had made a grave error.

Daniel grinned and answered, "Sure, Josh. Do you know if Neely is going?"

"I think so. We're gathering at the gate right after supper. See you then."

"Right."

The partners continued on toward the bath house. After washing off the day's grime, they went to the hall for supper, and Daniel noticed nothing unusual in Zach's silence. The youth often remained uncommunicative, though much less so lately. He answered readily enough when Tadi asked him a question, and even smiled at a joke Hedy made. But when the meal ended and Daniel turned from listening to a story of Hutch's, he found his partner gone. Assuming Zach had gone ahead to join the berry picking group, Daniel wandered out with Hutch to the gathering, unconcerned. But he didn't see Zach amongst the small crowd of young people waiting at the gates.

"Where's Zach?" Daniel asked.

He received only blank looks and shrugs in answer. Rad sneered, "Don't expect us to babysit your runtling outlander while you go off smooching in the bushes with Neely. Wherever he is, he can stay there."

Daniel just ignored Rad, not even acknowledging his comment with a glare. He just turned on his heel and headed back inside to look for his partner. After a bit of searching, he found Zach in the deserted dorm, sitting on his bed, braiding strips of rawhide into a rope as Daniel had recently taught him.

"What are you doing here, Zach? Aren't you coming berry picking with us?"

Zach didn't even look up. "They invited you," he said, "not me."

Daniel eyed his partner in dismay. He had just assumed the invitation included both of them. It had never occurred to him that it might have seemed otherwise to Zach.

"*I'm* inviting you, Zach. Please come. I don't want to leave you here alone."

"Alone is better than company where I'm not welcome."

Daniel studied his carefully expressionless face in silence for a moment, then sat down on his own bed, next to Zach's. "Fine then," he said, "I'll stay here with you."

"Dammit, I don't need a babysitter!"

Daniel swung his feet up onto the bed and settled back comfortably. "Zach, I think I've gotten to know you fairly well in the past few weeks. Well enough to know when you're hurting anyway. I'm not going to leave you alone when you're feeling like this."

He contemplated the ceiling, waiting to see if he got a response. Zach studied him searchingly, seeing his determination and recalling Neely's excited anticipation at supper, and the warm, lingering glances exchanged between the girl and his partner.

"Fine, I give up! I'll come."

When they got back out to the gates, some of the group had already left, but Hutch, Tye, Neely, Rennie and half a dozen others waited for them. It was Hedy's turn for kitchen duty, so she had to miss the outing. Zach felt disappointed. Her friendly presence might have made the whole thing a little more bearable. But Tye gave him a friendly slap on the shoulder and Neely smiled at him. At least he *thought* she smiled at him . . . she might have been looking past him at Daniel. Even Hutch's expression seemed a little warmer than its usual careful neutrality. But then, lately Hutch had seemed considerably friendlier anyway. Zach wondered if the holder was finally beginning to forgive him. Zach didn't know that Daniel had quietly taken Hutch and Tadi aside and told them what the youth had said about the shooting being an accident, adding his own remembrances and the fact that he believed Zach. Tadi had commented, "I suspected as much. The better I got to know that boy, the harder I found it to believe he would deliberately hurt anyone." He and Hutch passed the news on to others and the story began to quietly circulate throughout the hold. Not everyone believed it, but most seemed willing to give the young outlander the benefit of the doubt.

The berry pickers headed off into the desert. The berry patch lay two miles south of the hold, and the young people made the trip amid a great deal of lighthearted laughter and joking. Neely linked one arm with Daniel and the other with Zach and began singing a quick-tempoed marching song. Others soon joined in and Zach's spirits began to rise. After a while he and Daniel began to join in on the simple, repetitive choruses.

The berry patch covered a little over an acre of dry, dusty desert, creating a maze-like mass of sandberry bushes. The thorny brambles seemed to grow in an almost organized pattern of spiraling, twisting rows, creating dozens of nice, private little enclosures. The bushes had thick, leathery leaves that conserved water, and fruit the size of cherries, with a mealy texture and a tart-sweet flavor. They made excellent pies and preserves and dehydrated easily for winter storage.

The sandberry picking was traditionally left to the young, unmarried folk, and had more to do with romance and the choosing of a life mate than with foraging for food. Upon reaching the thickets, the group immediately splintered into clusters of two or three, each girl going off with one or two male partners. Hutch and Tye wandered off together with Serene and Rennie went with Tansy. Zach watched as the others quickly dispersed into the tangle, wishing Hedy could have come. Next to Daniel and Neely, Hedy had become Zach's closest friend and ally, often inviting him to partner her in a game or help her with some project.

"Are you coming, Zach?" Daniel asked. Neely smiled, but Zach could see the disappointment she tried to hide. She had looked forward to having this time alone with Daniel. The only reason Zach had agreed to come was because he knew how disappointed she would feel if his partner backed out of the trip. He had no intention of spoiling their pleasure.

"I'll just stay here and stand watch. You two go ahead."

Daniel felt reluctant to leave him alone, but Neely gave Zach a radiantly grateful smile and drew the mutant away with her. Zach climbed a low outcropping of rock and settled cross-legged with his rifle across his knees. He smiled, thinking about Daniel and Neely. After the bits and pieces he had heard of Daniel's background, and considering the brutal scars as an illustration of the parts untold, Zach had begun to realize what Hutch meant when he said Daniel had known more pain than the outlander could imagine. Zach felt his partner deserved a little happiness.

*   *   *

Neely led Daniel to a quiet, secluded little corner of the thickets, almost surrounded by high thorn bushes. They could hear others nearby, talking and laughing, but their privacy remained completely protected by the screen of brambles. For a while they picked the fat berries diligently, shoulder to shoulder, enjoying each other's company and the chance to linger alone together. Before long they had filled their buckets and they settled on the sand, close together, and talked in quiet intimacy. Daniel put his arm around Neely and she leaned against him, filled with contentment. She fed him a berry and followed it with a light kiss. Knowing they had Tadi's approval had started a growing hope in Daniel that he might actually have a chance with Neely. He hugged her and wondered what the other holders would think of such a union. Neely kissed him again, more demandingly, and he responded shyly, afraid of letting his hunger for her get out of control. Neely was no veteran at this either, but at least she'd had the example of loving, affectionate parents and a host of young couples over the years, as well as an experimental clinch with one or two of the boys as she grew up. Daniel on the other hand had mostly lived isolated, with no one to teach him such things. The only guides he had now were instinct and Neely, so he relaxed and let her lead him, gently introducing him to what she knew of the ways of love.

* * *

The sun gradually slipped lower as Zach sat listening to the sounds of chattering voices and occasional shouts of laughter from off in the distance behind him. He was not unhappy sitting here alone. He actually felt good, having given his two friends the gift of privacy. But after a while he began to feel strangely uneasy, as if watched by unfriendly eyes. He felt a prickling sensation as the hairs on the back of his neck stood up. A furtive movement caught the corner of his eye and he slowly, casually turned his head in that direction, searching the landscape. At first he saw nothing unusual, then a minute flicker of movement drew his eye and he saw them, three of them. Their dusty, greyish brown color blended with the desert as if they were made of sand. Another one crept forward a few inches and he realized there was a whole pack of them, virtually invisible when not in motion. Their movements looked neither innocent nor random. They were stalking the noisy, preoccupied berry pickers. They didn't seem to have noticed Zach yet, or if they had, they ignored him, deeming him too hard to get at. He scrambled to his feet, levering a bullet into the firing chamber of his rifle. "Dags!" he shouted in warning. "Dag pack!"

With the element of surprise ruined, the pack dashed into the brambles, intent on securing a meal by force if not stealth. Four animals rushed Zach's position. He fired, hoping he stood high enough so they couldn't reach him. One of the dags collapsed in a heap and lay still and the other three used the momentum of their charge to scale the rock face. Two fell back, but the third managed to catch the cuff of Zach's breeches in its teeth, and the weight of its fall yanked the feet out from under him and dragged him off the rock. His hand cracked against the stone, a numbing blow, and he dropped the rifle. He landed on his back on the sand and one dag immediately sank its fangs into his shoulder. Zach screamed as teeth ground against bone. Another animal lunged for his throat. He managed to grab a handful of its neck fur and hold it off. It raked his chest with its claws, struggling to pull itself closer. The third dag still tugged harmlessly at his breeches. Zach screamed for help, knowing he would be dead in seconds if no one came.

* * *

Daniel began to feel edgy even before Zach's warning shout. He rose to his feet, listening intently, the finely honed instincts of the hunted warning him that something was amiss. When the cry of alarm came, he sprang into instant action. He caught Neely's hand and headed back toward Zach's position at a run. They encountered another couple and Daniel caught a glimpse of Carly's frightened face over Rad's shoulder as he shoved Neely into their arms and said, "Take care of her." Then he stretched out into a dead run, spurred by Zach's scream of pain and his cry for help.

Daniel burst into the open and saw his partner half buried beneath a trio of dags. He fired at the one worrying Zach's leg and it gave a yelp and turned tail. He'd only creased it. He swore, longing for his bow. He didn't trust his aim so close to his partner, so he flicked on the safety and waded in, swinging the rifle like a club. He brought it crashing down with all the power in his back and shoulders, onto the head of the beast struggling for Zach's throat. The youth's arm gave out under the blow and the animal collapsed across his face, its skull crushed. The other dag released its bulldog grip on Zach's shoulder and lunged for Daniel's thigh. The mutant swung the rifle butt around and smacked the animal across the side of the head, staggering it. Before it could recover, he spun the rifle around again, flicked off the safety and fired. At that distance he could not miss. The animal's head disintegrated.

Daniel scanned his surroundings tensely, searching for more enemies, hearing shots and shouts and yelping from the thickets. For the moment the area looked clear, so he reached down to grasp the dead dag and fling it off his partner, going down on one knee beside him.

"Zach?"

The boy's eyes looked wide and glazed with shock and terror, but they slowly focused on Daniel's face. Zach visibly pulled himself together and tried to sit up, saying shakily, "I'm fine, Daniel. They only got my shoulder."

But the mutant gently pushed him back down and held him there with a firm hand in the center of his chest.

"Just lie still, Zach. You've been poisoned."

Zach stiffened as he suddenly remembered hearing that dag bites were poisonous. Where he came from the animals had been virtually wiped out because of their fearless predations on human settlements. This was his first close encounter with them. His heart started to pound again and he stared up at Daniel, scared to the core.

"Easy, partner. It won't kill you. You'll just feel mighty sick for a day or two. But the more you move around, the worse it will be. Here, roll over a bit. I'll see if I can draw some of the poison."

Zach bit his lip to keep from making any sound as Daniel sucked at the wound and spat out the bitter venom. The mutant shook his head and said, "Son of a bitch got you good." He looked down at the youth with deep concern in his green eyes. Zach reached up and wiped a smear of blood from Daniel's lip.

"You look like you're the one who's been chewing on me," he joked with a weak smile.

Hutch and Tye came bursting from the thickets, ready for anything, saw the position was secured and Zach was down.

"Zach! We heard you call, but we were under attack ourselves. We came as soon as we could. How bad is it?" Hutch asked worriedly.

"One of them took a pretty good bite out of him," Daniel answered.

Tye pressed Zach's good shoulder gently. "You saved lives here today, lad. Well done."

The others came straggling out of the maze now, appearing shaken but unhurt. No one else had been injured. Neely hurried over to kneel beside Daniel. She squeezed Zach's hand reassuringly and he smiled up at her. She seemed a long way above him. They all seemed strangely distant, even Daniel.

256

Rennie looked worriedly at the blood pooling beneath Zach's shoulder.

"Don't you have any of those leaves, Daniel? We should stop the bleeding."

"No, the leaves would only seal in the poison. Let some of it bleed out."

Daniel carefully slit the sleeve of Zach's shirt and cut it away, then used it to make a light bandage over the wound. He and Hutch helped the youth to his feet. Zach felt strange, as if his head might float away.

"You shouldn't walk, Zach," said Hutch, "you're going to have to let us carry you." He glanced at Daniel. "Chair lift?" The mutant nodded.

At that moment, Carly spoke up in a loud, carrying voice. "Well, at least none of *us* got hurt."

Zach stiffened and everyone else turned to scowl at her. The glares from her brothers and Daniel should have turned her to stone on the spot. Rad smirked. With his head down, Zach missed seeing the indignation her callous remark had caused. Her words stabbed him to the heart, making him feel even more the unwanted outsider. He shrugged off his friends' hands, muttering, "Leave me alone. I can walk. I don't need any help from a damned mutant lover and a freak."

He stumbled away. Tye told Carly bitingly, "Sister, you are turning into a front-line bitch. One of these days I'm going to sew that mouth of yours shut for good."

Hutch and Daniel hurried after Zach, trying to persuade him to accept help. He shook them off, and when they tried to force the issue, he struggled so hard they feared he might do more damage than walking would. So they let him go, flanking him on either side, ready to support him if he would allow it.

Zach could hear them talking, pleading with him, but they seemed far away and somehow disconnected from him, like listening to strangers arguing in the next room. His head seemed to be filling with air, getting bigger and lighter, floating further and further from the ground. He could no longer feel the rest of his body. He only knew it existed because he could feel the jarring impact of his feet each time they hit the ground, every footstep echoing through his skull like a slammed door in an empty, cavernous building. His vision started to go dark, and one scared, still-rational corner of his mind realized what was happening. The venom was coursing through his bloodstream, poisoning his system. He was going to die! No. Daniel said it wouldn't kill him, just make him sick. He trusted Daniel. His partner had never lied to him. Freak. He had called Daniel a freak. Zach's faltering footsteps stopped and he wavered, torn with dismay.

Hutch and Daniel immediately moved in on either side of him. Strangely enough, he could feel their hands on him, supporting him, even though he couldn't feel his body. He sagged against his partner.

"I'm sorry, Daniel. I didn't mean it. I'm just . . . I'm lost. I don't have anywhere to go."

"You have friends, Zach. Let us help you. We'll take care of you."

They gently drew his arms across their shoulders and he didn't even wince when Daniel lifted the injured limb. He offered no resistance this time as they locked hands, making a seat for him, and lifted him off the ground. He slumped, barely conscious. Tye and Neely walked behind, ready to lend assistance if needed, and Rennie flanked them, upset and worried. He would certainly never have wished anything like this on the outlander.

"I've never seen anyone have so quick or so bad a reaction to dag venom," Tye commented. "That animal must have pumped a helluva dose into him."

By the time they reached the hold Zach was unconscious. They rushed him into the infirmary and Margit quickly examined the wound. It looked inflamed and the whole arm had begun to puff up.

"Did you bring back one of the bodies?"

They looked at each other in consternation. "No. Should we have?"

"If I had venom from one of the poison sacs I could make an anti-toxin. For him to be this far gone this quickly, I would say he's had close to a lethal dose. He needs that anti-toxin. Without it, even if he survives, he could be left crippled with nerve damage, blind or even mindless."

The five young people exchanged a look of horrified concern. Hutch put a hand on Daniel's shoulder and said, "You and Neely stay with him. Tye and Rennie and I will go back."

Daniel didn't argue, he just said, "Be careful. They might still be hanging around."

The trio of young men left and Margit went to the surgery to begin setting up the equipment she would need.

"I feel like it's my fault," Daniel muttered to Neely. "I should never have left him alone out there."

Neely put her arms around him comfortingly and said, "Then it's my fault too. He did it for both of us. He knew I wanted to be alone with you."

"But it was my responsibility to protect him."

"And you did. You killed two dags. You saved his life."

"Did I? I hope so. I sure hope so."

* * *

The first awareness Zach regained was a sensation of burning alive. The poison had irritated the nerve endings and every inch of his body felt on fire. If he moved, the flames erupted from a smolder to a conflagration, so he lay still, trying to understand what had happened. He remembered the attack and parts of the walk back, but then his recollection became a blank, a void. He strained his eyes, trying to see something in the darkness. He couldn't remember the hold ever seeming this dark, even at night. With a sudden stab of panic, he realized he was blind. He gasped, and for an instant the fire flared up and then slowly settled again. He heard a rustle nearby. At least his hearing seemed unimpaired. Small comfort.

"Zach?"

"Daniel?" he answered, trying unsuccessfully to keep the panic out of his voice. "I can't see! I'm blind!"

"Easy, partner," Daniel said soothingly, "it's only temporary, I swear. You're all puffed up from the toxin. Your eyes are swollen shut. You look such a sight, your own mother wouldn't recognize you." The affectionate humor in Daniel's voice reassured Zach and he relaxed.

"Margit stuffed you full of antivenom. She says the swelling should start going down by tomorrow. You had a close call, my friend. For a while there, I feared I might lose you. I swear to God, Zach, I had no idea how much poison that dag put into you. If I had, I never would have let you walk home."

"Short of knocking me on the head, I didn't give you much choice, did I? I wasn't exactly rational at the time, but I was sane enough that I remember how crazy I acted. It wasn't your fault, Daniel, none of it was." After a moment's pause he added anxiously, "You know I didn't mean what I said out there, don't you, Daniel? What I called you?"

"I know, Zach. I knew it then. You were sick and hurt. That damned Carly! I could have cheerfully wrung her neck! You know you have as many friends here as those who think like Rad and Carly."

Zach was not so sure. The only real friends he had were Daniel and Tadi. And Hedy. And Neely. Maybe Tye and Cam. He wasn't sure about Hutch, but he suddenly realized how the list had grown and he felt warmed.

*　　　　*　　　　*

By the next morning, the swelling had subsided enough so Zach could open his eyes a little, but two more days passed before he recovered sufficiently to leave the infirmary. Even then he felt slightly brittle, as if the wrong move would send his nerves into spasm again. He had felt surprised by the number of people who came to see him while he lay abed. Besides frequent appearances by Daniel and Tadi, Neely and Hedy both spent time sitting with him, telling him stories to keep him from getting bored. Tye and Hutch visited every day, and Cam, Rennie, Serene and Cochita each came to wish him well. Even Aaron made an appearance, and twice Tadi's wife Salla accompanied her husband. The most surprising visit though, came from Joshua Tayler. Josh was older than Zach by about a year, but he came into the room with a guilty, sheepish air that made him seem younger. He only stayed a few minutes and didn't say much, but before he left, he said, "I didn't mean to snub you that day, Zach . . . oh, hell, that's not true. I did mean to, but I was wrong, and I'm sorry. I just want you to know, I don't agree with Rad." He hesitated for a second, then added, "I hope there's no hard feelings. Maybe . . . maybe we could be friends?"

The offer startled Zach, but he smiled and answered, "I'd like that, Josh."

Zach was young and healthy and his shoulder healed quickly. For a few weeks he could only stoke the fires and pump the blower during the smithing lessons, but he learned a lot just watching Daniel's efforts. The combat training got temporarily postponed as well, and he missed those sessions a great deal. Even his time spent drawing and painting, tainted as it was by that sense of doing something shameful, couldn't give him the feeling of being at peace with himself that those training sessions with Daniel did. They ran together every day anyway. The shoulder didn't hinder that at least. Zach's endurance had increased tremendously and he could run for miles now at Daniel's side without getting winded or tired.

The survival training continued as well. One afternoon Daniel took him out on an overnight trip, telling the youth they were reversing roles for a while, with Zach acting as the guide and senior partner while Daniel played the greenstick. Zach had to provide the necessary elements for their survival . . . a shelter, a fire and food. While building the lean-to, Zach glanced at Daniel several times to see if he approved, but his partner returned his look with a blank expression of total ignorance, as if the mutant hadn't the faintest idea how to build a shelter. Zach decided snares would take too long to provide a meal, so he fashioned a fish trap out of willow withes. This was not something he had learned from Daniel, but from his father, who had no patience for sitting on a riverbank with a fishing pole. The mutant watched with genuine fascination as it took shape and followed Zach as the youth searched the river shallows for a likely spot to set the trap. A few hours later, after gathering a pouch full of wild onions, watercress and biscuit root, they returned to find the trap had caught two medium-sized fish and three small ones. Daniel grinned. This was something the Old Man had neglected to teach him. They took their catch back to the shelter and Zach built a small fire, baking the biscuit root and onions beneath it. While they waited for the meal to cook, Daniel sat down with the fish trap, studying its construction and how it worked. He cut some willow withes and made a copy of it. At first Zach thought he was just playing along, pretending to be a greenstick, until he looked up and asked, "Why did you set it in that particular spot?"

The youth looked surprised. "Haven't you ever used a fish trap before?"

"Never even seen one before. The only ways I know to catch fish are with a hook and line or a net. Or if you're desperate enough and patient enough, by tickling them."

"Tickling them? You'll have to show me that one sometime."

Zach sat down beside Daniel and told him about a few other types of fish traps, explaining where and how they should be set, with a vee of stakes leading the fish into the mouth of the trap. It felt good to have something of value he could share with his partner.

They cooked the fish on greenwood skewers over the flames, and along with the wild roots and greens, it made a tasty and satisfying meal. They talked long into the night, lying side by side in the shelter of the lean-to. At last they fell asleep, and when a brief shower pattered down on the camp, sizzling in the hot ashes of their fire, the lean-to kept them completely dry. The sun roused Zach the next morning and he got up quietly. Daniel woke as soon as the youth moved, but he lay still, pretending to sleep while his young partner checked the snares he had set the evening before and rekindled the fire to roast the grouse he had caught for breakfast. When the smell began to make Daniel's mouth water, he sat up and stretched lazily, smiling at Zach as he asked, "Breakfast ready yet, partner?"

On the way back to the hold later that day, Zach asked Daniel nervously, "Well, how did I do?"

Daniel appeared surprised by the question. "How do *you* think you did, Zach? We survived, didn't we? We didn't go hungry. We didn't get cold or wet when it rained. If you found yourself suddenly alone out there, or with someone who didn't know the woods, do you think you could keep yourself and your companion alive? That's what survival is all about. It doesn't matter what I think, or anyone else. When it comes down to a life or death situation, all that counts is knowing how to stay alive and having the grit and determination and sheer boneheaded stubbornness to not give up."

Chapter Fifteen

She found the place where I've been hiding;
Have I the grace to let her in
To where my love has been residing,
Far away from the joy and pain again?
~Hal Ketchum

The time of harvest quickly approached. Already the holders had reaped and stored some of the earlier crops. Gathering groups went out almost every day to glean the rich bounty of the wild meadows and forests, the nuts, fruit, mushrooms and wild roots.

Daniel strode purposefully down the corridor toward the weaving room, a gleam of excitement in his green eyes. Today he and Zach and Hutch were escorting a group of ladies on a foraging expedition. Daniel and his partner had escorted gathering groups before, but today for the first time Neely would join them, the first opportunity Daniel had ever had to take the woman he loved into *his* world and show her some of the things he loved about it. They would be limited and hampered by the company, but they cherished any time spent together.

He was still far down the corridor when his keen hearing picked up the sounds of the ladies chattering. As he drew closer, one voice seemed to draw attention above the rest. In fact, the others stilled as if to listen.

"Well, I don't know how you can stand it! Those eyes!"

Daniel froze in mid step, sure that voice spoke of him. He wanted to turn and walk away, but something locked him in place and forced him to listen.

"I mean, can you imagine making love with those eyes shining at you in the dark? It would be like making love to a wild animal!"

He could almost hear her shudder.

"And he's a mutant! I think the council should disapprove it. I mean, what about your children? Every time you get pregnant, you'll have to spend nine months wondering if you'll give birth to a baby or some horrible, deformed monster!"

Daniel turned away blindly and fled. If he had stayed a moment longer, he would have heard the loud crack of Neely's hand connecting with Carly's cheek and the noisy flood of reproach from the other weavers in his defense.

In the side court garden, Zach worked with Josh, helping him harvest the peas and beans while waiting for the foraging group to gather. The boys heard the door slam and glanced up to see Daniel striding across the courtyard with a strange, frozen expression. When he realized his partner was headed for the gates, Zach ran after him.

"Daniel, where are you going? Don't you want to wait for the group?"

Daniel didn't even turn and all Zach got in response was a muffled, "No."

"Well, let me get my rifle, I'll come with you."

Daniel turned on him with a tormented expression. "No, Zach! I don't want you with me! I don't need some lead-footed, greenstick outlander following me around all the time! Just leave me alone!"

He whirled and stalked out the gate, leaving Zach open mouthed, too stunned to even feel hurt. He just stood there as if turned to stone. Josh came trotting over from the garden and Rennie clattered down from the guard-walk.

"Zach?" Rennie touched Zach's shoulder and the youth turned to him blankly.

"You know he didn't mean it," Rennie said. "Something must have upset him. It's just not like Daniel. You should go tell Hutch about it. He'll know what to do."

Zach nodded dully and turned without a word to go search out Hutch. He looked like he'd had the heart cut out of him. Rennie and Josh exchanged a worried glance, then went back to their duties. By the time Zach had located Hutch, worry had eclipsed his hurt over Daniel's rejection. He found Neely and Hutch just leaving the weaving room, ready to join the foraging party. Zach told them what happened and finished by adding anxiously, "He didn't even take a rifle!"

"Oh, Lord!" Neely cried, "I think I know what upset him." The young men turned to her expectantly. "He must have been coming to get me and overheard what Carly said. Oh, Hutch, I know she's your sister but I would like to just strangle her! She said horrible things about Daniel's eyes and about what our children might look like. If he heard that, he must feel terribly hurt. You have to find him."

"We'll certainly try. You tell everyone the trip is off for now. Zach and I will go scour the woods."

They searched for four hours and found no sign of Daniel. They even went to the refuge but found Darius away and no indication that Daniel had visited recently. At last Hutch gave up in helpless frustration.

"Believe me," he told Zach, "if Daniel doesn't want to be found, there's no one in the hold good enough to track him. Not even Tye. We may as well just go home. He'll return when he's calmed down a bit. I just hope that bitch hasn't hurt him so badly he won't come back."

"He'll come back," Zach said with conviction. "He won't reject a dream come true because it's not perfect. Even half a dream is better than none. I just hope he'll stay safe out here."

Their eyes met in a worried glance, shared concern for Daniel bringing them closer than they had ever been, even before the shooting. When they got back to the hold, Tadi asked Zach to help him with the pups and the youth felt glad of something to keep him busy and his mind off the multitude of disasters that might befall his partner. Hutch worked in the gardens, keeping an eye out for Daniel's return. Near suppertime, as he helped Josh dig potatoes in one of the outer gardens, Rennie came trotting up.

"He's back. He's up on the guard-walk. I tried to speak to him, but he wouldn't even look at me. I've never seen him like this. He's just staring out at the desert, not saying a word. Whatever is bothering him must be pretty serious."

"Thanks, Rennie. I'll go talk to him."

Rennie and Hedy moved around to the other side of the guard-walk, leaving Hutch some privacy for his talk with Daniel. Hutch walked up beside his friend, noting the bleak, frozen stare.

"You know, Neely is worried sick about you. Zach too."

Daniel glanced at Hutch with a strangely blank expression, as if he didn't even recognize his friend.

"I know you're hurting, brother, but you shouldn't listen to anything Carly spouts. She's always had more mouth than brains. No one else gives any credit to what she said, least of all Neely. You do love Neely, don't you?"

Daniel nodded silently.

"Then why don't you ask her to marry you?"

"Marry me?" he muttered. "What girl in her right mind would ever want to join with me?"

Hutch made an exasperated sound. "Look at yourself, my brother," Hutch murmured, "You have everything a woman could want in a man . . . honor, courage, loyalty and gentleness . . . besides being damned easy on the eyes. Why wouldn't any girl want to marry you?"

Daniel shook his head. "I'm a goddamn mutant!" he choked out bitterly.

Hutch gave him a thump on the shoulder. "No one even thinks about that anymore except a few lackwits like Carly. Danni, we love you! Neely loves you! Give yourself a chance!"

Daniel hesitated, torn between hope and doubt. "Do you really think the council would allow me to marry and have children?"

"Of course I do. They wouldn't have invited you to become one of us, only to deny you such a basic right."

Daniel turned to face Hutch with an anguished expression. "But what if our children aren't normal? What if they're deformed? What if they're little monsters? Hutch, how can I ask Neely to live with that uncertainty?"

Hutch studied his friend's troubled face and realized that this was the root of Daniel's despair, the fear he might bring immeasurable pain and anguish to the woman he loved.

"Daniel," he said gently, "it's a possibility we *all* live with. Were your parents mutants? They weren't, were they? And just because you are a mutant doesn't mean your children will be. Even if they are, this isn't the civilized lands. We don't kill mutant babies or sell them into slavery. We never have. If they are capable of surviving, they survive and we love them. We don't believe that mutants are spawn of the devil the way the Armageddonist bible says. Or that we need to preserve the purity of the human form. We believe that *all* men are brothers. It doesn't matter what they look like, it's what's in here that counts." He tapped Daniel on the chest, over the heart. "And what you have in here is worth passing on." He paused and smiled, then added, "Besides, if your mutation should happen to breed true . . . well, it's not exactly a deformity, is it? A few more little Daniels running around might even improve the human race."

Daniel stood speechless. Hutch saw him trying unsuccessfully to blink back the shine of tears.

"Ah, Danni! You've been hurt so many times and so deeply. Do you find it impossible now to accept happiness? Life is a gamble. We all have to take chances. Talk to Neely. She knows what the risks are as well as you do. Let her decide for herself what risks she's willing to take."

Daniel closed his eyes and nodded. "You're right, Hutch. She has the right to choose. Lord!" he choked out. "Have I ever told you how much your friendship means to me?"

*   *   *

Daniel found Zach in the tranquility garden, back in a secluded corner. The youth hunched over a piece of paper with the paint box open beside him, laying careful washes of color over a sketch of Tadi, his concentration so total he seemed unaware he had company. Daniel watched him for a moment, then broke the silence by saying quietly, "Don't ever do that where you're alone and unprotected. If I was an enemy, you'd be dead."

Zach looked up, startled, and an expression of relief washed over his face. "Daniel!" He set aside his brush and scrambled to his feet, starting towards his partner. But then he stopped, uncertain, remembering Daniel's last words to him.

"Are you alright?" he asked anxiously.

"I'm fine." Daniel smiled and sank cross-legged onto the grass. "Tadi told me I'd find you here."

Zach seated himself again, finding it hard to meet Daniel's eyes.

"Zach, I'm sorry about what I said. I was . . . upset. I just lashed out without thinking. I didn't mean to hurt you."

Zach shrugged. "It's alright, I guess I deserve it. I've done the same to you more times than I can remember."

"No, it's not alright. You know I care about you, Zach. You're my brother as much as if we'd said the bonding vows. I didn't mean what I said. I *like* having you for a partner. And you're not a lead-foot . . . not anymore anyway. You're almost as quiet as Hutch, and that's not bad for someone who's only been in the woods for a few months." He paused, studying Zach's face seriously. "Forgive me?"

"I forgive you for the words. I don't forgive you for going off unarmed and alone and worrying me half to death. I've spent the entire afternoon picturing every kind of mishap that could befall you . . . raiders, slavers, dags, a broken neck from doing something stupid! And wondering if it was somehow my fault."

"Why in creation would you think it was your fault?"

The youth shrugged. "Force of habit, I guess. Disasters are a specialty of mine." Zach picked up his brush, carefully cleaned it and put it away.

"That doesn't mean every disaster that happens is your fault, Zach. We're only responsible for each other to a certain point. We each have to make our own decisions and live with them." Daniel paused for a moment, realizing this was almost exactly what Hutch had been saying. "If you decided to go out and hand yourself over to the raiders tomorrow, would you feel it was my fault when they started toasting your toenails?"

"Probably," Zach grinned. "Point taken, Daniel. But if you ever do it again, you'd better watch out for your own toenails. I might do a little toasting myself."

*   *   *

Neely felt equally relieved to see Daniel. When he walked into the weaving room, she leaped to her feet so fast she nearly knocked over the loom. She ran to Daniel and threw her arms around him and he held her tightly, though he reddened a little under the friendly, approving gazes of her co-workers. Carly had taken herself elsewhere, vanquished by the silent, icy disdain of the other weavers. Not even Meta would speak to her.

"I need to talk to you," Daniel said. "Can we go somewhere?"

She nodded, half afraid of what he might say. They made their way out to the tranquility garden. Zach had left and the garden lay empty and private. For a while they just held each other in silence, then Neely said, "I'm so sorry, Daniel, about what Carly said. Even she never meant for you to hear that. It was cruel. And none of it matters anyway. I love you. I want to be with you always. I want to join with you and bear your children and grow old with you while our grandchildren grow up and get married too. Please, please, don't ever leave me."

Daniel's arms tightened around her. In a choked voice he said, "Ahh, Neely! I love you so much it hurts. But Carly was right. With me for a father, the risk of mutant children is a lot higher. They could be monsters, just like she said."

"I don't care. I will love them anyway. With you for a father, they couldn't help but be beautiful inside. But if I ever lost you, if I ever lost your love, it would hurt more than a thousand mutant or stillborn births. Time might dull the pain but it would never leave me. I would spend the rest of my life dreaming of you, remembering you and all the things about you I love. I need you."

She turned her face up to him and they kissed, awkwardly at first, still being new at it, then with growing assurance and hunger as mutual passion obliterated any sense of shyness.

"I know it's pushy of me to do the asking but . . . will you join with me, Daniel?"

With one gentle finger he traced the line of her cheek and her soft, rose-colored lips. He thought of Darius and smiled. Rose was the color of love. "If the council will allow it, I would be honored to join with you."

They hugged each other tightly.

"Let's tell Daddy right away. He'll assemble the council," she said, her voice muffled against his chest.

"And what will happen then?" he asked, a little apprehensive.

"We'll go before them and tell them of our commitment. They'll ask a few questions, maybe take a few days to research my genetic background . . . though with you being adopted they might not have to do that. Then they'll give their approval and set a time for the ceremony. Probably not until after the harvest."

"You sound so confident they'll approve."

"Of course they will. The only time they don't is if the couple is too close genetically, like if I wanted to marry my first cousin."

"But I'm a mutant."

"If they objected to that, they never would have accepted you for adoption. They knew then you would eventually want to marry and have a family. Most people do."

"Tell me about the ceremony. I've never seen a joining."

"Well, it's a lot like a bonding ceremony. Spring is the best time, when the flowers are blooming. But I don't want to wait that long. We'll both have our closest friends to attend us and help us prepare. We'll dress in our special wedding clothes . . . "

"Not the ceremonial whites?"

"Sometimes, but we're allowed to dress as we wish for a joining, as long as we observe the proprieties. I have a special dress I made, dreaming of this day. We'll each have one close friend to stand beside us and we'll come together before the gathered assembly. They'll all sing the joining song for us and then we'll say our vows to each other. Our families will join hands in a circle around us and each will offer a blessing or a wish for our future happiness. Then the assembly will sing the song of blessing. We'll have a huge feast with all our favorite foods and afterwards we'll have music and dancing and a bonfire."

"And after that? I can't very well take you back to the dorm with me. The boys would love it, but I don't think it would be quite proper." He began to almost believe it might happen. Neely giggled at the image he had conjured.

"Once we're joined, we'll be assigned a room of our own. We're not allowed to see it until after the circle dance. Our friends and families will have it all specially fixed up for our first night together. They'll leave little gifts for us and a breakfast tray so we don't have to get up the next day until dinnertime if we wish."

The thought of sharing a bed with Neely filled Daniel with excitement and terror. What if he disappointed her? What if he frightened her with his wild animal eyes? He had never been with a woman in that way before. In his isolated life the opportunity had just never come up. What if he didn't know what to do and fumbled it or hurt her? He shivered and she sensed his fears, his self-doubts.

"I love you, Daniel. As long as we love each other, that's all that matters."

They went to Tadi hand in hand, and one look at their faces, Daniel's full of wonder and apprehension and Neely's radiantly happy, informed him of their decision without a need for words. He put his arms around both of them and hugged them.

"Nothing could please me more than to see you joined," he said, "nor bring me more joy than to see you happy together. Let's go find Salla and tell her. And Aaron and Cochita too."

They found Neely's mother working in the nursery, helping to care for the babies and toddlers. When she heard the news, she hugged Neely tightly and then embraced Daniel. She smiled up at him with tears shining in her eyes and laid her palm against his cheek.

"When they brought Neely home all torn and bleeding from that encounter with the beastman, you were all she would talk about for weeks. I knew then that she would love you . . . that one day she would go to you. And I felt afraid . . . so afraid that you would take her away and we would never see her again. I'm very glad that instead of losing our daughter, we can welcome a son."

* * *

When Hutch came to the table at suppertime and saw Salla sitting at Tadi's side and Neely's hand tightly clasped in Daniel's, he knew his friend had acted on his advice. Salla usually ate in the nursery with the little ones. Her presence meant something special was happening. Zach looked very pleased as well, though he couldn't know about the joining unless he had guessed. No formal announcement would be made until after the council had approved the union. Hutch sat down on Tadi's left and smiled across the table at the young couple, loving them both and pleased for them.

Hutch wondered briefly if he would ever know this sort of passionate love. He realized that, if Daniel had never come along, he probably would have married Neely himself, but he felt no jealously. What he had with Neely was not a thing of fire and passion, but of friendship. It would have felt like joining with his sister. One day, he thought, he would have to go out into the world and find his special love and bring her home to Haven Hold.

*   *   *

As soon as everyone finished eating and the food had been removed from the council table, the hall cleared and the council convened. The young couple stood before them self-consciously. Neely could feel Daniel's tension and she squeezed his hand reassuringly. Except for Alison's dour face, the council members all smiled. Three of them were family anyway, how could they disapprove?

"So, I understand you wish to get married," Aaron said kindly.

"Yes," they answered together, exchanging a fleeting smile.

"Well, I can't say it's unexpected. Everyone in the hold knows you care for each other. We must ask a few questions first however. It's really just a formality in a case like this, since you, Daniel, are not related by blood in any way to Neely. For our records though, we would like to know a little about your genetic background. We realize this may be painful for you, but please, can you tell us a little about your parents and your grandparents?"

Daniel hesitated. "My . . . my mother was a trader's daughter."

"Her name?"

"Jaylene. Her father was a Kithtrekker, a tool maker. Avron . . . Sertise I think. I never actually met him."

"Are they still living?"

"No," he said softly, "my grandfather died before my birth, and my mother died when I was eight."

"And your father?"

"Jude Arbennis. He was the blacksmith in the village hold of God's Mercy." Daniel just barely kept the bitter irony out of his voice as he named the place.

"He's living?"

"I don't know. He was alive when I saw him last, fifteen years ago."

"And your paternal grandparents?"

"I don't know. No one ever told me about them. I was . . . unacknowledged. I think they existed, I just never knew who they were."

"Did you have sisters and brothers?"

"Three brothers. Maybe a sister. A child was born the night my mother died, but they never told me for sure."

The faces of the council filled with compassion. They could sense something terrible had happened to him that night, something more than the grief of losing his mother.

"Can you tell us the names of your brothers?" Aaron asked gently.

"Seth, Joram and Yakop."

"Do you know anything about your maternal grandmother?"

"Only that she died when my mother was very young. I think her name was Ellan, or Allaina."

"Alright, that should be enough for our records. As the father of the bridesman, I have no objection to this union. Cochita?"

"No objections." In fact, she looked delighted.

"Any objections from the bride's parents?"

Tadi and Salla answered together, "None."

"Margit, Alison, do you see any just cause to deny this union?"

"Not one!"

"None." Alison actually cracked a smile. Daniel almost sagged with relief.

"Good," Aaron said, looking immensely pleased. "With harvest time almost upon us, perhaps we should wait and have the ceremony after we get the crops in. That way the shepherds will be back and Sev and Jesse will be able to stand up for their brother and sister as well." The council leader smiled at the young couple. "Do you think you can wait half a month?"

"We can wait," Daniel said breathlessly.

"If we have to," Neely added.

"You must understand of course," Aaron cautioned them, "now your commitment is officially acknowledged and approved, you won't be allowed time alone together until after the ceremony. Only in a group can you be together."

They nodded. The restriction didn't concern Daniel in the least. Half a month seemed like nothing when he had spent his entire life with little more than closely guarded dreams to warm him. He could wait a little longer.

Chapter Sixteen

The greatest love of all is easy to achieve;
Learning to love yourself is the greatest love of all.
And if by chance that special place
That you've been dreaming of
Should lead you to a lonely place,
Find your strength in love.
~Linda Creed

Aaron announced the joining of Neely and Daniel before the assembly and they accepted it without question. If anyone might have raised objections, they wisely kept silent in the face of obvious majority approval.

The shepherds returned with the flock a few days later and the harvest began in earnest, with teams of reapers and stookers laboring from dawn to dusk, breaking only for a few hours to eat dinner and supper, falling into bed exhausted as soon as they had cleaned up from the fields. At this time of year, the weather became chancy and they raced to beat the first hard frost, wind or hailstorm. Field after field went down before their determined assault, leaving sheaves of grain piled behind them in golden pyramids.

For the first two days of the grain harvest Margit forbade Zach to do any reaping. She felt unsure his shoulder could take the strain of such prolonged and strenuous work, so Alison relegated him to stooking with the younger boys and the women. But on the third day, when he showed no ill effects, no soreness in the newly healed muscles after the grueling work of the last two days, she allowed him to take up a reaping hook.

The partners started out that morning working side by side, and for the first three hours Zach managed to keep up with Daniel, matching him stroke for stroke, trying to imitate his easy, graceful rhythm. Daniel remained aware of his partner trying to pace him but he kept silent about it, until he heard a sudden sharp oath and turned to find Zach staring down at blood dripping from his left hand. Daniel laid down his reaping hook and strode back to have a look at the injury. Blood welled from a deep gash in Zach's palm. Daniel pulled off the bandana he had tied around his head to keep sweat and hair out of his eyes.

"You should go see Margit," he said as he gently bound up the wound, wishing he had some bitterberry leaves to stop the bleeding. "You might need a few stitches."

"No, I'm fine. It's not that bad. Damn! I'm such a..."

"Don't!" Daniel said sharply. "Don't say it, Zach. It's not true." He knotted the crude bandage and looked up, meeting his partner's dark eyes. "Don't try to keep up with me, Zach. This isn't a competition. Just relax. Set your own pace, your own rhythm. You're doing your share and that's all that counts. You don't have to prove anything . . . not to them, and certainly not to me." He put a hand on his partner's shoulder and gave him a little shake. "Understood?"

Some of the tension went out of Zach and he almost smiled. "Understood."

They both went back to work, and by the time the dinner bell rang, Zach had fallen into a steady, efficient rhythm, and without realizing it, had almost caught up with Daniel again. The crew gathered, talking and laughing, and headed homeward. Zach trailed a little behind and Daniel dropped back to walk with him.

"How's the hand?" he asked quietly.

"It's fine," Zach answered, trying to keep the injured member out of sight. Daniel caught him by the wrist and pulled his hand up. The bandage looked stiff and rusty with dried blood. Daniel shook his head.

"Damn it, Zach! I said you should go see Margit. Why do you do this to yourself? This is just like walking home after I'd told you you'd been poisoned. It's like you're trying to punish yourself. "

Suddenly the truth of what he'd said struck him like a revelation. He pulled Zach to a halt and stood staring at him.

"That's it, isn't it? They had you all wrong, all of them. I never could figure you for a mutant hater. You may not trust mutants, but you don't hate them any more than I do. It's yourself you hate, isn't it, Zach?"

Zach turned his face away, as if he didn't quite know how to answer, or didn't much like the question. "I don't think I actually hate myself," he replied at last. "Maybe sometimes, when I've caused a major disaster. Like when I shot you. It just seems that . . . no matter how hard I try, nothing I do is ever good enough. And no matter how well things seem to be going, there's always a disaster waiting to happen. I'm always making mistakes, always screwing up and it seems like it's always someone else who gets hurt."

"And you don't like seeing people get hurt, do you, Zach?" Daniel put an arm around his partner's shoulders and they started walking again.

"You know, you can't take the blame for every accident that occurs around you. Other people make mistakes too and get into trouble all by themselves. And sometimes when people get hurt through their own stupid mistakes, they like to blame it on someone else so they won't feel so foolish." Daniel looked down at his young partner. "But that doesn't mean you have to accept the blame. If the mistake was yours, fine. It's important to recognize when you're wrong, even if it hurts to admit it. But to make yourself a whipping boy for anyone who trips over his own feet, that's just plain foolishness. In the time I've known you, I've seen you make a few small mistakes, mostly out of inexperience. But those kind of mistakes are human. They're part of growing and learning. No sane, reasonable person would fault you for those."

"My father used to swear at me," Zach confessed, "and tell me how useless I was whenever I did something wrong. Or sometimes he would just look at me and I could see it in his eyes. I never could do anything good enough for him."

"He was a damned fool then. Any man should be proud to have you for a son. Or a brother," Daniel added. "Twice now in the past two months you have found yourself in situations where other lives depended on what you did. The first time, you risked your life for me on that slide, and probably saved mine. The second time, you gave warning of the dags and drew their attention to yourself. You probably saved a number of lives that day. You certainly prevented a lot of people from getting very badly hurt. In both cases you handled the situation as well as anyone could have. Better than most."

Zach gazed up at Daniel thoughtfully for a moment. He started to grin a little. "Maybe there's hope for me yet."

"You've got more than hope, Zach. You've got value. You just have to learn to recognize it. You're smart, you're talented, you learn faster than anyone I've ever met, and you rarely make the same mistake twice. You've got a lot to be proud of."

Zach didn't answer. His head was down and Daniel couldn't see his expression, but after a moment his hand rose to rest on Daniel's shoulder.

"You know, I never had any brothers. I really loved my little sisters . . ." For an instant a deep pain flickered in his eyes. He looked away quickly and his voice sounded a little husky when he continued. ". . . but I always thought it would be nice to have a brother."

Daniel noticed Tye and Hutch waiting for them at the gate and answered, "Sometimes it's better to choose your own brothers than to trust fate to provide them. I had three natural brothers, and I wouldn't trade the lot of them for just one of my chosen brothers."

Hutch and Tye smiled to see the partners approaching, arms around each other's shoulders. Zach looked happier than he had since before the shooting.

"If you two moved this slowly in the field," Tye commented teasingly, "we'd have to set you to peeling potatoes for Cochita."

The brothers fell in on either side of Daniel and Zach and the four of them entered the dining hall together. Later, after the meal, Daniel saw to it that his partner visited Margit. As she stitched up the cut in Zach's hand, she shook her head in exasperation.

"You two!" she complained. "This is the fifth time in as many months that I've had to patch one of you up! You have to be more careful." She set the last stitch, brushed the wound with antiseptic and gently bound it up. "No more field work for you, young man." Zach started to protest and she added, "No arguments. They can always use extra help in the kitchen at harvest time. I'm sure Cochita can find something for you to do. Or if you prefer, you can stand guard duty and free one of the others to take your place in the fields."

Zach thanked her for the doctoring, and as the two young men left, she overheard him complaining dolefully, "What a choice . . . kitchen duty or guard duty." And Daniel replied, "If I were you, I'd take kitchen duty. More interesting. All those pretty girls around to comfort you in your convalescence!"

Their chuckles faded down the corridor and Margit smiled. It warmed her heart to see them friends, to see the growing strength of the bond between them after the near fatal shooting. The council had decided wisely in letting Zach stay, she thought. He was going to work out just fine.

*   *   *

Three days later, the grain harvest began to wind down. Only two more fields of flax remained uncut, and they needed another week or two to ripen yet. The field crews finished sheaving the last of the wheat and barley late in the afternoon and declared the rest of the day a holiday. They collapsed in the shade of the walls, exhausted from six days of dawn to dusk, backbreaking labor. With preparations for supper almost completed, Cochita released most of her helpers to take the rest of the day off as well. They had worked every bit as hard as the field crews, slaving over hot ovens in the late summer heat. Zach wandered out to sit with Daniel and his brothers where they sprawled in the shade, resting and talking quietly.

A few of the more energetic young men started a game of tag ball out on the flats. Daniel sat up to watch as Tye explained the game. Played in two-man teams, anywhere from two to a dozen pairs could play at the same time, the number varying as tired players dropped out and new ones joined in. With a goal set up at each end of the field, the objective for each team was to score as many goals as possible at the same time as preventing the other teams from scoring any. The only deliberate physical contact permitted was a light tag with the hand to the carrier of the ball, which froze him in position until he lost the ball, either by passing it to his partner or through having it stolen by whoever had tagged him, or anyone else near enough to snatch it. The role of the partner, or second, was to flank his mate and run interference, blocking taggers if possible. If his mate got tagged, he attempted to retrieve the ball before it could fall into enemy hands, thereby releasing his partner and switching roles. It was a game of speed, agility and teamwork.

Many non-participants began lining the field to watch and shout encouragement. Jesse urged Hutch to come and play with him and Hutch groaned, complaining, "You're going to wear me out before I'm twenty." But he went and soon became enthusiastically involved in the game. Daniel watched a while longer, then turned to Zach.

"How 'bout it, partner? Want to give it a try? It looks like fun."

Zach shook his head doubtfully. "I'm not much good at games."

"It doesn't matter, Zach. It's just for fun."

"Maybe Tye will . . ." But Rennie was already dragging Tye onto the field. Zach saw the disappointment in Daniel's eyes and gave in. "Alright," he said, trying not to show how reluctant he felt.

As they entered the game, Josh was running with the ball. Skeet, his second, covered his left flank, when Jesse dashed in on Josh's right and tagged him, then raced on ahead of the crowd, leaving Hutch to snatch the ball from Josh's hands before he could throw it to his second. Skeet tagged Hutch just as he released a long pass to his partner. It sailed over the heads of the other players, right to Jesse's waiting hands. The boy turned and ran for the throw line, well ahead of any opposition. The goal was a flat wooden board the size and shape of a door with a hole cut in it, slightly larger than the circumference of the ball. Jesse stopped ten feet back at the throw line and flung the ball. It hit the rim of the hole and bounced away. No goal.

The others reached him then and Tye snatched the ball from the ground, whirled and threw it to Rennie, who had dropped back when he saw his partner pulling into the lead. Again, the ball soared. Rennie jumped and caught it out of the air and was off, sprinting down the field with the pack in pursuit. The next scoring attempt had to be made at the opposite end of the field. Hal caught up with Rennie and stole the ball, then Skeet took it from him, and so it went, with the ball passing from hand to hand in a mad scramble. Zach caught a glimpse of the wild exhilaration on Daniel's face and felt suddenly glad he had agreed to play. To Daniel, scarred by childhood isolation and rejection, being allowed to join in and play with the group seemed the ultimate in acceptance. He didn't care if he won, he just wanted to play.

Just then, an opportunity presented itself and Zach tagged Hutch, then snatched the ball from his hands. Rennie tagged him almost immediately, but before he could lose the ball, he threw it to Daniel. It was a slight overthrow, and Daniel moved with it, catching it on the fly. Zach stretched out, running hard, trying to catch up with his partner to give him some protection from taggers. All those hours of daily running with Daniel began to pay off as Zach pulled ahead of the pack. He drew further and further ahead of the crowd, gaining on his partner, when Rad suddenly came onto the field, bearing in on Daniel's right, with his cousin Andi following as second. A stab of concern and a sudden premonition of disaster sent a jolt of adrenalin into Zach's bloodstream. He uttered a breathless shout of warning and extended himself even further. He was still a few paces behind when Rad reached Daniel, but close enough to see clearly as the holder's elbow stabbed viciously at Daniel's side, just below the ribs. The mutant stumbled and went down, doubled over in breathless agony. Rad snatched up the ball and started to turn away, when Zach came flying at him and struck with all the power in his slim body and all the force of his driving run. The youth aimed for Rad's jaw but overestimated and struck high on the cheekbone. Zach didn't even watch to see if Rad went down. He turned immediately to see to Daniel. He went down on one knee beside his partner, who was curled up, struggling for air.

"Daniel?" he asked anxiously.

Then rough hands seized him from behind and flung him away so he landed sprawled on his stomach. Before he could react, a knee came down in the small of his back and pinned him helplessly, while hard fists began to pound at him. The ground trembled with the thunder of approaching footsteps as the others caught up. The weight suddenly lifted off Zach's back and he rolled over to find Cam shaking Rad like a rag doll. Hal put a restraining hand on his brother's arm and said, "Easy, Cam. Don't break his neck."

Tye helped Zach up and held him loosely with an arm looped around his upper chest, as if afraid he might go after Rad again. But Zach's eyes went to Daniel, getting assisted to his feet by Hutch. The mutant still hunched over, one hand pressed against his side. He met Zach's worried gaze with a rueful grin and said in a strained voice, "Never turn your back on an enemy. Sorry I couldn't help you, partner. I was sort of paralyzed."

Tadi and Aaron arrived on the scene. They had been watching from the sidelines, keeping score and acting as referees, but from that distance they couldn't tell exactly what had occurred. Daniel might just have tripped, but Zach had most definitely fouled Rad, and Rad's method of retaliation seemed unsporting to say the least.

"Alright," Aaron growled, "what happened?"

As usual, one glimpse of the council leader's stern, forbidding visage rendered Zach mute. He stared at the ground, going rigid with tension. Tye's arm tightened around him and suddenly felt more comforting and protective than restraining.

Rad spoke up loudly, "This plague-rotted dag bait just attacked me for no reason! He's a damned troublemaker! We should have thrown him out when we had the chance!"

"Enough!" Aaron thundered. He glared his son into silence, then turned to Zach and said, not unkindly, "Go ahead, Zach. Tell us your side of it."

Zach hesitated, then seeing the arrogant, contemptuous expression on Rad's face, his anger flared again and he spoke up indignantly. "Rad fouled Daniel . . . deliberately elbowed him in the side right where . . . where he was wounded."

Aaron turned questioningly to Daniel and the mutant nodded in confirmation. Rad snarled, "Well, of course the mutant is going to agree. This dag bait is his partner."

Tadi looked around at the gathering. "Did anyone else see what happened?"

They all shook their heads and murmured denials. It all happened so fast, and no one had been close enough to see why Daniel went down. Then a voice spoke up.

"I saw," said Andi Tayler, who was not only Rad's second, but his cousin and his partner. Rad's face relaxed into a smile, sure his friend would back his story. But Andi said, "It's true. Rad fouled Daniel."

Rad went white with shock at this betrayal, then red with anger. He didn't get the chance to speak though. Aaron had turned back to Zach and asked, "When you hit Rad then, you were simply defending your partner?"

Zach reddened and looked a little shamefaced. "I guess it was more like vengeance than defense. Rad was already turning away."

To Zach's amazement, Aaron smiled at him. "One blow doesn't seem very vengeful, especially considering the way my son has harassed you in the past."

The council leader turned a stern eye on his errant offspring. "You, young man, have time and again shown yourself to be no true believer in the philosophies of the Haven. Time and again you have acted with unreasonable violence and cruelty. Your assault on Zach last spring was far from your first misdemeanor. It seems no punishment we mete out is strong enough to curb you or to teach you acceptable behavior. Don't assume that because you are Haven-born you are immune from exile. It's not unknown for undisciplined young men like yourself to be banished for periods up to a year, to teach them to appreciate the subtleties of hold law and honor. If the next two seasons don't see a marked improvement in your attitude, spring may find you making your way alone. Is that clear?"

Rad looked stunned and thoroughly chastened. "Yes, sir," he answered, with none of his usual insolence.

"I think you owe apologies to Daniel and Zach," Aaron added.

Rad nearly choked on the words, but he said them, then turned and stalked away. No one followed him, least of all Andi.

Chapter Seventeen

*'Till all the lonely, 'till all the lonely,
'Till all the lonely's gone, gone, gone,
Let's hold on to each other
'Till all the lonely's gone.*
~Pam Tillis/Bob DiPiero/Scot Sherrill

On the day of the joining ceremony, Cochita asked the young men to get her some fresh fish for the feast. With Hutch and Tye occupied elsewhere, Daniel, Zach and Jesse took a picnic lunch and went fishing. The errand was partly a ruse to get the bridesman out of the hold while his friends made preparations for the afternoon's ceremony and the celebration to follow. Neely's girlfriends hustled her off to the big orchard to pick windfall nuts for a pudding. She had participated in joining preparations before and the excuse didn't fool her, but she played along, pretending to believe in the deception.

The three young men spent a lazy, relaxed morning beside the river. They could easily have made a couple of Zach's fish traps and had all the fish they needed in a few hours, but this peace seemed just what Daniel needed to calm his nerves. Not that he felt any doubt about marrying Neely, but the thought of standing before the assembly, the focus of all those eyes, still had the power to shake him, even on a happy occasion.

After two hours Jesse had caught three fish, while Zach and Daniel had only tentative nibbles on their lines. The mutant turned to his youngest brother and said, "Alright, Jess, hand it over."

Jesse grinned sheepishly and produced a chunk of rubbery cheese. Daniel cut a piece each for his partner and himself, grumbling humorously, "Damned spoiled fish won't even eat worms anymore. Now they gotta have cheese!"

As they rebaited their hooks, Daniel asked his partner casually, "Will you act as my honorman this afternoon, Zach?"

The outlander regarded him in silent shock. Over Daniel's shoulder, Zach saw the stunned protest in Jesse's eyes. Everyone knew Hutch was Daniel's first and closest friend. The place of honor should be his. Jesse glared at Zach and the outlander turned away. He knew Jesse still harbored animosity over the shooting. Having remained away at the Meadows all summer, the boy barely knew Zach and had missed seeing the slow growth of friendship between Daniel and his partner.

Disturbed by his lack of response, Daniel glanced at the youth. "Zach?"

His partner stared at the tufts of coarse grass lining the riverbank, his face a study in troubled confusion. "You know I'll do whatever you ask, Daniel. I would never do anything to spoil this day for you. But . . . what about Hutch? I don't want to . . . offend anyone."

"No one will feel offended, Zach, least of all Hutch. I've already spoken to him about it. He'll be there at my side as my brother, just like Jesse and Tye. But you're my partner and my friend. I want you there too. I . . . I need your support."

Zach's dark eyes studied him solemnly. Daniel had just said three of the most powerful words in the human language, 'I need you'. It no longer mattered what Jesse thought, or anyone else. At that moment Zach would have walked through fire for Daniel.

"I would be honored to stand beside you," he said with choked sincerity. "I'll try to be worthy of you."

"Zach, you don't have to try, you *are* worthy. More than worthy."

By midafternoon they had a good catch of fish and they started back to begin their preparations for the ceremony. Hutch and Tye met them at the gate and the hunter took their catch to the kitchen while his brother hustled the trio straight to the men's bath house. Tye soon rejoined them and they spent a lengthy time scrubbing, shampooing and purifying the bridesman and themselves. They dressed in the ceremonial whites, but Daniel refused the tunic shirt, saying he had something else he wanted to wear. When he attempted to leave to get it, he found his way quickly blocked by Hutch and Tye.

"Oh, no you don't!" Tye said laughingly. "You're not allowed out of here until it's time for the ceremony. Just describe what you want and I'll go hunt it down for you."

A short time later, Tye returned with a leather-bound bundle, which Daniel carefully unwrapped. He shook out the folds of the shirt Neely had made for him over a year ago, never worn until now, and slipped it on over his head. It settled onto his scarred shoulders like a caress.

Hutch nodded approvingly. "Perfect," he said, "Neely's friendship gift."

Daniel stroked the softness of the fabric. "I nearly broke off the trade agreement that day, you know. I was so afraid of being betrayed again that I almost turned my back on the only real friendship I'd ever known." He shook his head over the memory of what he had been like, so distrustful and suspicious. It was a wonder Hutch hadn't given up on him. "I've learned a lot since then." He smiled at his bond brothers. "Thank you for teaching me. Thank you for being my friends."

They embraced him wordlessly and Zach watched, feeling a bit left out and envious until Daniel reached out and drew him into the circle.

A sharp rap on the bath house door warned them the time had come. Tye and Zach left to escort the bride and her honormaid to the great hall. The tradition of the honorman escorting the bride dated back to the days not long after Armegeddon, when young men of wealthy families searched the ravaged land for a genetically sound mate. Since such mates were not always particularly attractive, nor even of a similar age, the bridesman was disallowed by custom to see the bride before the ceremony. Therefore, he would choose his most trusted and honorable friend to escort her and guard her safety and virtue on the journey to her new home. The honormaid accompanied the bride as her handmaiden and chaperone, charged with seeing that the honorman remained honorable.

Tye tapped on the door to the ladies' bath house and heard a spate of giggling from inside. Then Kelda opened the door, her eyes bright with excitement. Serene emerged first, the honormaid preceding her mistress. She took Tye's arm, smiling up at him shyly. In the white ceremonial shift, with her braids coiled about her head like a crown and entwined with flowers, the plain young woman looked almost beautiful. Then Neely emerged and the young men gasped. She took Zach's arm and he felt suddenly graceless and awkward. As if sensing his shyness, she patted his arm and gave him an impish smile, and then it was Neely again and not some exotic foreign queen he escorted. Zach could not wait to see the look on Daniel's face when he first saw his bride.

In the meantime, Hutch and Jesse accompanied Daniel to the great hall. The holders had decorated the corridor with fall blossoms and leaves and turned the doorway to the great hall into an archway of flowers with masses of late roses and bright yellow asters. The assembly had gathered and seated themselves, waiting with hushed anticipation. Tadi, Salla, Sev, Hedy, Cochita and Aaron stood in a semi-circle at the head of the room. Hutch showed Daniel where to stand. Jesse stepped back to join the family circle, but Hutch stayed at his friend's side until the bride's party at last appeared in the archway.

Tye and Serene moved forward first and took their positions and Hutch stepped back to his proper place with the family. Then Daniel caught his first unobstructed view of Neely and froze with awe. A concerted gasp swept the room as she glided forward on Zach's arm. The youth looked as proud and excited as if he had invented her himself as a gift for his partner. The bride's dress was shimmery white satin printed with large, bright red blossoms. A circlet of red, white and yellow roses crowned her head, and over her shoulders and back, trailing out behind her, she wore a mantle of flowers. The ladies had spent hours making that cloak for her, pinning each blossom and leaf into place. She looked elemental, queenly, like the spirit of autumn. Zach guided her to her place facing Daniel, then moved to stand at his partner's side, just behind his left shoulder. The rest of the bride's attendants found their positions.

The Joining Song began as a wordless humming from the assembly, gradually swelling as more voices joined in. Then Aaron's deep bass boomed out the first lines to the song. Cochita added her contralto and Tadi and Salla joined in counterpoint, their four voices twining and harmonizing in a rising anthem of joy. The rest of the family members came in on the chorus, and soon the entire assembly added their voices. As the final notes died away, Daniel and Neely clasped hands and quietly said their vows to each other.

They had chosen for themselves what promises they wished to make, and each had sought the advice of others in the matter, Daniel going to Kelda and Cochita, and Neely asking Hutch what he thought Daniel needed to hear. Daniel pledged to love Neely always, to defend and provide for her to the best of his ability, to remain forever true and constant to her, to listen to her cares and consider the wisdom of her advice, and to always remain her friend as well as her husband. Neely vowed to love Daniel always, to nurture and take joy in any children of their union, to never harm or betray him or anyone he cared for, to try to never cage his spirit with her love, and to count the brothers of his heart her brothers as well. That last addition was Hutch's wording, and she didn't quite understand the significance of the vow, since she had known and loved Daniel's bond brothers longer than he had and was growing quite fond of Zach as well. But Hutch had been thinking of Darius.

The bride and bridesman embraced and a cheer rocked the room. The families joined hands in a circle around them and sang the song of blessing on the union. Then starting with the parents of the bride, each family member spoke a personal blessing for them.

Tadi: May your love grow deeper and richer with the years.

Salla: May your joys outweigh your sorrows tenfold.

Aaron: May the Lord of Light strengthen your spirits and make your love shine.

Cochita: May your children and grandchildren hold you as an example of what love should be.

Sev: May your pastures be ever green and your forests ever peaceful.

Kelda: May all your babies be strong and healthy.

Tye: In times of trial, may you stand together in the heart of the Flame.

Hutch: May friendship always remain the comforter that warms the bed of passion.

Hedy: When you are apart, may your hearts remain always together.

Jesse: May all your best wishes and dreams come true.

Serene: May your children be as beautiful as both of you are.

As the honorman, Zach gave the final blessing. He reddened a little self-consciously and said, "May this day live forever in your hearts, like a flower that never fades."

A sigh rose from the assembly and Neely smiled, tears in her eyes. The crowd began to sing the Song of Blessing and she reached out to hug Zach, enveloping him in the scent of roses and wildflowers. Then Serene hugged Daniel and suddenly the family circle closed around them and everyone was embracing everyone else. The assembly swept forward as well and Zach began to feel like he was drowning. He got pushed up against Daniel in the press, and he could feel the mutant trembling. Zach forced himself to relax. He rubbed Daniel's back soothingly and said in a calm voice, "Hang on, partner, it'll be over soon."

The assembly began to move out into the courtyard, sweeping the wedding party with them. Aaron and Tadi quickly organized the mob into a reception line, and with people at a more comfortable distance under the open sky, Daniel's claustrophobia eased. He put an arm around Zach's shoulders and gave him a quick, grateful squeeze.

"Thanks, Zach. I felt ready to bolt if I could only find a way out."

By the time everyone said their congratulations and wished the couple well, the kitchen crew had laid out the meal. They had used their most treasured recipes, saved for only the most special occasions, and had created a sumptuous feast. After dinner, the musicians set up in the courtyard and began playing lively music . . . bright, energetic reels and round dances and slow, romantic couple dances, befitting the occasion. Finally, as the hour grew late, the holders performed the circle dance and spoke their benedictions, many of them blessings for the new couple and thanks for the bountiful harvest. The circle broke up and folk began to head wearily to bed amid many wishes for a happy and fruitful joining night. A circle of brothers, sisters and friends gathered around the wedding couple, and with a great deal of good-natured teasing and laughter, escorted them to their new quarters, ushered them inside and quietly but firmly closed the door behind them.

Alone at last, Daniel and Neely looked at each other, feeling suddenly shy and awkward. She slipped her arms around his waist and leaned against him and he held her gently, as if holding a priceless, fragile treasure. He gazed around the room. It looked tiny, with just enough space for a large bed, a night table and a dresser. His spirit lamp burned on the night table and dimly lighted the room. Its light, familiar fragrance soothed Daniel's frayed nerves and began to ease the tensions of the day. He noticed another door and a shuttered window and asked, "Does that door open into the garden, Neely?"

"Yes," she answered, smiling up at him. "These outside rooms are usually reserved for senior members. This one was Alison's. He couldn't bring himself to leave it after his wife died. It held so many memories for him. But Mother and Daddy were going to give up *their* room for us. Daddy said a man like you should not be shut up in a windowless box, you need to be able to see the sky. So,

Alison said it was time he moved into the bachelor dorm anyway and left the privacy of this place to the young couples."

Daniel felt touched by the gesture. It was true, he would have felt trapped in an inside room. He would have to make a point of thanking Alison. Perhaps he had misjudged the man.

"Oh, look at this!" Neely cried, running her hands over the quilt on the bed, lovingly stitched in a pattern of linked hearts. "The two large hearts in the center symbolize you and me," she explained, "the inner ring of smaller hearts represents our families, and the outer ring of even smaller ones are all our many friends. Oh, it's so beautiful! It's Gemina's design. She calls it Circles Unbroken."

"It is beautiful," Daniel agreed, admiring the bright colors of the quilt. Neely drew him down onto it and for a while they just lay in each other's arms, content to be alone together in privacy. Then Neely began to slowly undress him, gently exploring his body as she removed each article of clothing. He submitted trustingly, watching her with breathless wonder, amazed that anyone like her could love such as him. She paused, her eyes going wide and welling with tears when she felt the ridges of permanent scarring on his back and shoulders. He held her close and said, "It's alright, Neely, it doesn't hurt anymore. Even the inner wounds have healed now, thanks to you and Hutch and Tye and all my friends and family here. I never thought I would find a place like this, people like these. I didn't think such existed."

He kissed her eyelids gently, tasting the salt of her tears, and began to remove her clothing in turn. He loved the feel of her dress, as smooth and cool as water against his skin. And when he found the flesh beneath it felt warm in contrast, soft and velvety like well-cured doeskin. He began to tremble with eagerness as the rising heat in him built to a feverish pitch, but he forced himself to go slowly, gently exploring her body as she had his. She had scars too, but Margit had done a good job of repairing the damage done by the beastman. White lines traced Neely's right breast where the monster's claws had torn her, but it remained as firm and shapely as its mate. She gasped and shuddered with pleasure as his hand lightly brushed over her breast and ribs and on down to her flat stomach. As he leaned forward to kiss her, Daniel saw her eyes suddenly go wide with wonder and he froze, realizing the light of the lamp reflected in his eyes, making them shine. He quickly turned his head away, afraid of what he might see in her expression . . . fear, loathing, disgust. All the names, the curses came back to him. Devil's eyes. Animal eyes. Monster, freak. He started to pull away but she held him.

"Danni," she said softly, "I love you. All of you. Your eyes are beautiful and I love them too. They are the most beautiful eyes I've ever seen, as green as new leaves and full of your humor and kindness."

"It doesn't . . . scare you when they shine? Like a wild animal?"

"No. Not like a wild animal, like the man I love. Danni, there is nothing about you, nothing you would ever do or say that could make me fear you or love you less."

He hugged her tightly, aching with the wonder of her. Before long, their embrace turned into stroking and exploring again and their inexperience no longer mattered as instinct took over.

*   *   *

They made love again the next morning, more confident now, feeling deliciously wicked to laze in bed while the hold came to life around them. After a while Daniel rose and cautiously opened the shutters. Early morning light spilled in cheerfully through a sheer curtain drawn for privacy. He turned to pick up the breakfast tray from amongst the pile of small gifts atop the dresser and stopped with a gasp of wonder. Resting modestly in the corner, half hidden by other items, stood one of Zach's sketches. Daniel drew it out carefully and examined it.

"Neely!"

The strange, almost strangled sound of his voice sent her scrambling out of the blankets to stand at his side. She too drew a breath of amazement. It was a likeness of the two of them in their wedding finery, but it was more than a simple portrait. Neely was an exquisite, womanly earth spirit, clothed in flowers, gazing up at the man beside her with loving eyes, while Daniel was a proud, fiercely gentle wind spirit, a wild, wing-free hawk, returning always to her hand out of love, not bondage.

"Oh, Daniel!" Neely breathed in awe. "Where did it come from? No one in the hold is capable of this!"

"Zach. I've seen a few of his sketches before, but this is far better than any of them, even the one of Hutch. It's incredible!"

He showed her the inscription on the back, written in a neat, precise hand -- Zach's blessing, 'May this day live forever in your hearts, like a flower that never fades'.

Neely hugged Daniel and said, "I used to worry about you going out alone with him after the way he shot you. But now I know Zach, I realize he would never have done it on purpose. I'm glad we didn't send him away. He's sweet, and he loves you. He's certainly not a killer."

"No, he's not. In fact, if the time ever comes when he has to kill to survive, I hope he is capable of it."

"We'll have to give him a special thank-you for this," Neely said, placing the sketch on the night table beside their bed. They sat on top of the rumpled quilt and shared the fruit and cheese on the breakfast tray while they examined the other gifts . . . a matching set of house slippers from Serene, a pair of hand-carved wooden candle holders from Denys with two sweet-smelling beeswax candles from Davin and Kelda, perfumed soap from Hedy, a small jug of elderberry brandy from Sev and a pair of polished copper goblets from Cam. Jesse had given them a small wooden flute, laboriously carved from a piece of kindling. Neely tried it and found the notes a little off key, but it was the first time her brother had ever even attempted such a thing and she loved it. Margit had filled a basket with herb teas, each small pouch labeled with the ingredients and their uses, mint for indigestion, chamomile and sage for nerves, dandelion root as a laxative, rosehips and pipsissewa to waken and refresh, and valerian to bring on sleepiness. One even claimed to aid conception.

Tye's gift seemed unique and rather odd . . . a small, plain white ceramic bowl from the kitchen containing a handful of carefully chosen multi-colored river pebbles in just enough water to cover them. Neely wondered at it, but Daniel understood. There was something mystical about Tye that set him apart and kept him solitary. Few amongst the down to earth holders really understood him, even Hutch. But they accepted him without question and loved him despite his differences, or perhaps because of them . . . just as they accepted Daniel.

"He has given us a part of himself."

Neely still didn't understand, but she could see that Daniel valued this strange gift. He placed it on the night table beside the spirit lamp, with Zach's sketch a safe distance back from both. The three objects seemed to fit together. It took him a moment to realize why.

"Look at that, Neely. The four elements, earth, air, fire and water. It's like a shrine."

They held each other and contemplated the arrangement.

"We'll have to put fresh water in the bowl every day."

"And keep the lamp filled and the wicks trimmed."

"Do you think Denys could make a frame to protect the picture?"

"We'll ask him."

They exchanged a smiling glance, arms encircling each other.

"I suppose we should make an appearance soon," Neely said regretfully, bending to pick up her dress, left in a neglected heap on the floor last night. She found Daniel's clothing in the same state. Laying it all on the bed, she opened the closet curiously and found it filled with all their belongings, brought from the women's quarters and the men's dorm and carefully arranged on the shelves and hooks by their friends. But what rested on the floor drew a cry of delight from Neely. She drew out a long, recurved bow and wordlessly handed it to Daniel, along with a leather quiver containing ten iron tipped arrows. He took them breathlessly, stroking the smooth wood of the weapon with awe. It was mahogany from the southern territories, the absolute best. He had missed his bow desperately and had thus far been unable to find a suitable piece of wood to make a new one. He strung the bow and tested it for tension. It felt strong. It would take a good pull. The arrows, fletched in his own style, had to be from Hutch. He was the only one who knew Daniel's way of fletching.

A beautiful, liquid sound drew his attention and he turned to see Neely stroking and plucking the strings of a redwood lap harp. She met his eyes and they sat in silence for a moment, overwhelmed by the generosity of their friends and family.

"They must be from our parents," Neely said at last.

"And Hutch," Daniel added. He laid aside the bow and knelt beside her, taking her into his arms. As they clung together, he said softly, "I don't ever want to die. Heaven could not possibly be better than this."

HAVEN HOLD: BOOK 3

A NOVEL IN THE HAVEN HOLD SERIES

COMING SPRING 2022

Acknowledgements

Thanks to my dear husband, John, who puts up with my single minded creative focus. Thanks to my beta readers: my BFF, Marcia Green, my writer's group friends, Garry Cameron, Shaun Adams, Bob Frankow, Marilyn Buekert and Marilyn Daily, my dear family readers, Sid Morton, Dave and Gail Morton and Linda LaRochelle.

Thanks to the copy editor for catching all my typos, grammar and spelling mistakes.

Thanks to Colton Nelson, my publisher, who is constantly challenging me with exciting new projects..

About the Author

A long time ago in a town far, far away, Shelley Penner came into the world, and neither she nor it have ever been the same since. Shelley has always been a creator in many disciplines -- drawing, painting and photography as well as writing. She says, "I have always had a head full of stories. As a child I would put myself to sleep by living scenes in my imagination until I dozed off. I didn't just make up stories, I became a part of them, I felt all the emotional nuances of the characters. Eventually, my head became so full of those imaginary people, demanding their chance to be made real in words, that I just had to start writing."

Early literary influences include the queen of sci-fi, Andre Norton, and Marion Zimmer Bradley, both of whose novels still maintain a permanent place in Shelley's personal library. You can find more about Shelley Penner at her website shelleypenner.com

ALSO TRY

Both Sides Now is a thought-provoking collection of short stories by Vancouver Island writers Derek Hanebury, Vicki Drybrough, and Libbie Morin. Ranging in time from the 1950s to the present, these stories will draw the reader in to the world of a boy and his younger brother who struggle to find the perfect gift for their ailing grandfather, a troubled veteran who tries to escape the past by settling in a small community, and a young girl who goes to the circus alone and encounters more than she imagined. From beginning to end, you will enjoy stories that are crafted with empathy and insight to give the reader a satisfying experience.

PRAISE FOR BOTH SIDES NOW

"This is a rich varied set of stories. It offers a wide pallet of narrative styles and situations to carry readers more deeply into thoughtful consideration of the world." - Peter Mcguire, Author of The Art of Twelve

"If you are wanting to read a book full of diverse subject matter, incredibly detailed settings and interesting characters, then you will appreciate this compilation as much as I did." - Laura Sturgeon, Author of The Big Ugly Sweater

"A kaleidoscope of human stories, from a little girl alone with a potential predator to a hilarious, disastrous camping trip, from prejudice to compassion, love and friendship to fear and loss." - Shelley Penner, Author of Haven Hold

AVAILABLE WHEREVER BOOKS ARE SOLD

Find out more & get a free preview at **www.bothsidesnowbook.com**

Other RCN Media Titles

Just Being Human
by Colton Nelson

Rough Diamond
by Derek Hanebury

A Kind of Seeing
by Shelley Penner

King of Dhamma
by Huei Lin

The Fifth Planet
by Joan Jedy

Responsive
by Colton Nelson

Double Cross
by Joan Jedy

Ms. Holliman's Employer
by Laura Sturgeon

Both Sides Now
by Derek Hanebury, Libbie Morin & Vicki Drybrough

Alberni Aquarium Cookbook
by The Alberni Valley

Haven Hold
by Shelley Penner

Something Else Altogether
by Derek Hanebury

Afraid of Heights
by Joan Jedy

A Nickel a Bucket
by Laura Sturgeon

More coming soon
To see a complete list go to:
www.rcn.media

RCN Media KIDS Books

The Adventures of Bob and Avery Series:
By Kay J Douglas & Eric Gardiner

1. Bob and Avery Help Helga The Witch
2. Bob and Avery Go to Space
3. Untitled 3rd Bob and Avery Adventure

By Gail Morton
1. Two Weeks With Charlie
2. The Giving Raven
3. Rockfish

More coming soon
To see a complete list go to:
www.rcn.media

Lightning Source UK Ltd.
Milton Keynes UK
UKHW022221130421
381938UK00005B/201